The eagle fell, spiraling down to the ground... landing

with a thud on the earth...

There he lay immobilized, crippled, with his broken

wings and shattered dreams...

He sent out great eerie cries to the heavens, hoping

to be healed, his saddened voice filling the night

sky...

Chapter 1

Reanna awoke with a start, feeling that something was slightly amiss, and attempted to gather her sleep clouded thoughts. It was then that the sound of the carriage pulling away intruded upon the silence of her bedroom. Throwing back the crisp white sheets, she jumped from bed, her bare feet landing with a soft thud upon the hard wooden planks of the floor, and with a light step, she ran swiftly to her window, pulling aside the sheer lace of the curtains to peer inquisitively out.

"It's Papa!" she exclaimed, "and he is leaving without saying goodbye. It must be after eight already!"

Smiling fondly, she remembered the long evening she had shared with her father the night before. She played first the piano, and then her guitar, singing many of the beautiful songs that she had learned growing up. Her father, relaxing in his favorite chair, had leaned back, and grinned dreamily, listening raptly, as if there were nothing more pleasant in all the world.

It was always the same, whenever he went away on business, he would ask her to sing and play for him the night before he left, so that he could, he had explained to her, carry her music with him in his heart, and she vividly recalled the conversation they had just before retiring last evening.

"How is the Golden Girl coming along, Reanna? I have not had the opportunity to watch you work with her recently."

"Oh, Papa!" Reanna cried fervently, ready as ever, to heap praise upon her golden mare. "She is doing wonderfully, and I am so happy with her. She is the very best birthday gift you could have given me! She is intelligent, responds readily to my commands now, and I have come to love her so very much in the short time I have owned her."

"Good, my dear. I must admit, I was a bit skeptical about allowing you to train her yourself at first. She is young and high spirited, but then, I also wanted to show confidence in your abilities and horsemanship, and that confidence is well earned, it seems. Remember, I have to leave early tomorrow morning."

"Yes, Papa", Reanna answered dutifully as she kissed his weathered cheek, "good night."

Reanna had long realized that her father was a very lonely man, for he missed her mother, his only love, terribly. Because of this she tried always to treat him with deference and respect, and to allow her cheerful disposition full rein, but there were many times when she would catch him unaware, staring out a window toward the snow covered peaks of the mountains where they rose above the timberline, a melancholy look upon his weather beaten face, his craggy features etched deeply with the pain of loss and his gray eyes misty with memories.

Her mother had died nine years ago giving birth to a baby girl. There were complications, both mother and child had been lost, and her father still grieved deeply.

Reanna blinked back the tears that threatened to spill from her lovely green eyes and quickly pulled her soft, white nightshirt off over her head, acknowledging the fact that she also was instantly saddened by thoughts of the loss of her beautiful mother, remembering that long night so clearly, despite the passage of years.

She moved to the water bowl and filled it with fresh water from the pitcher, then hastily washed her face, blotting it dry with a clean, soft towel before she began to dress, choosing her dark green riding habit. Pulling the green split skirt up over her long slender legs, she fastened it at her tiny waist.

Next, she donned a beige lace trimmed blouse, buttoning it just high enough to cover her full round breasts. Over the blouse went a short bolero of the same color and fabric as the skirt. Last of all she slipped her dainty feet into her beige riding boots, made of the finest quality leather. Stepping to the full-length mirror, she smoothed her clothes over her supple form, and picking up her brush from the dresser, she worked the tangles from her waist length, dark copper tresses. As she brushed, the sunlight, filtering through the window, struck the waves of her hair, creating an illusion of flaming sparks among her lustrous curls.

Giving those wayward locks a final pat, she hastened down the large, whitewashed staircase, pausing to trail her fingers down the elaborately carved newel post, and entered the kitchen, inhaling the fragrant aroma of freshly baked bread.

Carmelita, their Mexican cook, was preparing Reanna's breakfast.

"Ah, good morning, Reanna, I heard you get up. Your Papa has already gone. Here, eat your ham and eggs now, before they get cold, and don't forget, you go to your uncle Bob's house today for it is your cousin Jared's birthday tomorrow, and you must help your aunt Martha to prepare for the picnic."

Reanna, who was ravenously devouring her breakfast, paused to take a sip of coffee, while listening to the woman's ceaseless chatter glancing up at Carmelita, her gaze softened as she met the cook's friendly brown eyes.

Carmelita had been a part of their family ever since she could remember and had filled the role of mother in the long years since Reanna's own mother's death, showering the young girl with all her warmth and affection. Reanna, in turn, loved Carmelita for all her patience and kindness, and the cook would always hold a special place in her heart.

4

"Reanna, why are you dressed for riding? I thought that you were going to take the buggy to your uncles. Have you got your bags packed and ready to go?" Carmelita worried.

Used to Carmelita's overabundance of loving concern, Reanna smiled and answered soothingly, "Aunt Martha and Uncle Bob do not expect me until this afternoon, so I thought I would go riding this morning. I can pick up my bags later when I come back to change my clothes, and then I will take the buggy."

Carmelita's expression grew even more worried. "You be careful and do not go too far on that new mare", she admonished.

"Carmelita, please don't worry so, I'll be fine. You know that I have been riding all my life. I will be perfectly safe," Reanna attempted to placate the nervous cook.

"All right, Chica, but do not be overly long. You know that your Aunt Martha will worry if you are late."

"Not nearly as much as you," Reanna answered as she rose and brushed the woman's cheek with a fond kiss. "I promise to return soon." She grinned broadly, recalling similar conversations, for Carmelita insisted upon fretting over her in her father's absence.

Leaving by the back door, Reanna's step was free and light as she traversed the short distance to the stables. A light rain had fallen the day before, so the usual dust was not stirred by her boots as she walked. The morning was bright with the sun beginning to climb in the cloudless blue sky, and the air smelled fresh and clean, a perfect morning for a ride!

She found Pier, Carmelita's husband, in the stables. He glanced up as she entered the shadowed interior, dark eyes dancing with his usual good humor as he hailed her.

"Good morning to you Reanna!" he called as she approached. He was a small, wiry build in contrast to his wife's large, buxom figure, and his dark skin was wrinkled with the texture of worn leather.

Reanna breathed deeply of the smell of horses, and clean, fresh hay.

"Good morning, Pier. Could you saddle Golden Girl for me? I am going to take her for a ride to the pond near town."

Golden Girl was the palomino mare her father had given her, with a sleek golden coat and cream-colored mane and tail, large intelligent brown eyes, finely tapered muzzle, and perfect conformation, her excellent breeding was quite obvious.

Reanna stroked the mare's soft velvety nose as Pier cinched the saddle. "Watch her; she seems a little skittish this morning."

"Yes, Pier, I'll be careful. Do not worry about me," Reanna called as she mounted and waved goodbye.

Pier smiled, his eyes growing distant as he thought of how swiftly the years had passed. It seemed that only yesterday a young, curly haired hoyden had followed at his heels, and now she had grown into a beautiful, poised, young woman. With a long sigh, he returned to the present and busied himself with his work.

Reanna rode hard and fast, free as the wind, enjoying the cool rush of air in her face. Her copper hair billowed wildly about her, like a dark, soft cloud, and the suns' rays reflected off the dark mass, shimmering in its lengths, gleaming like red fire. Her cheeks grew flushed with excitement, and her large green eyes glittered with enthusiastic joy from beneath long, thick lashes.

She had to follow the north road almost into town, and Golden Girl's long eager strides covered the distance quickly, passing through fleeting patches of shade as the mare carried her rider beneath the great overhanging branches of gnarled old trees that grew alongside the dirt track where minute glimpses of yellow were blooming dog violets that grew in the shadows around the thick trunks.

Up ahead loomed the large, thick stand of pine that Reanna would pass through before reaching the turnoff that would lead her to the pond. As she entered the engulfing shadows of those pines a moment later, Golden Girl's hoof beats were muffled by the thick, aromatic carpet of needles that covered the ground. Reanna's attention wandered, thinking of how she loved all the activity around the town of Carson City, such a change from the relative calm of everyday life on her father's ranch.

She enjoyed just sitting on the banks of the pond, her feet dangling nonchalantly in the cool water as she watched the bustle of children who came from town to swim and frolic in the sun-drenched shallows, and occasionally she would spy a young couple strolling slowly hand in hand around the pond's perimeter, sharing their dreams as they walked in their own private world. Reanna pensively recalled her own former beau, and lost in her saddened thoughts, too late took note of the huge, rough coated shape that burst from among the trees as she approached the opposite end of the pine wood.

The animal veered and charged at Golden Girl, and Reanna felt the sickening lurch of her stomach, as with eyes gleaming madly and saliva dripping from his open jaws, the large dog raced straight at them with sharp white teeth bared menacingly.

Reanna tried desperately to turn the mare from the dog's path, but it was too late. The rabid animal bunched his muscles and leaped, slamming into Golden Girl's left shoulder with his great weight, attacking the horse in a mindless frenzy. Golden Girl stumbled from the force of the impact, and the snarling, brindle colored dog slid downward, leaving open gashes in the mare's shoulder that quickly spurted blood as he renewed his attack, charging the trim fetlocks of the gold horse. The mare, shaken and terrified, reared and twisted away in an attempt to avoid those cruelly slashing teeth, but mad with blood lust, the huge dog pressed on, the mindless urge to kill driving him past all caution. Reanna's scream blended with Golden Girls cry of terror, as the mare's hooves flashed in the bright sunlight in an effort to escape the brutal assault.

Reanna felt herself slipping from the golden horse, but as she tried desperately to regain her seat, the dog lunged again, his fangs ripping into the mare's neck; narrowly missing the jugular as the terrified horse whirled and reared, seeking to rid herself of his heavy weight and deadly teeth. She tried valiantly to hold on, but the panicked mare, her eyes rolling in terror, would have none of it. She reared again, screaming in rage and pain, as she snaked her head to and fro, hooves slashing at her attacker as the dog, losing his grip was flung off.

Reanna was thrown from the horse and landed on her side with a bone jarring thud. Her head struck a rock, just grazing the edge, sending her into a world of blackness.

When Golden Girl came down on all fours once again, the vicious, maddened beast was ready, and lunged with an open mouth, his powerful jaws snapping shut on the mare's delicate foreleg. Bone cracked as the horse stumbled sideways, and she shrieked in pain, lowering her head to snap her own large teeth shut on the dog's unprotected back. Snarling savagely, the dog loosed the mare's leg to lash out at her muzzle. And Golden Girl struck out again and again, flailing the beast with her sharp hooves while the dog writhed beneath them, snarling madly until those flint hard weapons ended his life. She then stood there wheezing from exertion, her muscles trembling, as she pushed at the carcass with her bloodied muzzle, assuring herself that her enemy would indeed not rise to torment her any longer. Her plaintive cry echoed in the silence that followed, and she limped toward her fallen mistress, unable to bear any weight on her fractured foreleg. Crying out in her distress, her golden coat marred and bleeding, she stood next to Reanna who lay where she had fallen, still as death.

*   *   *   *   *   *

Chance Nolton rode into town early that morning, having received word that his friend Bob Dublin, the sheriff of Carson City, Nevada, needed help.

He did not particularly relish the idea of being paid to work with the law, even though they needed a hand bringing in a vicious gang of cutthroats to justice. It smacked too clearly the role of bounty hunter, his former profession, and one that he was presuming to leave behind. A fast gun riding into town always seemed to instill fear and mistrust among the populace of the law-abiding citizens, and bounty hunters were not generally looked upon with acceptance. In fact, they were often times shunned as much as the outlaws they brought in – dead or alive – so he much preferred his present occupations of businessman and rogue, both of which he pursued with a zealous competence, but Bob was a friend, and Chance did owe him a loyalty. Hell, he owed him his life, and since when had he ever cared about what people thought of him? He had no intention of lingering over long when his job was done.

Chance had left home at the age of thirteen and had never stayed in one place longer than a couple of months since. He was a loner, through choice, and had done quite well for himself, considering the fact that he had been no more than a boy when he had left his family.

He now owned his own trading vessel, a ship called the Ellen Dorothy, after his mother, who remained with him in heart, no matter how far he roamed. She was the most gentle, loving woman he had ever known, with such a quiet, serene grace about her, even when his father would come home drunk, and he would ... the bastard!

Bile still rose in his throat when he thought of his father, a useless piece of filth ... the reason that he had left home at such an early age. He had not been able to stand helplessly by, watching his mother be humiliated time and again, any longer.

He had tried in earnest to get her to leave, to bring his three brothers and go away with him, but she would have no part of it. She had been pregnant, ready to give birth in a month's time, and preferred the familiarity of her own home, shack though it was, to an uncertain future on the road.

And so, he had left, never to return, never to look back. Oh, he had written to her a few times through the years, just to reassure her that he was still alive, but he would not ever venture into those Tennessee hills again.

Reminiscing, he thought about the soft golden color of his mother's hair, the gentleness of her touch, the love and endless patience she had shown to all her children, but as always, memories of his drunken father intruded. An inebriated swine, lying with her night after night, begetting children. The recollection of her cries and sobbing echoed still in his mind, making him ill. If he had not left, he would have killed the lecher.

Chance entered the comfortable lobby of the only hotel in town, called the Shamrock, his spurs jingled resoundingly in the silence as he leisurely approached the front desk to register.

The clerk, a small, bird like man, glanced up from his ledgers to give Chance a cursory examination before the customary fear flickered in his eyes, and in a positively simpering voice, he hastened to assure his silent guest of most comfortable accommodations in his, as he put it, respectable establishment, stressing, fearfully, the word respectable.

A smile without mirth thinned the stranger's full lips, and he signed the register with a flourish, and then reached across the polished oak desk to take the key to his room. The clerk relinquished it with a sickly smile, as if he expected to be shot where he stood, and Chance released an aggrieved sigh as he crossed the length of the lobby to ascend the stairs, dismissing the tiny man as he continued with his musing.

He had worked diligently, doing odd jobs at first, saving every penny he earned, except what he needed to purchase a decent mount, a bedroll, and after the first time he was robbed of his hard-earned wages, a used, but serviceable six gun. This he practiced with for days on end, in his every spare moment, until he was quick enough to outdraw anyone who came up against him. He learned to track through the most desolate of country, to fight with whipcord movements, and to bury his true feelings deep inside, never showing the slightest compunction or remorse when it became necessary to kill.

He earned large bounties bringing in wanted men, which he saved toward the purchase of a trading ship. Also, through wise investments and large profits realized from his vessel, he had gained certain properties in the various port towns of California. He collected rent on these bi-monthly and spent much of his time traveling from place to place simply reaping the profits and assuring himself that the businesses were running smoothly. He had read any books that he could get his hands on, continuing the education that his mother had started as he spent long nights alone near a campfire.

When he felt the need for company, he would pay for the services of a whore, availing himself of their pleasures all night, free to leave in the morning, with no involvements. He was truly a self-made man, with everything he wanted when he wanted it. He certainly could ask no more of life. After stowing his gear and, as was long his habit, investigating every avenue of possible entrance or escape from his room, and the whole second story of the hotel, he decided to waste no time in riding down to the sheriff's office to let Bob know that he had arrived.

Finding the office empty, he headed his horse around in the opposite direction and rode slowly on, viewing the everyday activities of small-town life at his leisure. There were the few inevitable women of less than sterling character in fancy dresses, a few old peddlers selling their wares, children with dirty faces playing and hooting with laughter in the quiet streets, while the few horses and carriages carried their riders slowly about their business. It all looked very cozy, but to Chance Nolton's mind, a bit dull. He had become used to the hectic bustle of the port cities of California with their teeming mixtures of populace and excitement.

He had reached the outskirts of town near what was called the north road when he heard the frantic screams of a horse in pain. Kicking his own mount, Lancelot, into action, he turned and sped toward the sound, and the sight that met his eyes caused his innards to clench in trepidation.

The large body of a dog lay broken and bloody in the middle of the road, and a trim golden horse stood on three legs over a still form which lay beside the well-worn passage. As he drew closer, he ascertained that the form was that of a female, and he reined in and swiftly dismounted to find that he was bending over the most beautiful woman he had ever seen.

Her exquisite, long, copper-colored tresses sprawled out in disarray over the ground, and her full, rosy lips looked as though they were made to be kissed. Her lush, shapely figure could not be hidden by her clothing. Her skirt, in fact, had risen above her knees, and Chance felt his blood stir unbidden at the sight of her pleasing contours.

When he had assured himself that she still breathed, he turned his attention to the golden mare. He could easily see that she had been a valuable animal, but now her front leg hung useless at an odd angle, mangled, and broken, and her smooth gold coat was marred, torn and bleeding in many places, and lathered with sweat.

He turned to the dog, noting at a glance the foam flecked lips still turned up in a savage snarl, an almost sure sign of rabies. Even his jaded heart sank at what he knew would have to be done, but even without the broken leg, the mare would most likely have to be destroyed.

Drawing his pearl handled revolver from its leather holster, he led the golden horse, hobbling, to the side of the road. His mouth a thin, grim line, he took careful aim and fired. The sound of the shot reverberated in the stillness, and the lifeblood of the palomino ran red as she sank slowly to the ground, her blood mingling with the earth as her pain filled eyes glazed over in death.

Chance shook his head; saddened at the loss of such a fine animal, holstered his pistol, and went to the aid of the injured woman. Bending down, he carefully lifted her in his strong arms, gently bracing her across the withers of his mount. Then, hoisting himself into the saddle, he placed his arms around her still form to keep her from falling as he slowly made his way back into town.

Arriving back at the Shamrock Hotel, he noticed a young boy playing on the boardwalk, who he immediately sent, with a gruff command, to fetch the doctor. The lad, wide-eyed, complied without hesitation, scurrying to do the tall strangers bidding.

He carried the unconscious woman easily up to his room and laid her gently upon his bed. Working the knot from his black neckerchief, he jerked it swiftly from around his neck and dipped it into the pitcher of fresh water that stood on the bed stand, bathing her forehead as he leisurely regarded the incomparable beauty of her features and her smooth, flawless complexion.

Reanna slowly opened her eyes in response to the gentle, cooling touch upon her brow, and was astounded as the visage of a dark, powerfully handsome man with concerned sable eyes filled her clearing vision.

"Wh…where am I? And who are you?" Reanna asked in confusion, certain that she must be dreaming.

Chance found himself to be thoroughly enchanted by the deep green depths of her eyes, and he allowed a slight smile to cross his features.

"You, fair damsel," Chance began in a playful tone, "are in my room at the Shamrock Hotel, and my name is Chance Nolton." In a more sober voice, he continued "You seem to have taken a rather nasty spill from your horse. I found you by the side of the road and brought you here. The doctor is on his way."

"Well, I first thought you to be some dark angel of mercy, but I realize now that you must be a knight in shining armor, come to rescue a … how did you put it - a damsel in distress?"

Chance laughed heartily, enjoying her soft, cultured speech and her innocent remarks.

"Hardly either of those descriptions suit me, I fear. I have been likened more often to the devil, in fact."

Growing serious once more, he questioned, "Are you in any pain?"

Reanna, realizing now how foolish she had sounded, smiled wanly, aware of a throbbing pain at her temples. Her ribs felt as if there were a great weight pressing in upon them and she winced, answering her benefactor in a carefully controlled voice, "I do feel quite bruised and shaken," she admitted, then sat up abruptly, causing her head to pound, as she belatedly remembered Golden Girl.

"And what have you done with my mare? She will need medical attention also."

Chance, noting her sudden pallor, eased her back down to lay upon the pillows. Oddly discomfited, he glanced away, hesitating before he met her inquiring green gaze.

"I'm sorry, but she had to be shot," he began, wishing that he did not have to tell her. "Her leg was broken … there was no other way."

Reanna's wide green eyes filled with tears, and in a horrified voice she choked out, "No! Oh, no!"

"Do you remember what happened?" he queried lamely.

She paused in an attempt to control her quivering voice, "A dog – he must have been mad – came from the wood and attacked us. Golden Girl was fighting him off when I fell. She … she was a birthday gift from my father just two months ago."

Chance bent and clasped her hand comfortingly, unsure of how to proceed in such a matter. "Please don't cry. Believe me, if there had been any other way … but the dog, being rabid –"

The sound of rapid knocks at the door cut him off; much to his relief.

Chance crossed the room to open the door motioning for the doctor to enter the room, stepping out into the hallway to wait while the doctor examined the lovely patient.

"Well, Reanna, just what kind of mischief have you gotten yourself into this time?" the doctor, a short, balding man with kind gray eyes looked sternly through his wire rimmed spectacles toward the girl resting on the quilt covered bed.

"I was riding out to the pond on Golden Girl, and a dog attacked us. Golden Girl started to fight him off, but I fell and hit my head. The next thing I knew, I woke up here. Mr. Nolton, it seems, found me on the side of the road and brought me here, but… but" tears streamed anew from her lovely emerald eyes at the loss of her beloved horse. "He had to kill Golden Girl," she finished in a broken whisper.

Dr. Farley patted the distressed girl's hand in gentle commiseration. "I am very sorry about your horse, Reanna. I know how much store you set in her, but we must be thankful that you will be all right." He had deftly finished his examination.

"You have several bad bruises, and that bump on your head bears watching, and although you have broken no bones, I suggest that you rest for the time being." Dr. Farley then summoned Chance back into the room, assuring him that Reanna would be fine with a bit of rest.

Chance turned to Reanna, relieved that she was not seriously injured. "Well, my lady, do you think you can ride? I can see you home if you don't mind riding double." In fact, he thought to himself, he was quite looking forward to the prospect.

Reanna had been sitting up, but her head was throbbing so, she did not think that she dared to try and stand.

"I … I don't think …"

"That's quite all right. Listen, I was supposed to meet someone; attend to some business. So, while I'm gone, why don't you just rest here" I can lock the door so that you won't be bothered."

"No, I think that I have caused you enough trouble for one day," Reanna replied softly.

Deciding that he really did not want to let her go, Chance remained firm, "Oh, believe me, it's no trouble at all. In fact, I could … insist."

Reanna gasped, shocked, "Really, sir! I don't think-"

Doctor Farley broke in, thoroughly scandalized, "Mister, you can't really mean to keep Reanna locked in your hotel room like a trollop! Don't you realize who-"

A loud rap on the door cut the doctor off. Chance irritably swung the portal open, ready to do battle. He was not used to being opposed in his desires. But it was his friend Bob Dublin, who stood on the other side.

Bob, a tall husky man with thick gray hair and laughing blue eyes, smiled broadly in greeting. He gave Chance a friendly clap on the shoulder.

"Nolton! Good to see you. How the hell have you been? I heard that you arrived early this morning. It's good to see you, old friend!"

Chance returned Bob's smile, forgetting his irritation of a moment ago. "It's good to see you, Bob. How long has it been" Let's see, it must be three or four years since I last saw you."

"Five, but who's counting?"

"Uncle Bob?" Reanna was horrified at what it must look like to her uncle, finding her in a man's hotel room, in his bed.

"Reanna! What in God's name child?" Bob questioned suspiciously and turned an accusing eye toward Chance.

Chance, astonished, managed to blurt out, "Uncle?"

Reanna quickly sought to waylay her uncle's fears. "Oh, Uncle, it's not what you think! Golden Girl and I were attacked by a dog. I fell and was knocked unconscious. Mr. Nolton found me, brought me here, and sent for Dr. Farley."

The doctor, chuckling now at Chance's discomfort, was swift to assure the sheriff, "That's right Bob, and Reanna will be fine. She's bruised and shaken a bit, but all she needs is a little rest."

He then turned to Reanna with a twinkle of amusement in his eyes. "Leave it to you, young lady, to stir up all this commotion!"

Reanna managed a small smile, but it quickly vanished at her uncle's next words.

"I'm certainly glad that your father is out of town! He would worry himself sick if he knew about this. You know how he dotes on you."

"He'll have to know," she said sadly, "Golden Girl had to be killed. Her leg was broken, and the dog was surely rabid." As Reanna spoke, tears threatened to spill once more from her eyes.

Bob looked at his niece with tender concern. "Damn!" he swore softly, "That's too bad, Reanna, a real shame. She was as fine a horse as I've ever seen, and I know she meant the world to you. I will have the bodies … taken care of."

Dr. Farley took his leave, admitting that he had left patients cooling their heels in his waiting room to rush over.

"Jeremy said only that you were hurt, and that a strange man had carried you in here. I had no way of knowing what to expect."

Bob said, "I'll walk you out. I must see about getting a carriage to take Reanna home. That way," he glanced pointedly aside to his niece, "she can't get into any more trouble, and Martha will see to it that she gets the rest she needs."

With Bob and the doctor both gone, Reanna found herself once more alone with Chance. He slowly unfolded his lithe form from where he had been lounging with arms crossed against the wall, and advanced toward the bed with smooth, catlike grace, never taking his eyes from the beautiful girl. He reminded her of a sleek feline.

Reanna swallowed dryly, feeling as if she were a morsel to be devoured as he locked her in his mesmerizing dark gaze. His raven hair hung to his shirt collar, and his virile features looked as if they had been chiseled in granite. A neatly trimmed mustache accented his full, sensuous lips. He bent his tall form over her and murmured in a deep, husky voice, "My fair lady, I hope you do not feel your bruises too painfully … or for too long."

Reanna swallowed nervously, struggling to speak. His very nearness made it difficult even to draw breath, and for some reason, her heart quickened its beat. "I – I thank you for your concern, Mr. Nolton."

At the sight of her shy smile, and becoming pink blush, Chance felt something stir within him. Not recognizing the feeling, he interpreted it as lust, since he had little other experience with women. He abruptly straightened and moved away, continuing from a safer distance, "I am really very sorry about your mare, Miss Dublin."

"There was little else you could have done Mr. Nolton, and I thank you for doing it. I would not have been able to bring myself to … to do it," she finished in a whisper.

At that moment Bob Dublin returned, announcing in a hearty voice, "Well, Reanna, let's get you home. Chance, be at my house at six for dinner. We can discuss business then."

He carefully helped Reanna from the bed and to the door, where she turned and offered Chance another shy smile. "Goodbye Mr. Nolton. I hope that I'll see you again."

This time Chance returned her smile. "Goodbye Miss Dublin."

As he closed the door after them, he thought, you will see me again Reanna Dublin, of that there is little doubt. He smiled, remembering those shapely legs he had glimpsed earlier, her full lips, long silken hair and bewitching green eyes. He had never seen eyes so green, so compelling, as if the sea danced within their depths. Laying on the bed with arms crossed beneath his head, his smile broadened as he caught the fresh scent of roses that lingered even after Reanna had gone.

Fortunately for the object of his thoughts, the ride to her uncle's house was a short one, for the jostling of the carriage brought renewed pain to her aching head and bruised body. She heaved a sigh of relief when they pulled up in front of the whitewashed fence that surrounded the immaculately kept house and gardens, and Bob helped her from the carriage and along the short stone walk to the door.

As they entered the house, Aunt Martha, a tall, large framed woman with graying brunette hair worn in a chignon, came from the kitchen to greet them.

Noting Reanna's pallor, she was immediately concerned. "Reanna, you don't look at all well. Is something wrong? What has happened?" Her kindly brown eyes were full of worry.

"Martha, if you will see Reanna to her room, I will explain everything. Right now, I think she needs to lie down."

When Martha had bustled Reanna off and comfortably settled her in the bed in the upstairs guest room, she softly closed the door and hurried back down to her husband.

"Well, Bob, what has happened?" she demanded. "That poor child looks awful!"

After hearing his account of the accident, Martha, although saddened by the death of Golden Girl, was also concerned with the damage that might have been done to her niece's reputation.

Anger at Chance made her speak more sharply than she meant to. "Whatever possessed that man, bringing Reanna up to his hotel room instead of to Dr. Farley's office? And don't give me any of your innocent looks, either! You know how people will talk. They will think the worst!"

Bob answered, defending Chance, "I'm sure that he meant no harm. I guess it's just that he is not exactly used to worrying about a lady's reputation. And I invited him to dinner tonight, so please don't stay too angry with him."

Turning on her heel and muttering to herself about the inconsideration's of the male race, Martha returned to her kitchen.

Reanna's dreams were filled with visions of Chance Nolton: his face, his dashing manner, as she slept peacefully on through the afternoon, but as she slowly came awake, she discovered that her conscious thoughts were filled with his handsome presence, as well. She sighed with pleasure, recalling that he was tall, and bronzed from many hours in the sun, with a broad chest and shoulders, and long, lean torso and legs. When he had smiled and gazed down into her eyes with his penetrating deep brown orbs, she felt as though he had seen what lay hidden beneath her clothing. She flushed at the thought and glanced nervously around the room, chiding herself for the bent of these foolish musings. For all she knew, he might be a married man with children, likely a very pretty wife, much more so than herself. She would do well to keep a tight rein on her wandering thoughts if she did not want to blush all evening when he joined them for dinner.

She stretched, glancing fondly around the familiar room in which she had slept so many times through the years. The bed, wardrobe, and dresser were made of oak and gleamed softly with a polished sheen. The waxed floorboards were covered with a braided rug and a colorful, soft quilt neatly blanketed the bed.

A breeze fluttered the sheer white curtains that hung at the window as Reanna's glance took in her bags that were set by the door. Uncle Bob must have sent her cousin Jared after them while she slept, which meant that everyone at the ranch would know of her accident by now. She hoped that they would not worry overmuch on her account, but she could almost hear Carmelita's aggrieved tone now.

Deciding that she had best change for dinner, she climbed from the bed and removed her soiled clothing. Washing off the dusty residue of her ill-fated ride, she donned a simple dinner dress, wincing slightly as she pulled it on. Her bruises would without a doubt be painful for several days.

The dress was fashioned of green muslin sprigged with tiny yellow embroidered violets, and the moderate neckline and long sleeves were trimmed with yellow lace. She buttoned the bodice up the front and pulled a dark green velvet belt around her slender waist, tying it in a large bow in the back.

Next, she brushed out her long hair and braided its long length down her back. Winding the large braid about her head, she fastened it back with a green bow that matched her belt, but stray tendrils escaped at the nape of her neck and in front of her ears, framing her face with wisps of curls.

She pulled green slippers onto her feet, and last of all fastened a simple gold chain about her neck. With a last critical pat of her hair, she turned and lightly descended the stairs.

Reanna's head felt much better, the pain dulled now to a slight headache. Her body ached here and there, but she realized that this would fade also as the days went by. It was not the first time that she had been thrown from a horse, and it probably would not be the last.

As Reanna entered the parlor, she saw that Chance had already arrived and was sitting with the family enjoying drinks before dinner.

"Good evening, everyone." Reanna's greeting included her two cousins, Michael, who was fourteen, with light sandy brown hair, a liberal sprinkling of freckles across his nose, and blue eyes that reflected his personality, full of boisterous good fun, and Jared, seventeen tomorrow, with his thick black hair and large brown eyes framed with thick lashes. His strapping build showed the promise of becoming a strong, handsome man when fully grown. In fact, his glance in their direction set many a young girls' hearts aflutter, even now.

The men stood as everyone returned her greeting and besieged her with questions regarding her health. After reassuring them that she was indeed going to be fine, Aunt Martha rose from the settee and poured her a glass of sherry. She thanked her aunt and took a tentative sip, glancing up to find that Chance was standing before her. He certainly had a disconcerting air about him, the way he could approach one without their knowledge.

"Miss Dublin, I had no idea that we would meet again so soon. When your uncle said that he was taking you home, I didn't know that he meant to his house. Do you live here?" He smiled and moved closer, his gaze boring down into her eyes.

That smile could surely melt even the coldest of hearts, Reanna thought. "No," she answered, "I live on a ranch with my father, Uncle Bob's brother. I had every intention of helping Aunt Martha prepare for tomorrow's picnic, but as it turned out, I have not been of much assistance. My father prefers that I spend time here when he is out of town, claiming that it helps to keep me out of trouble."

"And I would venture to say that he would consider it trouble to have been attacked by a mad dog, thrown from your horse, and finally, winding up in a strange man's hotel room. I must apologize for that last, I can see that he would worry, and I suppose if I had a daughter as beautiful as you, I would want to see that she was properly watched over, myself."

Reanna flushed deeply at his compliment and turned away in confusion to find a chair. "Excuse me, Mr. Nolton," she mumbled.

Chance arched a dark brow, immensely enjoying the sight of her narrow waist and softly swaying hips as she moved gracefully away.

Uncle Bob, watching the exchange, cleared his throat noisily, saying, "Let's all sit down, and Chance can bring us up on all he's been doing since we've seen him."

After they were all settled, Chance filled them in.

"Well, as you know, I've made excellent profits off my trading ship, which has enabled me to purchase a few business properties, and a few acres of land in California, which should greatly increase in value within a few years. One business that is doing exceptionally well is the hardware supply, which caters mostly to the needs of the miners. I was able to acquire it for a very reasonable sum from an old miner that I've known for years, who wanted to retire."

"I bet you could really make a bundle from mining", broke in Michael, and Chance smiled at the lad's enthusiasm.

"No, most people realize very little profit in digging for gold," he answered. "In fact, you can earn much more from shrewd investments, and studying the needs of the miners."

Reanna found herself completely immersed in the conversation, interested in learning any facet of this captivating man's life, and so Aunt Martha announced that it was time for dinner. They sat down to a feast of baked ham with glaze, mashed potatoes, fresh creamed peas with carrots, and dessert, warm apple pie with fresh whipped cream and coffee.

All through dinner they enjoyed themselves, laughing and conversing lightheartedly, but each time she ventured a glance in Chances direction, it would be to find his brow arched, dark eyes speculatively studying her. She would blush and quickly avert her eyes, feeling suddenly self-conscious, but before long she would be drawn back into the conversation and find herself laughing again.

Reanna loved being in her uncle's house, because of the light, happy atmosphere that surrounded his family, unlike home, with papa often so lonely and sad. The only time her father seemed completely happy was when he listened to her play her music. Her mother had loved music, and used to play the piano quite proficiently, and often.

Audra Dublin had begun teaching Reanna to play when she was only five years old, and she had just mastered it and begun to play well when her mother died, so papa had engaged tutors to further her education. She not only learned to play the piano and guitar, but also to sew fancy stitches, read, write, and decipher numbers. Her education was perhaps more complete than if she had gone to school in town, having had the advantage of many varied and well-read teachers.

Finishing the meal, Uncle Bob and Chance excused themselves and went into the study to discuss the business Chance had come for. Bob got right to the point. "I've been busy putting together a posse to go after the Corey gang. They are a notorious bunch; rode into town one night, terrorizing the citizens, and then robbed the bank. There are four of them, and they're unusually hard, cruel men. I won't tell you it's going to be easy, but then I suppose that you already know that."

Chance poured himself a brandy from Bob's desk and agreed without preamble, "Yes, but I always get what I go after."

He was thinking not only of the Corey gang, but of a certain copper-haired beauty as well.

Reanna retired with the rest of the family to the parlor, where Michael asked if she had her guitar.

Jared replied for her, "Yes, I brought it with her clothes. It's on the chest in the hall. I'll get it," he said to Reanna as she started to rise.

Both cousins love to hear her play, especially when her soft voice joined with the chords to fill the room with song.

Chance and Bob, working out a feasible plan of action in the study, were treated to bits and pieces of her soft serenade, and hearing the music, Chance could contain his curiosity no longer.

"Is that Miss Dublin singing?" he questioned.

"Yes, it is Reanna. She often plays and sings for us and is really very good. Has a voice like an angel" he boasted, hoping that he did not sound overly doting, although he knew he was. He had missed not having a daughter to spoil, and Reanna was the next best thing to having his own.

Chance found it increasingly difficult to concentrate on the business at hand. "Are we just about done here, Bob?"

Bob felt much the same. "Yes, by all means. Let's join the family in the parlor," he suggested.

When Reanna finished her song to spirited applause, she glanced up to find that Chance Nolton stood before her once again. His smile was wide, and his dark eyes shone with approval.

He certainly was disarming, she thought once again, with his enticing smile, but his prying eyes frightened her somewhat.

He reached out to take her hand in his, raising it to his lips where he placed a light kiss upon her palm, sending a swift, warm current unexpectedly through her. If she were not already seated, she very likely would have swooned.

"Miss Dublin," he began in his smooth, deep voice, "that was easily some of the most beautiful music I have ever heard. May I impose upon you to play another melody before I leave?"

She shivered from some force that she did not quite understand, and finally found her voice. "I'd be happy to, sir."

Now it was Chance's turn to be disarmed, for when Reanna turned the full force of her dazzling smile upon him, he knew that he was caught, that he must have this lovely, talented creature. He found it hard to look away, his glance being drawn to the way the gown she wore clung to the shape of her full breasts.

Suddenly it dawned on him that she was attempting to pull her hand from his. "If I could have my hand back, sir," she said softly, her eyes sparkling with amusement.

Chance laughed almost awkwardly, likening himself, in his own mind, to the fourteen-year-old Michael, and quickly relinquished her hand to turn and find a seat.

Reanna chose a ballad she learned from her Indian friend, Mansunama, many years ago. It told of the sea and the birds that flew free there, receiving life and giving it back again. It was a song that she thought Chance would enjoy after hearing his talk and enjoy it he did.

Chance thought that he would have found pleasure in anything she sang, with her clear, soothing voice and matchless beauty. In fact, watching her graceful movements afforded him as much pleasure as did her singing.

When she finished, Chance reluctantly rose to take his leave. "I really must go now, but I will see you all tomorrow, as Bob has invited me to the picnic. Thank you all for a wonderful evening. Martha, the meal was delicious. It was a welcome change to have a good home cooked meal. And Miss Dublin, thank you for the enchanting entertainment."

He crossed the room to where she now stood, and taking her hand again, he watched her beguiling smile, the way her eyes sparkled and glittered like the deep green sea and caught the faint scent of roses that clung to her.

"I will see you tomorrow, Miss Dublin," he assured her softly, and brought her hand up once more to brush a light, almost teasing kiss across the back of it, watching intently for her reaction.

Reanna was indeed tantalized, feeling as if she wanted more, much more of this man's attention.

He smiled as if he knew her thoughts before he turned and walked with Bob to the door. To her acute embarrassment, she found that three pairs of eyes were watching her closely.

Aunt Martha smiled and queried, "What do you think of our charming rogue, Reanna?"

"I think he is really only coming to our picnic to see Reanna," Michael declared.

Reanna simply smiled affectionately at the teasing remark and bid them all good night.

Morning dawned bright, clear, and warm, a perfect day for a picnic. Aunt Martha rose early and fried an abundant supply of chicken to crispy perfection and baked dozens of soft, flaky rolls, with a fresh rhubarb pie for dessert.

Reanna rose and joined her aunt in the kitchen, wrapping and packing the food into large wicker baskets, and simmering baked beans into crocks to keep them warm. She also added fresh strawberries, and the last of the dried apple and pear slices preserved for the winter gone by. As she worked, she became engrossed with vivid thoughts of

Chance's gentle touch and dark burning eyes, the smooth timbre of his voice.

Suddenly she realized she had stopped working and was foolishly smiling at nothing, and that Aunt Martha was watching her with a knowing smile. Blushing furiously, she returned to her work, determined that she must keep her mind off of Chance Nolton, for she had no desire to be caught standing around grinning at nothing in particular.

Bob had gone into his office in town early to check for messages and to complete some paperwork, and when he returned, Martha started some breakfast cooking while Reanna set the table.

Michael and Jared; waking to the pleasant aroma of sizzling bacon, hurriedly dressed, bounding down the stairs and into the kitchen with their usual ravenous appetites.

When the meal was finished, Martha and Reanna restored some semblance of order to the kitchen and did the dishes while the men loaded and hitched up the wagon that would carry them all to the pond for their picnic.

Reanna hurried up the stairs to change for the day's celebration, carefully unpacking the Indian outfit that she planned to wear. Her friend Mansunama had gifted her with the unique creation at a time when she had been stricken with grief over the death of her fiancé, in an effort to lift her flagging spirits.

Running her hand over the softly tanned doeskin, she allowed her mind to dwell on the close companion of her youth, Mansunama. She did not see him now, for he was the tribal Shaman, or medicine man, and as such had assumed a heavy burden of responsibility to his people.

Slipping the sleeveless, waist-length top over her soft white shoulders, she began to lace the front closure with a strip of rawhide, admiring the fine pattern worked in the tiny beads and porcupine quills that bordered each side of the front opening. The calf length skirt hugged her narrow waist before flaring out to the full, fringed hemline and laced up both sides in a crisscross pattern and tied at the waist, the ends of the laces embellished with rawhide medallions worked in the same pattern of bead work as the top, and lastly, she pulled on knee high moccasins which lace up the front and were also trimmed to match.

Parting her hair in the center, she secured each side in a leather thong, crisscrossing its length to bind her tresses for a short way before allowing it to tumble free, to spill over her shoulders, and after a swift glance in the mirror, ran lightly down the stairs.

Hearing Aunt Martha call to her from outside, she crossed hastily to the front door and was about to pull it open when it swung wide, stopping her in her tracks as Chance's tall frame filled the doorway.

"Ah, Miss Dublin, I was just coming in to call you. Everyone is in the wagon, ready to leave."

His eyes boldly swept her length, appreciating the way her unusual attire clung closely to her very feminine curves. Coming to rest on the soft swell of her bosom, his gaze lingered speculatively for a moment before he proffered his arm asking, "May I Miss Dublin?"

"Thank you, sir," she answered, shyly taking his arm. "That's a very becoming outfit, Miss Dublin."   She replied shyly, " Some friends made it for me."

After assisting Reanna into the wagon with a great show of gallantry, Chance climbed in next to her, and they were on their way, Chance laughing and joking with her cousins as they sat among the hay and picnic baskets in the bed of the swaying conveyance.

Arriving at the pond just outside of town, they disembarked and spread several blankets on the ground to hold their supply of food and to provide resting places when desired.

The rest of the morning was spent playing various games, including horseshoes, races, and scavenger hunts. They were having a wonderful time, and even Chance found himself really enjoying the frivolous, carefree atmosphere. The sound of his deep laughter mingled gaily with the others, until, exhausted, everyone sat down to partake of the picnic feast.

Replete after their meal, they all relaxed in the shade. Chance, leaning back lazily against the trunk of a tree, noted that Bob and Martha were dozing off, their arms entwined, while the sound of droning insects filled the heavy afternoon air.

Michael and Jared had shed their shirts and shoes with the intention of going for a swim, and Chance pulled his hat down to shade his eyes, thinking to nap for a while. He quickly changed his mind, however, when he glimpsed Reanna near the woods, heading down a path he had taken note of earlier. A slow smile spread over his features, and pushing his hat back up, he rose with slow, deliberate grace and went to join her.

Reanna started when Chance appeared suddenly at her side, and he offered an apology. "It wasn't my intention to frighten you, Miss Dublin. I just thought that you might enjoy some company on your walk."

"Yes, that would be nice, Mr. Nolton."

They strolled down the narrow path through the woods, side by side. Sunlight filtered down through the dense canopy of green leaves to dapple the earth with slowly moving light, and Reanna spied a mockingbird high in the bough of a tree, singing a bubbling song. They stopped to enjoy the refrain for a moment.

"Mr. Nolton, may I ask you a question?" Reanna ventured hesitantly.

"Certainly, sweet lady, what is it?" Chance answered, turning to face her.

"Will it be very dangerous? The posse, I mean. I will worry greatly about you and Uncle Bob, and the rest of the men."

"Miss Dublin," Chance smiled, "I thank you for your concern, and yes, there is always the possibility that some of us may not return. But we have worked out a good plan, and the men, I'm told, are good men. And your Uncle Bob is totally adept at taking care of himself, as am I. In fact, your uncle saved my life once."

"What happened?" Reanna queried her eyes wide in astonishment at this unexpected information.

Chance stared down at her, suddenly, painfully aware of the alluring curve of her mouth, and he longed to sear those softly parted lips with his own. His gaze dropped and he burned to undo the laces that held her softly molded breast, to feel those ample curves that beckoned to him. Dragging his gaze from so tempting a sight, he found himself drowning in her wide green, innocent eyes, and he curbed his less than honorable desires. The fact that she was Bob's niece, a lady, so obviously innocent of men, caused him to think that they might be safer in the company of others, before he succumbed to his male longings.

"I will tell you all about it sometime. Right now, why don't we go back: I'm sure that Bob and Martha are awake and wondering where we are by now."

Confused by his suddenly brisk manner, she allowed him to hasten her back to her family, and the rest of the day passed quickly, until it was time to pack up and go home for an early evening, as everyone was tired. Chance took his leave, but stopped to reassure her as he noticed Reanna's pained expression.

"Miss Dublin, try not to worry, please. I will see that no harm comes to your uncle, and I promise you, I will see you again … Good night." His eyes lingered upon hers for a long moment, as if he wished to say more, but then he turned and walked down the darkening street.

Reanna spent a restless night, tossing and turning, unable to sleep, and she heard Uncle Bob rise and leave to meet Chance and the rest of the posse well before daybreak.

Chapter 2

Reanna and Martha took a carriage into the center of town, intending to do some shopping. It was really just an excuse. What they were after was anything that would take their minds off wondering about the posse, even if just for a while.

The men had been gone for five days now, and the two women could not abide sitting at home and waiting any longer.

As Aunt Martha pulled the carriage to a stop in front of the dressmaker's shop, they could see a group of rough looking young men lounging about the boardwalk a few feet away. Reanna groaned silently as they alighted from the carriage, for they had attracted the attention of the group, who were now sauntering toward them with distinctly unpleasant expressions on their faces. She held no hope that she and her aunt would be allowed to pass without some sort of distasteful incident.

Even though she had been expecting trouble, Reanna started at the sudden loud, nasal voice that addressed them, sending a shiver of fear up her spine.

"Well, well, what have we here? I do believe that it's the proper little Miss Dublin and her fat aunt!" Larry McPherson spat and included a growing group of onlookers, who were attracted by the disturbance, in his glance, while his brothers chortled at his wit.

Reanna had always feared the McPherson brothers, and rightly so. Larry McPherson had narrowed hazel eyes that burned with hatred, fueled by the constant consumption of whiskey. They were eyes that held no warmth for his fellow man, only a barely repressed fury. His nose was protruding and hawk-like, and bent to the side, the result of having been broken countless times. His skin was deeply pockmarked, and his thin, cruel lips rose in a vicious smile over broken, blackened teeth. Also, Reanna assumed the result of his constant brawling.

His hostile voice rose loudly for all to hear. "And you from a rich, respected family too, Miss Dublin. Tell me, where were you, Auntie, when your sweet little niece was up in a man's hotel room, a dirty bounty hunter and known womanizer? Has our sweet, innocent, and respectable Reanna been taking lessons in the art of pleasing men?"

Reanna drew in her breath sharply, wondering how anyone could be so cruel and abusive, and those who knew her gasped in outrage. There were others, strangers in town, who now eyed her with keen interest, however.

Aunt Martha drew herself up to her full height, and with her nose high in the air, grasped Reanna's hand and pulled her through the crowd, shouldering a path to the shop's front door, and entering to the hooting and jeers of the McPhersons.

"Why, Aunt Martha, are they always so mean?" The sheen of unshed tears glistened in Reanna's wide eyes. "It is bad enough that I lost Golden Girl, but for them to turn what Chance did into something dirty … oh, why are they so hateful? We have never done them any harm!"

"Hush, Baby. That is the way they treat everyone." Aunt Martha drew a lace embellished handkerchief from her purse and gently wiped the tears that had begun to fall from Reanna's eyes. "There is not a kind bone in any of their bodies," she continued, "and the way they were brought up has a lot to do with it, I'm sure. Their father actually encouraged them to be nothing but ruffians and brawlers. He was an evil one, that man. I say it was the whiskey, and the sons are all the same. All cast from the same mold, the lot of them."

"Not all of them, Aunt Martha." Reanna laid her hand upon the older woman's before she went on. "Not Billy. He is different from the rest of them, kinder. And he doesn't frequent the saloon half as often."

Martha looked thoroughly disgusted. "Now Reanna, you just forget those childish, romantic notions of yours. If you had your way the whole world would be painted pink with roses. Real life is just not that way, child. Those McPherson boys are nothing but filthy vermin, and don't you worry, they will all stick together no matter what, like ticks to hounds, including Billy."

Martha looked so ruffled that Reanna made no reply. But still, she felt that Billy would someday be something better than his brothers.

"Oh, how I wish that your uncle could run them off, but they have done nothing that is against the law, really, at least not that anyone can prove. They were suspected in a few robberies, but without proof, nothing could be done, so here they remain," Martha added, and as she turned to the clerk to inquire after the dresses that they had come to pick up, Reanna heard her aunt mutter, "Fat, indeed!" and had to hide a small, tremulous smile of amusement. Aunt Martha preferred to think of herself as large boned.

When they finally left the dress shop, Larry, and the crowd he had attracted had dispersed, but there was another grouping down the road in front of the sheriff's office now.

The two women hurried to deposit their packages into the carriage and hasten to the jail.

"Your Uncle Bob is back!" Martha cried, and fairly pulled Reanna along. They squeezed through the growing crowd and entered the small brick building.

"Ah, the best part of my homecoming is always having you here to welcome me back, my love." Bob declared and gave Martha a hearty kiss on the cheek as they embraced, tears of relief shining in Martha's eyes.

Reanna, having determined that her uncle was unharmed, glanced about the small office at the trail-weary and dusty men. They stood in small groups recounting their successful mission. Two of the Corey gang had met with death; two would reside in Carson City's jail to await judgment of their crimes. It was a foregone conclusion that they would hang, however. This ruthless gang had terrorized the town and robbed the bank, shooting two men down in cold blood. There was no shortage of witnesses to their deeds, and the townsfolk were eager for vengeance.

Although she heard a few negative comments bandied about concerning Chance Nolton, the bounty hunter, Reanna found that the general opinion held was that if it were not for his expert gun-hand and tracking abilities, the posse would not have brought in the entire gang.

But where was he, Reanna wondered?

"Where is Mr. Nolton?" She asked her uncle. "I do not see him."

"Doctor's office, Reanna," he answered, but taking note of the automatic concern in the girl's eyes, hastened to remedy it. "He wasn't hurt too badly, but he did take a bullet in his arm that will have to be removed. He will survive. In fact, the doctor may have finished by now."

Reanna started for the door, asking, "Would it be all right if I go to him?" but then noticed the amusement on their faces, she added "Just to see if he needs anything."

"Certainly, Reanna," Uncle Bob gave his permission.

"I will come with you Reanna. Your uncle will have his hands full here for a while, and I would like to see how Chance is faring myself."

Entering Dr. Farley's office, they were surprised to see that Chance wavered unsteadily on a chair, grasping an empty whiskey bottle by the neck in one hand while the doctor did his best to bandage the bounty hunter's injured arm and support it in a sling.

"Missss Dubalinnnnn, how nice to ssseee you again," Chance drawled, inclining his head in an exaggerated gesture of greeting. He was having difficulty focusing his eyes, but he knew he saw the copper-haired maid, or were there two of her now?

"Dr. Farley!" Reanna began, "Why, he is drunk!" She sent the doctor an accusing glance.

"I had to make him drink to deaden the pain when I dug the bullet out and stitched his arm," the doctor defended.

"Oh … is there anything we can do to help?" she inquired in a gentler tone.

"If you two ladies could assist him to his room … I doubt that he could get there on his own. He just needs to rest for now. In fact, his head will likely feel worse than his arm does by tomorrow. I did not intend that he drink quite so much. But … he insisted."

Chance merely grinned at them all. He had lost track of how much liquor he'd consumed after finishing the first bottle on the ride back to town.

The women guided Chance to the hotel, where the disgruntled clerk assisted them in helping Chance up the stairs, complaining the whole way.

"I told him, I run a respectable establishment here. Then what did he do? He brought you to his room, Miss Dublin, and now … this!"

Reanna hid a smile at the clerk's nervous protestations and Martha snapped, "Really, Edward! He is not going to cause any trouble. In fact," she glanced aside at Chance, raising a speculative brow, "he will probably sleep like a baby until tomorrow morning."

They entered Chance's room and helped him into bed, and Reanna sat in the chair next to it while Martha and Edward wrestled the boots from his feet.

Chance turned and reached for her murmuring, "come here."

Reanna leaned closer and he touched her face, lightly running his fingers down her cheek. "Now it iss you who playsss the part of anngggell." His arm dropped to his side, and he closed his eyes, instantly asleep. Reanna smiled, pulled the quilt up to cover him, and left the room with her aunt.

For the next two days Martha and Reanna were in a flurry of activity, busy preparing for the large yard party held at the Dublin's every year to celebrate the advent of summer. All their friends and neighbors would attend, eager to partake in the mountains of food, plentiful drink, gay music, and lively dancing.

They had not seen Chance since the day of his return, but Bob assured them that he was progressing nicely. Reanna hoped that he would attend the party but could not bring herself to ask if he had been invited. Her cousins teased her enough as it was after hearing her question her uncle about the bounty hunter the other night, but at least now she knew that he was not married.

Friends and acquaintances of the Dublin's began to fill the backyard on the afternoon of the party. It was a beautiful, sunny day, if a bit on the warm side, with light clouds drifting across an azure blue sky.

Reanna had taken a place beside one of the long cloth covered tables that groaned with the weight of many condiments, serving a delicately spiked punch to the older ladies present, and the men availed themselves of the harder liquors. Most of the younger ladies helped themselves to wine or sherry. Reanna preferred the latter, although both her aunt and her father disapproved of more than one glass of any alcoholic beverage, so Reanna sipped only sparingly at a few small glasses when Martha was not watching too closely.

Several of the younger, single men had gathered at Reanna's table, greeting her warmly as they vied for the honor of her promise of a dance later on. She was happily looking forward to the coming music and chatting gaily when she suddenly felt as if she were being observed very closely.

She glanced up to find that Chance Nolton had arrived and stood just a few feet from her. He treated her to a rakish smile as he casually closed the distance between them, while his eyes devoured her in a boldly assessing fashion. His admiration was evident when he met her eyes, and Reanna blushed, feeling for the first time, the extreme heat of the afternoon.

She smiled widely showing even white teeth, and her heart began to beat faster as he approached.

"Miss Dublin, you are a vision to behold," he said softly, and his eyes lowered to her breasts and lingered for a moment, watching their rise and fall at the low, ruffled bodice as her breathing quickened noticeably, causing his smile to broaden as he duly noted this fact.

Her attire suited her admirably, he thought. A white cotton peasant blouse with a wide band of crocheted lace edging the deeply ruffled neckline contrasted nicely with the skirt she wore, a many tiered confection of ruffled sating, its narrow green and blue stripes gleaming dully in the sunlight. Her unbound hair cascaded in heavy waves around her face and over her creamy shoulders to her waistline, shining with fiery highlights in the sun.

Reanna felt naked beneath his penetrating gaze and found herself wishing that she had worn something a bit more modest. "Thank you, Mr. Nolton. You look quite handsome yourself," she complimented him shyly.

Chance wore a white silk shirt, gathered to fullness at the shoulders and above the wide buttoned cuffs, with a few of the top front buttons undone that exposed a portion of his bronzed, furred chest. His black breeches fit snugly, showing to advantage his thick, muscular thighs.

"You seem to be quite popular with all the young men Miss Dublin. How can a rogue such as myself ever hope to compete with them all for your affections?"

Reanna's smile faded as she became staidly serious, "Would you really want to, Mr. Nolton?"

Chance had no time to form an answer, for Bob appeared at that moment, interrupting their conversation. "Reanna, the barbecue is ready, and your aunt could use your help for a while."

They had slowly roasted many large beef roasts on spits over pits filled with hot coals for most of the day, turning them now and again to assure even cooking. The men had taken them down, and now they needed to be cut into thin slices, something that several of the women had been delegated to do.

With a last quick glance at Chance, she turned to go, but was stopped by his deep voice. "Miss Dublin, we will talk later."

She smiled again and hurried away, leaving Chance to admire once again the graceful sway of her skirted hips.

When everyone had eaten their fill, Jared brought out Reanna's guitar and, at many neighborly urgings, she agreed to play just a few songs while everyone relaxed, for she longed to dance this day.

Chance watched with rapt attention as her long, elegant fingers began to coax a melody from the instrument, deftly working the strings while her soft, mellow voice rose in song. He agreed with everyone else gathered around, Reanna had great talent. There were few who could match her in melody,

41

and, he thought privately, there were few women who could match her in any way. She was exquisitely perfect, with the face, form, and grace of a goddess.

He had learned many things about her in the time he had been here. She was very well admired by everyone, treating her elders with respect, and always ready to help a friend in need. She was kind and gentle, loyal, and understanding, and even though her father owned the largest ranch in the territory, the High Ridge, and had plenty of money, she acted totally unspoiled and generous to all.

Reanna finished, tired of playing, and looking forward eagerly to the dancing, she handed her guitar over to Kenny, who would continue playing in her stead. Kenny and Molly Beckett were very good friends of the entire Dublin family, and especially to Reanna.

There were a few more guests who joined in, playing harmonicas, and a fiddle. The amateur musicians struck up a lively beat, and those who desired to do so paired off for the dancing.

Reanna was quickly claimed and whirled away by Tony, and danced the whole evening through, next with Joseph, then Gary, and Sean who worked for her father on the ranch. He was quite obviously smitten with his employer's beautiful daughter, although his blond good looks and bright blue twinkling eyes made him a favorite with more than a few unmarried young ladies.

Reanna was given no respite, for as soon as she finished with one partner, she was immediately whisked away by another, until finally, out of breath she begged Joseph to accompany her to one of the large tables for refreshments. She was exhausted, though pleasantly so, and exuberantly happy.

After they had rested for a time, enjoying their drinks, Reanna excused herself, taking time out to retire to her room, where she washed the sheen of perspiration from her flushed face, enjoying the cool water that touched her heated skin. She ran the cloth over her exposed chest and, lifting the heavy weight of her hair, the back of her neck. She closed her eyes and sighed with pleasure, relaxing for a few blissfully quiet moments before returning to the party.

Heading directly back to the table she had left, she found that Chance was there waiting for her. As she neared, he smiled broadly, saying, "I knew that I would have trouble competing with all of them." He gestured with a slight movement of his head toward the dancing crowd, then, becoming serious, he moved closer, so close that she could feel the faint tickle of his breath upon her neck, as his question sounded more like a gentle command "Now, Miss Dublin, might I have the pleasure of a dance?"

A strange shiver of excitement rushed through her, and although she had just washed, and the night air had cooled, she felt flushed with heat. She smiled faintly and found her voice, "I would love to dance with you, sir, but Joseph was waiting here for my return. I had promised him the next dance."

"I have taken care of that inconvenience," he informed her. "And now, may I?"

He offered her his good arm and escorted her to where the musicians stood casually grouped and leaned over to speak quietly to Kenny.

It occurred to Reanna to wonder just what it was that Chance had done or said to Joseph in order to ensure that this dance be his, but Kenny was nodding, the music had changed to a slow, intimate beat, and Chance turned to gather her in his one good arm. At the touch, all thoughts of Joseph fled her mind; she was caught in his penetrating gaze, which burned with an intense desire.

All night he had watched as she gracefully danced with the many full tiers of her skirt swirling gaily about her as her white booted feet kept perfect time and her dark hair billowed around her in a wild, silken veil, while he patiently waited his turn.

Now he led her through the waltz with practiced ease, and all the while his intense dark gaze never wavered from the deep green of hers. He loved the feeling of holding her close, while the soft scent of roses that drifted lightly about her teased his senses. He drew her more closely against his hard body and she did not protest, enjoying for the first time the faint stirrings of passion as a heat, which had nothing to do with the weather, suffused her body.

She gazed up into his eyes with a mixture of surprise, curiosity, and fear, for she knew that she could easily learn to love this man, and was equally sure that he could, and probably would, break her heart. Although she yearned with all of her young heart to know love again, she was terribly frightened of living with the heartache that love could bring, having endured it once before.

This man was as free as the wind, and she did not doubt that he wanted to stay that way. Yet even knowing this, his attraction was such that she felt she would not be able to resist if he pressed his suit hard enough. Therefore, she would have to have faith in her powers as a woman, and work to do all she could to keep him, for she was convinced that here was the man for her. All she had to do was convince him to return her love.

She suddenly realized that he had maneuvered her into a dark corner of the yard, and they were no longer dancing. He crushed her to him and hoarsely whispered "I curse this sling that keeps me from holding you properly."

She opened her mouth to speak, but in that instant his lips descended to hers, claiming them in harsh demand, hot, probing, insistent to taste the sweetness of her.

After her initial shock, she responded, slowly at first, then with increasing ardor as he masterfully awakened in her a heated desire. She leaned into him; pressing her soft curves against his lean male hardness as her knees grew weak and her heart hammered in her chest.

Belatedly remembering where they were, Reanna pulled sharply away, pushing him from her with shaking hands, and gasping for breath, turned abruptly from him to hide her blush of shame.

He moved to her, laying a hand firmly upon her shoulder, and she started as the heat of his touch burned her. The whisper of his soft, breathless voice caressed her ear. "I apologize, Miss Dublin, if I was perhaps too ardent in my desire for you. Please forgive me."

"No, Mr. Nolton, don't be sorry. I just …. Would you mind seeing me to the house? I am exhausted and wish to retire for the night. It has been a busy day." She closed her eyes for just an instant, her long, soft lashes dark against her creamy skin.

"As you wish," Chance answered quietly, and escorted her to the door. But before she could enter its promising quiet haven, he turned her to him and kissed her again, gently this time, brushing her lips lightly with his own, the way she was accustomed to being kissed by the few beaus that had courted her, even if he did prolong the tender contact. Even Daniel, to whom she had been engaged, had never kissed her as Chance Nolton had done. He lifted his head and grinned down in a knowing way, as if he sensed her inner turmoil, and he bid her good night.

Chance watched her go, then returned to the table where he had met Reanna earlier, determined to drown his desires in drink, so poured himself a glass of brandy, but then he stood, considering, staring blankly down into his glass. The red-haired maiden was beginning to get under his skin. He raised his drink and voiced his thoughts aloud. "Bob, old friend, I think that you have involved me in something a hell of a lot more dangerous than riding posse."

Hours later, when the party had dwindled to only Sam Dentin, the barkeep from the saloon, Chance wandered to the house, having been invited to spend the night. Martha had retired long ago and Bob, having imbibed in too much liquor, was arguing politics with Sam, and Chance was tired. His thoughts were on the enchanting Reanna, the taste of her sweet lips, the soft satin of her skin, and the tempting allure of her generous curves.

He suddenly became obsessed with the urge to see her, and after only a slight hesitation, made his unsteady way up the stairs.

Having stayed here once, years ago, he knew which room was reserved for guests, and assumed that would be where he could find Reanna. Knocking softly, he received no reply, so he silently entered her room.

She was sleeping peacefully, bathed in faint white light from the moonbeam as it streamed through her open window. One slender arm was raised above her head, and Chance stood, transfixed, gazing upon her slumbering beauty. Her creamy skin was smooth as satin, her long lashes dark smudges against her cheeks, and her hair tumbled and spread long lengths of curls over her pillow.

He swallowed tightly, longing to run his hands over her curvaceous form, covered only by a thin sheet. He should not have come here, and was turning to leave when her soft lips parted and he heard her murmur, with pain evident in her voice, "Daniel ... why, Daniel?"

Chance narrowed his eyes, his brows furrowing. Who the hell was Daniel? He felt, for the first time in his life, a painful stab of jealousy. It gave him something to think about as he softly left her room and closed the door, returning to the parlor without a sound. He did not ponder this new knowledge for long however, making his way only as far as the first comfortable chair before drink overcame him, and he sunk into the plump cushions, where he spent what was left of the night.

Reanna fairly floated down the stairs the next morning. There would be a huge amount of cleaning up to do, but she did not mind the work, and she had had such a good time last night!

She burned at the memory of Chance's lips upon hers, and it brought a heated flush to her cheeks. Then she stopped in her tracks, spying the object of her thoughts sprawled in a parlor chair, deeply asleep. A lock of his raven black hair hung down across his forehead, and his hat rested at an odd angle on his head. She could not suppress a giggle. Chance, who never seemed to have anything out of place, slept in his rumpled attire, the result, Reanna decided, of having imbibed in too much liquor, and he would awake feeling the aftereffects very strongly.

Martha was already in the kitchen, preparing a huge breakfast and much coffee, so Reanna went into the backyard to begin straightening the mess left by the guests. By the time she was finished, Aunt Martha was waking the men, fearful the food she had prepared would be ruined. She had kept it warm long enough.

Reanna was busy setting out dishes when Chance entered the kitchen, rumpling his hair with his good hand. She smiled brightly and handed him a steaming cup of coffee.

"Would you like something to eat?" she queried, receiving a miserable groan in answer as Chance found a chair and sat gingerly upon the seat.

"No thanks, Miss Dublin. The coffee will more than suffice," he finally stated softly.

Reanna could not resist the urge to indulge in just one gibe and widening her eyes in mock innocence, asked, "Why, Mr. Nolton, is there something wrong?"

He gazed hard at her for a moment from red rimmed eyes, as if weighing his words, and then with jaundiced brow raised, he answered "I found that I had need of drowning my ... sorrow, after your abrupt departure last night. Your sweet kisses had me yearning for much more – but I trust that you, at least, slept well?"

Reanna's face grew crimson as she lowered her eyes and toyed with the silver on the table. She sat uneasily on the chair across from his, wishing now that she had never spoken.

The silence dragged on as she searched for something – anything to say, and taking a deep breath, she began to talk avidly, ignoring what had just passed between them. She told Chance about the wonderful time she'd had last night, of how she so loved to dance, and then, without stopping for a breath, informed him of her plans for the day.

She was to ride out to visit old Mrs. Oliver, a widow who lived alone in a small log cabin in the hills. She was not able to get around very well, so, Reanna explained, she visited the old woman often, bringing her food supplies and friendship. She always brought her guitar along also, as Mrs. Oliver loved to hear her sing.

Before long Chance had forgotten his throbbing head, so intrigued had he become in Reanna's words. He was struck anew by her loyal generosity and compassion for those around her, and her passion for life.

He began to feel, in fact, like a heel for his earlier words. He should not have said something that he knew would embarrass her.

All too soon, it seemed, Bob and the boys entered the kitchen, and the sheriff requested that Chance accompany him to town, for there seemed to be trouble brewing over the men who were in jail, and he needed Chance's gun arm to help dissuade any from taking the law into their own hands.

Chance agreed, and the men left Reanna, but she stayed in the bounty hunter's thoughts throughout the day, and for the next several, as he was kept busy at the jail and had meetings set up with more than a few individuals who wanted to invest in his next cargo, or who needed his financial support for ventures of their own.

Somehow, her vision danced constantly before his eyes. He could see her soft beauty and dancing green eyes. He would catch the elusive scent of roses and feel the immense love she seemed to have for other people, indeed, for every aspect of life.

And Reanna, it seemed, suffered the same affliction as Chance. She wondered how long she would have to wait before seeing him again in other than her dreams.

Reanna's father Raymond returned, having successfully negotiated for the sale of several hundred cattle, and decided to celebrate the occasion by taking Reanna and his brother's family out to dinner.

The restaurant was actually a combined saloon, restaurant, and dance hall. The floors were smoothly worn, wide planked wood, and red velvet curtains hung in all the windows, the 'Horseshoes' only attempt at grace and charm. Above the front door, a weathered sign swung in the wind, a creaking testament to its existence since it looked much the same as the other buildings lining the main street of Carson City.

It was a comfortable place where respectable women could be taken out and courted, treated to a wholesome meal and an evening of dancing. Although there was an occasional quarrel, and even a brawl, the saloon was a separate room from the dining and dancing area, and so the diners were seldom bothered by the excessive binges of reveling cowhands.

The congenial group seated at a center table, enjoying before dinner drinks, and catching up on each other's news, included Raymond Dublin, Bob and Martha, and their boys, Michael, and Jared. Reanna had stopped to see her friend Avis, a plump, blond-haired young woman whose mother was a seamstress in the dress shop. She planned to join the party a little after the others.

An hour later Reanna was on her way to dinner, walking the short distance to the Horseshoe as she relived the troubling events of that morning. Her father had come directly to his brother's house, anxious to see his only child. And they had told him the sad details of her accident and Golden Girls' death. When Reanna described her savior, Chance Nolton, in glowing terms, telling her father how wonderful she thought him to be, he had grown increasingly angry with her, something he very rarely did.

Her father knew all about Chance Nolton. His reputation as a fast gun, his winning ways with women, and he was adverse even to the idea of the bounty hunter staying in town, anywhere near his beautiful daughter. The man was bad news, and certainly not good enough to toy with the affections of his only child.

Reanna could not understand it. After all, Chance had put his life in danger when he rode with the posse to apprehend the outlaws bedeviling their town and had also come without hesitation to her aid.

Sighing in resignation, Reanna entered the crowded, smoky saloon, and still deep in thought, made her way around the boisterous throng grouped at the bar, heading slowly to the door that opened to the large dining room. She was halfway there when someone grabbed her arm, pulling her to an abrupt stop. She turned in surprise to meet the cold, calculating eyes of Larry McPherson.

Frightened, she struggled in vain to pull away, but he only smiled at her efforts and yanked her roughly to him, bringing his mouth down harshly upon hers. Revolted, Reanna pushed at him with her hands, using all her strength, and twisted her head away, finally managing to break his hold.

"Pig!" she hissed as her hand shot out to slap him, so soundly that her hand burned from the impact, and Larry's eyes narrowed dangerously. "You shouldn't have done that," he warned, then grabbed her again, pulling her arms behind her to hold them in one punishing hand while he savagely yanked her hair with the other, forcing her head back with the intent of bruising her lips once again.

Closing her eyes tightly against the pain, Reanna brought her knee up hard, striking blindly, and hit home. With an exclamation of pain and indrawn breath, Larry abruptly released her, and she staggered back, but two of his brothers, Cal and Darrel, jumped forward to hold her immobile in an unbreakable grip. They were very drunk, laughing at what she had done, when Larry advanced on her once again, his mouth turned up in a nasty sneer. She knew that he was going to strike her and steeled herself to accept the blow.

Chance Nolton was seated at a corner table, deeply immersed in conversation with a business associate as they pored over a stack of paperwork. Becoming aware of some sort of disturbance, he glanced up and across the room.

Spying the long copper tresses, he immediately identified Reanna and leapt to her aid, pushing away anyone in his path as he purposely strode toward her.

Larry drew his hand back to strike, but halted immediately when he felt the sharp jab of a gun barrel in his back.

"I wouldn't," came the deep steely voice from behind him, and Larry raised his hands away from his sides as he turned to meet the cool, assessing gaze of the bounty hunter. Keeping his gun trained on Larry, Chance flicked a contemptuous glance to the two who still held Reanna prisoner and ordered in a deadly voice, "Let go of the lady now, and get out, or I'll blow his head off!" He slowly raised his gun and leveled it at Larry's head.

Cal and Darrel swallowed and wordlessly released their intended victim, backing away for a distance before turning and running out the door like frightened schoolboys. Chance once again focused his attention on Larry who wasted no time in following his brothers, albeit a bit slower in his movements, and only after a hate-filled glance in Reanna's direction.

Reanna took a deep, shuddering breath and wrapped her arms about herself, attempting to ward off the sudden chill that gripped her.

Chance placed tender hands upon her shoulders in an effort to steady her. His concern was evident in his dark gaze as he questioned softly, "Are you all right, Miss Dublin?"

Reanna was comforted by the warmth of his gentle touch and smiled bravely up at him with gratitude shining in her deep green eyes. "Yes, I will be fine Mr. Nolton, and I must thank you once again for your help.

The McPherson brothers have always been mean, but tonight they were much worse than usual, probably because they were so thoroughly inebriated. They reeked of whisky," she added as she wrinkled her nose in disgust.

Chance felt a surge of relief in the knowledge that she had not been harmed and glanced around the room to find that more than a few discomfited gazes slid from his in embarrassment, and he correctly surmised that they were all frightened of reprisals should they cross the McPhersons. He sighed heavily and said, "Miss Dublin, I am beginning to believe that you have need of constant protection. A ... knight in shining armor, I seem to recall you saying."

Reanna blushed at the reminder of her foolish words at their first meeting, and ventured shyly, "My father has come home, and I am to join him and my uncle and his family here for dinner. I ... I would like you to meet him, and perhaps ... you are welcome to join us."

Chance offered her his arm, and she suddenly noticed that it was no longer in a sling as he guided her toward the dining room.

"Regretfully, Miss Dublin, I am in the middle of an important meeting, but I will gladly see you to your table, and when I have concluded my business, if you are still here, I will join you then."

Her heart leapt with joy at his words. She had missed him these past days, and she was determined to prolong dinner as long as possible.

Reanna introduced Chance to her father, entreating him with her wide eyes to please not cause a scene, and to her relief, Raymond was polite, if only grudgingly so. He took full measure of the way his daughter's eyes were shining when she looked at, or spoke to Chance Nolton, and he did not approve at all. He could see no good coming of Reanna involving herself with the man.

During the meal, Reanna informed her family of what had happened on her way in, and of how Chance had once again been there to help her.

"I wish I could catch them at something besides malicious pranks," Bob growled in irritation, "and put them away for a long time. As it is, if you wish to press charges, Reanna, I could only lock them up for a week or so."

"If they hurt you ..." Raymond began, but Reanna interrupted.

"No, Papa, they didn't. Mr. Nolton was there ..."

"Mr. Nolton is here now," Chance spoke softly near her ear.

Reanna turned a dazzling smile in his direction and invited, "Mr. Nolton, please join us."

He pulled up a chair next to Bob, and everyone, especially Jared and Michael, clamored to hear the story again of how Chance had chased the McPherson brothers from the saloon ... even Martha laughed at the thought of them turning tail and running like frightened boys.

Reanna noted, however, that her father was not sharing in the mirth, but scowling darkly at Chance, who, if he was aware of it, gave no sign that he was. The bounty hunter was studying Reanna with a considering expression, and whenever she chanced to meet his eyes, they would hold her for breathless moments in their magnetic depths.

An old man seated himself at the piano in the corner of the dining room and began to play familiar and well-loved songs as people slowly congregated on the dance floor, and Chance turned to Reanna. "Would you do me the honor of sharing a dance, Miss Dublin?"

With a swift, dubious glance at her father, Reanna answered quickly, "Yes, I would love to," and rose to join him as he led her out, this time with two arms holding her close. Two strong, warm arms.

Reanna felt a tremor of excitement leap through her at his touch, and she imagined, as his eyes bore into hers, that he could see into her very soul, and then smiled at such a foolish notion.

"May I ask what you find amusing, Miss Dublin?"

"Oh, I guess … I guess that I am just happy when I am with you Mr. Nolton."

Now Chance was amused. "I am glad to hear that, Miss Dublin, for I am also very happy in your company."

The dance came to an end, and they walked slowly back to the table, arm in arm.

Raymond decided that he had seen enough for one night, and announced, "It is time to be getting home, Reanna. We must leave now."

Everyone agreed that it was getting quite late, all but Chance.

"With your permission, Mr. Dublin, I would like to see your daughter home a little later, so that we may enjoy a few more dances. We will not be late, and you have my word that I will take good care of her."

Raymond grimaced, aware that he could not possibly refuse such a polite request without appearing churlish, especially in light of Chances' earlier intervention on his daughter's behalf. He also realized that the rogue was quite aware of this, smiling blithely as he awaited Raymond's answer.

Bob was no help either, as he added, "After all, Ray, Chance and I are old friends, and I promise you, he is a man of his word." Bob seemed to be quite amused at his brother's discomfort.

"Very well," Raymond grumbled, and when they had gone, Chance led Reanna in several more dances, and they enjoyed a drink, by now Reanna's third. She was beginning to feel quite lightheaded, not used to indulging in more than one glass, and with Chance so close, it heightened the feeling.

Taking note of her flushed face and easy laughter, Chance decided that they should leave now, for he did not relish having to face Ray Dublin's wrath should he bring Reanna home intoxicated.

"Do you mind riding double, or would you prefer that I rent a carriage and drive you home?" he inquired solicitously.

"Oh, please don't go to all that trouble, Mr. Nolton. I would be perfectly happy to ride," she answered, and he escorted her out to where his stallion, Lancelot, was tied.

The large horse nickered in greeting, and Chance said, "Company tonight, old boy," as he assisted Reanna in mounting. He straddled the horse behind her, enfolding her in his arms as he took up the reins.

She giggled as they started toward the ranch, and he asked, "What do you find amusing now, Miss Dublin?"

His breath tickled her ear, and she giggled again before answering, "It's just that I never envisioned you talking to a horse, Mr. Nolton."

He made no rejoinder as they rode on, but her nearness and the touch of his thighs against hers quickly aroused his desires, surprising in their intensity.

Reanna, unavoidably aware of his blatant arousal, blushed profusely, and was grateful for the cover of darkness that hid her embarrassment from Chance's probing gaze. She began to prattle nervously, describing her life on the ranch, how her father had come to settle here, about the death of her mother, and about the loving bond she shared with Pier and Carmelita.

They had come to a brook that crossed her father's land, and Chance stopped the horse, dismounting and turning to help her down. His hands lingering immodestly close to her breasts sent the heat racing to her face again, and she asked uneasily, "Mr. Nolton, why have you stopped here? The house is just a bit further on."

"I'm aware of that, but it's a beautiful night, and I am sharing it with a beautiful woman, and I would like to make it last just a little longer."

The sound of his voice was like a soft caress and Reanna shivered as she looked up at the many stars in the clear night sky. "Yes," she agreed, "it is a beautiful night."

The light of the full moon glittered as diamonds upon the moving waters of the gurgling brook, and several cottonwoods lined the banks ... and Chances hands still rested lightly beneath her breasts, holding her close.

She really should ask him to release her, she thought, but he was lowering his lips ever so slowly to hers. So slowly, in fact, that she could not resist raising hers up to meet him.

He paused, savoring the anticipation, and then, as lightly as a butterfly sets down upon a fragile blossom, his lips moved slowly over hers, delicately teasing, barely touching, tantalizing her until she felt faint with wanting more. He straightened, watching closely for her reaction, and was pleased with what he saw. Reanna's deep green eyes were softly luminous in the moonlight and wide with wonder as she gazed up at him. Her full, soft lips quivered, slightly parted. He smiled his approval as he held her gaze with his own.

She should stop him now, she knew, but she had no desire to do so, for he had awakened new, strong emotions within her that left her weak and trembling, wanting for more.

"Reanna?" her name was a soft caress, his husky voice full of a yearning desire, but giving her a chance to refuse. She said nothing as he continued to watch her closely, and then his arms came around her, holding her close, crushing her to him.

His kisses fell lightly, first upon her forehead, then her eyelids, across her cheeks and nose, finally claiming her mouth once again, suddenly all-consuming in his heated passion, and she found herself responding, returning his kiss with a fiery ardor of her own. His hands moved over her back, cupping her buttocks to pull her even closer, up against his hard, throbbing manhood, and Reanna felt as if she would explode with the tumultuous feelings burgeoning within her.

She moaned softly, deep within her throat, as he deftly unclasped the hooks of her dress, ever so gently easing it over her shoulders and down, followed by the gossamer covering of her camisole, so that he could look upon her beauty unimpeded.

Her eyes were closed, but she heard the sharp intake of his breath, and she felt his hands warmly cup her breasts before he lowered his head to circle first one, then the other, lightly with his moist, warm tongue, teasing the rosy peaks until they were hard.

Reanna could barely manage to draw breath and felt as if she would float away on waves of pleasured ecstasy. She wanted more, much more, but knew if she did not stop him now, she never would, and was suddenly frightened by the force of their passions. She began to struggle against him, desperately repeating his name, finally pulling at his hair to lift his head from her breasts.

"Chance, Chance, please stop," she whispered urgently, and her words at last broke through the haze of his desire. He raised his head to look searchingly into her frightened eyes, and his own burned with such raging desire that they had taken on a reddened glow.

He groaned painfully, still caressing her plump breasts with his hands, and she suddenly sensed that she was way out of her depth, suddenly very fearful of this man, of the powerful feelings he evoked; she was no match for him at all. Never had she, in her limited experience, encountered such a fiercely sexual male.

She stepped back slightly, away from his roving hands, and frantically attempted to pull her camisole and dress back up over her shoulders, but the task proved to be difficult, for her hands were shaking so…

Chance read the naked fear in her eyes, but unfortunately, it did little to curb his fierce, raging desire. It actually seemed to fan it, for he realized that this beautiful creature had never been touched in the way of love. She was still a virgin … something he had little experience with, and it was that thought that finally sobered him. She was completely innocent and would need tender coaxing, and time for romantic courting.

Suddenly, instead of merely desiring to bed her, he felt almost protective of her … and something else, something that he could not quite define. He slowly reached out to turn her around, and gently began to hook her dress back up.

Reanna walked slowly to the edge of the brook and stared down into the flowing water with tear filled eyes, allowing the sparkling surface to mesmerize her. She was a fool, and she was deeply ashamed of her actions. She felt terribly confused, never having experienced these things with a man. She had never allowed anyone to touch her the way Chance Nolton had. He must think that she is terribly wanton to allow such liberties.

Chance thought no such thing. He walked over to where she stood in brooding silence and sat, pulling her down next to him. They watched the play of the water rushing over the stones in its bed, and the restless stirrings of the night creatures mingled with the soft sounds of the water, the far distant howl of a wolf, to pull at Reanna's heart.

"Reanna, look at me."

He had never addressed her by her first name before, and the soft command startled her, but she turned obediently to face him. His dark, burning gaze searched her features carefully. He wanted her badly, more than he had ever wanted another woman, and he had tasted the passion that lay hidden inside her, but he would have to wait until she was ready.

"Reanna, you are a very beautiful, exciting woman. Please forgive me if I ..."

She silenced him with trembling fingertips upon his mouth, and, laying her head on his shoulder, she stared once again at the water. She did not want to hear his apologies; it was she who should be making them. She led him on, allowing him to take those liberties, and she now felt foolish for having had to refuse him.

Chance did not think her foolish but fancied that he understood her. He knew he could be patient and wait until she was willing.

He also knew that he would not go to his bed alone this night, but it was not to be the beautiful Reanna that he took with him.

Chapter 3

Early the next morning Reanna asked Pier to saddle her a horse, and she rode in solitude up to a rocky, mountainous cliff that was a favorite place of hers, a place she visited when she needed time alone.

She sat up there for hours, at the edge of the cliff, basking in the warm sunlight and reveling in the breathtaking view; the thick evergreen forests and high, sunlit meadows below, and the sharply etched, distant Blue Mountains above. Braced by a freshening wind, she felt free of her normal daily responsibilities, as she did whenever she came here.

Her thoughts, however, were plagued by memories of the dashing Chance Nolton. His image refused to leave her mind, and she felt the heat of a warm blush suffuse her face whenever she remembered the things he had done to her last night.

When he delivered her home, his eyes had still burned with a raw desire that he made no effort to hide. His parting kiss had been warm and passionate, and she trembled weakly under his scorching lips, then, pulling his head back, he had looked into her eyes with intense deliberation and stated in a low, husky voice, "The sweet pleasure of this night will remain with me until we meet again, my lovely Reanna Dublin." Then he'd swiftly mounted his horse and ridden away into the night, leaving Reanna to gulp in great quantities of fresh air as she had tried to slow the rapid beating of her pulse.

Her thoughts turned to Daniel, realizing now how chaste his kisses had been compared to those of the charming rogue Chance Nolton, and with these memories came again the pain that the parting of their ways, and Daniels subsequent death, had brought. She had no desire to experience that pain again, so she must be insane to accept the attentions of a man like Chance Nolton, a roamer who would never allow himself to be chained by a woman's love. She determined to keep a distance between them, to be more careful of him and deny the glorious new feelings he had aroused in her, to remain aloof, so as not to be hurt by him in the end, for she knew that he would leave when he had what he wanted, knew without a doubt that she would be wounded terribly if she gave him her love.

She finally rode back to the house, and later that evening sat with her father in the softly lit parlor. He was relaxing in his favorite chair with the weekly paper, she restlessly pacing the room as she absently strummed her guitar, playing no particular tune, but portions of several as she sought to fill the silence of the house, which she found to be unbearable this day.

There was a knock on the front door and Reanna rose to open it. Chance Nolton stood on the porch, to her surprise, and he presented her with the largest bouquet of fragrant pink roses that she had ever seen. Her smile of pleasure was bright as she accepted them, her eyes glittered like the sea, and Chance had all the thanks he wanted with the privilege of watching the play of expressions on her lovely countenance.

"Mr. Nolton, thank you so much. They are lovely, and oh, they smell so heavenly! Come in, please. Papa and I were just relaxing after our dinner."

She led him into the parlor, announcing, "Papa, we have company. May I offer you a drink, Mr. Nolton, coffee, or brandy?"

"Thank you, Reanna, coffee would be fine."

Reanna gestured to the settee, "Please sit down. I won't be but a moment ..." she gracefully glided from the room, leaving Chance to the disconcerting stare of Mr. Dublin, who seemed to be most displeased with their guest, and Chance sought to ease the tension with conversation.

"Mr. Dublin, I trust that with all the fine weather your cattle are well, and fit for market?"

"Well and fit enough," Raymond answered gruffly before burying his face once again in the newspaper, for which Chance was almost glad. He was not used to making conversation with disapproving, over-protective fathers.

Reanna entered with a rustle of skirts and placed a large silver tray, containing a silver coffee pot, creamer and sugar bowl, China cups, and a crystal vase which held the flowers, onto the dark mahogany table that stood before the settee. Taking up the vase with the flowers, she set them down on the table next to her father's chair, calling his attention to them as she did so. "Papa, look at the lovely roses Mr. Nolton brought." Without waiting for him to comment, she whirled gaily to face Chance.

"It was kind of you to be so thoughtful. They really are lovely, and I shall enjoy their fragrance and beauty for days."

Chance, she noticed, was sliding her guitar away from him, so she said, "You can put that on the floor beside you. How would you like your coffee?"

Chance casually rose to his feet. "I'll fix my own. Did I hear you playing when I rode up?"

"Yes, but I was just strumming, making noise. I was not really playing anything."

"Would you play something now, for me?"

Reanna seated herself in a billow of skirts next to Chance and leaned forward to retrieve her guitar from the floor. Following the neckline of her snugly fitting pink velvet gown, his eyes warmed appreciatively as they watched the downward move, hoping for a glimpse of the tender fruits he knew to be hidden there, but a loud cough from Raymond caused him to meet the man's hard glare, and he immediately returned his glance to Reanna's face.

She began to play, singing a soft, sweet refrain, and Chance watched the changing expressions on her face with unwavering intensity. He was lulled; enchanted by her beauty and soft, peaceful melodies. She was truly a captivating woman. And he felt himself being drawn further under the spell she wove, vowing that he would not give up the quest for her seduction, for she would indeed prove a prize well won.

Finishing the song, Reanna rose to lay the guitar aside and pour herself a cup of coffee.

Chance smiled warmly in her direction. "That was beautiful, Reanna, and I thank you. You do play very well."

"I have had ample opportunities to perfect my skill, Mr. Nolton. Not only did I learn much from my music tutor, but also from friends and traveling musicians who passed through town. Theirs are the best songs, for they are both well-traveled and well versed," she said, thinking mostly of the ballads she had learned from her Indian friend, Mansunama.

He still gazed at her with such intensity that she felt a blush beginning to creep over her features, he spoke softly, "You are well versed yourself, fair lady, and it has been a rare pleasure to visit with you tonight." He turned towards Raymond, saying "With your permission sir, I would seek the privilege of visiting again soon."

Raymond treated Chance to a cold perusal, and then turned to his daughter. "Reanna?"

Both men turned their eyes toward Reanna, waiting expectantly for her answer. She knew what her papa wanted, but even if she wanted to deny Chance his "privilege", she would never be able to do so with his dark gaze holding hers and was suddenly stricken with self-conscious indecision. She was not sure who to address or what words she should choose. The heat of color touched her cheeks once again, and she hurriedly, shyly answered, "Yes, Papa, if it would … I mean, Mr. Nolton, it would be nice if …" she smiled in embarrassment. "I would like it if you would visit again, Mr. Nolton."

Chance smiled widely. She was actually opposing her father to ask him here, a very promising sign indeed. Aloud he said, "Well then, I will see you soon, and I thank you very much for your hospitality and pleasant company."

He turned to leave, and Reanna walked with him to the door, where he turned and raised her hand to his lips, pressing a warm, lingering kiss to her palm.

All of her earlier resolutions about this man seemed to dissolve as a thrill of excitement rushed through her.

"Good night, Miss Dublin."

Reanna's voice was little more than a whisper as she gazed at him with wide eyes, "Good night, Mr. Nolton."

She stood at the door and watched as he mounted Lancelot, and, removing his calf-leather, wide-brimmed hat, swept her an elaborately gallant bow before riding off into the darkness. Then, still smiling, she turned to close the portal and started when she realized that her father was standing right next to her, a black scowl creasing his face, which quickly sobered her mood.

"Reanna, I don't like it. That man is naught but a roamer. You had better guard your heart well, my daughter."

At Reanna's pained expression, Raymond softened his manner and gently grasped her shoulders as he spoke. "The man is an obvious womanizer, Rea, and if he should dare to lay a hand on you, to ruin your prospects of marriage …"

Reanna's face burned crimson, for he had come far too close to the truth of what happened the night before, but she said, "Papa, please! Do you take me for a complete fool? I can see plainly what the man is. I cannot help it though if he seems to sweep me off my feet. Still, you must not worry for my virtue, Papa; I can take care of myself."

"You don't know his kind, Reanna. He is not some lovesick boy, but a hard, dangerous man. I won't, however, worry over-much, for I intend to see to it that you are never alone with him again as you were last night. Chance Nolton will have little opportunity to press his advances on you!"

"Yes, Papa," Reanna murmured. "Good night."

She turned quietly and mounted the stairs to go to her room, angry that her father could insinuate that she would allow Chance Nolton to take her virtue ... How could he! She heaved a heavy sigh. She had no right to be angry with him, he was only trying to protect her from a well-known rogue, and she was foolish to be so taken with the scoundrel. Oh, but what sweet feelings he aroused in her! He made her feel as she never had before.

Raymond sank heavily into his chair. How had his daughter, who was so kind and good, come to desire a ruthless man like Chance Nolton? And all in the short time he had been gone. He had carved an empire here for himself, had battled to make and hold this immense ranch, yet it seemed that he was helpless in this instance. Of course he could lock Reanna up, forbid her to see the man, but this, he knew, would only serve to fire her determination to see him all the more. Well, Chance Nolton was not going to be spending any time alone with his daughter, not even if he had to post constant guards on her! He had plenty of men. He sighed and wearily rubbed his eyes. It was time he went to bed.

Reanna was restless and bored with only her father and Carmelita for company, which she found odd, for this had never been the case before. For two days she flitted from one activity to the next, unable to finish any attempt at sewing, reading, or going over accounts, her only required job on the ranch, before taking on a new chore.

Finally, disgusted with herself, she decided to put on her riding clothes and join her father out on the north range, but, once she found him, regretted that it had not been one of her better ideas. The men were building a new holding pen for cattle and horses, a large, fenced area, and they had removed their shirts in search of at least some relief from the heat of the blazing sun.

Sweat glistened on their chests, and their forearms were coated in a film of dust kicked up by digging holes for posts, but they toiled steadily on, at least until Reanna rode into view. Then, it seemed, all work stopped, as first one, then another of the hands paused to admire the graceful beauty seated before them.

Raymond's weary eyes flashed them, and then Reanna, a look of exasperation.

"What is it, Reanna?" he questioned impatiently. "I have asked you not to come around while the men are working. As you can see, very little gets accomplished when you are about."

"I'm sorry, Papa. It's just that I feel so restless, I don't know what to do with myself."

"Why don't you go shopping? Women are supposed to enjoy that," Raymond suggested a trifle impatiently.

Reanna noted that Sean, usually so diligent in his work, was leaning negligently on the handle of his shovel, mopping his brow as he watched with some amusement the exchange between father and daughter. His wide chest was darkly tanned, the stubble of a beard roughened his square jaw, and his eyes glinted in appreciation as his gaze swept the length of her body. He was very handsome, Reanna thought, and had always been very attentive toward her, but now that she had met Chance Nolton, she had eyes for no one else, including Sean.

"Perhaps we could go for a quick swim?" Reanna asked. "I don't really feel much like shopping."

Raymond glanced around once more at the enthralled men, and sent a particularly quelling look Sean's way, which did nothing to diminish the young man's attention to Reanna, so with an aggrieved sigh, he relented, "Very well, Reanna, we will go for a swim. I'll be certain to get more work out of them with you occupied elsewhere."

Reanna smiled happily. She was not fooled one bit. The idea of a swim sounded wonderful to her father, so after he had mounted his own stead, she kicked her horse into a gallop, shouting over her shoulder, "I'll race you!" and she bent low over the horses' withers, leaving her father to follow her billowing cloud of copper hair.

Reanna reined her horse to a sliding halt at the edge of the pond, with her father coming to a stop just behind her. "Looks like I won, Papa, but not by much," she admitted, her eyes sparkling and face flushed from the excitement. "Come on, let's get into the water!"

Raymond smiled at his daughter's girlish enthusiasm as she jumped from her horse and peeled off her dusty riding clothes, leaving on only her white cotton camisole and pantalets, neither of them realizing that a pair of dark eyes warmed appreciatively at the sight of the well-proportioned length of Reanna's legs. Her father shed his shirt and dove into the water.

Surfacing, he shouted to her, "You may have triumphed on land, Rea, but I have taken the sea!" he playfully splashed her with water, and shrieking in mock outrage, Reanna followed his example, diving beneath the refreshing surface to rise gracefully some distance out, glorying in the pleasure of the cool bath.

She was a proficient swimmer, having learned at an early age through the encouragement and direction of her father. His sister had drowned at a young age, so he felt it important to be a strong swimmer.

Raymond swam leisurely near the shore while Reanna darted and splashed, spraying up droplets of water to shine brilliantly in the sunlight as she ventured further from him, around the shrub lined edge that jutted out from the shallows, taking her into deeper water, where she tread effortlessly, resting for a while as she surveyed the opposite shore of the deserted pond.

Sensing a movement to the side of her, she turned sharply and gasped. Chance Nolton was wading toward her, and he was close enough that she could see the dark wet mat of hair on his muscular chest. He, it seemed, had been swimming before them, his black hair wet, and slicked back from his strong, virile features. She could only hope that he was clothed on the lower portion of his body. With him, one never knew what to expect.

He, too, was treading water now as he swam next to her. "Well, Miss Dublin, I never expected to meet you here," he grinned wolfishly as his eyes dipped to the top of her low-cut camisole. "Do you always swim with clothing, Miss Dublin? It is so much more comfortable without them." He ventured, as she moved uneasily away through the water until her feet could touch the sandy bottom.

She chose to ignore his comment about her clothing. "I'm surprised there is no one else here, seeking to cool themselves," she said.

Chance had followed her and stood so close that she could feel his warm breath on her ear as he spoke, "I find that I am hot all over again, now that you are near."

She should have been outraged at his words, but instead, her breath came more quickly, and her stomach tightened in excitement. Before she could react, he was pressing his mouth harshly to hers, searing her lips with his heat as his hand came up behind her head to hold her, so that she could not pull away, but the knowledge that her father could at any time spy them goaded her into action.

She used both her hands and feet, pushing against him until their contact was broken, and she was able to gasp out "Papa! He will see!"

Just then they heard Raymond's booming voice ring out, "Reanna, it's time to go!"

Chance had the decency at least to look slightly chagrined, "I only wanted to ask you ..."

"Please! I really must go!" Reanna said urgently, and turned, diving smoothly under the water to swim back to her father, while Chance moved to position himself so that he could glimpse Reanna's lush form as she waded from the pond in her wet, clinging attire, a lovely sight indeed.

Raymond did not say a word to Reanna about Chance, and she breathed a sigh of relief. He had not seen them. She did not want to incur her father's wrath, either upon herself, or upon Chance.

Now that she was away from his compelling presence, however, she grew indignant, and quite uncomfortable, when she realized that her feet had encountered bare skin beneath the surface of the water when she pushed Chance away. Her face flamed crimson as it occurred to her just what part of his anatomy her foot had inadvertently brushed. Reanna fumed to herself, allowing a soft oath to escape her lips as she angrily pulled her clothes back on. It was enough to make her never want to set eyes on the rogue again!

Her wish, however fervent, was not to be granted, as she discovered when she answered the knock on the door later that evening.

"Mr. Nolton!" She could not keep the blush from staining her cheeks.

"Good evening, Miss Dublin. I hope I'm not disturbing you?" he questioned politely, completely oblivious of her discomfort, and wearing that smooth, easy grin that had the power to completely disarm her.

"No, not at all, come in, please," she said softly, stepping aside so that he could pass.

"I thought that we might go for a walk," he suggested, "the night is warm, and the moon is bright."

Reanna was certain that she knew precisely what his idea of a walk would entail and thought the better of it. "I am sorry, Mr. Nolton, but Papa would not approve of that at all. If you would allow me to play for you, I will get some coffee and we could spend the evening here."

So, he would not get the chance to seduce her further tonight. "Well … It is always a pleasure to hear your music, and the coffee would be quite welcome, thank you."

Reanna smiled in relief. He did not seem to be upset about the walk. "Very well then, I will get some coffee right away. Please make yourself at home."

Reanna entered the kitchen just as Raymond, seated at the table, began to clean one of his rifles. "Papa, Mr. Nolton is here, and I am serving coffee. Would you like to join us?" she questioned as she arranged the necessary items on the tray. She wanted so for her father to soften his regard of the bounty hunter.

Raymond looked thoroughly exasperated and ran a hand fondly down the barrel of the rifle before he answered, "That man is becoming a thorn in my side! I have no desire to drink coffee with him. In fact, I'd love to run him off at gunpoint!"

"Hush Papa, he will hear you!" Reanna whispered urgently, "Doesn't it matter to you that I might enjoy his company?"

Raymond turned hard gray eyes upon his daughter. "Just remember, you better not enjoy his company overmuch, Reanna. You will only be hurt in the end!"

"Oh, Papa, you are impossible!" Reanna stamped her foot and turned with the coffee tray, stalking out of the kitchen in a huff with her green eyes sparking in anger. The contents of the tray clattered loudly as she irritably placed it on the table in the parlor.

Chance, having heard the raised voices in the kitchen, rose from the settee and spoke with mock innocence, "I do hope that the anger I see in your eyes is not directed toward me."

Reanna laughed, "You seem to have developed an obsession for music Mr. Nolton."

"It is your music that obsesses me, sweet Reanna, only yours." His brown eyes danced with golden lights as they met her sparkling green ones.

Reanna, filled now with an unreasonable shyness, turned to pick up her guitar, and once they were seated on the porch, played for a long time without stopping in an attempt to purge her feelings of confusion, restlessness, and anger of the past few days. Never had she fought with her father, and neither had she ever experienced the strong sense of passion she felt whenever Chance was near. She had no right to these feelings, these first stirrings of love, for he was naught but a roamer who would only leave her with a broken heart, and she knew her father was only trying to protect her. She really had no right to be angry with him, so she put the depths of her feelings into her songs. She sang the song of her soul; cherished memories and loss, the love that was stealing into her heart. The softly lilting ballad rose in sad refrains, swirling, reaching for the sky, touching Chance's heart.

Finally, he reached over and stayed her fingers with a gentle touch of his hand. Reanna gazed up at him with wide, questioning eyes.

"Have I satisfied your obsession?" she queried.

Chance smiled warmly and leaned close to her face, speaking in a low, husky whisper, "You made beautiful music, but have not come close to satisfying my true obsession with you, Reanna."

His kiss was light and soft, demanding nothing, merely asking, but it somehow stirred the flames of passion within her, having the same effect on the innocent maid as his hungry, demanding touch had. She was set atremble, and blush rose to stain her cheeks, which she attributed more to his words than his close proximity. When he raised his head her green eyes sparked in sudden anger, and her words were sharp.

"Perhaps you ask too much of me, sir rogue. I find your words to be without amusement, and it is plain that you do not show the respect befitting a lady. Now, if you would remove yourself from my path, I would bid you good night."

Chance remained where he was standing, in front of her chair, as he eyed her inscrutably for a few moments. Obviously, her father had been talking to her, perhaps warning her against him, but for some reason he could not fathom, this lady's anger smarted sorely, and he sought to ease it.

Executing a courteous bow, he stated, "You have my deepest apologies, sweet lady. I truly did not mean to offend you. I now see my folly and regret it, and I humbly beg your forgiveness."

Reanna rose from her chair to stand beside him, hiding a smile at his sudden change in attitude. He really could be quite chivalrous when the occasion demanded, and she found that she could not stay angry with him.

"I will accept your apology sir, only if you will promise to have dinner here tomorrow."

Chance took her hand, raising it to his lips where he pressed a brief kiss to the back of it, and said, "It would be an honor, my lady. Good night then."

As he leisurely descended the steps of the porch, Reanna called after him, "We eat at six!"

He turned to face her and smiled; his handsome features bathed in moonlight. "Perfect."

She had the overwhelming sensation that she must have been stricken with temporary madness, asking him to dine at her father's table. Why should she entertain him, knowing full well the underlying reasons behind his visits, aware that she would never allow his purpose to be fulfilled? She supposed that she wanted to turn his thoughts to the more respectable ones of marriage, for she was undeniably and completely smitten with the wandering rogue. She perceived that there would never be another to compare, never would another man make her feel the way this one did. The love that she had felt for Daniel was, she now realized, no more than mere fondness. For the first time in her life, she wanted to bind a man with her love so that he would never feel the desire to turn away.

As Chance fitfully slept that night, his dreams were haunted with visions of the lovely Reanna Dublin. He had never been so completely enamored of any woman, and he did chafe under this desire, for he knew that it probably would not be eased. Not by Reanna, nor by any other.

Oh, he had tried. The night he and Reanna stopped by the brook, he had come back to the hotel, bringing a paid lady with him to his bed. But the whole time his body made love to her, his mind had been filled with visions of Reanna. He was driven mad by memories of her tender flesh, enchanting smile, deep, sea-green eyes, and soft, lingering scent of roses.

He had used the whore all night, but when she finally left, thoroughly sated, he was no more satisfied than before she had come. He was cruelly aware that he would never be happy. His agony would not be eased, until he had Reanna in his bed. He was hopelessly under her spell and meant to have her.

He would have to tread carefully, lest he frighten her away, but then he wondered, was he really capable of frightening a girl who had already rendered him helpless by her bewitching beauty? He was glad when the sky paled with early morning light, for with it, came relief from his fevered dreams.

Chance arrived at the High Ridge ranch promptly at six that evening, much to Raymond Dublin's chagrin, which he made no attempt to hide, speaking barely civilly and then only to answer questions put directly to him.

If he thought to put Chance off by his actions, he was sadly mistaken, for the bounty hunter was accustomed to this sort of treatment, and Reanna chatted on endlessly about all manner of subjects, occupying all of Chance's attention.

Chance felt his helplessness more sharply than ever, so completely enchanted was he with her endless, enthusiastic love of life and all that it offered. The sea glittered in her eyes and her gay laughter filled the room with music. She was a balm to his sore and travel-weary spirit, but he did not realize yet the full effect she had on him. He would not come to terms with it for some time, and only then when the fickle fates forced him to accept his place in her heart.

Carmelita had prepared a simple but elegant meal before leaving the ranch house for her own small home. They feasted on crisp succulent pork roast seasoned with fresh herbs, fluffy baked potatoes topped with butter, and carrots with a brown sugar glaze. For dessert she had prepared individual custards topped with rich caramel sauce.

When Chance left later that night, Reanna accompanied him to his horse, and he observed dryly, "Your father does not particularly care for me."

Reanna shyly averted her eyes, but then deciding to be bluntly honest, answered hesitantly, "It's not that he dislikes you so much. It's just that he thinks you are ... a ... philanderer and would ... steal my virtue and ruin my prospects for marriage." She blushed, thankful for the congealing cloak offered by the dark night.

Chance cupped her chin in his hand and tipped her face up so that their eyes met. "And what, fair maiden, do you think?" he asked in a low sensuous voice.

Reanna wrenched from his grasp and turned her back to him. "I know that what he says is true, but I worry not for my virtue, for it is mine to give as I see fit, and I certainly would not see it as fitting without marriage vows spoken between the two who would share it."

She kept her back to him, aware that he was mounting his horse, before he replied in the same smooth, low tone he had used before, "We shall see, my lovely lady fair, we shall see."

As he rode off, Reanna chafed under the tears that stung her eyes, aware that his deliberate purpose had not been altered by one notch, not one bit. Her heart sank, knowing as she did that he would not be swayed in the least by her belief in the sanction of marriage.

Chance's thoughts ran in much the same direction as he rode back to town. He had gotten involved with the wrong kind of woman, one who would not consent to his purpose without the promise of marriage. Still, she had responded most ardently that night by the brook, so he repeated his earlier words to himself, "we shall see," and for the next six weeks Reanna was swept into the whirling excitement of new romance.

Chance Nolton relentlessly courted her, always flawlessly playing the part of the perfect gentlemen, but of course it was seen to that they were not alone too often, or for too long, by Raymond Dublin.

Whenever he came to the house, which was nearly every day, he would bring some token of his esteem. Flowers of every shade and sort filled the house with their heady fragrance, reminding Raymond at every turn of the man that was pursuing his daughter. Reanna had more candy than she could ever eat, and one day Chance even brought her a beautiful carved rosewood music box depicting a knight in armor upon a charging steed.

"Is this supposed to be you?" she asked, and he laughed, answering, "If you wish it to be so."

Chance was introduced to Reanna's friends, and for the first time in his life was accepted by, and became, through her, part of a social group. They paid several visits to Molly and Kenny Beckett, who owned a farm just a few miles from town. Kenny's main interest was in raising horses, and Chance saw that here, with his serious hazel eyes and mop of unruly, dark brown hair, was a man determined to succeed, and he admired the man for taking great pride in his work and fearlessly pursuing his dreams.

Reanna smiled every time she remembered their first visit. Molly, who had long, raven hair and violet eyes, a slender build and pretty face, had taken her aside and whispered, "Oh, he is very handsome, Rea, a real find! If I were you, I would pull him in, hook, line, and sinker."

Reanna had laughed merrily, "Believe me, Molly, that is much easier said than done, but I do plan to bait my hook aplenty."

They had dissolved into helpless giggles, which drew the curious attention of the men. That sobered them enough so that they could go about setting the table for coffee with only an occasional stifled outburst of mirth and change the subject of their conversation.

They went into town often, and Chance met Reanna's other friends; Belinda, a saloon girl with a voluptuous figure, long, burnished gold hair, and laughing aqua-marine eyes, and Avis, who although quite heavy set, possessed a happy, very friendly constitution, always willing to help anyone she could.

Yes, he was becoming acceptable to the townspeople, for in a small town, everyone knew one another, and all of Reanna's friends and acquaintances admired her greatly, and they could see that she admired him.

He also had the questionable privilege of running into the McPherson brothers again one day as he strolled leisurely along the boardwalk with Reanna on his arm. They had just enjoyed lunching at the Horseshoe with Bob and Martha Dublin and had decided to do some window shopping to walk off their meal before returning to the ranch.

As they gazed through the window of the general store, admiring an intricately woven saddle blanket, the five brothers sauntered from the saloon and, noting the couple on the boardwalk, strolled toward them.

Chance and Reanna were about to go on, but at the sight of the ruffians Reanna hesitated a second and would have gone out of her way to avoid them, had Chance not been holding her arm in unwavering intent to proceed on their chosen course. She had no recourse but to do likewise.

Billy, the youngest and most amiable, with short cropped blond hair and sky-blue eyes, tipped his hat politely and spoke pleasantly, "Good day, Miss Dublin."

Reanna inclined her head graciously and smiling, returned his greeting, "Good afternoon, Billy."

Her smile faded quickly however, when Larry elbowed Billy roughly in the side and said loudly, "Can't you see that the lady is occupied, little brother? I told ya she's been gettin' lessons in the art of pleasin' menfolk, and that dirty gunslinger is teachin' her well, I'll wager."

His mocking laughter died in his throat, for in the blink of an eye Chance had smoothly drawn his gun and held it steadily pointed at Larry's chest. His eyes were hard as flint, devoid of emotion, and Reanna could not suppress a faint shiver of fear as she beheld his changed countenance. It was easy to forget just how dangerous he could be.

She pulled at Chance's arm, pleading, "Please, Mr. Nolton, their words do no harm, and I assure you, everyone in this town has at one time or another been subject to their rudeness. Please, there is no cause for a gunfight. I do not wish to see blood spilled for but a few unkind words."

Chance relaxed his stance slightly, but kept his gun leveled. His voice was soft, but held a deadly serious threat as he stated, "I will not have the lady's name, or reputation, slandered by the likes of you. Another word against her from your mouth will cost you dearly. You have my word on that."

Once again Larry backed down, but as Chance and Reanna moved away, he shot a venomous look towards their backs, muttering, "You ain't gonna be around forever, gunslinger. You ain't the stayin' around kind," and his grin was full of evil promise.

One day when Chance came to visit, Reanna was playing a tune on the piano and did not hear his knock. Carmelita admitted him, leading him into the parlor, and he stood and watched in amazement as her fingers flew lightly over the ivory keys and the beautiful, tinkling melody filled the room with sweet sound. It was almost magic, it seemed to him, the way she could so effortlessly weave her spell of music.

He was afforded an even greater pleasure however, as Reanna finished playing and stood to stretch, unaware of his presence. She tipped her head back, and Chance swallowed painfully as she raised her hands above her head, and he was treated to an uplifting view of the full curve of her breasts. She gasped in surprise as she turned around.

"I am sorry Mr. Nolton. I did not know you were here."

"Don't be," he answered wryly, but his eyes were lit with pleasure, "I did not mean to startle you. It was Carmelita who let me in, and you have surprised me as well. I had no idea that you played the piano, and just as beautifully as you do everything else. It was truly a pleasure to hear."

"Thank you, Mr. Nolton," Reanna giggled, "But did you think that we kept the instrument in our home merely for decoration?"

Amusement glinted in his eyes as he answered, "Very funny, Reanna. Actually, I thought perhaps it had been your mother's, and you kept it for sentimental reasons. I am glad to find out otherwise."

Carmelita entered with a pitcher of cool mint tea and glasses, observing, "It is a hot day, and I thought the two of you would like some refreshment. This must be the young man that has been burying us in flowers."

"Carmelita, I would like you to meet Chance Nolton. I am sorry that you haven't been introduced sooner, but you have gone home or were busy with other things whenever he was here."

Chance raised Carmelita's hand to his lips briefly and smiled down into her eyes. "I feel as if I know you already, kind lady," he said suavely, and from then on Carmelita would hold Chance in the highest esteem, lost to his charm.

Chance and Reanna both reveled in their enjoyment of each other, and in their friends, during those weeks of courtship, but Chance was rapidly growing impatient with their lack of privacy. Everywhere they went, there was one or two of Raymond Dublin's men to follow, leaving them only when they were in the company of others. Normally Chance would not have stood to be trailed everywhere he went, but how could he do otherwise without chancing a rift between him and his prey?

He did, however, complain one day, scowling darkly at the man on horseback that followed their carriage at some distance, as Chance drove them into town.

He growled out his words, "Your father guards you well."

Reanna answered him softly, "What is his, he keeps."

"And what I want I take," he rejoined meaningfully, but Reanna, softly adamant, informed him, "Not this time."

She loved him, but the attention he bestowed so freely upon her was merely part of his effort to compromise her virtue, a point that he never attempted to hide even subtly.

Even when her father was present, he would boldly allow his gaze to linger hungrily upon her breasts or sweep longingly over her entire body. Her face would burn and turn pink with a blush under his intent perusal, and at night when they said their goodbyes, his kisses were long, hard, passionate demands; his eyes would remind her of the burning coals of a hearth, flaming with the heat of raw desire. At such times she would become just a bit frightened, but overriding her fear was breathless excitement, a longing to give herself entirely up to his strong arms and searching lips, if only he would share his passion as her husband, not as a drifter, just waiting to satisfy his hunger before leaving.

It was an exceptionally hot day in July, when Chance arrived at the Dublin home only to be informed by Carmelita that Reanna was to be found out back, so he promptly went to find her.

She was lovingly tending the rose bushes that grew in profusion in the large, formal garden that her mother had insisted upon having, despite the wilderness she had settled in.

Her hair was pulled back and tied simply with a bright green ribbon, but as she worked, many tendrils had escaped confinement and the stray locks wisped damply around her face. She wore gloves to protect her hands, and an old, thin yellow dress with short sleeves and a square neckline that strained tightly across her bosom. Drenched in perspiration, she was just thinking that she must be crazy to be working so hard in this heat.

"You must be crazy to be working out in this heat."

Reanna jumped to her feet, startled that her thoughts had been spoken aloud, and turned to face Chance. Brushing self-consciously at the hair that fell across her face, painfully aware of her filthy, bedraggled appearance, she cried, "Mr. Nolton! I did not expect you until much later. I am sorry to be such a mess, it will ... I will run in and get cleaned up."

"Nonsense Reanna, you are as lovely as ever, dirt and all."

He stepped close and took her gloved hand, his grin turning to a wolfish leer as he lazily drew the garment off her soft hand, his eyes darkening with the thoughts that lay behind them.

His voice caressed, "Milady tends the blossoms with loving, tender hands. Ah, but that those hands would tend this man in the same fashion." He awaited her reaction with lights of fiery mischief dancing in his dark eyes, and she decided two could play this game.

"Ah, but that the man would tend to this woman's honor."

"Would you say then that there is no honor in love?"

He raised a sardonic brow as he waited for her answer, but having no retort, she pulled away from him in anger. Toying with a rose bloom, she sought to change the topic of conversation.

"It's funny, but when you spoke about the heat, it was as if my very thoughts had been repeated aloud ..."

Her voice trailed off, at a loss for further words, and Chance gave a full-throated laugh, "Well then fair damsel, you can see that it must be a matter of fate that I have arrived to carry you off to the cool waters of a certain pond."

To Reanna the idea of a swim sounded heavenly, and it showed in her expressive green eyes, but reluctantly, she had to refuse, "I'm sorry but I couldn't. Papa would not allow me swimming with you without a proper chaperone."

"I have thought of that, so I brought your two cousins along for company. With Michael and Jared to accompany us, you have no excuse. Come with me."

Reanna was still reluctant. "Michael and Jared are young boys; they can hardly be considered a proper escort. I am sorry Mr. Nolton, but Papa would…"

Chance grasped her shoulders and spoke urgently into her ear, "To hell with Papa, Reanna! You are a grown woman and have every right to make your own choices. What could possibly happen with two boys along? Do you think me to be some sort of monster that I would try to take you in the presence of …?"

"Cad! I never meant any such thing! I … I only meant … well, boys are given to wandering …"

"Then there are always your father's henchmen, who will follow at a discreet distance, just waiting for me to make a wrong move, so that they can … castrate me more than likely, since they are all half in love with you themselves! Your father plays the game very well!"

"You are a rogue! A scoundrel!" Reanna cried, having turned crimson at his words, though more from embarrassment than anger. She turned and began to stalk toward the house, but Chance caught her arm.

"From the beginning I have been only honest with you about my intentions. You speak of honor, lady, what honor has a man if he is not honest? I am weary of playing games, and I will not pretend to you things that will not be."

Reanna's green eyes narrowed in glaring anger now, as she berated him, "Honestly? Games? Honor? Tell me Mr. Nolton, what honor has a woman if she does not play these games, if she does not believe in the honesty of marriage? You, being a man, have no care. You may take your pleasures and leave to seek your freedom. But where would my honor be if I was left with your seed planted in my belly? I must be quite blunt in saying to you that I will not be dishonored in such a way. I will have marriage vows spoken first by the man to whom I would give myself in love!"

"All right Reanna, you've made your point," Chance conceded, "but for now, for today, will you come with me?" he pleaded. "Just enjoy each other's company?"

Reanna, with a sinking feeling in her heart, felt that there was something much more behind his words, a hint of regret, or sadness. She thought with a painful stab of sorrow that he must be thinking of leaving her life.

Softly she inquired, "Tell me Sir Rogue, what would you wear this day into the water?"

Heartened by her sudden capitulation, Chance's laughter boomed out, and he answered, "Milady, I'll grant you this honor, at least. In lieu of embarrassing your tender feet further, I promise to wear my pants all day."

"Oooohhh! You are a cad! A hopeless cad!"

The next day, Reanna found herself dreamily reliving the events of the past eight weeks, when Chance had first arrived in Carson, and she was thankful, when she remembered the passion that had ruled her that night by the brook, that she had only been spared a few moments alone with Chance. Her face burned hot with the memory of it. He was much too accomplished at the delights she had only just glimpsed.

Chance, at the same time, was cursing his bad luck. He had been celibate for too long now and was painfully aware of the fact. How had he come to be so infatuated with her charms? Why did this girl – woman hold such power over his physical abilities as a man and wreak havoc upon his emotions. She had bewitched him, and he damned her for it, damned himself for allowing it to happen. He began to question his sanity. Why did he stay, pursuing a girl whose father would just as soon see him dead, one who would not deviate from her moral upbringing? Sighing, he realized that he just may be falling in love with her, and that frightened him more than anything else had the power to. He had no room in his life for love, especially if it involved marriage. That was what they expected of him, to do everything in the proper way, right down to the wedding day. Well, he was no man's fool, was not about to commit himself to one woman for the rest of his life, would not give up his free and easy living arrangements. Yet, for these past weeks had he not done exactly that? It was time to get the hell out, to put an end to this nonsense, and he would do so tonight.

He was to take Reanna to the Becketts for a dance, accompanied by, of all people, her father. Chance smirked inwardly at himself.

The old man was no fool; he knew the powerful allure of his innocent daughter.

Chance arrived right on time; Reanna and her father were waiting on the porch, and the delight that radiated from the young maid's face as she glimpsed him gave the bounty hunter pause, but he sternly reminded himself again of his vow. It was time to move on.

He could not help, however, catching his breath as he appreciatively eyed the lovely picture she presented. She had chosen a gown of dusty rose with a low, enticing décolletage. Her dark copper tresses were swept up on top of her head and fastened with a wide strip of ribbon that matched her gown. It then cascaded down her back in soft waves, with a few unruly wisps escaping to frame her face. Damn, but she was a bewitching vixen! He silently cursed the thoughts that crept into his mind as he leaped from the carriage and with panther-like grace, handed her up. As Raymond climbed in after her Chance stalked around the vehicle to take his place as driver.

Curse his thoughts though he did, he could not halt them. It dawned on him with violent certainty the reason he continued to play this game. He wanted this woman as he had wanted no other. Definitely in his bed, but it went much further than that, the feelings she aroused ran deeper, cutting him to the quick as he recognized the long-forgotten yearnings she had stirred within him. He wanted her with him, by his side, to laugh with him, to love with him, to share his every moment.

His meditations were interrupted, as usual, by Reanna's excited chatter, and it was not until they arrived at the Beckett's farm, and she was immediately swept into other conversation that he had a chance to ponder this new turn of his heart.

He helped himself to a good-sized drink. He did not know how or when it had happened, but he definitely was in love with Reanna Dublin. The question was what to do about it? He certainly was not going to marry her. He just was not ready for that kind of commitment. Tie himself to the same woman forever? He remembered well the bitterness of his parents' union. No, marriage was not for him. Perhaps, if he renewed his efforts, he could convince Reanna to go away with him, to travel with him, to live with him without the trappings of church, without speaking senseless vows. That way, when they tired of one another, they would each be free to go their own way. She may want their union sanctioned by the church, but he stood a good chance of convincing her otherwise. She was totally in love with him, of that he was certain. She had not yet learned to disguise her feelings and wore her heart on her sleeve.

Reanna noticed that Chance stood off by himself. He downed his drink and poured himself another. He was deep in a brooding silence, bringing to mind her recollection of a sleek black panther, dressed as he was in dark clothing, silent, poised, and deadly. The muscles in his lean jaw worked tensely … Reanna approached and lightly touched his arm. "Mr. Nolton, you look as if you are miles away."

He slowly set his drink down and turned hard eyes to her. "I was just thinking of you Reanna. Dance with me," he commanded, but his voice was distant and sad.

She laid her hand upon his arm, and he led her to the middle of the dancing area, taking her into his relaxed embrace, but his steady regard for her never wavered. She smiled up at him, but he remained serious. His eyes bored into hers until she felt that he wanted to devour her very soul. He lowered his dark head until his warm breath tickled her ear, starting the now familiar tremors of excitement building within her, and, closing her eyes, she reveled in the sensation that she had come to completely enjoy.

Chance's voice, a husky whisper, was rough with the raw hunger of his desire, and her knees grew weak at his words, "I want you Reanna Dublin! I am tired of playing games. We need to talk, now … outside!" he pulled her unceremoniously through the crowd and out the door, where the sudden rush of night air cooled them. He led her to the far end of the barn where they could speak in privacy. The night was dark, with little moon, and he stood close to her.

"Mr. Nolton, if someone …"

Chance grasped her shoulders, more roughly than he intended, and shook her once, "Damn it Reanna, enough! I have had enough of the formalities, the conventions, the proprieties! I want you! I want you to come away with me, to be with me every moment, to be my woman. And my name is Chance. I cannot stand to hear another Mr. Nolton, not from you. It is just another of your ways of keeping me at a distance. And I've had enough of it!"

Reanna felt as if her heart had taken wings, so great was her joy, and it lent a deep, breathless quality to her voice, "Are you asking me to marry you, Mr. N ... Chance?"

Her hopes, however, were cruelly dashed at his next words, "No, Reanna, not marriage. Maybe someday, but I am not ready for that right now. I am asking you to live with me and share my life, but also to retain your freedom, as I would have mine. That is all I am prepared to offer."

Bitter, crushing disappointment threatened to overwhelm her, a terrible weight settled in the pit of her stomach. She had lost, but she should have known better. She could never do as he asked, and he would not bend in his own convictions.

"You are asking me to be your mistress then, Chance, to live with you in sin, to go against everything I've ever been taught, and to break my father's heart. Did you ever stop to think ... what if I was to have a baby?"

"I am asking you to love me as I love you, to give our love a chance before it is smothered beneath the strictures of your society. And any child that you may produce will be well taken care of, you have my word on that. I am a very wealthy man."

"Chance, I have only known you for eight weeks. Please give me time. I need time to think about this ... proposal."

She wanted to laugh at the duplicity of her own words but felt the sting of tears coming to her eyes instead. She attempted to turn away, but Chance would not release her, increasing the pressure of his forceful grip on her shoulders.

"No Reanna, there is no more time. I will leave here soon, and I want you with me when I go."

The finality of his words served to numb her senses.

"When Chance?" she asked, terribly afraid of his answer.

Chance allowed his hands to drop quietly to his sides and strode a few paces from her. It appeared that he was considering his reply.

"How soon Chance?" she repeated, no longer able to hold back the tears. They rained freely down her face.

Chance turned back to face her, and his words were harsh, "Two weeks, Reanna. I will wait two weeks for your answer, and then I am gone."

Why she wanted to bother with him in the two weeks left, Reanna did not quite understand. Her answer, the only one she could give, was inevitable, and she thought that he had sensed it too. But it was two more weeks to be with him, to bask in his love. He had said that he loved her, and she would hold his words close to her heart, for she loved him as she had never loved anyone, would ever love anyone again.

He stepped close once more and gently dried her tears with his handkerchief, then kissed her tenderly. They shared no words, there were none left in either of them. They simply reentered the gay atmosphere of the party, allowing themselves to be drawn into the dancing, drink, and conversation so they would not have to dwell upon the future, a future in which they were both destined to part.

Later, when Reanna woodenly informed her father of Chance's imminent departure, she could not hide the tears that sprang quickly to her eyes. Raymond Dublin's heart ached for his beautiful, loving daughter, and he attempted to ease her anguish. She was all he had left, so he spoke as gently as he could.

"Reanna, I tried to warn you about the danger of falling in love with a man like Chance Nolton. I told you he would only break your heart. But I am not so old that I don't remember that your head does not rule over matters of the heart. If you have only two weeks left to be with him, you should take full advantage of the time, so that you might try and convince him that you are worth staying here for."

He took note of the shock that registered on her face at his words, and smiled indulgently, "Reanna, I am not blind. I can see how much you love this man, and although I may not have shown much approval of him, I do not either wish to see my daughter lose the only man she could be happy with."

Reanna hugged her father, hope springing anew within her breast, saying, "Oh, Papa, you are wonderful!"

"A word of warning Reanna, never forget that he is a potentially dangerous man, and you are enough to make any man, especially one such as him attempt various … indiscretions, shall I say? Do not give me cause to regret my decision. You do understand?"

"Yes, Papa, and you needn't worry," she promised.

The young couple took full advantage of their newfound freedom with picnics, daylong horseback rides, and long, leisurely walks together. Reanna showed Chance around the vast acreage of the ranch, where they roamed at will.

He used this time to try and convince her to go away with him, would take her in his arms and kiss her tenderly, then with increasing passion as she responded with a fire of her own. He touched her softly, his roaming hands branding her skin with heated desire, and whispered sweet words of love and longing into her ears. His eyes remained ever watchful, burning with the fiery intensity of his passion, gauging her reactions.

Reanna would always pull away, despite the fires that he ignited within her. She felt that he would consume her very soul, and she could not, would not give in, and would not offer her whole being up to a man who was not willing to give all of himself up to her. She feared that she would never be given his complete love in return for hers, leaving her ever empty.

Because Chance did love her, he respected her feelings, and allowed her the courtesy of retreat, but it was growing increasingly difficult to do so. There came a day when he could not stop. In spite of her whispered pleas, he pushed her back until she lay in the grass, his lips captured hers in a fierce, brutal assault to still her denials as his hands worked feverishly at the buttons on her blouse, exposing the smooth, creamy mounds of her breasts to his view. Her curves were too generous, her very slender waist accentuating them even more, her beauty was so great that he would go mad if he did not have her. He had been waiting far too long. He lowered his head and his large body covered hers as he took one of the rosy peaks into the moist heat of his mouth, sucking eagerly at it, then the other, until they were stiff, and Reanna lay moaning in desire, her eyes half closed in drowsy passion.

Chance worked his hand up under her skirt, lightly running his fingers up the soft length of her thigh as he returned his lips to her mouth, plundering the sweetness within as his tongue, hot and experienced, drew her artless response.

Waves of pure pleasure washed over Reanna. She forgot her virtue, her shame, everything except the wonderful things that Chance was making her feel. She felt she would die of a longing that she could not quite even understand. Until his fingers reached the juncture of her thighs, rubbing the mound of her womanhood, probing gently for entrance. She felt the hard shaft of his desire pressing into her leg, and she panicked, struggling against him in earnest. She twisted her head to the side as she pushed at his chest with her hands, managing to gasp out, "No Chance! No!"

He attempted to grab her chin and recapture her lips, but she was desperate, and jerked away as she bucked against him, trying to wriggle from beneath him.

"Chance please, please stop!" she cried, panic edging her voice and tears springing to her eyes.

Her fear reached him, and he eased the long length of his body from hers, but his breathing was labored, his eyes burned with red heat and his face taught as he fought to bring his rampaging hunger under control.

"Jesus Reanna!" he finally managed to say, "I'm sorry, I did not mean to push you, or frighten you," he added as he gazed into her eyes, noting the emotion replacing the warmth and trust previously there.

"I think it would be best if I leave you now," he stated quietly, staring as Reanna, with shaking fingers, re-buttoned her blouse, "before I am overcome once more by your charms. You will forgive me if I don't see you back to the house?"

Still frightened by her narrow escape, Reanna could do no more than nod mutely.

Chance rode back to town, still trying to bring his lust under control. The powerful force of his need surprised even him; he did not dare trust himself with Reanna, for she was far too tempting.

He left Lancelot in the livery stable and after assuring himself that the stallion was properly curried and fed, strode purposely to the Horseshoe, and entered just as dusk was falling. He ordered a bottle of whiskey and sat at a corner table to drink in solitude. He was in a foul mood, spoiling for a fight, and the whiskey was not helping to curb his raging desire in the least.

Several acquaintances came in, but after one look at his scowling face, steered clear of him. Even Cal and Larry McPherson, lounging against the bar, knew better than to irritate him with their usual taunts.

Aggie, the saloon girl that worked nights, eyed Chance surreptitiously as she sat conversing with other patrons and serving drinks. He sure was handsome, even if he was glowering in anger, and she'd bet that it had something to do with Reanna Dublin. If she knew men, which she did, she would say that he had the look of a man far too long thwarted in amorous desires. She suppressed a shiver of excitement. Reanna Dublin did not know what she was missing, of course, but she herself would never refuse such a man! To be held in his arms …

Chance watched with narrowed eyes as Aggie approached, deliberately pronouncing the seductive sway of her hips. He had seen her take many men upstairs to her bed in the short time he had been in town, but with her enormous breast and hips, and narrow waist, it was not surprising that they were only too eager to pay for her services. Her lips were full, generous, and moist, and he wondered absently at the things they could do for a man.

She stopped in front of him, and in a deep, husky voice asked, "Mind if I have a drink?"

"Suit yourself," Chance said neutrally, sliding the bottle and his glass toward her.

She leaned forward to pour the drink, and a thrill of excitement leaped within her as she noted that his eyes, as she had planned, dipped to where her large breasts threatened to spill from her gaping, low cut bodice. His eyes seemed to burn her where they rested, her nipples swelled, and she felt the familiar tightening of need in the pit of her stomach. He said nothing, so she slid onto his lap, smiling into his eyes as she felt his pressing need through their clothing. She hooked an arm around his neck, pressing her breasts into his chest as she looked him in the eyes and deliberately ran the tip of her tongue around her lips.

Still, Chance did nothing. He sat perfectly still, tensely holding his raging desires in check, and stared back at her with hard, angry eyes.

Her face, up close, had the hard, mercenary look of a seasoned whore, but then, as she began to wriggle her ample bottom against his painful erection and teased his lips with the warm tip of her tongue, it did not matter. He could no longer deny his fierce need, and with a low growl, slanted his lips over hers in hard demand and cupped one hand over her bodice, squeezing one large, heavy breast as Aggie leaned into him, quite impatient for more.

Chance, breathing heavily, tore his mouth from hers and rasped, "Let's go."

She rose, and he followed, grabbing the bottle of whiskey in one hand while with the other he grasped Aggie's wrist and half dragged her up the stairs to her room, where he kicked her door closed with a resounding crash and pressed her down onto the bed.

Downstairs, Larry smiled evilly after witnessing the two head up the stairs, and in his loud, nasal voice, observed, "I guess just one-woman ain't enough for some men. I wonder if Miss Dublin knows that her dirty gunslinger is so hot for old Aggie."

"She will, she will. I wonder if she's always as ready for a good tumble as Aggie is." Cal wondered, and they both laughed uproariously, while the few men seated near, and Sam the barkeep, looked distinctly uncomfortable. It was, by now, well known that beautiful, well-respected Reanna was in love with Chance, and no one wanted to see her hurt.

Reanna was supposed to meet Chance for lunch the next day at the Horseshoe, and she arrived early to visit Belinda, who served drinks in the saloon during the day. She greeted Sam, who gave a guilty start at her entrance, exchanging a long look with Belinda, and nervously began to arrange glasses at the far end of the bar.

Belinda was left to gaze sadly at her friend, wondering just what she should say, if anything. Then, deciding that she had better tell Reanna gently before she heard it elsewhere, Belinda took Reanna's hand and led her to a table.

"I have something to tell you Reanna, that you won't want to hear. Please sit down," she offered gently, and Reanna sat.

"What is it, Belinda? Is something wrong?" Reanna questioned in concern.

Belinda took a deep breath. Best to get right on with it. "Chance is upstairs … with Aggie," she said, as gently as she could.

"Up … but, why? We are supposed to have lunch."

Belinda searched for a tactful way to make her friend understand. She knew that Chance had brought Verna, the other girl who worked the saloon at night, in and out of his hotel room, but no one else knew about that night, Belinda herself aware of it only because Verna had pointed him out as a most enthusiastic lover. Since he hadn't seriously been courting Reanna then, there had been no need for her to know, but this! Everyone in town knew by now, thanks to those McPhersons.

She cleared her throat and said in a flat voice, "Reanna, they have been up there all night." She could have bitten her tongue off when he saw Reanna's stricken look, and she attempted to console her, "Honey, men do …"

"I think I better go home now," Reanna interrupted in a sick voice, "Goodbye, Belinda."

Reanna stood and ran from the Horseshoe, climbing into her carriage and urging the horse into a fast trot toward home, as tears of hurt and humiliation stung her eyes.

Belinda stared at Chance with an air of reproach when he came down, and said, "She was here, and she knows. I think that she was deeply hurt, she has such high ideals you know."

"Unlike me, who has the morals of an alley cat?" Chance questioned, wishing that the pounding in his head would stop.

"No, it's Aggie who has the morals of an alley cat. You, I suspect, could not help yourself, wanting Reanna so, but not being able to have her for all this time …" At his quizzical look, Belinda added, "I know my proper friend well."

Chance had no retort and continued on his way, stopping at the hotel to bathe and change his clothes before commandeering Lancelot for the ride to the High Ridge ranch.

He found her in the rose garden, idly watching the bees that hovered around the fragrant blooms. She was composed now, but he could tell that she had been crying.

"Reanna, I'd like to explain," he began, but she turned to face him, and he saw the deep hurt in her large green eyes.

"You told me you loved me," she whispered, and Chance stepped near to pull her into his arms.

"I do, Reanna, but men have needs …"

"Don't tell me men have needs," she accused, "my father is a man, and I don't see him running up to Aggie's room!"

Chance, unable to help himself, laughed heartily, and Reanna looked at him as if he were mad.

"My dear," he explained, "you are such an innocent. What do you suppose that your father does on all those business trips that he takes?"

"He doesn't!" Reanna gasped.

"No?" Chance inquired in a silky voice, "Then tell, me why doesn't he ever invite you to accompany him?"

Reanna had no answer for that and quietly tried to absorb this unexpected new insight into her father's life.

Chance gently cupped her chin and raised her face to his, "Reanna, surely you realize that I almost took you against your will yesterday?" She said nothing, and he continued, "No? Well, take my word for it. I have wanted you so badly, for so long, that I was nearly crazed with it. Aggie means nothing to me. She just served to take care of my ... physical needs, but I am left still unsatisfied. I want you, Reanna, but not as I would have taken you yesterday."

He kissed her very gently on the lips, then moved to the column of her neck, pressing his warm lips softly against her throat, following with the tip of his tongue as his head dipped lower, brushing her skin at the neckline of her dress.

"I want you warm and willing," he continued as he raised his head once again, staring down into her passion glazed eyes, "I want to love you as you deserve, slowly and thoroughly. Reanna, I would rather tutor you gently in the ways of love. Tell me you want me to," he whispered into her ear, and Reanna's knees grew weak. She was filled with longings that threatened to take her breath away, and she had to lean on Chance's broad chest for support. Her heart was beating wildly, and she could feel the steady pulse of his through his shirt. Her eyes were dark with desire as she gazed up at him.

In a breathless whisper she stated, "It would make for a wonderful wedding night."

Chance smiled sadly and gently ran his finger down her lovely cheek, brushing tenderly at the curling tendrils of silken copper hair. She had given him her answer. She would not be going with him. It hurt him to look at her, she as so beautiful, filled with gentleness and grace.

"I have a business meeting, some things to attend to," he said, "Why don't I pick you up tomorrow at six for dinner and dancing? I will make arrangements for you to stay at your uncles in town in case we are out too late."

She murmured her assent, and after a long, gentle kiss, he left her.

Reanna felt bereft, numb with pain. He had not said it, but she was certain that he would be leaving the day after tomorrow and had planned an evening filled with people and activity to make saying goodbye easier.

Reanna dressed to the hilt, wearing her best gown, a dark bronze velvet, embroidered with rows of golden roses that shimmered and sparkled as she moved. The short, puffed sleeves sported golden lace trim and the low-cut neckline was edged in the same. She wound her hair in a coronet of braids, as she had the first night at her uncle's, and wore a golden locket that nestled against the tender flesh just above the bodice of her gown, and golden slippers peeked from beneath her skirts when she walked.

She noted that Chance had done the same, as he wore a dark brown, double-breasted suit made of the finest linen, a cream-colored silk shirt, and he even wore a dark brown silk tie. With his lean, muscular build and aura of potent masculinity, Reanna knew well that she would be the envy of many of the women attending the dance tonight. He looked so darkly handsome that she could have burst into tears at the sight of him, certain that this would be her last evening with the man she loved so much.

They rode to the Horseshoe in silence, each absorbed in their own thoughts, and when their dinner arrived neither of them could eat more than a few bites, although their steaks were cooked to perfection.

They were on their second dance, and Chance was tired of trying to make small talk.

"What is troubling you, Reanna? You are very quiet tonight and have graced me with your smile no more than once or twice. It is not like you."

They had ceased moving to the music. It seemed to Reanna that time suddenly stood still, and as her sad, empty eyes searched his, he noted that the deep glitter of the sea no longer sparkled in her green eyes. There was none of their former liveliness, only the dull hue of pain in the knowledge that they would part. Chance felt something constrict around his heart.

Tears sprang into her eyes, threatening to choke her words, "It is tonight, isn't it?"

Chance could no longer bear to look into those eyes. He bent his head, expelling a long breath. He wondered how she had known. Ever so softly he managed, "I will be leaving at first light, Reanna."

If he were not holding her, she would have swooned. She could not fight back the tears any longer and they rained freely down her face, turning quickly into body wrenching sobs, and Chance guided her quickly through the crowd and out the door.

Once out in the night air, he held her tightly against his chest, stroking her head and back, allowing his warmth and nearness to comfort her. She cried, heartbroken, for some time, and slowly her sobs quieted, but she could not stop the tears that rained down her cheeks in abandon.

Chance moved her to a nearby bench and bade her sit, "Let me get you something to help. I will be right back."

He returned with a glass of brandy and raised it to her lips. "Drink this Reanna, it will help to calm you," he ordered.

She took a sip and shuddered, gagging as the fiery liquid slid down her throat. She pushed the glass away, but Chance was insistent, and she finally managed to finish the draft surprised to find that it did relax her, and she no longer cried. But she could not face again the gaily lit atmosphere inside. She wanted to go home, to sleep, and to forget.

"Take me home Chance, please."

"I will see you to your uncles. It is late, he will be expecting you."

"Yes, you are probably right, but I don't think anyone would be waiting up at this hour." She sighed, "Let's not take the carriage. I feel like walking."

They strolled in heavy silence to Bob Dublin's front gate, where they stood together, Reanna with her head bowed. Chance reached out and touched her hair, and she looked up at him in the half darkness, just beyond the reach of the lantern's light on her uncle's front porch. They had left it burning for her.

"Reanna ..." Chance began in a husky whisper and then stopped, at a loss for words.

"Go if you must, my love, and Godspeed. But do not forget that I have given you my heart, and you carry it with you. I only pray that you bring it back to me someday," Reanna spoke softly, but she felt her heart was shattering to splinters. She raised her lips and kissed him lightly, a bittersweet, sad caress, and turned to let herself into the yard.

Chance finally found his voice and called softly, "Goodbye Reanna Dublin. We will meet again someday; of that you can be sure."

He turned and walked slowly through the silent darkness, never dreaming just how soon his words would prove to be true.

"Goodbye, my heart," Reanna whispered, and watched until he melded with the blackness beyond.

Chance found that he had no taste for staying another night in this place. He wanted to be on the move, to quit this town and leave its memories behind as swiftly as possible. He collected his belongings from his room, settled his account, and packed everything on Lancelot, riding off into the night.

Larry McPherson had been in the saloon that afternoon, had heard Chance talking with Sam, the barkeep, so he was privy to the knowledge that Reanna Dublin was staying at her uncles for the night, and that the bounty hunter would be leaving at first light.

So ... he thought, he might finally get his chance after all. His eyes narrowed in contemplation. They would all get their chance, but they would have to play their cards right. No mistakes, and that they did, unfortunately so for Reanna.

She turned to walk up the stone path to her uncle's porch when she heard a strange noise, almost as if someone were moaning in pain. She listened intently, then called out, "Michael? ... Jared? ... Who is there?"

She received no answer, and her natural concern for others led her to investigate. Someone was hurt. She could finally make out the form of a man lying on the ground, his legs pulled up to his chest, his arms crossing his stomach as he rolled in agony. She ran to him and knelt by his side, touching his shoulder lightly to attract his attention.

It was as she leaned over him that it hit her. The sour smell of whiskey and tobacco was so strong that it choked her. He turned his head to face her. Larry McPherson! Strange, but he did not seem to be in pain at all, for he was laughing, an ugly, malicious sneer split his face.

He grabbed her, and she tried to scream, but there was a sharp, cracking pain in her head, and she slumped motionless to the ground, plunged into a darkness blacker than the night.

As Chance rode determinedly through the night, an inexplicable sense of doom rode with him, growing stronger as he traveled farther. He felt as if it had something to do with Reanna, that some terrible fate had befallen her, but then he cursed himself for his trepidations. He himself had wronged her, had broken her heart. He would never forget her parting words or the deep sadness in her eyes.

He hated himself for what he had done, a new, and not overly welcome sensation for him. He had purposely pursued a beautiful, innocent maiden with the express purpose of seducing her, and captured her gentle heart, only to throw it back at her feet. He had to leave it behind, to forget her and find his free and easy way of life again. He kicked Lancelot into a mile consuming lope. He would ride ... and he would forget.

Chance had no way of knowing that no matter where he ran, how fast, or how far, he would never forget. For he could not leave Reanna behind when he carried her with him in his own heart, forever.

Chapter 4

Martha woke early and padded quietly down the stairs to the kitchen, where she put a pot of coffee on and began to slice bacon for the morning meal. As it sizzled, she began to scramble the eggs, absently humming a tune as she inhaled the aroma of the coffee beginning to fill the room.

"Good morning, dear," Bob greeted her, placing a fond kiss upon her cheek as he hugged her broad form.

"Good morning. Reanna seems to be sleeping late; she's usually up long before this. Well, she and Chance must have had a late night; I didn't even hear her come in."

"Well, let her sleep," Bob said as he sat down to eat. "You know, Martha," he added in a thoughtful voice, "I have suspicion a that our Reanna may be getting married in the near future."

At her dubiously raised brow, he continued, "Yes, I know what you are thinking, but I know that Chance is in love with her. He has that look of a man in love, which, I don't have to tell you, is a first for him."

Martha chuckled and admitted, 'If anyone could capture that rogue's heart, it would be Reanna. She is a very beautiful, compassionate young lady, and if you call that darkly brooding look he's worn lately that of a man in love, well then, I guess you're probably right."

"Of course I am," Bob said as he dug into his food, "men know these things."

At Martha's snort of derision, Michael and Jared burst into the kitchen and the conversation ended.

"Mornin' Ma, mornin' Pa," they barely managed to say before ravenously attacking the portions placed before them.

Martha cleaned up the kitchen and prepared a pot of stew to simmer on the stove while the men went out to their chores, then, thinking that Reanna had slept quite long enough, went to wake her. "Funny, her bed has not been slept in," Martha mused, surprised to find that Reanna was not there, "She must have gone home to High Ridge after all."

When she informed Bob, he agreed. Reanna must have gone home.

Hours later, Raymond Dublin sat alone at the table, absent mindedly toying with the supper Carmelita had left before going home. Reanna should have been back hours ago. It was not like her to stay at Bob's and not send him a word. Well, maybe she had gone out with that bounty hunter again. Still, she would have told him, would have come home for a change of clothes. He continued to push the food around on his plate, lost in his thoughts, and an elusive worry began to gnaw at him. Finally, he pushed back his chair and strode purposely to the barn, where he saddled a horse and rode into town, to his brother's house.

Martha hurried to answer the loud insistent knocking at the door. "Why, Ray! Come on in. Whatever brings you here at this hour? Usually, you and Reanna are relaxing after dinner, listening to music by now."

"Is she here?" Raymond demanded, "She never came home today, and I became worried. She always lets me know if she has other plans."

Now Martha was concerned and puzzled. "But Reanna has not been here at all! You mean she never went home last night? Her bed was not slept in, so we just naturally assumed that she had gone back to the ranch, instead."

Bob came up behind Martha, placing comforting hands upon her shoulders. "What do you mean Reanna never came home? She had to. She certainly has not been here," he said, knowing, with a sinking feeling in the pit of his stomach, that his words were but a spoken denial of an obvious truth.

Raymond's accusing eyes met those of his brother, and scowling, he said, "This is all your fault Bob. That bounty hunter you hired has taken her away! I knew he was no good from the moment I set eyes on him, and I told her to stay away from him!"

"Now Ray, calm down," Bob lectured, "you cannot know that for sure. I really don't think that Chance would do anything like this, even though he has done exactly as he wants his whole life. I say we check around town before we jump to any conclusions. She may turn up after all, and we can start by asking Chance himself," he recalled with an increasing sinking feeling the day Chance had first come to town, and where he had found Reanna, but, no, he was sure that Chance cared too much for his niece to openly compromise her by keeping her in his hotel room all last evening and today.

They inquired at the Shamrock, but Edward, the clerk, informed them that Chance Nolton had checked out last night, suddenly, and yes, he had been alone.

They began a methodical search, enlisting the aid of Michael and Jared to knock on every door, questioning friends and acquaintances for any knowledge of Reanna's whereabouts. They all came up with the same empty answers. No one had seen her since she had left the Horseshoe with Chance and she had been very upset about something. Only Sam, the barkeep, had anything further to add, and that was that Chance had intended to leave in the morning. So why the sudden early departure? They were at a dead end. The only other thing Sam knew was that Chance planned to go to Nevada City, California, on business, and after that, well, who knew?

Raymond and Bob returned to the sheriff's office with their shoulders hunched in defeat. Reanna was definitely missing; her friends knew nothing.

"I told you; he has taken her away with him," Raymond said, his voice hollow. His poor, lovely daughter!

"I will admit, it does not look good," Bob ventured, "but I still cannot accept it. Has it been so long that you no longer recognize the look of a man in love?"

"Love, hell! If he has so much as touched a hair on her head … I just hate to think of her out on the trail with him, day, and night. He will ruin her! I am going to find her. I'm going back to the ranch for some of my men, and if he has touched her, I'll take care of him in my own way!"

Bob prayed, for Chance's sake, that he did not have Reanna with him, and that some word of her whereabouts would reach him in the meantime.

As Raymond Dublin rode through the night with a small posse of men at his back, he thought of how unnecessary it would have been for Chance to kidnap Reanna. Of course, Nolton would not force her. If she were with him, she would have gone of her own free will. He found this fact very hard to accept, but Reanna was nineteen, old enough to make her own decisions, right or wrong, and she was very much in love with the bounty hunter. Still, the man would do the right thing by his daughter, he would see to it.

It was a three-day ride to Nevada City and Nolton had a twenty-hour head start. They could make the trip in forty-eight hours if they wasted no unnecessary moments and pushed the horses to their limits. But halfway through the night, the sky clouded over and they were forced to stop because of the total darkness, leaving Raymond to fume over the delay. In the end it took the full three days for them to reach their destination.

Chance had ridden that whole first night, pushing Lancelot as fast as he dared, and all the next day he pushed onward, stopping only to water his horse. The following night he was forced to stop, if not for his own exhaustion, then for that of his horse, which was beginning to stumble with weariness.

At first light he was again on the trail. It took him only two and a half days to reach Nevada City, and he took care of his business as quickly as possible the next day, collecting rental monies from his agent, who had never seen Chance so agitated.

Chance hated the restless stirrings within his soul, and wanted to move on as soon as he possibly could. He was never able to shake the feeling that something was terribly wrong with Reanna and kept reminding himself that it was he who had wronged her and was now paying the price. He would forget, in time. Maybe a bottle would help in this endeavor. He planned to leave in the morning, but he had to somehow make it through the night.

Last night had brought him only fitful snatches of, by now, longed for slumber. He had suffered the worst dream he could remember in his life. Reanna was screaming in pain, and he could not reach her to help. Something was holding him from her, something that he could not see, and how could he fight that which he could not perceive? Reanna was slowly being drawn into a swirling void of inky blackness, her screams growing more distant …

He had awakened drenched in a cold sweat, with an ache in his heart, and chilling dread in the pit of his stomach. All day he had been unable to shake that feeling of cold dread. Yes, a bottle would surely help him through the coming night.

He spent the next five hours in a saloon, silent and morose, with only his own black thoughts for company as he slowly drank two bottles of whiskey with cold deliberation, drank until he passed out in his chair and his head hit the table with a loud thud.

The barkeep, along with two other men, had not dared to invade the dark, menacing stranger's privacy while he drank, but sensing his heartache, carried him to the back room, where a cot was supplied for just such occasions.

Chance opened his eyes the next morning in response to something cold and hard prodding him in the ribs. Bleary eyed, he blinked to clear his vision, and a harsh, angry voice demanded, "Where is she, Nolton?"

He could not place the voice to a face, yet there was something vaguely familiar about it. His head was throbbing so badly that he thought it would explode, and his tongue felt swollen in his mouth. It was his damn binge from the night before, he should have known better, but the sweet surcease ...

The voice was louder now, more belligerent, "Where is my daughter, Nolton? She left with you; I know it. What the hell have you done with her?"

Chance felt the cold steel dig painfully into his ribs as cold dread gripped his heart. Reanna! His throat contracted so tightly that he could barely breathe.

He reached up with swift accuracy, his instincts honed by years of living by his wits, and grabbed the barrel of the rifle, rising up to push it away with all his strength, and the sudden force knocked Raymond backwards, causing him to nearly lose his balance.

Chance rolled to his side and gained his feet in one lithe movement, but checked his forward lunge at Raymond, brought up short by the sight of six-gun barrels pointed threateningly in his direction.

"I'm going to ask you one more time, Nolton, and then things could get nasty. Where is she?"

"I have not seen your daughter since the night we went dancing, Dublin. I left her at your brother's gate, and left town immediately after," Chance said levelly. Was Raymond mad? Fear began to clutch his innards, and Raymond was still glaring in accusation.

Chance sighed in resignation. Obviously, this was going to take some blunt speech.

"If I had your daughter with me, which I don't, as you can plainly see, you would not have found me in the filthy back room of a saloon, but between sheets of a room in some hotel, and I would be …" Chance sat gingerly back down on the cot, holding his throbbing head between his hands, "perfectly sober."

Several of the men, a cold-eyed Sean among them, started forward at Chance's bold words, but Raymond raised his hand in a gesture to stay them.

"Believe me; I haven't touched her," Chance continued, "although I will admit, not through any lack of effort on my part."

Sean started angrily toward Chance once again, and once more Raymond stopped him, carefully considering Chance's words. Deciding that the bounty hunter spoke the truth, he slowly lowered his gun, and his men did the same.

"Reanna apparently never went into Bob's house that night, Nolton. Her bed was never slept in. we could only assume …" his words trailed off, and he slumped in defeat.

Chance nervously came to his feet. "You've checked everywhere?" he asked softly, knowing the answer to his question already. Still, he had to ask. The tightness in his chest threatened to suffocate him.

"Yes."

Chance was suddenly very clear headed, the truth slamming into him with cold vengeance. His dream, his feeling of dread … something had happened, something terrible had happened to Reanna!

He reached the door in a few strides and flung it open, suggesting in a controlled voice, "We'll go back. Split up and fan out on the way in case she tried to follow me. I don't think she would have, but we must explore every possibility. And maybe there is some word in town by now. She is sure to have turned up."

But his words held the hollow ring of hopelessness, even to his own ears, and resounded in his head as they rode furiously back in the direction they had come.

Chance allowed them no rest. He would not, could not stop the frantic pace. He had the dreadful premonition that Reanna was not going to be found, would not be there when they arrived back in Carson City. Why had he not heeded his own gut feelings? He pushed on, mindless of the horses labored breathing, mindless of everything but the cold terror screaming through his very soul...

Reaching town on the evening of the second day, they hauled their exhausted, lathered mounts to a sharp halt in front of the sheriff's office and dismounted in a cloud of dust kicked up by the horse's hooves. Chance almost pulled the door from its hinges in his haste to ask Bob for any news, but there was none. They had not heard from, nor found any traces of Reanna.

Chance ran a shaking hand through his matted hair; his eyes held a feral gleam, reflections of his inner torment and impotent rage, which had built within him until he felt like a caged lion, desiring to lash out, to sink his fists into someone, anyone. Even Bob would not dare to cross him now. He began to pace restlessly, and when Bob handed him a drink, he downed it, then without a word or backward look he left them, slamming the door with a deafening crash on his way out.

Chance canvassed the entire town, desperately asking questions of everyone he met, even stopping carriages in the middle of the street, searching for some word or clue to Reanna's location. He knew that Bob had already initiated a thorough search, but he had to do something while they awaited the return of the rest of Ray Dublin's men, who were still scouring the distance between Carson and Nevada City's borders for information. It was an effort in futility, however. People shook their heads sadly or looked after him as if he were mad.

The riders came in with nothing more to add. It was growing late, he was no closer to finding Reanna, and he was exhausted, having gone without sustenance or sleep for over two days. Raymond rode, dispirited, back to the ranch with his men and Chance took his old room at the Shamrock. He could endure the ache in his heart no longer and thankfully slipped into a deep, dreamless slumber.

He had not slept nearly long enough when an insistent rapping on his door forced him from this haven of oblivion, and he mumbled a groggy acknowledgment as he stumbled, still fully dressed, to the door.

"I found this attached to my office door," Bob said grimly, stepping into the room as he handed Chance a crumpled piece of paper.

He swiftly skimmed the childish scrawl, then, in stunned silence, raised disbelieving eyes to Bob's anguished gaze.

It was a ransom note, demanding ten-thousand dollars, to be delivered by Bob Dublin, alone, the next day, which was by now, today, and Chance's stomach congealed with a terror he had never before known. Those filthy scum, the McPhersons, had Reanna!

"We must do as the note says. We can't just ride in there, guns blazing. They may kill her," Bob said softly.

"I know," Chance could barely manage a whisper.

Ten thousand dollars was a lot of money, even for Raymond Dublin, but Chance had no doubt that between himself and Reanna's father, they could raise it.

"Chance, I want you to ride out to High Ridge right away and show this to Ray. Find out if he can raise that much money."

Chance nodded curtly and wasted no time in reaching the ranch, only to be greeted by an overwrought Carmelita.

"He just sits in that chair, holding her guitar," she explained as she led Chance into the parlor, wringing her hands helplessly, "he won't eat, and he never went to his room last night, just sits in that chair without moving."

Chance stood before the man that had wanted to kill him just days ago and was shocked by the change that a few hours had wrought. Raymond looked as if he had aged ten years and gave no sign that he even knew that Chance was there, just clutched his daughter's guitar as if he would never let it go.

It was the uncertainty, the not knowing, Chance realized, that had done this. Well, he could remedy that, but the truth would not be easy to accept either.

"We have received word of Reanna," Chance began stiffly, and Raymond's eyes seemed suddenly to focus on his visitor.

Chance reached out to take Reanna's guitar, and held it, staring down at the fine wood, and in his mind, he could see her gaily playing her music, singing her sweet melodies with sparkling eyes, her whole face alight with the joy of the life she so loved. He closed his eyes and swallowed painfully at the memory, then ran his fingers over the strings of the instrument a few times, the discordant notes hanging in the waiting silence. He turned to place the guitar gently on the top of the piano before continuing, "a ransom note. It was on Bob's office door this morning."

"Where is she? How much do they want? Where is my Reanna?" Raymond demanded, coming to his feet.

"Read it." Chance handed him the note.

"My God … my God, the McPhersons have her!" Raymond groaned, and a look of complete understanding passed between the two men as Carmelita gasped in horror.

"It's worse than you realize," Raymond said. "Bob killed their father a few years ago. He was always in trouble with the law, it was self-defense, but the five boys never accepted that. Claimed that Bob shot him in cold blood, and … they are going to make Reanna pay," he predicted in a sick whisper.

"For that, and other things, I'm sure," Chance agreed, remembering the painful kick Reanna had dealt Larry, and the McPhersons humiliation at his own hands. He turned to the teary-eyed Carmelita and asked gently, "Do you think you could find something for us to eat, quickly? I haven't eaten in three days myself, and we do not have much time."

"Of course, I have some stew all ready," she hurried into the kitchen, grateful to have something to do.

The men made plans as they sat at the table, inhaling the robust aroma of Carmelita's stew before delving into it heartily. Now, at last, they could make definite arrangements.

Suddenly, Raymond's face fell, and Chance queried, "What is it, Dublin? Surely there will be no problem getting the money. If there is, I can help, and I offer it readily."

Raymond looked defeated and answered in a tired voice, "I have no need of your money, but today is Sunday, the bank is not open, and Dell Johnson, the banker, always leaves early Sunday morning to visit his parents' home in Virginia City. It is impossible to get the money to them today, he will not return until late tonight."

Chance was on his feet in an instant, saying, "I will ride out there and bring him back. I'm sure that he won't argue once he knows the urgency of the situation, and if he does, well it will do him little good. I can make it there in an hour and a half."

"Nolton, it's one o'clock now. That will make it at least four o'clock before you make it back. Then, withdrawing the money, getting things organized … do you think it will be possible to do all this before dark?"

"Get all the men together and meet Bob in town, Dublin, she's already been their prisoner for six days, and who knows what horrors she has endured. I will not leave her there another night if I have to break into the damn bank myself for the money!" Chance declared vehemently as they walked to the door, leaving Raymond to stare after him as he urged Lancelot in desperation toward Virginia City.

He returned with Dell Johnston in tow, by four o'clock, just as he had promised, and found that Bob and Raymond were waiting at the sheriff's office with a large group of men, ready to move.

They had a plan all worked out, and briefed Chance as they collected the ransom money and headed out to the McPherson farm. When they were some distance from their destination, the men would leave their horses and silently converge on the house, taking whatever cover was available, while Bob rode in alone with the money, demanding to see Reanna outside. Once he handed over the ransom and got his niece off to a safe distance, the men could move in and hold the brothers for arrest. They had finally done something that would send them away to prison for a good long time. Would to God that it was not at Reanna's expense.

As they neared the farm, there was more than one nervous glance exchanged between the men as they noted Chance's deadly calm features and coldly intent dark eyes blazing with the urge to kill. All of them made it a point to stay well away from him, and his laboring black stallion. The animal looked by now as menacing as his owner.

They reached the outskirts of the farm, and the men dismounted, creeping silently to their respective positions surrounding the house. Two of the brothers were in sight, Cal in the side yard chopping wood, and Larry, lounging lazily on the front porch. They could not know where the others, or Reanna, were. When all was ready, Chance gave Bob a signal, and the sheriff rode alone into the dusty yard, meeting Larry's terrible smile with a cold, unblinking glare.

*   *   *   *   *   *

Fragments of disjointed conversation intruded upon, then receded from the fringes of awareness that slowly dawned in Reanna's mind, increasing in volume and clarity as consciousness returned.

She heard laughter, a short, loud burst, and intermittent wagers punctuated with the sharp clink of coins. The acrid stink of tobacco smoke filled her nostrils, and when they fluttered open, burned her eyes as it hung in a heavy haze over the small room.

She attempted to raise a hand to her aching head but found that she could not move. Confusion scattered her thoughts for a moment, but then her eyes focused on the five men sitting at the table. The McPhersons!

As Reanna watched in disbelief, they continued playing, unaware that she had recovered from the blow to her head. They were wagering … for her now! She struggled to rise, but she was bound tightly with a length of rope to a chair in the corner of the kitchen. The small movement brought a flash of pain to her head, and she could not withhold the small moan of distress that escaped her parched lips.

Billy, who was nearest her, heard it and rushed to her side with a cup of water, "Miss Dublin, here, drink this, it will help some." He held the cup to her lips, and she gratefully sipped the cool liquid, easing her dry throat before she fearfully whispered, "Billy, what have they done? Why am I here?"

Billy, shamed by his brothers' intentions, averted his eyes, and she followed his gaze, an inexplicable fear beginning to take hold of her as she noted the hard, interested attention directed her way by the four men at the table.

Larry and Darrel, wavering slightly, stumbled to their feet, and sauntered slowly toward her, their gazes raking her body. She realized that they were drunk, for three open bottles of whiskey, in various amounts of consumption, stood on the table.

Larry was so close that she could feel his foul breath against her face as he spoke, "So the little princess is finally awake, and I 'spose you're wonderin' why you're here? First, for our enjoyment, and when we had our fill of you, we're gonna send your daddy a little present," he threw his head back and laughed evilly, "a ransom note. Once he pays, he can have you back, but you won't be nothin' better'n a whore by then. You already are, just no one realizes it, you bein' so rich and respectable." He laughed once again, amused by their plans for her.

Darrel, a large, dumb brute of a man, leaned over her, his protruding stomach coming close to her face. "We was bettin' which one of us would get to have you first," he informed her, reaching out to roughly finger her silken hair as he smiled lasciviously, his thick lips parting over rotted teeth and his small, dark eyes glittering in anticipation, "Larry won."

Reanna wanted to scream, but she was so terror stricken that she could not find her voice. Her head was spinning; her mind wanted to refute the dreadful circumstance in which she now found herself. No one could be this cruel, this insane. It was all just a bad dream, it had to be. How could they hope to get away with it? But the pain in her head, the choking odor of whiskey and tobacco, the disgusting touch of this madman … her senses recoiled, but reality settled into her brain with forceful clarity. It was not a dream; this was really happening.

Larry reached behind her and roughly jerked the knot from the rope, chafing the tender skin of her wrists as he pulled the length swiftly from around her. He ran his finger down the creamy column of her neck and on to where her locket lay resting in the valley of her breasts. He smiled a nasty smile and said, "I won, and you lose."

He dragged her roughly up out of the chair and began to push her toward a room separated from the rest of the cabin by a worn curtain.

Sobbing now, Reanna frantically turned and tried to break away, to run, but there was nowhere she could go. The others had circled around her, a pack of wolves with leering grins, and everywhere she turned, strong arms were there pushing her back toward the inevitable fate.

Then, there was only Larry. He wasted no time, but viciously grasped her shoulders and forced her down upon the bed, a filthy, stinking bed that made her skin crawl. He pawed at her clothing with eager hands, uncaring that he ripped and tore the luxurious fabric of her gown in his haste to free her breasts, and in a moment, they were bared. He feasted his eyes upon their round, creamy perfection, glowing in the half light of the lantern that filtered through the thin curtain at the door. Grasping them with sadistic pleasure, he squeezed and pulled vehemently, and Reanna's low moan of pain only served to inflame his lust even further. He bent his head over the soft mounds, smiling in malicious pleasure, and plunged down to ravish their tempting rosy peaks with his teeth, indifferent to Reanna's pitiful sobs.

He raised his head finally to eye her in cold-blooded anticipation. "Now, my little whore, I'm gonna show you that I'm bettern' that dirty bounty hunter, bettern' your dead fiancé was and bettern' that Indian friend a yours, too."

Reanna's mind reeled in shock at his crude words and painfully cruel touch. The suffocating odor of his whiskey laden breath filled her nostrils until she could barely breathe, and she suddenly could stand no more. She began to fight him as furiously as a wildcat. Writhing violently beneath him, she kicked him with all her strength and raked her nails sharply down his face.

"Damn you, bitch!"

Raising a hand to his face, he brought it down covered in blood, and his eyes glowed with more cruelty and malice than she would have thought possible of anyone.

She knew deep, chilling fear as he pinned her arms above her head, while he said, "If you liked havin' a dirty bounty hunter ruttin' you, I'm sure you'll like what I do." Then he ground his lips down upon hers with a savage, intense fury, raking his teeth callously over their tender fullness.

She made a wrenching sound deep within her throat and tried to break away from his stinking embrace, but he held her easily under his body, his lips continuing to abuse her until he finally raised his head, angered by her reluctance, releasing her swollen mouth.

His breathing came rapid and harsh, and his narrowed hazel eyes burned with unappeased lust. "You damn whore!" he spat, "You think you can bed everyone but me?"

"What'sa matter, Larry, she don't want ya?" Darrel called.

"Maybe ya need someone to show ya how to handle her," offered Cal, breaking into another round of laughter.

"Shut up!" Larry screamed, "Alla'ya just shut up!"

He looked down at Reanna, hate twisting his features, and slapped her face with vicious force again and again, venting his savage temper, keeping at it until she lay in a dazed state of shock. Then when he was sure that she would not be capable of further struggle, he pushed her skirts up to her waist.

Tears of pain and fear streamed from her eyes as her mind screamed a silent denial of that which she was helpless to deny any longer. She had never seen a man unclothed, and the sight of his erection filled her with horror …

Reanna began to plead weakly, knowing that it was to no avail, "Please … no … please don't …"

Larry's thin lips parted in a leering smile, hate burned in his eyes, and suddenly he was upon her, unable to curb his lust a minute longer. His large organ throbbed against her, demanding entry. He quickly forced her legs apart, and her pleas turned to a scream of anguish as he rudely invaded her. She felt herself being ripped and torn without mercy until his savage assault was halted momentarily by the barrier of her maidenhood.

Surprise registered on his face, then a malevolent cunning as he withdrew from her. Licking his lips in anticipation, he gloated over his discovery.

"A virgin! Ya sure had me fooled, but now," he paused to smile at her fear and rub himself tauntingly against her, "now I'm gonna really make you pay for all you and your family done. This …" he lifted and drove into her with a deep, savage thrust as Reanna screamed in agony, suffused in total burning pain, unlike anything she had ever known, "is how I'm payin' you and your uncle back!"

He increased the tempo of his thrusts, brutally sinking into her untried depths, wreaking his vengeance with terrible cruelty. He kept on, abusing her relentlessly in depraved pleasure until he finally shuddered with longed for release, filling her with his seed.

Reanna's screams grew weaker, and she thankfully lost consciousness, a defense against the pain, so was spared any humiliating tortures that the others would have given her this night.

She woke the next morning to puzzling silence. Perplexed, she listened for any sign of movement. There was none. Maybe she could use this chance to make her escape from this nightmare. She attempted to rise, but the effort proved to be too much for her. She lay back down upon the smelly, rumpled bed, moaning in pain.

Every muscle in her body ached, and her loins burned with the unbearable after-effects of Larry's ruthless assault. She began to sob piteously as she recalled the brutal rape she had been subjected to. Better that she had given herself to Chance, who she loved more than life itself. Chance, her knight in shining armor. He would never want her now, and she wept for all that she had lost.

The sound of gunfire cut through the dull haze of her thoughts, and she tried once again to rise from the bed, gaining her feet after much effort. Her eyes were brilliant with the sheen of tears and her soft lips were swollen and sore, her temples still throbbed from Larry's beating, but she managed to slowly shuffle to the kitchen. Her head was spinning and for a moment she knew only blackness, but she grasped the back of a chair to save herself from falling to the floor.

Reanna opened her eyes once again, to a fresh jolt of fear as she saw that Cal sat in one of the chairs, eyeing her with steady, cold regard as a chilling smile spread slowly over his face.

He was strikingly handsome, with classically chiseled features and bronzed complexion, white-blond hair, and neatly trimmed mustache.

It was a well-known fact that he had no trouble at all finding women willing to bed him, even married ladies. What was not so well known was the fact that he had a penchant for battering his hapless lovers.

"That sound … the guns …" Reanna could barely force the words from her parched throat, then stopped as he continued his cold, unfeeling regard of her, his slate gray eyes assessing, and she was filled with a paralyzing fear.

He crushed his cigarette out in a dirty bowl, and then rose slowly from his chair. Ignoring her curiosity about the gunfire, he ordered her, "Ya want coffee, ya git it. Then ya can git us some breakfast. I'll be damned if I'm gonna cook when there's a woman around."

Reanna closed her eyes and swallowed against the tears and utter hopelessness that threatened to engulf her. Surely, they did not expect her to cook for them! Hadn't they done enough? Why didn't they just ransom her and get it over with? She moved with halting steps to the stove, every move bringing a renewed stab of scorching pain between her legs. She poured her coffee, and then slowly moved back to the chair, intending to sit down, but Cal quickly slid his foot in front of the chair leg and moved to tower over her.

"I jest tol'ya to git our breakfast." Despite the quiet tone of his voice, there was something sinister and threatening in the way he spoke, and Reanna hesitated in her answer.

"You … you really do not expect me to …"

Cal picked up his foot, and then brought the booted appendage down with such force upon her bare toes that her breath caught in her throat and tears of surprised pain filled her eyes. He grabbed her braid and roughly yanked her head back.

His gray eyes glittered with malice, and he sneered, "You'll do as you're told, little lady."

Reanna was terribly frightened of his cruel grip and without thinking; she dashed the hot coffee she still held into his face, breaking free of his hold to bolt for the door.

His bellow of rage and pain followed her as she struggled desperately to open the door, but before she could succeed, she was caught in an iron grip from behind and spun around to face him. She struggled valiantly, but her efforts were in vain, his arms easily held her imprisoned.

She looked up at her captor in terror, and his lips slowly parted in a lustful smile. She realized too late that her gown had torn more, and gaped open, exposing a generous portion of her breasts.

"Looks like I'm gonna havta teachya a lesson little lady," he drawled, and his smile broadened at the thought, "one ya ain't gonna be too likely ta forgit."

He threw her violently to the floor, and the breath left her body at the sudden impact. She tried to sit up, and he roughly yanked her up to her feet, pulling her forcibly by her hair. She screamed in pain, and salty tears again stung her eyes.

He brutally slapped first one side of her face, then the other, leaving large red welts on the tender skin of her cheeks, then he slammed her up against the wall with such powerful force that her breath was taken away. He pinned her there, his large body easily holding hers.
Shaking with fear and shock, she attempted to reason with him once more, "Please, I beg of you, please let me go."

"Shut up!" he screamed, slapping her violently once more, smashing her face into the rough wood of the wall.

Reanna sunk weakly to the floor, weeping. Unmoved by her tears, he gazed down at her with cold, steel gray eyes and a slow smile of evil intent spread over his face.

"Now, little lady, ya gonna git our breakfast, or do ya want more a what I just gave ya?"

Reanna looked up at him with apprehension and could no longer keep the bile from rising in her throat. "Sick, I'm going to be ... sick," she managed to choke out, and he roughly lifted her and shoved her to the table, where she grabbed the dirty bowl Cal had used for his cigarette and wretched violently into it. She had never felt this sick, degraded, and utterly alone and abused, but she had no time to dwell on the fact, for as soon as she finished, Cal forced her to take the bowl and mercilessly shoved her out the door, guiding her to empty it into the shrubbery next to the house.

Reanna stumbled, nearly falling in her misery as he pushed her back through the door, to the stove and shelves where the food was kept.

"Now, the meal," his tone was menacing.

Reanna's stomach contracted in mortal fear, and she thought she would be sick again. They had always had Carmelita and she had never learned to cook, hadn't the slightest idea of what to do.

Her tears were back, running down her face to burn the livid grazes left by this pitiless monster. She stared at him in wide-eyed fear, trembling uncontrollably, and admitted, "I ... do not ... Oh, please! I ... never ... learned to cook."

This struck Cal as humorous rather than angering him as she thought it would. He laughed heartily, saying, "Well, that's just another thing you're gonna have ta git the hang a, and quick, won't ya, little lady?"

Reanna quaked in fear, and realized that she must do as he said, or suffer more of his brutal treatment.

"Won't ya?" he repeated, more loudly this time.

"Y ... yes," she whispered fearfully, and he reached up to grab a slab of bacon off the shelf, slapping it down with a small thud next to a basket of eggs.

"Just slice this here piece a meat and fry it, then the eggs, in a pan. And make it quick, honey, all that exercise made me hungry."

Somehow, she managed to cook and serve the meal under Cal's unnerving scrutiny as he sat at the table calmly smoking while she trembled in nervous apprehension, expecting to be cuffed for some misdeed at any moment.

As the brothers gathered around the grease-stained table, Reanna hesitantly began to dole out the food while one by one, they began to eat, ravenously devouring the fare, and she was able to breathe a sigh of relief. She would not be meted out any punishment for now, at least.

Larry finished his meal and wiped his shirt sleeve across his mouth before rising slowly from his chair to grab her arm in a bruising hold, anger distorting his sharp features as he bellowed wrathfully, "How dare ya serve us this slop, bitch! It ain't fit even fer hogs!"

He raised his hand to hit her, and she ducked from the coming blow, but Cal's burst of roaring laughter halted the expected downward swing of his arm, and he turned to his brother in open mouthed amazement, unsure of the cause of his sudden mirth.

"What the hell er you laughin' at?" he demanded, and Cal answered good naturedly, "Screwin's not the only thing she's never did afore. Ain't never cooked nuthin' either."

He burst into renewed laughter, and after a tense moment, Larry let her arm go and followed suit, allowing Reanna to stagger to a chair in the corner, where she sat dejectedly holding the edges of her torn gown together as the others joined in the merriment at her expense.

All of them, save Billy, who rose and went to the stove to fill a plate for Reanna, then, brought it to her and gently began to coax her to eat, but she shook her head miserably, and tears once again welled in her large green eyes. She was much too sick to even think about taking any nourishment.

Billy stared down at Reanna's bowed head, revolted by what his brothers had done to this beautiful, kind woman who had always spoken so cordially to him, regardless of the vast differences in their circumstances. Her large green, sparkling eyes had lost their luster, her unblemished, creamy skin was now scraped and bruised, and he had become almost ill last night ... they had all heard Larry's words, that she was a virgin ... listening to her screams of agony as his brother brutally raped her. He wished to help her, but how? There was no way they would allow him to walk out with her, to return her to her family. They would likely kill him for trying.

"Come on Billy, she don't need nuthin, and ya gotta help me an Cal chop some wood."

Billy sent Reanna a look of silent commiseration before turning away to set her untouched plate on the table.

"Oh, an make sure ta clean the place up real good," Cal ordered as he turned to go.

Reanna dismally surveyed the filthy kitchen, piled with dirty pots and dishes, empty whiskey bottles, and assorted refuse, all coated with smoky layer of grease, and began to cry again. "But ..."

"Just do it!" Cal snarled, and Reanna, frightened out of her wits, jumped to do his bidding.

Darrel and Joel remained seated at the table, ostentatiously to make sure that she was working, but consuming a great amount of whiskey in the process. Their eyes followed her as she labored to scrub the dishes and the stove, Darrel, with his beefy arms and large paunch and Joel, his long mousy brown hair hanging to his shoulders in greasy strands.

As Joel watched their prisoner, his light hazel eyes began to gleam with the stirrings of his drunken desire. He lowered his whiskey bottle slowly from his mouth, running his tongue sensuously around the perimeter of the opening in anticipation of the pleasures which would be forthcoming.

Darrel, noting his brother's look, heaved himself to his feet, intending to be the next to sample Reanna's lush body.

She stopped, letting the bucket drop as he advanced on her then brought it up to dump over his head.

"Not again," Reanna pleaded desperately, all the while knowing it was useless, but unable to keep herself from fighting Darrel off until he knocked her unconscious with Joel laughing all the while.

She did not know how much time had passed before she woke, screaming. She dragged what was left of her bronze gown around her sore body and crawled to a corner of the kitchen, where she huddled in misery, waiting for the next act of cruelty to descend, and her heart called in silent appeal to her love, to Chance.

Filled with as much horror as the first, the next three days were full of suffering. Reanna was never left alone in the house, for fear she would try to end her life, and was not allowed outside for any other purpose than to use the outhouse or draw water from the well, even then she was escorted. Much of that time she spent in a state of numbed exhaustion, for she was given no respite, no peace. If she was not being forced to cook, carry water, stack firewood, other necessary household chores, Larry had her in bed.

Larry now had claimed her as his own, only his, and the others feared him enough to allow it. He reeked with the sickening odor of whiskey, tobacco, and his unwashed body, which threatened to suffocate her at every turn.

A few times she rebelled, anger surfacing to replace her fear, and fought like a wildcat, kicking, biting, doing all she could to inflict pain, to break away, always to no avail. The only thing it accomplished was to bring her more beatings and much rougher treatment. She no longer ate at all, and her sleep was filled with tortured dreams, so that even when he was not rutting over her, she would wake screaming in terror many times each night.

She was no longer the same Reanna Dublin her handsome bounty hunter had professed to love. Her hair hung in a matted dull mass, tangled and filthy, around her bruised and swollen face, and her lifeless eyes, once so sparkling and clear, were dulled with shadows of pain and defeat.

Chance... she could not even bear to think of him now, but her mind would not release her from its memories. She recollected with great clarity his warm, dark eyes, the lean planes of his handsome face, the welcome thrill of his strong embrace. Her heart would cry out in despair, her soul become too heavy a weight to uphold, and she would wish desperately for the peaceful surcease that only death could bring to her battered body and mind.

Quite unexpectedly, the perfect opportunity presented itself for Reanna to make her escape. She lay beside Larry, who had drunkenly bedded her before falling into a deep intoxicated slumber, and nothing stirred in the rest of the cabin, dark, but for the wane moonlight that streamed in through the filmy windows.

Now was her chance, perhaps the only one she would have, and she quietly left the bed, creeping stealthily to the door, and silently opened it. Holding her breath, she listened for movement behind her, and hearing nothing, she slipped outside into the cool, fresh air, unaware that a pair of menacing light hazel eyes watched her every move.

Joel swiftly grabbed his shotgun and followed her, and Billy, who had also been unable to sleep, trailed in his wake, fearing for Reanna's life.

Reanna drew a deep breath of relief. It had been so simple, too simple maybe, but she had yet to put distance between herself and her captors. She felt icy fear stab through her like a sharply honed knife. What would they do if she were caught? But still, she had to try, in spite of her fear. She began to run, desperation giving wings to her feet. She rounded the house, darting past the dilapidated well, onward to the decaying barn, where she could commandeer a mount and make good her escape. The hope for freedom burgeoned in her chest at last, she was almost there!

Suddenly, out of nowhere it seemed, the sharp crack of a rifle shattered the stillness of the night, and Reanna stopped short, shock permeating her every pore. She stood frozen, unable to move, and someone grabbed her from behind, whirling her around. She saw the remorse in Billy's eyes as his fist came up to graze her temple.

As she went down, his gentle arms caught her, and he regretfully carried her unprotected form back to the cabin. Although her senses had been dulled, she had not lost consciousness, and as Billy tenderly laid her back down upon the bed, she heard him whisper, "Reanna, I'm sorry, but I had to do it. Joel might have killed you, and I won't see that happen."

Her eyes met his, so filled with compassion for her plight, and she wondered for the thousandth time why this gentle young man stayed with his onerous siblings. He was the only one who had not harassed her, and in small ways, he tried to ease some of her pain. He showed her kindness, treated her with respect and concern. He argued numerous times with his brothers, heatedly defending her when they grew more obnoxious than was usual, even for them, and one time Larry had dared to pull a gun on him, his own brother. Reanna shuddered as she remembered that time. So full of hate that they had no room for love or pity in their hearts, they were twisted and cruel, bringing to her mind the image of the mad dog that had attacked Golden Girl in what now seemed another lifetime.

Billy had given her a shirt to wear the day she cowered in the corner, which she gratefully accepted. The others would not have bothered, having no care for her modesty.

He stayed here, she supposed, through some misguided sense of family loyalty, although he seemed to become increasingly distressed at his brothers' actions and temperaments. Even though they raised him after their father died, he was eighteen now, and beginning to realize that theirs was not the right way of life. She was grateful for his presence in this nightmare of pain.

Reanna sighed and slowly closed her eyes, emotionally and physically drained, and Joel burst into the room, shoving Billy out of the way. He ruthlessly bound her wrists tightly together with a length of rope; then tied them to the bedpost.

"Ya won't find it so easy to escape again," he promised, then yanked cruelly on her arms so that the ropes bit into her tender skin. "I swear," he continued, "you're more trouble than you're worth!"

Reanna gave no sign that she heard him. A single glistening teardrop slid from beneath her dark lashes and traced a path across her cheek before she succumbed to a deep, dreamless sleep of total exhaustion.

Snatches of conversation drifted into her as she prepared breakfast the next morning. The McPhersons lounged about the front porch, waiting impatiently to eat, with the door open, allowing the cool morning breeze to circulate through the overly warm kitchen, heated by the wood burning stove.

"... Virginia City ... the little chinaman that sells the opium ... ought to have us a high ol' time!"

A chill ran down Reanna's spine and her hands began to tremble at the thought of what they would do, what new tortures they would heap upon her, when they were all high on the drug. She had no idea that they meant it for her.

"Hey Larry, wanna have her smoke it now?" Darrel's voice, loud and eager, startled Reanna as she sat quietly in a chair after cleaning up the supper dishes, as inconspicuous as she could be, while they drank and smoked, as was their usual habit.

Larry's glance shifted to rest malevolently upon Reanna, who paled instantly under his perusal, and an evil smile spread across his face.

"Go ahead, Darrel. Make her smoke it."

The softness of his command did nothing to quell her rising fright, and she sat bolt upright in her chair, her eyes widened in disbelief, as Darrel approached and held a pipe to her mouth, lighting it as he coaxed, "Come on an' smoke this like a good girl, now. We got it just fer you."

Reanna gasped in fright and shoved the pipe from her mouth. Darrel slapped her face. "Smoke it!" he ordered.

"No!" Reanna cried, averting her face, and stubbornly refusing the proffered drug.

Larry narrowed his heartless hazel eyes in malice, slowly rose from his chair and walked over to stand in front of the rebellious prisoner. "Ya will smoke it, bitch!" he hissed, but Reanna still refused.

Larry, in no mood for playing, reached down and pulled a knife from his boot strap. Placing it threateningly to her breast, he demanded once again, "I said smoke it, bitch!"

Reanna, beginning to sob in near hysteria, refused him.

He drew the sharp edge of the knife almost gently across her skin just above the shirt's low neckline, caused by missing buttons, making a long cut in her tender flesh.

Reanna gasped in pain, unable to believe, after all this time, the extent of their cruelty, and Billy rose from his chair pale faced, ready to spring to her aid.

"I can cut ya up real bad, won't kill ya, but ya'll have scars aplenty," Cal promised.

Something in her mind snapped. She could no longer focus on reality. This was not her own blood she watched running in bright red paths down the creamy skin of her breast, staining her shirt. Nothing was real, and she was not really here. She resignedly accepted the pipe, drawing on it, at Larry's insistence, over and over until her world took on the shadowed oblivion of unreality. There was no hate, no love, no beauty nor ugliness, no words, nothing mattered. She was soaring, as high as the birds in the sky. Her spirit floated as free as the wind, bending, dipping into space. She became one with the darkened sky, catching fleeting glimpses of the passing clouds below her.

"Whore, you're my whore. From now on, ya'll always be a whore." Larry realized that he was about to strip her of the remnants of her pride, a fitting recompense to her and her family, and he smiled evilly.

Reanna woke late that night when all was quiet. The bile rose to her throat, she needed to vomit, and her body retched over and over, but there was nothing there. She hadn't eaten in four days, or was it five? She had lost count. She felt so incredibly weak, desolate; so alone. Then all she knew was blank, empty space.

The next time she woke up, bright sunlight was filtering through the window. She rose shakily to a sitting position and attempted to stand, but her legs were weak, incapable of supporting her weight, and she sank to the floor.

Billy heard her fall and hurried in to help her up, she leaned against him weakly as he walked her slowly into the kitchen and sat her in a chair. He offered her a steaming mug of broth, insisting that she eat, but Reanna pushed it aside.

"Reanna, I made it just for you. You have to eat something. Don't let them beat you, Reanna. Don't let them win. They want you to feel so low that you lose all self-respect. I think I have found a way out for you. After last night … after what they did to you … I …" Billy was so choked with emotion that he could not go on, and a trace of tears welled within his eyes.

Reanna raised the cup to her lips and drank woodenly, tasting nothing but bitter heartache.

"So, our little whore is up at last," mocked Cal, coming in from outside. He laughed vengefully as he made a playful grab at her breast, then he turned toward Billy, his smile fading.

"And where did you git to late last night, little brother? Ya didn't come back till early this mornin'," Cal noted suspiciously.

Billy shrugged nonchalantly, "It's really none of your business, but if you must know, I went for a ride."

Cal's eyes narrowed as he studied his brother, "Getting' pretty uppity ain't ya? I just may hav'ta teach ya a lesson in respect. What'sa matter, ya fallin' in love with this whore?" He threw his head back and laughed heartily at the idea.

Billy fixed Cal with a glacial stare, meeting the cold gray eyes of his brother for some moments before he turned and stomped from the cabin, slamming the door behind him.

Reanna watched this episode with detached interest, numb to everything now. She thought that she had lived with shame these last days, but her pain and humiliation had reached a new level, she ceased to care what happened to her. Maybe she was a whore.

Larry, Joel, and Darrel came in and Larry sauntered up to Reanna, reaching out a calloused hand to finger her matted, tangled hair, a lecherous smile breaking over his features.

"You proved to be the whore I knew ya ta be last night. Maybe I'll keep ya around fer a spell, since ya got ta be so good 'tween the sheets." Laughing, he strode toward the front porch, calling over his shoulder, "Make me a good dinner whore. I gotta keep my strength up fer ya."

He laughed wickedly as he left the cabin, brushing past Billy who had come back in to keep his brothers from hurting Reanna further. Billy seemed nervous about something, Cal thought as he followed Larry outside, but dismissed it as unimportant.

Reanna cared about nothing. She rose unfeeling from the chair and quietly assumed her chores in the kitchen, far beyond tears by now. As she began to peel potatoes, the sound of a horse and rider reached her ears, and she moved cautiously to the door to peer out.

Larry was moving to meet the rider and Reanna stared, almost disbelieving her eyes, as Uncle Bob, on his horse, filled her vision.

Larry stopped in front of Bob's horse, and in a decidedly threatening voice asked, "what the hell are you doin' here?"

Bob answered tensely, "I have the ten thousand dollars in ransom for Reanna's return. It's all here in this saddlebag, but I want to see her first."

Cal and Larry exchanged puzzled looks, but ten thousand dollars would make them rich men. It was a lot more money than he planned to ask for her return. But an idea was already starting to form in his devious mind. Kill the sheriff, he was alone, take Reanna and the money with them when they fled.

"Cal, git in there and git the bitch!" he ordered, licking his lips in nervous anticipation, his eyes glittering with avarice. All that money! Who would have thought that things would work out this good?

Cal entered the cabin and glanced at Reanna, who was held in a tight grip by Joel, with a hand covering her mouth to prevent her from giving her presence away. Then his cold gaze fastened on Billy, and he demanded, "You have anthin' to do with this? Sheriff's out there with ten thousand dollars fer her. That where ya went last night?"

"You wanted to ransom her, and I decided it was best ta do it afore all a ya killed her," Billy answered, "She would not have brought much then."

"We weren't gonna kill her, but he's here now, so say goodbye to yer lady love, little brother."

He grabbed Reanna from Joel's grasp and shoved her through the door. She stumbled slightly on the porch, and he pushed her forcefully from behind, sending her sprawling to her hands and knees in front of Bob's horse.

Cal quickly stepped from the porch to stand beside Reanna, and raising his booted foot, kicked her viciously in the ribs, yelling down at her, "Get up, bitch, and show yer uncle what he's buyin' back!"

Reanna cried out sharply in pain and rolled to grasp her bruised, aching side with her arms, fearful that she would be sick, so great was the hurt. She staggered to her feet, but Cal, impatient with what he considered her clumsiness, brutally grabbed her arm, and yanked her to stand before her uncle, trembling with fear and head bowed in humiliation.

Bob deliberately steeled himself not to react. The threat of worse treatment or death to Reanna kept him from it.

Chance placed a restraining hand on Raymond's arm as he instinctively started forward in his daughter's defense. They were hidden behind some scrub growth several yards from the house and could see and hear the exchange clearly.

Chance himself had all he could do not to make his presence known, had to stifle the oath that sprang to his lips. There was a consuming fury that raced through him at the sight of Reanna, his Reanna, the woman he loved, beaten, and abused. She stood now, dejected, with livid bruises covering her once beautiful face and her flowing copper tresses hanging in limp, filthy strands, the man's large shirt she wore torn and stained.

Chance felt a murderous lust rise within him, a cold, calculating, brutal rage burned in his narrowed eyes. His mind screamed in outrage at the injustice done to this beautiful girl. His lovely, gentle, proud Reanna was at the mercy of those animals for days!

Then came the move, just the excuse he was waiting for. His sharp eyes caught the subtle movement of Larry's hand toward his holstered gun as Bob threw the saddlebag containing the ransom money to the ground. He aimed as if on reflex, and a deafening explosion rent the air. Larry dropped to the ground, staring through sightless eyes, as Chance stood to his full height, and raising his arm, brought death just as swiftly to Cal. There had been no room for mistakes; Cal had stood right next to Reanna. She screamed as his blood sprayed her arm. She was in hell, and it had exploded almost in her face. She stood rooted where she was, incapable of movement, and something crashed into her, bearing her down to the ground as gunfire filled the air, echoing back from the distant mountains, filling her head with the very real horror of what was taking place before her eyes.

Billy, Joel, and Darrel burst from the cabin returning fire, and one by one they fell to the ground, their blood spilling to mingle with the dry, desolate earth upon which she lay.

All around her, death and destruction reared their heads, and it was over in a moment of time, yet it seemed an eternity. A dark devil rose from the spilled blood in a towering rage, as if Lucifer himself, bellowing a harsh edict. "Burn it! Burn it all!"

And the flames of hell shot skyward, the fire licking greedily at the dry tinder of the cabin, roaring with its mighty appetite, and then the devil was taking her into his gentle arms, repeating her name, rocking her as she lay still in shock, and Reanna slowly came to realize that this was not Lucifer at all, but her own dark angel that held her steady in his arms in a careening world gone mad.

She wanted to reach out to him, assure herself that he was, indeed here, but she could not raise her arms, the world around her was no longer clearly in focus. She slumped against Chance, succumbing to the web of peaceful black escape that wove itself around her.

Chance lifted her tenderly in his arms and carried her from the heat of the fire, holding her in his comforting embrace for what seemed to be hours, rocking her softly as he whispered to her unconscious form of his love, praying to God that it would be enough to give her the strength to survive.

The men found two wagons and hitched horses from the barn to them, then torched that building, as some of them lifted Kenny Beckett into one of the vehicles. He moaned in pain, a bullet in his back, and Bob Dublin attempted to staunch the flow of blood from his arm, where he had been wounded.

Raymond ordered one of his men to drive them to town, to the doctors, and was finally free to see to his daughter's welfare. The last he had seen, the bounty hunter had flung himself at Reanna, knocking her to the ground so that she would be out of the line of fire when the McPhersons had burst from the cabin with guns blazing. It had taken him a moment to recover from the sight, firsthand, of the deadly speed and accuracy with which the gunfighter handled himself. Bob would surely have been killed, and Reanna probably so, if not for the man's timely intervention. But his avenging rage was a terrible, destructive thing to witness, giving no quarter, taking no prisoners, no chances. He was definitely one man that should not be crossed.

Now that same man sat with Reanna cradled gently in his arms, rocking her still form, the anguish that he felt for her was plainly evident in his strained features.

Raymond walked thoughtfully to the well and drew a bucket of water. Perhaps he had been wrong about Nolton. He soaked his bandanna and almost fearfully approached Reanna, wondering just what her state of mind would be, and just how badly she was beaten. He had gotten only a quick glimpse of her bruised face before the gunfire started, but his fears turned out to be well grounded, he realized, when he knelt beside her and began, very tenderly, to bathe her swollen features, exchanging a long look of concern with Chance before Reanna's dark lashes fluttered, and she uncertainly opened her eyes.

Chance Nolton, his dark brown eyes entered her vision, and he tried to subdue the overwhelming rage he still felt at the sight of her bruised and swollen features, the pain that showed in her eyes, desiring that she know only his gentle concern. She blinked, unable to quite believe that he was not just a figment of her imagination, then his smooth, deep voice filled her ears, and she knew that he was really with her.

"Reanna, my heart, my love, I am with you now. It's over; everything will be all right now."

Reanna reached out to touch his face, and then his words registered in her mind. It's over. She recalled the blazing crossfire, the pools of bright red blood. Dead … All dead. She sat slowly up, panic creeping into her voice as she whispered raggedly, "No … Not Billy!"

She struggled to her feet and hesitantly made her way through the remnants of the death and destruction, the garish forms of the dead, to Billy's side, where he lay face down by the light of the dying flames in the gathering darkness.

Reanna knelt at his side and began to tug on his shoulders, trying to wrest him to his back, sobbing, "Billy ... oh, Billy, you cannot die, please don't die! They did not know, Billy. They could not have known."

As Chance and Raymond lifted her to her feet, she could not control the wrenching sobs that shook her body. "NO!" she screamed, "NO! We can't just leave him to ... he is not like the others ... we cannot leave him to die!"

Chance's throat constricted with emotion, he pulled her tightly against his broad, warm chest and stoked her hair in a comforting motion. "It is already done, my love. It is finished."

"He is still alive," Raymond's words pierced through Reanna's grief.

"Then get him to the doctor. Hurry, please help him!" she demanded, pulling away from Chance to face her father.

Raymond studied his daughter closely, and Chance began tentatively, "Reanna ..." He wondered if the horrors inflicted upon her in the last days had affected her mind, he feared for her sanity. Certainly no one, not even Reanna, could forgive these animals their terrible transgressions.

She turned, her pleading eyes met his, and she begged him to understand. "Chance, Billy tried to help me. He was the only one who was kind to me, the only one who did not ... hurt me," she was unable to voice aloud what had happened, as yet, to Chance.

"He is not really one of them," she continued, "and I will not leave him here to die. Please help him!"

"Very well Reanna," he agreed, more in an effort to calm her than from any gratitude felt towards Billy. He knew what she had been about to say, and his anger boiled anew.

Sean approached the small group and questioned Raymond, "Fires just about out sir. What do you want done with the bodies?"

"Leave them!" Chance snarled in contempt, and Raymond nodded curtly in agreement. "For now, at least."

"We're ready to pull out then. I sent a few men back to fetch horses," Sean informed them, and spared a surreptitious glance toward Reanna, but she leaned against the wagon as if for support and stared studiously at the ground, afraid to meet his eyes for fear of the censure she imagined would be there.

When Sean walked away Reanna broke into tears, weeping uncontrollably, and Chance hurried to gather her into his arms. She had thought that she had no more tears left, but her heart was overwhelmed with sadness. A sadness so deep she felt as if she would drown. She was suffocating, falling … when she collapsed, it was Chance who caught her and held her from sinking to the ground. Her beloved Chance Nolton.

He lifted her and laid her in the bed of the wagon, and then he and Ray laid Billy beside her. They brought Reanna home to High Ridge and Carmelita's loving care, sending the wagon on to town with a ranch hand, and instructions for Doctor Farley to come for Reanna just as soon as he could.

Chance and Raymond sat down to a hearty meal of beef, corn, gravy, bread, cheese, and fruit while Carmelita bathed and changed Reanna upstairs, then the men went into the parlor, gratefully sinking into the soft chairs as Raymond poured them each a measure of brandy.

"Join me?" Raymond queried, and Chance accepted the drink, feeling the need for several glasses of the calming liquid.

"I feel that I have wronged you Chance," the older man began, "I … I want to thank you, first of all, for all the help you've given me, for my brother's life, and for Reanna's. I will never be able to repay you the debt I owe. I should have guarded her from others, not you."

"No, you don't owe me a thing," Chance assured him, "and you were right not to trust me with your daughter. My intentions were not of the most honorable sort, and Reanna is too beautiful a woman not to desire her."

"I think it goes much further than that," Raymond announced. "I do realize now that I have been wrong about you all along. I can plainly see how much you love Reanna, even if you can't quite yet, and I see how much she loves you. Neither of you will ever be happy, you know, unless you are together. The kind of love you two share is of the rarest sort. Few people ever find that kind of love in their lifetime. It would be very foolish of anyone to throw it away if he was lucky enough to find it. Think of it Chance. Think on it hard and long. I'll let you know now; I would not stand in your way if you chose to wed her. Whatever you decide, one thing you can be sure of, you will always be welcome in my home. In fact, I would like to invite you to stay here in our home, if you would like. We have an extra room near the kitchen, you could use that. Reanna's grandmother used to stay there. There was a time, you know, when this house was full of people's laughter and happiness. I would like to see it so again one day, before my time on this earth passes. I suddenly have a compelling urge to see my grandchildren running through this house. Reanna's children and perhaps Chance Nolton's children, eh?"

Chance choked on his mouthful of brandy, and the burning liquid went down the wrong way, causing him to cough fitfully before he could find his voice. "M ... marry? Even if I am in love with her, I am not a marrying man," he insisted, "That is why I left town without her. She would not consent to be my mistress."

"Nor will she ever," Raymond sent Chance a hard look. "However," he continued, "she loves you, and I believe you will be able to help her to recover from this … incident. And who knows, you may yet change your mind about marriage."

"To the victor belong the spoils," Chance said wryly, "Is that what you're saying?"

"Of course not, my daughter is the prize," Raymond answered, unperturbed by Chance's caustic remark about marriage.

Oh, hell, it was all too confusing for him at the moment, Chance thought as he downed the rest of his drink. First the man wanted to kill him, now he was being invited into his home and given his daughter. But he did want to help Reanna if he could. Hell, he may as well take the room. He was bone weary.

"I'll stay," he told Raymond, "But I can't say for how long."

Chapter 5

A voice pierced the protective barrier of dark slumber, slowly crumbling the walls of her quiet sanctuary, and although Reanna's mind protested the intrusion, her father's worried summons was repeated until she finally woke.

Her peace fled in an instant, to be replaced with blinding pain, stabbing at her heart, filling her mind, battering her body. Strangely, she could not recall from where the many discomforts had come.

Groaning in protest, she rolled over and pulled herself to a sitting position. Her head was spinning, and she held it tightly, pressing her hands to her temples in the hopes that it would somehow help the pain.

"Reanna! Reanna?" Her father's inquiring voice seemed to come from a great distance away.

"Ah-h-h-h, I'm all right, Papa." Reanna's voice rattled in her throat, grating at her ears, and she began to sob in wrenching agony. "Oh, Papa … Papa."

It was all coming back to her now. Like a damn bursting, all the terrible memories of the past week came flooding back, threatening to sweep her from the brink of sanity, to drown all reasonable thought, but her father kept her afloat. He held her tightly, crooning softly and rocking her gently as he had when she, as a child, had turned to him with her hurts. Gradually her sobs became slow, deep sighs, and after she had quieted, her father took her chin in his hand, turning her to face him, forcing her to understand.

"Reanna, Doctor Farley is here. He wants to examine you. You have been beaten pretty badly, and we must be sure that there is no permanent damage, no internal injuries."

Reanna was emphatic in her denial. "No, Papa! He must not … I cannot … Papa, no!" she could not bear the thought of anyone gazing upon her bruised and battered body, and even more repulsive was the thought of any man touching her, examining her as the doctor would certainly do.

Suddenly conscious of the fact that she had been bathed and dressed in a clean, white, lacy gown, of her own, she gasped aloud, "Papa, who …?"

Raymond knew the reason for her discomfort and understood her automatic alarm, also her rejection of having the doctor look at her, and he patiently explained, "Reanna, it was Carmelita who bathed and dressed you. You have to allow us to help you now. You must understand that it is necessary, that there is no shame in it for you, only the love that we feel for you. Take that love and draw strength from it. Here, drink this. it will help to calm you."

He reached over to her night table and took up a glass of brandy, pressing it to Reanna's lips. She obediently swallowed the offered liquid and let the tingling warmth spread through her body, but her father's words, meant to be a comfort, lent to her, instead, an icy coldness that the brandy could not dispel.

He did not understand, no one could ever begin to comprehend the enormity of the nightmare she had endured in that dreadful week that had stretched on for an eternity, which would haunt her for the rest of her life. The very fabric of her gentle disposition and sheltered life had been shredded, torn beyond repair. All of her senses became numb. Her feelings, thoughts, and convictions … none of them mattered now. Everything was as nothing.

"Very well, send the doctor in," she relented, submitting to his careful examination with detached interest and answering his prudent questions with the cursory, hesitant manner of one who has retreated from the harsh touch of reality.

Doctor Farley frowned thoughtfully as he gazed at his patient. She had slept soundly all last night and late into the afternoon when Raymond had woken her upon his arrival. She would need lots more rest to regain her strength and help her heal, which she would do. It was her mental health that he was more concerned with at the moment.

Chance had spent most of that day in town, first visiting Bob Dublin, who was home recuperating from his bullet wound. The doctor had ordered the sheriff to take it easy for a few days, and he asked that Chance assume the duties of that office, starting tomorrow, for the next few days. Chance readily agreed.

He then visited the doctor's office to see how Kenny Beckett had fared, but the prognosis was grim. Kenny hovered near death, and there was little chance of survival. If he did somehow recover, he would be unable to walk. The bullet had gone into his spine, severing vital nerves.

Billy was there also. He had been shot in the chest, and although he remained unconscious the doctor felt sure that he would recover. Chance was not overly concerned whether any McPherson happened to live, and he said as much.

He then rode out to the Beckett's farm, to see if there was anything he could do for Molly. He had only met her a few times, but was genuinely fond of her, and she was one of Reanna's closest friends.

He found her working in the barn, hovering in a state of near exhaustion. Her long black hair hung in unkempt tangles, and her large violet eyes were shadowed with hopelessness and fear.

When Chance placed a restraining hand upon her arm, she stopped her methodic pitching of hay and gazed desolately into his eyes. "How is Reanna?" she inquired, and Chance hastened to assure her.

"She was sleeping when I left, and the doctor had not seen her yet, but I think she will recuperate, given time. I just came from visiting Kenny. Molly, is there anything that I can do to help?"

Molly flatly refused, saying, "No, Chance, thank you, but I must stay busy, or I will go crazy. It is the waiting," her voice broke, and tears sprang to her eyes, "I do not even know if my man will live or die. It is the waiting I cannot bear!"

Chance understood only too well, for he felt much the same.

"Well, if you change your mind, if there is anything, anything at all, just send word to the Dublin ranch."

Molly nodded mutely and went back to her work, leaving Chance to ride back to High Ridge in hopes that the doctor had been able to get there by now.

He was impatient to see Reanna, having had to bide his time last night while she slept, and again now while the doctor was with her. Like Molly, he could not stand these idle hours.

As he paced back and forth like a caged beast, all he could envision was the sight of Reanna being pushed from that cabin, her clothing torn and covered with blood and dirt, her matted hair hanging limply around her swollen, battered face, and her creamy skin covered with cuts and bruises. And when the bastard had kicked her, he had signed his own death warrant at that moment.

Chance relived the shootout over and over in his memory, and it brought him great pleasure to see them all dead. A slow, satisfied grin spread across his face, and he found himself hungering to spill their blood all over again. Reanna should have let Billy die, for he did not yearn to look upon any of their cruel faces again unless it was with his hands around their vulgar throats, squeezing the life from them.

Doctor Farley entered the parlor, and his serious voice brought Chance from his cold-blooded reverie. Raymond offered them all a round of drinks, and as the doctor began his grave prognosis, Chance felt his heart sink with the man's words.

"Reanna is in a state of protective shock. In other words, she has the normal use of all of her functions, but her mind has locked her emotions deep inside, where they cannot be hurt. She will give no warmth, nor will she accept any that is offered. I can't say how long this behavior will continue, a day, a week, a month or maybe longer. In this particular situation you must be careful to follow the few guidelines that I will now explain to you. She has accepted you, Ray, and Carmelita, because you have both given her a lifetime of love. My presence she merely tolerated because she knew it to be necessary and she would barely speak to me. We must be extremely careful not to upset her in any way. If anyone is to see her, it must be with her approval; if anything is to be done to, or with her, it must be with her acceptance. We will be here to offer her suggestions, encouragement, and love, but we cannot shock her any further by trying to force her to recover too quickly. It could drive her over the edge."

"In other words," Raymond began nervously, pacing the floor now as Chance had done earlier, "she needs this state of shock that she is in to recover properly?"

"Precisely. Physically Reanna should recover quickly. Right now, she is weak and bruised, but in a weeks' time she should be on her feet again. Now, gentlemen, I must get back to my other patients. Do not hesitate to send word if you have need of me, though."

When the doctor had gone, Raymond returned to Reanna's side, coaxing her to take a cup of broth that Carmelita had prepared. When she finished, he asked, "Will you see Chance Reanna? He has been waiting downstairs and is very worried about you."

"No!" Reanna's emphatic reply surprised him, and he wondered that it would be so, when she loved the man that waited downstairs, but he did not dare to push her any further.

"Very well then, Reanna, try and get some more rest."

Sighing tiredly, Raymond rose and descended the stairs with flagging steps, attempting to postpone telling Chance for as long as possible, but Chance was waiting at the bottom landing.

"She will not see anyone right now Chance."

The bounty hunter peered at Raymond closely for a moment, then, shrugging his shoulders, said, "You don't mind if I have a drink, do you?"

"No, help yourself," Raymond offered, then went to answer a knock on the door, admitting Sean into the parlor.

"Sir," he began, sending Chance a level look, "I have come to ask for your daughter's hand in marriage."

Chance scowled darkly and Raymond coughed politely, observing, "I was not aware that you were courting Reanna."

"Well, sir, I haven't been, not exactly," Sean ventured another look at Chance's decidedly unpleasant countenance, "but I have always … admired her, and surely, she will need a husband now, I mean, what happened … I'm sure that you could make her see the advantages of being wed as soon as possible."

"I see," Raymond said, "I will keep your offer in mind, Sean. It is kind of you to think of her and I thank you."

This time it was Chance who coughed after taking a particularly deep draft of his brandy. There was nothing kind in Sean's offer at all, but then Raymond undoubtedly realized that himself. Sean wanted Reanna and he wanted High Ridge even more. Marriage would guarantee him both, but he would not care enough for Reanna's feelings, would not give her the time she needed to heal.

How Chance knew these things, he could not say, but he would bet money on these intuitive judgments. The thought of Sean marrying Reanna made his blood boil.

Reanna would not see Chance in the morning either, so he was glad to go to town and assume the duties of sheriff. Something that would occupy his time and thoughts to make the waiting easier, but she would still not see him when he returned just before dark.

"She just needs more time, Chance." Raymond could think of no other words to soften his daughter's flat refusal of the man.

Chance quietly left the house and rode Lancelot to town, where he spent the night in the saloon. That was where he woke in the morning, in fact, with his head throbbing from overindulgence. Well, at least he had had the presence of mind to refuse Aggie's overly ample charms this time, and she had been most persuasive. But he simply could not take the chance of hurting Reanna more. He wondered at the fact that he hadn't cared enough to think this way before.

After his duties for the day were complete, he hesitated at the idea of returning to the ranch, not wishing to bear Reanna's rejection of his person once again, but neither could he stay away. What if she decided that she did want to see him? It was that thought that carried him back to High Ridge.

Things remained unchanged, and he thought that he would go mad, forced to play this waiting game. Hell, it was time to end it, he decided, bounding up the stairs to knock loudly on Reanna's door.

Carmelita asked, "Who is it?" and Chance stuck his head around the door, just to make certain that Reanna was decently clothed before he entered uninvited. "It's only me, 'Lita. I had to finally see her for myself."

Carmelita attempted to stop his approach, but he was heedless of anything but the need to be close to Reanna. He stood next to her bed, but she did not acknowledge his presence. She stared straight ahead, her emerald eyes blank, and unseeing.

"Reanna … Reanna, look at me," Chance demanded, but she continued to look from vacant eyes, as if lost in some other world that did not really exist.

"Reanna, for God's sake, look at me. I'm here for you. I care for you; I want to help you." Chance pleaded softly, feeling an empty, unfamiliar ache in his heart.

He cupped her chin, turning her face toward him, and saw that there were tears streaming from her eyes, but they remained dull and frighteningly empty. He tried once more, "Reanna."

He elicited no response, so he turned and walked calmly from the room, closing the door softly on his way out. He went to his room and threw himself on the bed, staring vacantly up at the ceiling, haunted by the empty waste he had seen in Reanna's eyes.

Unable to continue there, thinking, a moment longer, he got up and went outside to walk, quickly changing his pace to a steady, distance covering lope, which he kept up for miles before returning to his bed, exhausted, in the early morning hours and mercifully found sleep, if only for a few short hours.

Joseph, the young man whom Chance had frightened away at Bob and Martha's party, arrived at mid-morning, hat in hand, with another proposal of marriage. He was more nervous than he would have been however, with Chance standing at Raymond's side, glowering angrily.

"S – Sir – Mr. Dublin, I have come to tell you that I would be honored to take Reanna as my wife, should she desire it. I love her, I have for years, and I promise you that I would treat her well, to give her anything she wants."

"I'm sure that you would, Joseph, and I will tell her of your proposal as soon as she is feeling better." Raymond spoke politely, and Joseph nodded shortly, anxious to be gone from Chance's hard glare, and took his leave stammering, "Yes sir, thank you sir … good day, sir."

Raymond, duly noting the frown Chance had directed toward Joseph's retreating back, smiled benignly, commenting, "Nice boy, that Joseph."

It could not hurt for Chance to know that there were others waiting to marry his daughter if he would not.

Chance thought privately that Joseph would never be man enough for the woman he was sure that Reanna would someday become and would never be able to run this ranch. Didn't Raymond see that?

"I have to get to town, I'm late," was his only comment to the man, though, as he crammed his brown leather Stetson onto his head with more force than was necessary.

Later that night he crept silently into Reanna's room just to assure himself that she was really here and safe, gazing upon her beauty for a full half hour. Her face looked improved, the swelling had gone down, and the bruises had faded slightly. He reached out to gently touch her lips, having no fear of waking her, for the doctor had left laudanum to help her sleep. As he slowly withdrew his hand she stirred, and Chance heard her murmur a name. Not his, but the same one he had heard her use one other time as she slept. Daniel. He was sure that he had met no one in town by that name, and it gave him something to puzzle over for the next few days, causing him more than a little worry. Who the hell was this Daniel?

On the seventh day of Reanna's return, Chance was dumbfounded as he entered the kitchen to meet her calmly drinking a cup of coffee.

"Reanna?"

"Good morning, Chance." She spoke in a level voice, devoid of emotion. "Papa said that you have been worried sick about me, but I'm fine now, really."

Just like that, she was fine? He noted the lack of her smile, the icy self-control with which she held herself, and the unfeeling tone of her words. But she was fine?

He stood there gaping at her, unsure of how he should respond to this new Reanna, until she rose and swept gracefully out the door. He was in motion, out the door and after her, and it seemed that the tight reins of tension he had held in check for the past days snapped when he caught hold of her. Then all the agonizing, pent up emotions of the past two weeks spilled forth uncontrollably, demanding that he get through to her somehow.

He shook her in anger, unable to stop himself, throwing the words in her face, "Damn you, Reanna! No more! You've got to let me in, to help you. I love you and I know your pain as my own. You've got to understand that you need my love now, as I need yours. I am here for you, love."

He stopped shaking her, realizing that he was still not getting through, and she stared at him coldly, speaking in that same icy, controlled voice, "No, Chance, it is you who must understand. Everything that was alive in me has died. They took it, all of it, and I will never get it back. My heart is gone, and my soul has been soiled beyond any possible cleansing."

Chance changed his tactics, thinking that at last he had found an inlet. His voice, when he spoke, was extremely tender, softly insistent, pressing into her numbed senses despite the quiet timbre of his tone.

"You are wrong, Reanna, very wrong. They could not take from you that which you did not have to lose. When they kidnapped you, you had no heart. You had already given it away, freely to me, that night when I left you. Remember your words to me, Reanna. You said that I was taking your heart with me and that you hoped I would bring it back someday. Remember it, Reanna. They could not take your heart, or hurt it, because I carried it with me. Like a burning cross, I carried it and protected it, though it scorched me with the burning intensity of its love. I'm here now, and I'm giving it back to you. You must take it Reanna, for I cannot bear to carry it alone any longer. You must take it so that we may share the love it holds."

Reanna began to sob, drowning in the love that she felt Chance pouring over her, and she held him tightly, her island in a sea of stormy emotions.

Chance sat down, pulling her with him onto his lap, where he held her, rocking, crooning soft words of endearment, for nearly an hour, until she finally lifted her head and he saw that her eyes truly held some feeling once again.

She began to talk to him, and as she sobbed out her story, he almost wished he didn't have to hear. Reanna attempted, as well as she could, to describe the hell she had gone through, why she felt such a terrible sense of loss and shame, and that her life would never be the same. She put special emphasis on Billy's kindness towards her, for without him she felt she would never have survived.

When she began to tell Chance about the last night, with the opium, she could barely form the words, so great was her shame, but she had to force him to understand why she must reject his love, why she did not deserve it.

Chance realized, perhaps better than Reanna herself, why she had tried to lock herself away from all that she had held dear. Not only had she been taken against her will, which would have been debasing and painful enough, but she had been stripped of every shred of dignity that she possessed. The pain of that would stay with her for far longer than any injustice done to her body. He only hoped that she would allow him to help her heal. It would take a long time, and she might yet reject the love that he offered, but he had finally made a decision. If she pulled through this, when she was fully recovered, he would make her his wife. He no longer wished to live alone, without Reanna, and he certainly did not wish to see her wed to Joseph or Sean.

Reanna's thoughts were running in quite the opposite direction, and Chance's fears were realized when she voiced those considerations aloud.

"Chance, I thank you for allowing me to unburden myself, for making me see that I cannot completely close myself off from life, but I can never share my love with you now. I feel so dirty, incapable of accepting your love. I may even be pregnant, and one thing I know for sure, I would be repulsed by any man's touch, even yours."

"You will get over that in time, Reanna," Chance murmured.

"Will I?" she whispered. "Will I get over it if I carry their child, or some filthy disease? No, Chance, I want you to leave. Go back to the life you love."

Chance grasped her shoulders, and his gaze burned, holding hers, that she might know the truth of his words. "It is you I love, Reanna. That life no longer holds any interest for me. I want only you, and I will not leave, not ever again. No matter what happens, no matter how you deny me, I'm staying. You will heal, my love, and I will be here to help you every step of the way."

In the next two weeks, Reanna gradually resumed her active lifestyle, and once again bloomed in good health as her body healed and she began to eat properly. She was just as beautiful, perhaps more so, as before.

One night as she was upstairs changing for dinner, Chance answered a knock on the door to find Billy, hat in hand, standing uneasily on the front porch.

"Let's see," Chance growled sarcastically, "you wish to marry her too, I suppose."

"Why yes," Bill answered in surprise, "I would like to speak to her father, if you don't mind."

Raymond, who had come to stand next to Chance, eyed Billy coldly for a long moment before making a decision.

"It took great courage for you to come here, young man. Either that or you don't have a lick of sense in your head. We may speak in my study. You too, Chance," he added, leading the way.

As soon as Raymond closed his study door, Chance stated menacingly, "It seems that there is an over-abundance of love-sick swains ready to marry Reanna, but I will save you the trouble of proposing, McPherson. If anyone is to marry her, it will be me."

Raymond raised an inquiring brow. When had Nolton reversed his views on matrimony? Well, of course the old man knew it be only a matter of time. But it was to the look of relief that passed over Billy's face that he addressed himself.

"You did not want to marry her? Then why ask?"

"Sir, I felt somewhat responsible for what my brothers did to her, although I did not take part in any of it. And I would not mind marrying her, if it would help her, for she is very kind and beautiful. I do know, though, that she could never love me, and she deserves to be happy."

"Mmmm, very well put, young man. Perhaps you would not mind staying for dinner? I'm sure Reanna would be most pleased to see you."

Chance stewed at the thought of sitting down to dinner with a McPherson, but Reanna was glad to see Billy, and delighted that he had recuperated from his wound so well.

Reanna had tried to tell him of Billy's kindness to her during her abduction, and as they conversed, Chance formed a grudging respect and even a liking for the boy, himself. Billy had already taken a job tending bar part time in the Horseshoe, and it had been Billy, they learned, who had delivered the ransom note that night, opposing his brothers to do so. If not for him, Reanna might still be subject to their less than tender mercies.

Although Reanna regained her strength, there was something very important missing. Her former sparkle, her zest for everyday life was gone. She showed no real pleasure in anything, never really smiling much. Chance found that flowers, candy, or any of the little gifts that he purchased failed to renew that missing spark, even for a moment. But there had to be something …

One day, on the way back from a visit to Bob Dublin's, he was sure that he had found the answer. He remembered Reanna expressing interest in the Gordon Setters owned by a couple in town.

He decided to pay the Lamar's a visit and discovered that their dogs, a rare and beautiful breed with rich mahogany markings against a silky black coat, were becoming well known for their superior hunting abilities and ease in training. A good-sized dog with a sturdy build, they would make excellent companions for Reanna.

He wired a telegram to his lawyer in California, for the Lamar's had purchased their dogs from breeders in Sacramento, to send two pups, a male and a female that could be bred, to him in Carson City, and he was there to collect them when they arrived.

Presenting them to Reanna, he wore such a foolishly self-satisfied grin on his face that she could not help but hug him tightly and kiss his cheek in her enthusiasm, and his grin changed to laughter at her reaction. It was the first spontaneous action she had shown since her capture, and the first time she had voluntarily touched him.

The pups jumped at her, exuberantly licking her face, and Reanna's pleased giggle was music to his ears; her smile was genuine and wide.

It was one more steppingstone behind them on the way to recovery for his beloved, the one he was sure would someday be his wife.

Chapter 6

For the next two months Reanna spent her days working furiously in the gardens and barn, with many hours dedicated to the training of the pups. She was determined to push herself past the limits of her endurance in an effort to avoid the vivid nightmares that crept in upon her sleep. Terrible dreams where she was forced to relive the searing agony of pain, the wretched emptiness of her soul, the days and nights with the brutal animals who had taken such perverse pleasure in shredding her dignity and self-respect to the tattered remnants she was left with now.

She would wake screaming, shuddering in revulsion, and her father would suddenly be there, pulling her into his arms as if she were a small child again, the pain in his heart reaching out to hers, but there were no words of comfort that could chase away her fears; she would merely sob brokenly against Raymond's solid chest.

Chance noted in growing alarm the gradual changes in Reanna's demeanor, her pale, drawn features, loss of weight, her darkly circled, haunted eyes, for even during daylight hours the demons that drove her gave no respite, but lingered, constantly seeking to take possession of her every thought.

It was Reanna's father who finally suggested that Chance take her to Lake Tahoe for a day, as she had always loved the wild beauty of that particular place, and it held nothing but fond memories of happier times and carefree days.

There was nothing Chance wanted more than to recover the emotional intimacy that he and Reanna had shared before her kidnapping, but she insisted upon keeping their relationship light and easy, as if they were nothing more than friends, making small talk, sharing laughter, but allowing him no glimpse of her innermost thoughts and feelings.

There was a time when Chance would have welcomed this distance in a woman, but no more, not in this woman. He simply had to find a way to melt the icy barrier she had erected to keep the world from touching her again. She had to find the softness and warmth of loving once again, to regain her faith in the human race. He almost laughed aloud at this last thought. He, Chance Nolton hardened bounty hunter, seasoned killer, seeking to restore to a wounded girl the tender heart she once possessed, and believing in the truth of this desire most strongly.

Early the next morning Carmelita packed a basket full of a few of Reanna's favorite foods, tender portions of pink ham, thick slices of freshly baked bread with a crock of pale-yellow butter to spread on them, fresh apples and pears from the ranch orchard, and a bottle of light, fruity white wine.

As Chance loaded the horses with the items that they would need for a day at the lake, Raymond approached and added Reanna's guitar, strapping it over the pommel of her saddle as he said thoughtfully, "She has not touched this in a long time. Perhaps today if things go well ... I think it would help her."

Chance met his gaze squarely and nodded once in perfect understanding. It could be a very good thing for Reanna to put her inner feelings into her music, so that she could face and overcome her doubts and fears. The music could put them to rest as none of them had been able to. He could only hope.

Leading the horses, Chance went in search of Reanna. He found her as he thought he would, patiently working with the pups, which she called Modock and Tasha, teaching them to lay down on command. They were growing healthy and strong under her loving care, which came as no surprise to Chance, as Reanna spent most of her time with them. It was becoming an obsession with her which left Chance feeling quite left out.

Today he was determined to put another steppingstone behind them. "Good morning, Milady."

Chance's deep voice drew their immediate attention, and the pups rushed forward to greet him in a burst of enthusiasm. Reanna's gaze grew quizzical, taking in the unexpected sight of the two burdened horses he led.

"Good morning, Chance. This is certainly a surprise. I thought that you were riding round-up with my father."

There it was, Chance thought, and he winced inwardly. That polite distance again, which he craved to put aside, and vowed that it certainly would come about if only she would agree to accompany him for the day.

With a definite twinkle in his dark eyes, Chance bowed low, sweeping his arm toward the waiting horses in a grand gesture.

"No Milady, not today, for I gallantly volunteered to take you away, along with these ferocious little beasts," his eyes indicating the pups, "for a day of pleasure in an idyllic paradise."

He raised a dark brow, glancing down at the pups that were having a playful tug of war with the bottom of his trouser legs, each of them planting their front feet and shaking the hem furiously clenched in their sharp little teeth.

Reanna was intrigued and could not disguise her mirth in his playful display, or the pup's antics. She crossed her arms and tapped her booted foot, smiling as she demanded, "Chance Nolton, what have you got up your sleeve this time?"

"That Milady, is a secret, and one that is much better off up my sleeve," he glanced down at the scuffling balls of fur, continuing dryly, "than up my leg." He bent and disengaged the growling pups, offering Reanna his arm.

"Come on, you all need a break. What do you say? Step upon your fast steed and we will ride off into the blue yonder."

Reanna pursed her lips, about to protest, but Chance would not hear of it.

"Reanna, how can you possibly refuse this reformed rogue, who has totally given up his heart to you? Besides, Carmelita has gone to great lengths to prepare us the most tempting of delicacies. I will not take no for an answer."

Reanna hesitated another moment but found that she could not resist the appeal of his engaging grin.

"Very well Mister Nolton, but pray tell, to what destination will these fine steeds carry us?" Swinging up onto her horse she noted her guitar, and a sharp feeling of regret pierced her heart, for she did not think that she could ever take up the instrument again.

"Follow me, sweet lady, and you shall be apprised of our destination in good time," Chance announced happily, as he swung to seat his own mount.

Reanna called the pups, and they followed the slow pace Chance set, darting off on short side trips often to investigate an item of interest, and then hurrying to rejoin Reanna when she summoned them to come.

Halfway there, Reanna correctly divined their destination to be Lake Tahoe, for she had often ridden this trail during the past years. She and her father had shared many good times here, many times accompanied by her aunt, uncle, and cousins. They would picnic, play games on the banks and meadows, and swim in the clear waters of the lake.

The ride there took a little over three hours, but those hours were filled with bright warm sunlight, the sweet sound of birdsong, and periods of dappled sunlight in iridescent pools on the tips of pine needles as they rode with muffled hoof beats through pungent glades of the towering evergreens.

Something stirred deep within her as they neared the water, for here Reanna had experienced nothing but good times, had felt nothing but the abundant love of her family as they had frolicked in the warm, peaceful bosom of nature. She had always come away with a feeling of renewal and contentment, fulfilled in a way that she could not explain, even to herself.

She sighed longingly, wishing that she could somehow recapture those feelings, but she had become resigned to the fact that whatever it was that kept all of her old emotions locked deep inside of her was here to stay. She would never be allowed the luxury of loving Chance again, as she had in the past. Although she had tried, she inevitably failed herself and him.

Chance was almost awed by the beauty of this spot as he dismounted and turned to help Reanna down, but as he held her in his arms and she looked down at him with her hair billowing about them in a silken, fragrant cloud, her beauty paled all else and he felt the hard stirrings of his urgent passion, which he had kept under such rigid control for so long now. Whenever he made advances toward her, she invariably recoiled, but his heated need for her, and only her, burned ever more strongly. Yet all he could do was to hold his desire under firm control for as long as it would take her to heal. He did not dare to do anything that would push Reanna even further away.

Reanna pulled gently but firmly away from Chance as he set her on the ground, trying to ignore the look of pain that crept into his eyes as she did so. They walked in unspoken agreement to the water's edge, and there stood, silently gazing at all the splendors of nature that suddenly engulfed them.

Birdsong filled the air with a myriad of various melodies. The sun reflected off the bright silver scales of a large fish as it leapt in a graceful arc from the water, making a soft splashing sound as it returned to its own environment, sending out ripples from the point of return in ever widening, sparkling circles across the surface of the lake.

A flock of Canada geese flew overhead in the V formation that was their eternal habit and circled a few times, making loud honking cries that lingered, rippling upon the currents of air after they were gone. Having decided not to alight upon the mirrored surface of the lake, they left its reflective image of steep mountains and dense forests unmarred.

Blue winged teal ducks floated about on the crystal water, sending small ripples over the smooth expanse, and strange waves of undefined longing through Reanna's soul. When she watched them bobbing up and down in the water, skidding across its buoyant lap with rapid speed, she could not suppress the bust of laughter that issued forth in gay abandon. Then, noting a doe and her yearling fawn on the opposite bank nervously lowering their graceful heads to drink, she became more animated than Chance had seen her since the day he had presented her with the pups. It was then that he realized this day would indeed prove to be a healing one for her.

"Come, walk with me awhile, my love," Chance urged softly, and they strolled slowly through the woods, their senses filled with the forest; the sight and smell of the earth, moss, leaves, and trees; the majestic snowcapped peaks of the mountains above them, causing them to feel unimportant in this land of magnificent beauty. Reanna drank it in, as a newborn babe absorbs a mother's love, and was able to experience, at last, the first stirring of her tormented soul reaching out to be healed.

Returning to the clearing where they had begun, Chance noticed a few late blooming black-eyed susan growing at the edge of the woods, their yellow heads rearing up toward the warmth of the late morning sunlight. He bent to collect several of the blossoms, presenting them to Reanna with his usual charming aplomb.

"A simple gesture of love, Milady, from the heart of a rogue who has fallen hopelessly in love with you." Although his words echoed his earlier playful banter, his voice had taken on a quiet, serious tone, and he stood so close that Reanna could feel the warmth he exuded.

"Oh Chance," she murmured, as stinging tears sprang to her large, green eyes, which she immediately blinked away. Touching the golden softness of the flower's petals, she bent her head to inhale their warm, fresh scent.

Nature's bounty, her varied beauty, overwhelmed Reanna. The delicate blooms, the stately trees serving as silent sentinels of the craggy mountain lofts above, the crystal air and bright sunshine, the brilliant blue sky with the steady earth and clear water below, all spoke to her of healing qualities of life, endlessly renewed. But the greatest beauty of all was in this man standing before her, in all his magnificence, offering her his undying love in spite of everything she had told him that happened in that week of hell, and what she had done.

When Chance leaned, ever so slowly, to place a gentle, delicate kiss upon her softly parted lips, she did not turn away, and she realized then that she never would again.

Chance was joyous at her shy acceptance of his kiss. She had not responded, but neither had she pulled away, nor retreated into her hidden, distant world as she had so often of late, one that he could not reach.

"I don't know about you, Reanna, but I am famished. Let's have that picnic lunch now." Chance suggested, turning from Reanna's wide-eyed gaze with difficulty to retrieve the blanket and food from the packs on the horses. Spreading the former smoothly over the luxurious grass, he neatly arranged the various assortment of food upon it and then, taking Reanna's hand, gently led her to sit amidst the bounty.

She whistled for the pups, and they scampered from their fruitless explorations, bursting from the woods to land noisily in her lap, licking her face with their rough tongues and leaping about so excitedly that Reanna fell back upon the ground, giggling like a child.

"If I did not know better, I would fear that I have fallen in love with a child, the way you carry on with those pups," Chance teased, causing Reanna to dissolve in helpless laughter as he joined in the fun, romping playfully with the pups.

After they had eaten their fill and sipped a few cups of the wine, Chance decided that he could no longer resist the beckoning call of the clear water. He pulled off his shirt and boots to wade hastily in and dive beneath the surface, splashing about while Reanna ventured in, keeping close to the water's edge so that the cool liquid lapped gently about her feet.

"Come in and cool off," Chance called to her, but she shook her head, smiling gently as she refused his offer.

Determined to lure her into the water, Chance thoughtfully lay back to float in the watery expanse, then a broad smile slowly stole across his face as it occurred to him just how this might best be accomplished, a ruse he was sure would work.

Disappearing suddenly beneath the surface, he came up coughing and sputtering, then lurching forward in the water several times before he shouted frantically, "Aagh! What the hell? … Reanna, quickly! My leg seems to be caught on something under the surface. Bring my knife and come cut me free!"

Reanna reacted automatically, rushing to doff her gown without further thought and grab the knife they had used for lunch, before she dove into the water, swimming unhesitatingly to his rescue. Her heart was beating in furious panic, but when she reached him, his coughing and choking had somehow turned into howls of laughter. Had he gone mad? No, it was all just a trick! And the beast was still laughing!

"I knew you would fall for that, you really do care," he chortled gleefully, his laughter increasing as he noted the expression of shocked disbelief and anger that had settled upon her comely features.

"Oh! You, you …!" Reanna began furiously, at a loss for words wicked enough with which to berate him.

Thoroughly piqued, she began to splash, sending large sprays of water into his face, and his cough now was not a trick as he sought to catch his breath, his laughter abruptly dying.

Reanna railed at him loudly, "You once told me you were a devil, and I didn't believe you, but now I know it to be the truth!"

She splashed him again with all the force she could muster, but slowly began to see the humor in the situation as her anger dissolved, and she found herself smiling, and then giggling, in spite of her best efforts not to.

Suddenly Chance was there before her and holding her arms at her sides in an iron grip, his dark brown eyes penetrated her gaze to the very depths of her soul as he lowered his head to kiss her with all the fierce passion he could no longer hold in check.

At first Reanna could not respond, as all of the horrible memories of the McPhersons clouded her head, rushing in to shock her with their vengeful force.

Chance, pulling back to look into her eyes, could see the pain he caused, but was not yet ready to give up his quest. He raised his hand to stroke her hair gently, whispering sweet words of love as he pressed soft, light kisses over her eyelids, cheeks, nose, and mouth.

"Rea, my love, my heart," he pleaded, "let me back in. Take my love into your soul and be filled with it. Be filled to overflowing so that you may give some of your own love back to me. Love me, Reanna, my darling, as I love you."

His soft words slowly penetrated through her fear, shattering icy barriers as if they were glass and allowing the feelings that had been locked somewhere within her for so long to fill her with their warmth. Rising from the depths of her soul so that she was finally able to share them with Chance once more, the look of wonder and love that filled her large green eyes was enough to make him shudder in joyous elation.

Greatly encouraged, he pressed on, showering Reanna with a rain of delicate kisses while he touched her so tenderly that she shivered with the first soft stirrings of desire, then, suddenly, responding with her own fierce passion. Desperately she whispered his name, caressing his strong body as she forgot all about the cruel McPhersons, mindless of everything but the fire that had been ignited between the two of them.

Chance dragged her closer into his embrace, his hands beginning to roam over her sodden undergarments, the curve of her hip, the length of her thigh, and she made no protest as she pressed eagerly against his broad chest, her own hands running roughly through his thatch of raven hair. He ran his fingers gently up the soft flesh of her inner thigh, and his roving hand encountered something rough and hard, a scar of some sort, but he passed it by, not giving it another thought.

Reanna, in her fevered state, had noticed his slight hesitation at the scar, and Larry McPherson's face appeared before her again, twisted with cruelty. She was once more filled with the pain and suffering she had been forced to endure at his hands, and those of his brothers.

She fought and clawed against the images that invaded her thoughts, screaming her fear and heartbreak aloud, and Chance realized immediately what had happened. He held Reanna close and whispered soft words of comfort, letting them wash over her, a balm to her suffering thoughts. As his words soothed her, she collapsed in tears against him, and as she clung tightly, she asked him to help her, to forgive, and to hold her. Chance, despite his great frustration at not being able to proceed any further with his advances, dared not press on.

Later, as they sat together on the blanket in the warm sun, they spotted a large, beautiful golden eagle circling above them. His shrill cries filled the air and Reanna watched this king of birds with keen interest, for it brought to her mind a bittersweet memory. That of Mansunama, the Indian friend of her youth, and the song he had taught her of the soaring golden eagle. She had played it for him on her guitar often, and she suddenly realized how very much she missed her friend. They had not seen each other in over three years now.

He told her goodbye, mindful of the fact that there could never be any future together for them. He loved Reanna deeply, but could not have her, and he could not bear the pain of this knowledge. Reanna held him dear to her heart, but did not return his love in kind, and he had to assume responsibilities he was born to, as shaman to his people.

The song, she recalled, told the story of a great eagle who had broken his wings and sent out his eerie, sad cries on the great wind, which carried his plaintive calls to the heavens. The heavens opened and swallowed the eagle, and he was able to soar high and free for all eternity.

Reanna now felt a strange kinship with that maimed eagle, and lost in her thoughts, she unconsciously took up her guitar and as she began to run her fingers over the strings, the melody came back to her with strong clarity. She sang the words with cutting emotion, her inner feelings in complete accordance with the touching phrases, and Chance began to wonder if, indeed, she had flown with the eagle, soaring aloft to touch at heaven's door.

When she finished, she raised her eyes to find that the eagle had vanished, but in his place glimmered the barest hint of pastel colors, as if a rainbow was beginning to form, and it was then that Reanna knew her own broken wings would heal, and that she would someday soar above the clouds herself. The knowledge brought her the light buoyancy which only true inner hope can impart.

She stood and walked to Chance, sitting in his lap, and his dark, inquiring gaze tugged at her heart; she kissed his warm lips in that light, delicate way that he remembered with such fondness.

They talked through the waning golden sunlight of the peaceful afternoon, as Reanna attempted to explain her earlier behavior.

Chance, well aware of her reasons before she voiced them, assured her that none of it mattered. If she would be secure in his love for her, together they could surmount any obstacles put before them.

With that settled, Chance held her lovingly within his protective embrace until it was time to start back to the ranch. Reluctantly, they began to pick up the remnants of their feast and called to the wandering pups.

Before mounting their horses however, Reanna stayed Chance, gently laying her hand upon his arm. "Chance, I just … I want to thank you for giving me this beautiful day."

Chance felt his joy surge at her words, and as his brown eyes held her green gaze, the love that showed plainly within their dark depths pulled at her heart, so intense was his obvious longing.

"Reanna," he breathed softly, "I would have every one of your days filled with all the wonders and joys of life, if you would but allow me."

Suddenly shy of him, she broke eye contact as she blushed, and then turned to mount her horse, and they left the quiet sanctuary of the lake to ride home.

Raymond, anxiously awaiting their return, noted the changes in his daughter immediately. She glowed with happiness, and whenever Chance directed his rakish, intimate smile her way, she answered with her own, and that certainly did not escape her father's close observation. The next few days were filled with joy for Chance and Reanna as they began their courtship anew, delighting in their rediscovery of one another, and in the renewed love that they had found. They spent every spare minute together, talking, laughing, and playing, which did not escape the notice of all her other would-be suitors, and they gradually gave up any hope of marrying Reanna, for it was obvious that the bounty hunter had once more claimed her affections.

Once again, Chance was taking advantage of every opportunity to seduce Reanna, although with a new, more sensitive respect for her limits, which were soon made apparent to him. Although she more than welcomed his advances, she could tolerate no exploration of the most private part of the lower realm of her body, apologizing as she invariably stopped him.

"I – I am sorry, Chance, but I am not ready for that. I just … I cannot help it. Please forgive me."

She burst into tears, ashamed that she was unable to share with Chance the love she knew he desired, and that she wanted so greatly to give, but he, with a seemingly never-ending flow of love, would wrap her in his warmth and ply her with understanding until she was smiling once more. He took comfort in the fact that she had come a long way on the road to recovery, and would someday heal her wings and fly, like the golden eagle.

The fourth day following their return from the lake, Reanna came down to breakfast dressed in her riding clothes, having decided that she had been sadly remiss in visiting her friends Kenny and Molly Beckett. She knew Kenny had been instrumental in her rescue, but she had been so wrapped up in her own problems these past weeks that she had failed to find time to ride out to their farm to personally thank him. She had been hoping to run into them on one of her trips to town, but for some reason she never had.

Raymond and Chance both wondered where Reanna was bound on her own so early in the morning, for she had been afraid to venture beyond the relative safety of the ranch without an escort, and her attire did not suggest a morning of strenuous chores.

Raymond took the initiative and casually questioned his daughter. "Reanna, are you planning on going somewhere today? You should have let us know."

"Why yes, Papa, I am, but I am going on my own. It is about time that I stopped taking you men away from your work to squire me around. I feel that I am quite ready to get out on my own, and past time that I paid a visit to Kenny and Molly. I have much to thank Kenny for."

Both men swallowed convulsively, and then exchanged mutual looks of dread. In their concern for Reanna's state of mind, they had neglected to tell her anything at all of Kenny's condition, having decided between themselves that she would not be able to handle the news of her friend's permanent paralysis at first, then … well, it had been too easy to put off telling her.

Heedless of the looks exchanged, Reanna went on. "I haven't had the opportunity to thank Kenny, as I have everyone else, for helping in my rescue. I thought that I would bring them one of the apple pies that Carmelita baked yesterday. I wonder how those new colts of his are doing. They must be close to full grown by now."

She flashed them both a wide, disarming smile, and neither of the men could seem to find his voice. Why hadn't they told her? She had been bound to find out. Chance had been riding out to their farm secretly, to offer assistance whenever he could, and Billy now made his home with the Becketts. In exchange for working on the farm, he rode back to town on weekends to work at the Horseshoe, but they hadn't told her anything.

Raymond cleared his throat, finally able to find his voice as Reanna stared curiously at their ashen faces, wondering at their continued silence. "Reanna, I … I really don't think that you should go to the Beckett's today. It looks like rain; I don't' want you caught in a sudden downpour. You know what the weather is capable of this time of year."

"Oh, Papa, you worry as if I were still a child, you always have. I have put this off for too long. What must Molly think? Actually, now that I think about it, isn't it strange that she has not come to call on me?"

Chance added his own appeal with a sense of impending doom. "Reanna, what your father says is true. Why don't you wait another day? One more day will make no difference, will it?"

At last, their strange behavior caught Reanna's full attention. They had said nothing to arouse her suspicions, but something in the air was not to her liking.

"Why don't you want me to go to Beckett's? I will certainly not melt in a little rain, and my mare is sure footed. I have never had a problem riding in the rain before, and you both know that I have done so many times."

"Reanna, we need to talk first. We can spend the day together, and I will explain things to you." Chance's nerves were so taut that for once his steel self-control was threatening to slip under an overpowering sense of guilt.

Reanna, immediately frightened for her friends' welfare, queried softly, "Explain what Chance? What are you two hiding? Has something happened to Molly?"

The raw edge of panic had crept into Reanna's last words, and Chance felt his throat constrict, his mouth go dry. Dear God, why hadn't they told her? To have to find out now, just when she was making such good progress … what would this do to her?

Chance did not answer her, but turned and strode into the parlor, with Raymond close behind, at a loss, for once, as to what to do.

Reanna followed the men, and Chance splashed a liberal amount of whiskey into a glass, offering it to her in silence. It was then that she was certain something terrible had befallen her friends. Becoming frantic, she moved to stand in front of Chance, pushing the proffered glass away from her.

"What is it? Tell me! What has happened?" she cried, "You both know something, and have not seen fit to tell me. I want to know, now!"

"Reanna, calm down. Please, sit," Chance urged, leading her to the settee, but she stood mutely, waiting for him to continue.

"You must try to understand that what we have kept from you was for our own good. We meant only to protect you … and, well … we were concerned only with your immediate recovery." Chance drew a deep breath, and continued, "That day at the McPhersons … when the shooting started … Kenny was wounded badly Reanna. A bullet went into his spine. It severed his nerves and left Kenny crippled. He will never use his legs again."

Reanna sat now, her face white with shock.

"No," she whispered, tears raining freely down her face as many damning emotions rose within her, fear, dread, and self-blame. But most of all, anger toward those who had kept this terrible news from her. When she could have been helping her friends, she had been … training pups and enjoying carefree days with Chance. What must Kenny and Molly think of her?

"You bastards!" she hissed "The lot of you!" thinking of all her friends in town who had kept silent as well. She bolted from the room, but Chance caught her just as she reached the back door.

"Reanna, please wait!" His protest was harsh with a deep-seated fear.

Sobbing hysterically, Reanna was barely able to choke out her words, "Get your hands off me, you son of a bitch!" she shoved him away from her, her eyes blazing with fury, the deep green of the sea within crashing with the force of wind whipped whitecaps.

Chance had never heard her use such harsh language, or seen her so angry, but he had also forgotten just how loyal a friend she was, and he could certainly understand her feelings of resentment at being kept from offering her help to those who may have needed it. The people she had trusted most had lied to her, all of them.

He attempted to reason with her, "Reanna, don't go there now. Not like this."

Reanna's anger was full blown, and through bitter tears she screamed at Chance. "How dare you, any of you! What could you have been thinking? Kenny and Molly have been my friends for over ten years! I will never forgive you Chance Nolton, you most of all. I trusted you, and you have betrayed that trust. Now get your hands off me. I cannot bear to remain in this house with either of you another minute!"

Chance had grasped her firmly by the shoulders during her outburst, and he continued to hold her tightly as their eyes locked, waging a battle of their own; Reanna's full of fiery fury and his filled with remorse, begging her to understand. He relented when she would not back down, and released her, though it was with misgivings.

Reanna fled to the barn and saddled the mare she had been riding of late, her vision blurred by tears, and careened recklessly from sight, headed toward Beckett's farm.

She had accomplished but half her journey when the skies opened and spewed forth a fury of their own, soaking Reanna thoroughly, but she was oblivious to anything but the necessity of seeing her friends as quickly as possible. She urged the little mare onward, pushing her to greater speed, heedless of the mud splattered by the mare's flying hooves to cover her clothes and hair, or the danger of the pace she set.

When Molly answered the insistent pounding on her door, Reanna was barely recognizable. Her hair and clothing were dripping wet, caked with mud, her eyes red and swollen from constant weeping, and her breath came in loud gasps. Taken aback by her friend's bedraggled appearance, Molly blurted out, "Reanna! Whatever has happened?"

Reanna dimly heard Kenny echo his wife's surprise as her shocked gaze found him, sitting in a woven caned chair with large wheels attached to the sides, gripping the arms tightly as if he wanted very much to rise, but could not.

Reanna's tenuous hold on her nerves broke completely, and with a strangled, unintelligible cry she brushed past Molly and ran forward, falling to her knee at Kenny's side.

"Kenny … Kenny … I only just learned of it … of your … oh, Kenny, forgive me. If I had known, I would have … but no one told me. If I had only known, I could have at least …" she could not go on. Great wrenching sobs racked her body convulsively as Kenny gently stroked her head, offering futile words of comfort, which did nothing to relieve the anguish she felt.

Molly quietly drew the drenched cape from Reanna's shoulders and wrapped a blanket in its place, then brought a towel to gently rub the excess moisture from her hair.

As Reanna's tearful cries subsided, Molly handed her a glass of brandy, insisting that she drink it to warm herself, while Kenny began once more to explain.

"Reanna, listen closely to my words, and believe them. It is true that I will never walk again, and I will not tell you that it has not been difficult, but I am gradually accepting that fact. It has been a long painful process, to be sure, but I have Molly, and the strength of our love helping me through it all. Now you must accept it as we have. In no way are you to blame for what happened. I mean it," he insisted, forestalling her protest. "None of it was your fault, you cannot help the hateful things those men did. Everyone who rode with your uncle and Chance that day knew what could happen, just the same as with any posse. Molly and I are just grateful that I survived, that we can still be together, and we are thankful that you are still here, and recovered. These are the important things. Reanna, all of us, including myself, thought it best that you recover from your own injuries, and healed emotionally, before giving you more to worry about. We knew that you would take it hard, and you already had enough of a burden to carry. We did not wish to add to an overly heavy load."

Kenny's voice became softer as he noted the expression of surprise that crossed Reanna's lovely features, for she had not once considered the fact that Molly and Kenny themselves had not wanted her to be informed of his injury. "Surely you must see that our secret was kept in your own best interest."

Reanna began to weep once more, this time overcome with tears of happiness for the unselfish love of her friends, while she felt a sharp sense of guilt enter her heart for the harsh words she had directed toward her father and Chance earlier.

Molly offered Reanna another brandy as she rose, sniffling, from Kenny's side and sat at the table. They spoke at length of all that had occurred since they had last seen each other and were joined by Billy as soon as he had finished his chores out in the barn, and they did not notice that dusk had fallen until a light rapping on the door drew their attention, for the room was lit by a blazing fire.

Reanna was quite surprised when Molly answered the door and Chance's broad, muscular frame filled the doorway. His dark gaze was immediately drawn to her, searching for understanding in the green deepness of her eyes, realizing that perhaps in their concern for her they had been guilty of neglect. She should have been told much sooner about her friends' difficulties.

Chance found that this friendship business was all very perplexing. In all his years of traveling from place to place, roaming at will, he had never formed any real, lasting friendships, only acquaintances, and those were formed mostly out of others' fears of his fast gun. No, Bob was the closest he had ever come to friendship, and he had seen him very seldom over the years.

"Reanna, are you finally ready to come home and forgive us? Following you here may not have been the best idea, for I have been cooling my heels out there for hours in the rain, but I must admit that I was more than a little worried at the way you rode out this morning. The roads are very muddy, and it is a long ride to make alone in the dark."

Reanna was overcome by the depths of her feelings toward Chance. That he would follow her through the pouring rain to see she arrived safely and then wait in it all day, hoping for her forgiveness, brought tears once again to her eyes, and she flew into his arms, her heart swelling with love for him. Feeling the slight tremors that shook his body as he embraced her, she insisted he take a chair by the fire, and Molly brought him a brandy as Reanna removed his hat and vigorously toweled his thick, dark locks dry.

Stretching his long legs out before him, he grasped Reanna around the waist when she stepped around to his side and playfully pulled her onto his lap, insisting that he would not need the blanket she had been on her way to get him.

Softly kissing her neck, he looked into her eyes, his own taking on that familiar sensuous red glow, and smiled rakishly. He spoke quietly, so that she alone could hear. "I have all the warmth I need right here."

He suddenly realized with a start, the home he had not even known he needed was here, with this woman. Reanna would be his home forever more. Wherever they traveled, whatever they chose to do, it would be together, for his heart had finally found a place to dwell, a place he would never have to leave behind.

Two days later, Reanna was helping Pier to curry horses in the barn, daydreaming as she worked slowly, inhaling the fragrance of fresh hay as sunlight filtered gently in through the doorway and the soft drone of insects mingled with the low, contented whickers of the horses.

She started suddenly as she realized that Chance stood next to her, a smug smile splitting his face, and she knew immediately that he was up to something. She supposed that she was about to find out exactly what it was.

"Chance Nolton," she scolded, "you frightened me, sneaking up like that! Whatever are you up to now, you mischievous scoundrel?"

"Mischievous scoundrel, is it now? Just for that I think that I will keep the surprise I have for you secret for a while longer, and drive you mad with curiosity."

His eyes glittered with excitement, and Reanna knew that he was just dying to tell her, so she decided to tease him a little bit, just compensation for the fright he had given her. "That is fine with me sir, for I have had my fill of surprises these past months."

Chance was instantly contrite. He had not meant to remind her of any sadness. She was smiling, but he could not help but feel that he had brought back painful memories, and he gathered her gently into his arms. "Reanna, my love, this surprise is meant to bring you nothing but happiness. Come with me now, and I will show you. We have just to take a short ride."

Deeply touched by his sudden tender concern, she attempted to set him at ease once more, and smiled widely. "Lead on then, my dashing knight, and let me discover this well-kept secret."

An hour later they pulled up in front of the old Talmar homestead and Chance dismounted, leaving Reanna to look about in confusion.

"Chance, there is nothing here, the place has been closed up for years, ever since Mr. Talmar passed away. Mrs. Talmar moved to Virginia City to live with her sister, but she refused to sell this property, even though she has had several fair offers. What are we doing here?"

Chance could not hide the superior grin that lit his face. "I have been well informed as to the history of this place, and Mrs. Talmar. But she has finally decided to sell, and just who do you think has purchased this rare jewel of a house, and all the land for miles around?" he questioned with a grand sweeping motion of his arm.

Reanna's green eyes narrowed as she studied him closely, watching his proud grin widen further. "Chance! You? You bought this place? But whatever for, Chance? You know that you will always have a home with Papa and me. And how were you able to purchase this when the widow was so set against selling?"

"You forget, Rea that I am very wealthy, and everything has its price, eventually. It's all in how you go about it."

Yes, Reanna was perfectly aware of how charming Chance could be when he wished. Between his charm and his money, the widow hadn't stood a chance.

"Also," Chance continued, "I rather thought that this would make us a good home, together."

They had dismounted, and he reached out to hold her face, softly stroking her long, silken tresses. "I mean to marry you, Reanna, my darling," he whispered as he bent his dark head to place a soft, passionate kiss to her lips.

When she did not respond, Chance drew away to study her expression. What he saw was not to his liking.

Reanna was astounded. This was what she had wanted, had dreamed of … once, before the McPhersons. Now, what kind of wife could she be? Chance would not be happy for long with half a wife, one who could not stand to be intimate with her husband. Although, she thought with a blush, the things that they had shared so far had proved to be highly enjoyable. If she could only be certain that she would someday overcome her fear. Damn! She could think of nothing to say to him, left, for once, completely speechless.

Knowing the reason for it, he was unable to stand the silence any longer. Chance took her hand and slowly led her toward the back door of the house.

"Come, let's have a look around. The house itself needs very little work, and the grounds will be beautiful with just a minimum of weeding and pruning. There is plenty of rich pasture, and Reanna, there is even a special place for Modoc and Tasha. It's as if the place were built just for us, my love."

"Chance, I always assumed … if I were ever to marry, my husband and I would make our home at High Ridge, with Papa," Reanna ventured.

"Your father of all people will understand the need for a man to make his own way and not just live off his wife's father," Chance answered her, thinking of Sean as he led her into the large, sunny kitchen which had a wide planked floor and many cupboards, all built of light, waxed oak.

A small but comfortable bedroom led off one end of the kitchen, to the right of a large cast iron stove, perfect for a live-in maid. Double doors opened off the other end to an enormous parlor, complete with a large stone fireplace, and glowing with the rich hand rubbed sheen of mahogany, visible even through the layer of dust. Imported French doors made from the same wood surrounding small panes of glass opened from one side of the room to a private stone patio that caught the morning sunlight. Here, myriads of flowers would bob their heads in the spring, lending their subtle fragrance on a balmy breeze.

Solid, dark mahogany doors opened to what would be an office and library on the opposite side of the room, and as they ascended the large, curved staircase, Reanna ran her hand up the smooth, dark banister, admiring its dim luster.

The upstairs housed five airy, sunlit bedrooms, all opening across from each other, the windows placed just so they would catch any cool cross breezes in the heat of summer, and all equipped with small stone fireplaces, miniatures of the one downstairs, to ward off the chill of winter. The floors of the hall, and all the bedrooms, were also of rubbed oak, like those below, and Reanna began to feel the warm, friendly atmosphere and quiet elegance beckon to her. She found herself wondering what it would be like to fill this house with the happy laughter of Chance's children.

The barns needed some work, but were built solidly, as was the house, meant to weather any storm. As they wandered from the second of the two outbuildings, Reanna finally found her voice, asking tentatively, "The barns, the house, they are beckoning to be filled, aren't they, Chance?"

"Reanna," Chance said excitedly, heartened by her query, "just wait till you have seen it all. It was made with you in mind, I think."

He showed her the chicken coop, and finally led her to a large pen with a covered section built with wired runs. "This, Milady, is for Modoc and Tasha. Now, if you harbored any doubts before, this should convince you once and for all. It will be the perfect place to raise little setters."

She sighed, glancing around at the still beautiful, but neglected grounds. An herb garden stood just outside the back door, and around the well grew a profusion of rose bushes, which lent their heady perfume to the warm air as they bloomed.

Chance explaining his plans for the future, used the words ours, and we, as if she had already consented to be his wife. They had just reached their tethered horses, and Reanna decided that she must put a stop to what she could only interpret as Chance's persistent assumptions. Her eyes were filled with painful regret as she turned to face him.

"Chance … I do love you; you must know that … but … I just cannot consent to marry you, now … and I don't understand how you could want me, knowing that I cannot bear to … be intimate." Tears pricked her eyes, and try as she might, she could not fend them off.

Chance wrapped her tightly in his arms. "Reanna, my love, my heart, my very soul, we have been through this many times. You know it does not matter, together we can overcome our fears, and our love will conquer the hate. Love can conquer all, Rea, if it is strong and sure enough, it can conquer hate, can even overcome death. And our love is strong Rea, certainly powerful enough to overcome the evil of a few men. Simple, evil men did the damage, Reanna, now we must let our undying love heal the wounds and scars that they have left."

Reanna, touched by his murmured message of comfort, chose her words carefully. "Chance, I know your words to be true. I know it, and yet … I need more time, Chance. What you say is well and good when the words are spoken, but applied to our everyday lives, well, it may be much more difficult than you imagine. I am sorry Chance, deeply sorry, but I must refuse your offer of marriage. And please Chance, if you feel you cannot wait for me, or your passions … well, overwhelm you … you are, of course, completely free to find another. Do not worry about hurting me, for I would truly understand."

Her last words cut through Chance's heart as if with a sharp blade, causing deep hurt, and he wanted to wound her as well. He pulled roughly away from her and mounted Lancelot, grating out his words as he did so. "Reanna, if you don't want me, why don't you just say it out plain? I have tried everything I can think of, to no avail. Damn it! I am tired of wasting my time."

Reanna followed him, attempting to explain. "Chance, wait! You misunderstand me … Chance!"

She screamed his name, but he was gone, his image swallowed up in the dust of the unused road that led from the house.

Chapter 7

Reanna, heartsick over her misunderstanding with Chance, climbed wearily onto her mare and turned her mount toward home. She reasoned, though, that Chance would never have returned to the ranch, not as furious as he had been. She should follow him; try to explain her position once again. Tell him that she had only been thinking of what would be best for him. It certainly was not what she desired. In fact, the thought of Chance seeing another woman left her feeling violently ill.

So why was she still headed home? She had to find him, and she was fairly certain of where he would go to ease his hurt. She pulled the mare to a stop, indecisive of her next actions. Would Chance deem it far too forward of her if she followed him? Then a mental image of Aggie's smiling face appeared, and Reanna shuddered.

"To hell with proprieties, girl. We're going to town," she told her mare, and, her decision made, set off at a brisk trot toward Carson City.

Just as she had surmised, she found Lancelot tied outside the Horseshoe, and she wasted no time entering the establishment. It took her eyes a moment to adjust from the bright sunlight outside, and in that short space of time she was overcome by the stench of tobacco smoke and whiskey; the odor of unwashed bodies as cowhands, fresh in from the trail, gathered to squander their hard-earned wages away on drink, gambling, and women.

She scanned the crowded, boisterous room for Chances tall form, to no avail, and she was becoming more nauseous and light-headed by the minute. She spotted Belinda and began to squeeze her way through the crowd.

"Belinda, have you seen Chance? His horse is outside, but I can't seem to find him anywhere." Reanna was feeling more faint by the moment, her breath came with difficulty, as Belinda, overjoyed to see her friend, grasped her arm, spouting enthusiastically, "Oh, Reanna, I'm so glad to see you … I have the most incredible news! Joseph Stranton was in yesterday, straight from California. He said that he saw, you'll never guess who, so I'll have to tell you. Daniel Macon! Said he was in a prison somewhere on the coast, I can't remember the name of the town now."

Reanna's shock at this news combined with her spinning head to make her knees buckle, but Belinda slid an arm around her, easing her into a close chair.

"Oh Reanna, I'm so sorry! I just didn't stop to think about how the news would upset you. Are you all right honey?"

"Belinda, could you get me something, some sherry maybe?"

"Of course, you just sit right there," Belinda answered, and hurried away, returning with a generous amount of the liquor, which Reanna promptly tossed down her throat, gasping at the sudden fire that choked her.

"I never saw you drink like that before! Anyone who knows you knows what a true lady you are, but I swear Rea, sometimes you act just like a cowboy!" Belinda giggled, embracing her friend in a loving hug, and then sobered quickly when she realized Reanna's consternation.

"It can't be true, Belinda. There must be some mistake. There just has to be another explanation. Daniel is dead. He was killed fighting the Indians, you know it as well as I. Joseph was in error and saw someone that resembled Daniel, that's all."

"No, Reanna, I'm afraid not. Nick Barber was with him, and he, too, swore that the man they saw was indeed Daniel."

Reanna became so dizzy that she clutched at her head in an effort to keep the room from spinning.

"Reanna, what is wrong? You look ill, like you need a doctor. Reanna?"

Belinda, truly shaken by her friend's appearance, rose from her chair just as Reanna swooned, but she was not fast enough to prevent her from sliding to the floor.

"Reanna! Someone help me with her!"

Reanna was dimly aware of a pair of strong arms lifting her, and then she was outside, the fresh air reviving her as she drew in great lungful's, able to breathe at last, away from the closed, smoky atmosphere of the Horseshoe. She opened her eyes to Chance's grave, worried frown, and was barely able to manage a whisper, "Chance."

He failed to hear her, but carried her directly to the doctor's office, where he laid her gently on the examining table. Reanna became fully aware of her surroundings a few minutes later, and Dr. Farley stood before her.

"Reanna, how do you feel?" he asked, concern etched across his features.

"I feel a little dizzy, that's all Doctor. The saloon was so crowded and the smoke so thick, I just – I'm all right now I think." She sat up gingerly, unsure of her strength.

"Reanna, has this ever happened before, I mean within the past couple of months?"

"What, doctor? My fainting you mean? No, why do you ask?"

"What about nausea Reanna? Have you had any of that? Any other unusual symptoms?"

"Symptoms? Of what, Doctor? The only thing unusual is the terrible nightmares that still plague my sleep. Why all the questions? I already know the reason I fainted. It was the smoke and the noise, that's all. I'm fine now, really."

Reanna climbed down from the table and found Chance in the waiting room. He leaped to his feet as she entered, impatient to hear how the exam had gone.

"Reanna, what happened? Are you all right now? Maybe you had better sit down here."

Reanna hid a smile. Last she knew, he had been quite upset with her, yet here he was now, all loving concern once more. "It was nothing, Chance, just the atmosphere of the saloon. And I will sit down, but on my horse, not here. It has been an exhausting day, and I want nothing more than to get home."

"I agree with you my love, and if my earlier harsh words can be forgiven, I would deem it an honor to escort you home myself." Chance flashed her an entreating grin and Reanna answered him softly, "Forgiven and forgotten, my dashing sir knight. Lead on." She took Chance's arm and together they left the office.

Dr. Farley called after them, "Reanna, I want you back here for a full exam soon!" but Reanna's mind was on other, more important matters.

Later that night, as soon as the household was silent and she was sure that everyone slept, Reanna slipped out into the dark night. She told herself that it was something she just had to do. She had to speak with Joseph herself, so that she could set her mind at ease.

She cringed as Lancelot whickered in inquiry as she led her mare from the barn, but all remained silent. She expelled a deep breath, mounted, and rode to the Stanton's ranch, relieved to see that the lights were still burning when she arrived. She had feared that she would wake them and was glad now to see that she would not have to.

Mr. Stanton opened the door soon after Reanna's knock, greeting her in surprise. "Reanna Dublin! What are you doing out at this hour child? Come inside, my dear."

"Mr. Stanton, I do apologize for the late hour. But it is urgent that I speak to Joseph at once."

Knowing immediately the reason she had come to call, Mr. Stanton nodded in sympathy. "Ah, you heard the news of Joseph's discovery, then. He was going to ride out tomorrow to let you know. He swears it is true, and I don't doubt his word, hard enough as it is to believe, but he would not be mistaken with something as serious as this." He turned toward the back of the house and bellowed, "Joseph, Reanna Dublin is here!"

"Reanna," Joseph greeted her a moment later, taking her hand in his, "you are looking as lovely as ever. But I don't suppose that is what you came to hear, is it?"

"I came to ask you about Daniel. It is true then?"

Joseph, a bit sheepish that he had neglected to inform Reanna of his news first, was apologetic. "I was going to tell you tomorrow, Reanna. I should have done so right away. You should have been the first to know that your fiancé is alive, especially after the way you grieved over the news of his death."

He paused and grasped Reanna's shoulders gently. "We all grieved with you, but he is alive, Reanna. I have seen him. He is imprisoned, in a jail near the coast there, but definitely living."

"But Joseph, how can this be? Why is he imprisoned? How long has he been there?"

"I honestly don't know, Reanna. He wouldn't talk to me about any of it. He was angry that I'd found him. He made me promise not to tell you, but I had to. I couldn't let you go on thinking he had died when I knew otherwise. You are too good a friend."

"I blamed myself because we had parted in anger. He insisted upon fighting the Paiutes, although I begged him not to go. One of my best friends happens to be of that blood.

You know Mansunama, Joseph, and even though his tribe refused to fight, I still felt that Daniel was waging war on my friends. You could see the hatred in his eyes when he spoke of them. I kept hoping that once he was in the midst of the actual fighting, he would change his mind and come home. But he was gone so long that when I heard of his death, the anger didn't matter by then, hadn't mattered for some time. And I know now that our love was never meant to be, but I don't like the fact that he is alone, in a cold prison cell, with no one to help him. Joseph, you must tell me how to get there. I must go and do what I can for him, for the sake of what we shared."

"Reanna, that's crazy. It's a long journey, all the way across California. I will not tell you."

"But Joseph, I must go. Don't you see? How can I possibly rest with the knowledge that he is there, and not knowing the cause, or if he needs help? I will not go alone; I can take some men from the ranch. Oh, please Joseph, please help me."

Joseph relented in the face of Reanna's heartfelt plea, able to refuse her nothing, and drew her a detailed map, filling her in on all the information she would need, although not without misgivings. It would be just like Reanna to dash off to Daniel's side alone with no thought of her own safety. He sighed in resignation as she thanked him with a kiss on his cheek, and then watched until she rode from view.

She must see Billy. He would help her, she was sure of it, and he could be trusted to keep her plans to himself.

It was very late when she arrived at the Becketts, and Molly was more than a little surprised to find Reanna at her door alone. But that soon turned to incredulity as her friend explained her mission. She was of course glad to hear that Daniel was alive, but she turned a stern look upon the younger girl.

"You are crazy to think you should go to him Reanna. You have Chance now, and what will he think? The love that the two of you share should not be taken lightly Reanna, and you may well be throwing it to the wind if you go through with this scheme of yours. At least ask Chance if he minds that Billy accompany you. Maybe Chance would prefer to go with you himself." Molly turned to Billy for support, and he nodded in agreement.

Reanna paused to think about Molly's words, but how could she ask Chance to come with her into her past, something he could not possibly understand? He would assume that she was still in love with Daniel, especially in light of her words to him earlier today. No, she could not ask him to come with her. She wasn't even going to tell him until she returned, and her mission was accomplished.

"Molly, if Chance truly loves me then he will not be angry at me for doing what I must. If he cannot understand something that is this important to me, then our love may be in vain."

She recalled the words he had spoken today when they were outside the house he bought. If he meant all that he said, then she needn't worry.

"Billy, will you agree to come with me? I leave at first light, with or without you."

Billy did not hesitate, for he felt obliged to Reanna, still consumed by the guilt of his brothers' sins. "I will meet you at daybreak on the North Road."

Reanna rushed home to pack some food staples and personal items, all very quietly, so that she would not wake her father or Chance, and donned her only pair of pants, a shirt, and vest. Then she lay down to get a few hours sleep, which in the end eluded her.

She met Billy at dawn, and together they started out. She had decided to leave a note for Chance after all, explaining that she did as she felt she must, but she wondered, would he understand? It had seemed impossible to capture her feelings on paper, and now she had to wonder if it had been wise to leave an explanation at all.

It would take them at least a week to reach their destination, Albany, which was close to San Francisco, on the coast of California. They had to cross the Sierra Nevada Mountains, which would be the most difficult part of their journey, and Reanna did not look forward to it. She hoped that at least the good weather would hold, and that the trails were in good condition. It was late in the year, and it grew cold in the high elevations.

*   *   *   *   *   *

Chance, waking the next morning, failed to notice the carefully folded message bearing his name. Reanna had placed it on the mantle in the parlor, where he would be sure to find it, but he was much too preoccupied with his own plans for the day. His home would need a thorough cleaning, and a few minor repairs, and he wanted to find a cook. Someone like Carmelita, able to run the household in his absence, to clean and cook, which he himself had no desire to do. Reanna was used to having help with those kinds of things, having been brought up with someone to do the cooking. That she would one day say yes to his proposal of marriage he had no doubt, for he would not give up until she did, and he wanted her to have every comfort that she now enjoyed.

He could think of no one in town to fill the position, so he headed leisurely into Reno. The heat was worse than usual for this time of year, and Chance absently watched the dust particles stirred from their resting places by Lancelot's plodding hooves as they glimmered in the afternoon light before settling slowly back to earth, covering both him and the horse with a thin layer of brown dust.

He appeared to be dozing as he entered the town, his head nodding and his calf-leather Stetson pulled low to shield his eyes from the white glare of the sun as he proceeded indolently down the bustling main street.

There were those who watched him long after he passed, sensing that he was as alert as any bird of prey. His dark hazel eyes missed nothing as he casually, habitually surveyed his surroundings, and further up the road a group of men stood clustered outside the saloon, laughing drunkenly, and swilling from upraised bottles.

Chance grimaced in distaste. Loud, boisterous gatherings of this sort usually spelled trouble.

Suddenly one of the group smashed his bottle over the hitching rail and holding the jagged neck out in a threatening gesture, advanced to the center of the gathered assemblage.

Yes, definitely trouble for someone. More than likely some cowboy caught cheating at cards.

Chance continued on his way, nonplussed, until his interest was piqued by the sight of one burly member of the group hauling on a rope, grinning wickedly. He could not at the moment glimpse who or what was on the other end, but as he drew closer his eyes grew hard, with an unforgiving quality that had been the final sight of many who had dared to try to best him. He reined Lancelot in and casually, with the grace and ease of the panther that his actions had instilled in Reanna's mind, dismounted, raising a hand to push back his hat.

Lassoed at the waist was a strikingly beautiful Indian woman, and though petite in stature, was stoically resisting the large man as the others gathered around, laughing at the spectacle. The one with the broken bottle in his had held the sharp weapon out toward her face in a wordless threat, but her eyes showed no fear, no emotion whatever as the men attempted to drag her into the street.

Time reversed itself and it was Reanna who stood surrounded by the petty animals that had so hurt her gentle spirit.

Caught up in their exuberant display of abusive mockery, they failed to notice the lean, dark stranger that stopped nearby. In stony silence he drew his gun, effortlessly bringing it up as, with what was second nature to him, he took lightening aim and squeezed the trigger.

The sharp report took the rowdy group by surprise, effectively stifling their malicious laughter, and the burly cowboy tugging on the rope staggered backwards as Chance's bullet found its mark, neatly severing the rope six inches from his hand. He swiftly regained his balance and stared in disbelief at the dangling hemp left in his hand, then dropped it as if it had suddenly turned into something repulsive.

All eyes rested on Chance now, as in a deadly, smooth voice he asked, "Care to try your luck with me, gentlemen?"

His hard, penetrating gaze never faltered, sobering the men as well as if he had dumped icy water over them, and indeed a couple of them did shiver as the cold finger of fear ran down their spines, for it seemed as though they stared into the dark visage of death.

The drunk that held the broken bottle let it slip through his immobile fingers to land with a resounding clunk as it hit the worn planks of the boardwalk, rolled to the edge, and sent a small puff of dust upward as it landed in the dry street.

"Mister, we was just having a little fun, is all. Just an injun squaw, anyways. Ain't no good for nuthin," ventured one of the group tentatively, braver than the rest, or perhaps just not quite as bright.

An ominous silence met his statement as Chance raised his revolver to the speaker, his eyes promising more than his next softly spoken words.

"If I were you, I would crawl out of here as fast as possible and leave the lady alone, before I change my mind about letting you go!"

The men stood gaping for only a moment before they decided upon the safest course of action, and as one, backed down from the stranger, who's burning hate filled gaze promised nothing but a sure death if they dared to cross him further. Turning, they shuffled back into the saloon in somber silence, their fun for the time being, at an end.

"Thank you." The simple words of gratitude, plainly spoken, surprised Chance as the men faded from sight into the dimly lit interior of the building, and as he glanced her way, the Indian woman met his gaze squarely, with no fear.

"You speak English," Chance noted aloud as he took in her bedraggled appearance and the pinched, hungry looking planes of her thin, finely formed face.

At her affirmative nod, a sudden idea occurred to him, and he smoothly holstered his gun before speaking again.

"You need a job, a place to stay?" But it was more a statement than question, for Chance had accurately divined her circumstances without the benefit of words.

She nodded once again, surprised at the white man's astute observations.

"I have just purchased a house and have need of a cook and housekeeper. If you want, the job is yours, on the assumption of course that you can cook."

"I am an excellent cook," she answered proudly to the inquiring lift of his brow, "but what will your wife say when you return with me? A lot of people will not tolerate having an Indian in their home."

He surmised her to be from the Nez Pierce tribe. They were superior horsemen, noted for the appaloosas they raised. She was far from her home and had acquired a skillful command of the English language somewhere, but she had obviously fallen on hard times.

"I have no wife right now, but I intend to … just as soon as I can convince her to marry me."

A flicker of amusement passed briefly through the Indian's dark eyes. She instinctively trusted this tall, lean, handsome man and considered any woman foolish that would not agree to wed with him, but she wisely held her tongue on that account.

"And you need not worry that you will be unwelcome in our home," he added, "She loves everyone, and is very soft hearted. She treats everyone with respect, even those who do not deserve her kindness." Chance assured the woman, recalling times Reanna had stopped him from taking retribution on the McPhersons after very insulting behavior toward her in town, the memory bringing with it a painful twist in the region of his heart.

The woman smiled for the first time, revealing even, white teeth. "It is settled then. My name is Lada."

"My name is Chance Nolton, and I am very pleased to make your acquaintance. If you like, I'll rent a wagon for the ride home, after we have lunch. And I will make sure you have proper clothing. You can repay me from the wages you will earn." He added the last comment quickly, effectively putting to rest the protest she had been about to make.

"Thank you again," Lada said on the way back to Carson City, "I owe you much."

"I think Lada; it is I who has gotten the better of this arrangement." Chance answered and meant it.

Lada hadn't had much reason to trust anyone lately. She was the daughter of a chief, Running Wind, and had been fifteen years old when a white peddler came to their village. Thinking him the most handsome man she had ever seen; she fell in love and ran away with him one stormy night five years ago. She learned to cook the way he liked and mastered his language; learned to discern his every want and need before he asked. She had thought that he loved her also.

They traveled the countryside selling his wares, and she had been happy until they arrived in Reno two weeks ago, when he ran off with a buxom, flaxen haired saloon girl, leaving Lada without clothing or money, not even a goodbye.

She had survived, sleeping in barns or behind buildings, as well as she could, but hunger was her constant companion, and no one was willing to hire an Indian, it seemed, even for the most menial labor. Hunger and heartache, until now, was all she had known, left at the hands of the white man.

She could not return to her people, for Running Wind would only be forced to turn her away. She had disgraced them all, forsaking her tribes' teachings to become the whore of a white man. There would be no young braves willing to have her for a wife; she would be no more than a slave, begging for scraps of food.

Now, Chance Nolton had eased her hunger, but the heartache, would it ever go away?

With Lada settled comfortably in his new home, Chance rode straight to High Ridge to give Reanna the good news of Lada, arriving at dinnertime to find Raymond was more than a little put out with him.

"I really wish that you and Reanna had seen fit to tell me that she was going with you for the day. I had no idea until Carmelita went to wake her for breakfast."

Chance stopped dead in his tracks, his back ramrod straight. He heard himself ask in a confused tone, "What do you mean? Reanna was not with me today. I haven't seen her." Dread settled in the pit of his stomach.

Raymond's face grew haggard, his eyes instantly filled with keen agony. "Chance," he whispered slowly, "there is something that I have not told you. But now … well it appears necessary that I do so. There seems to be no other explanation but that he has come back and abducted my daughter. Oh God! She could not bear it again! Not again!"

Urgency surged through Chance, and he hissed, "What are you talking about? Get hold of yourself man and talk sense! What is it that you think has happened to Reanna?"

Raymond breathed deeply, forcing himself to explain calmly, "Cal McPherson. When the men went back the next day to check on the fire, they couldn't find his body. Not a trace. I sent men out for three days and they never found a clue. I did not want to burden you or Rea with the knowledge," he finished lamely. He should have made sure that Reanna was protected at all times.

Chance walked to the fireplace running his hand tiredly through his hair, but his thoughts were swiftly pursuing their options. Get up a posse. He could have gone anywhere with Reanna. One thing was certain, he could not take her back to that filthy cabin, since they had burned it. That left the whole countryside open for possibilities.

Something on the mantle caught his eye. A piece of paper with his name in Reanna's fine hand, a note! He snatched it from its resting place and quickly scanned the contents, incredulous for a moment at her words.

"That little fool!" he finally exploded, handing the note to Raymond. "Oh, don't worry, I'll find them. They have a good head-start, but I'll bring them back. It's whether or not to wring her foolish neck when I catch them that has me stumped, for you may be certain that this little escapade was not Billy's idea!"

He strode angrily into the kitchen, shoving a few necessary items into an empty burlap sack. As he swung his lithe form onto Lancelot's back he turned to Raymond.

"If you could kindly let my new housekeeper know that I will not return for a few days."

He let his words trail off as he spurred the great black stallion into a mile-consuming lope. Bred for stamina and speed, he had no doubt that Lancelot would overtake the pair he sought.

Later, as he sat alone under the dark sky staring into the flickering light of his campfire, he thought aloud, "You are a fool, Reanna Dublin, a damn beautiful little fool, who may just be in very grave danger."

*   *   *   *   *   *

"Would you like more to eat Billy? More coffee maybe?"

"Just coffee thanks." Billy held out his cup as Reanna refilled it, the steam rising into the cool mountain air.

Bending, she began to clear away the dirty dishes. "This works out well, Billy. You do the cooking, and I, the cleaning up. Although, you might let me attempt one meal, you know."

Billy ventured no comment as he swirled the dark, warm liquid around in his cup, staring solemnly into the fire, his blue eyes lost in thought. "Reanna?"

"Yes, Billy?"

"It's not too late to turn back you know."

"Billy, we've been all through that. You know that I have to do this. I have to find out why he is imprisoned, if he needs help."

"And Chance … what of him? What do you think he will do when he finds out that you have run off to see Daniel?"

"I left him a note explaining everything. I do not think that he will worry over-much."

"If you say so, but his being worried was not exactly what I had in mind, furious maybe." The tone of Billy's voice left Reanna in no doubt that he did not share her convictions. He also was beginning to feel a slight foreboding; something was going to happen. He shrugged the feeling off, putting his ill-ease down to the fact of having to face Chance's anger when he found them, which Billy was certain the bounty hunter would do.

Reanna finished the dishes, and brushed her long hair, which crackled with a fire of its own as the light of the flames struck the dark tresses which reflected back as molten copper.

"I guess we had better turn in now if we are to get an early start tomorrow, Billy."

"Yes, I reckon so. Good night, Reanna." Billy rose to bank the fire, and they rolled up in their blankets, thankful for their warmth in the crisp night air.

The red dawn crept silently across the lightening sky, touching the tops of the snowcapped mountain peaks to turn them a dusky rose. Reanna slowly opened her eyes as the aroma of crispy fried bacon and brewing coffee invaded her dreams. She stretched, throwing back her covers.

"Billy, when did you get up? Just look at those mountains! Aren't they beautiful? I cannot wait to see them close! We should be up there sometime today, shouldn't we? Why didn't you wake me up?"

Billy smiled at her chatter. She loved to see new things, and her excitement shone in her eyes. Like a child, he thought. Well, he wished that he had a better feeling about this trip. But he was not going to spoil her day with dire forecasts.

"We'll make the foothills about noon, I'd say. From then on, the going could get kind of tough. We'll have to stick to the trail. Come on and eat so we can get started."

The sun was high in the sky when Billy broke out bread and water for lunch. "It's not much but I want to get as far as possible every day now that we've hit the mountains, Reanna."

"That's fine Billy, I know that it's going to be a lot slower traveling now, and I do so want to get to see Daniel."

Billy just shook his head. Once Reanna made up her mind, there was just no stopping her.

They climbed ever higher into the Sierra Nevada's, those great mountains that dared to reach to the heavens, only to plummet down forever, it seemed. The trail became twisting and rocky, with the horses having to pick their way carefully around loose stones. One misstep could result in both horse and rider plummeting to their deaths on the rocks below.

The air was getting thinner, and Reanna felt strangely light-headed. She reached up to brush a stray tendril from her face and swayed in the saddle. She tried to straighten but felt herself slipping further from the saddle. She looked down to dimly view brush and rocks rising ever closer and managed to scream once before she hit the cliff and began to slide over the edge, scraping her hands as she fruitlessly grasped at the rocky outcrop.

At Reanna's panicked scream Billy turned in his saddle, his face drained of color and turned a sickly gray.

"Jesus Reanna!" he screamed, and the sound of his voice came back to him from the far mountain ridges all around them. He threw himself from his horse, careless of the narrow ledge, and ran to the spot where she had gone over the edge.

"Sweet Jesus, Reanna!" Billy knew the worst feeling of useless desperation in his life. Tears streamed unchecked and unnoticed down his face as he scrambled over the rocks, not wanting to see her broken, lifeless body far below, but knowing that he had to look.

He crept to the edge of the cliff, inching his way out on his belly so that he could peer over. There, to his amazement, was Reanna, hanging onto a piece of scrub brush for dear life.

Billy choked back his tears, "Reanna, hold on, I'm going to get a rope!" He staggered up to Reanna's horse and grabbed the length of rope from her saddle horn, tying it on before turning to hurry back. "Reanna, I'm coming down to tie this rope around you. Hang on!"

A strangled sob was her only answer. Hanging on to the rope, he inched his way down the wall to where Reanna's trembling arms gripped the limb for dear life. He tied the rope around her waist and held on above her.

"We've got to go up now, Reanna. Use your feet and keep your hands moving up along the rope. I'll be right behind you."

She nodded and they began the difficult ascent. One step, two … Reanna lost her grip, and Billy thought he was a goner, but he managed to hold on, and support her with his knees until she regained her balance.

After what seemed to be an eternity, they lay panting back up on the trail, attempting to regain their labored breath and ease the shuddering of strained limbs.

Reanna sat up and began to sob, "Oh Billy, how can I ever thank you? I thought that I would surely die. I was so frightened. I don't know what happened." She shuddered. "If you had not been here … I don't even want to think about it." She put her head in her hands and cried with body wrenching sobs as the full reality of what had happened hit her, bringing with it the very first doubts about what she was doing.

Billy rose and took her into his arms, wrapping her in comfort as she cried out her relief, rocking her gently back and forth, his own tears long forgotten.

"Do you think you are able to ride now? We should find a place to make camp for the night. It grows dark quickly in these mountains."

"Y ... yes, I think I'll be fine now. Please, let's get out of this place Billy."

They shakily climbed aboard their horses and slowly made their way up the narrow trail. An hour later they rounded a bend and stopped in amazement as the trail widened, winding down and opening into a large clearing surrounded by tall birch and pine trees. Above the tops they could see the grand vistas of the jagged mountain peaks breaking the blue of the late afternoon sky. Kestrels, or sparrow hawks, circled lazily overhead, gracefully riding on swift currents of mountain air, dipping, and rising, their shrill cries echoing back from the lofty summits in which they lived.

"Let's camp here tonight, Reanna. I don't think we'll find any better place, and you must be exhausted."

"Yes, I am, and it is so lovely here. I think we needed to find a spot such as this after all that has happened today."

Billy looked at her closely. There were mauve circles under her large green eyes, and shadows of past and not so distant pain appeared in their depths.

"Reanna, are you absolutely sure that you want to go on with this?"

Reanna sighed, "Yes, Billy, I must. Things could not get any worse than they were today, could they?"

"Well, no, I suppose not. But you sit and rest while I get a fire going. At least I can fill you with a good meal before we turn in. I hear the sound of running water through those trees, why don't you go get cleaned up while I get us settled."

"Billy, you talked me into it." With a waning smile Reanna fetched a bar of soap and a towel from her saddlebag and set off through the trees.

When she found a pool that had formed in a stream bed, Reanna shed her torn, rumpled clothes and stepped gently into the cold, clear water. Catching her breath at the icy shock of the water, she washed, and then swam leisurely around the deep pool as she grew accustomed to the temperature, stopping to soak her long locks, then became lost in daydreams as she relaxed in the healing water. Daniel's face drifted across her mind, as she had last known him; Daniel, who was dead, but is now alive. "Oh Daniel, what has happened? You were so gentle, so courtly and considerate." Suddenly Chance's dark visage floated into her mind, destroying her peaceful reverie. Shuddering from some unknown wanting, she swam to the edge of the pool and stood to dry herself, the late afternoon sunbathing her creamy skin with a golden light.

Quickly dressing, she toweled her hair dry and walked the short distance back to camp. Billy had taken care of the horses and had a warm fire crackling. He started coffee brewing, and was frying slices of smoked ham and potatoes, as Reanna suddenly realized how ravenously hungry she was. They both ate two plates of food and then settled down near the fire to leisurely savor their coffee.

"Dinner was delicious Billy. I feel so much better now." She did the dishes and Billy took care of the flame, and they lay down to welcome a deep slumber, as only those who are totally exhausted in mind and spirit are able to do.

On the third day in the mountains, they started to descend from the great heights, slowly winding their way through trees of great proportions, which completely blocked the sky from view, as their branches reached out their great lengths to form a canopy of green. Thick layers of needles dropping for untold years formed a deep mat that muffled hoof beats. It seemed as if Reanna and Billy were trespassers in a green forest of giants. If they spoke, it was in whispers, so silent and majestic were their surroundings.

As they broke free from the sheltering pines, they looked out at the great valley, shimmering in the afternoon light with its luxuriant mantle of tall, rich grasses, and stopped in wonder as they glimpsed, not far away, the largest deer they had ever seen. Larger than their horses, he lifted his head to stare at the interlopers, chewing the grass he had just bitten off, then slowly he turned and blended into the great pines from which he had come.

"Billy, did we really see that or was it just my imagination?"

"We did Reanna, but I can hardly believe it myself. Just look at this valley. It would make some prime grazing land for cattle, if someone had a mind to start a spread here."

"Like you, for instance?"

"No, I like it just fine around Carson City. It will have to wait for someone else, I'm afraid."

Reanna laughed, "Oh Billy, I swear you do not have an adventurous bone in your body. Come on, I'll race you."

Away they flew, through the tall grass, letting the horses enjoy the freedom of stretching to their limits after the days of slow going through the mountains.

After a time, they pulled up, walking the horses to cool them down. They decided to make camp early, to start out at daybreak again tomorrow. Hobbling the horses so that they could graze, they began preparations for dinner. After all the chores had been attended to, Billy and Reanna sat close to the fire to enjoy their coffee, as had become their habit.

"Reanna, will you ever marry Chance? He loves you and you obviously feel the same way about him. If you wait too long, you may end up losing him."

"I don't know Billy. I just cannot give him everything he wants. I don't want to be unfair to him, and he just expects more than I am able to give right now."

"Because of my brothers." Billy's eyes glazed to the hard blue of winter ice, and he turned away to look into the darkness of the distance, full of self-blame. If it had not been for his family, this beautiful, kind woman beside him would be whole, instead of a shell of her former self. He felt a gentle hand on his shoulder and turned to look into her wide green eyes.

"Please don't blame yourself. You did as much as you could do, as you dared to. And if not for you, I might not have lived, neither then nor yesterday on the cliff."

"Go to bed Reanna, it's been a long day."

Screams pierced Billy's consciousness to rend the still night air and he woke to hold Reanna's trembling form within his arms. She was incoherent, and bathed in a cold seat, just as she was every night, reliving the nightmare of her brutal days at the hands of his brothers. Billy could only hold her, offering the comfort of his gentle presence, and know the curse of his own guilty feelings, until she slept in peace once again. He wondered if it would ever end for either of them.

They approached a great, shining river the next day, and crossed its vast expanse by means of a ferry, which was rather like a large raft, pulled from one side of the river to the other along a rope attached to trees on both shores. Reanna was overjoyed as the ferry master pointed out a family of black and white ducks with bright ornate bills that were peacefully bobbing upon the smooth surface of the river, breaking the mirrored image of great tall trees on both sides as they dove beneath the water. They thanked the old man as they disembarked and continued on their way, watching as red-winged black birds cavorted among the tall shafts of gently swaying grasses. The terrain gradually changed to encompass them once again in huge trees, with the air becoming damp, the result of warm currents of air blowing in from the Pacific Ocean.

That night Reanna awoke again, in the pain of her memories, and Billy held her, sharing her pain as no one else could. And he felt the urge to turn back home more strongly than ever, but he fought it down and kept silent on the matter.

*   *   *   *   *   *

Late afternoon of the eighth day of their journey, Billy and Reanna reached their destination, the town of Albany. The smell of the sea air was stimulating, and gulls flew overhead as the breeze carried the scent of the salty brine and fish in its wake.

They stopped in front of the saloon – hotel, a small wooden structure, weathered before it's time by sand, wind and salt air, and they checked into their rooms, small and plain, but clean. Then they decided to get a hot meal before taking their horses to the livery and enjoying a walk along the shore, something Reanna had been looking forward to with great anticipation the whole trip.

They sat and enjoyed an after-dinner drink, discussing the visit they would make to the prison, when Reanna's face suddenly paled, the shocked expression that crossed her features caused Billy to lean anxiously toward her.

"Reanna, what is it? What's wrong?" Concern sharpened his voice.

Reanna lurched uncertainly to her feet, and her voice came as a whisper of sound, "Chance!"

Billy turned to look around him, and now it was his face that whitened as he glimpsed Reanna swiftly crossing the room toward Chance, who lounged against the bar, casually scanning the room as if he were searching for someone, and then she stood before him. Their eyes met and held; a sizzling current flowed between them so strongly that Reanna thought she would swoon with its force.

Chance's words, soft and tender, caressed her gently with the love that she heard in the depths of his smooth voice. "Reanna, how could you think that I would not understand, that I would allow you to suffer what can only be great hurt and disillusionment alone? Knowing you the way I do, I understand that you had no choice but to come, but remember, I am with you in whatever you do, here for whatever you need."

He did not say that his knees had turned weak with relief when he saw that she was safe from any harm that Cal McPherson would have perpetrated had he found her. Chance was sure that the man would exact a lasting revenge, but he dared not tell Reanna, for the knowledge was bound to have a devastating effect on her.

Then they were in each other's arms, clinging together. Tears smarted Reanna's eyes at the wonder of this hard man who seemed yet able to read her gentle heart better than his own.

Reanna slowly, reluctantly pulled from his embrace, whispering, "We are forgetting Billy."

Chance escorted her to the table where Billy sat in ashen faced turmoil, wondering whether he should try for a timely escape. He gulped audibly, but Chance simply nodded before sitting down to order a hot meal, and the younger man knew giddy relief when the bounty hunter gave Reanna a roguish grin, his eyes sparkling darkly with mischief as he noted, "Reanna, if you are going to visit this prison, then I would suggest a thorough washing and change of clothes. You look like a cowboy just in from a long, hard drive."

Reanna was taken aback for a moment, having forgotten the state of her travel weary clothing, but then she smiled brightly, quipping, "And I declare, Mr. Nolton, that you do not look much better. You smell of horse and sweat and ..."

Reanna's observations were cut short as Chance leaned over to press a tender kiss to her lips. When he pulled away, he looked deeply into her large green eyes, searching her gaze thoroughly as she continued.

"... and I love you, Chance Nolton, no matter what you smell like."

Billy smiled for the first time, assured now that Chance did not have murder on his mind. They kept him company as he ate his meal, and then went to their rooms to wash and change before walking the short distance to the prison.

Reanna insisted that she could do very well on her own, but Chance and Billy would settle for nothing short of accompanying her inside, Billy still fighting the feeling that something was to go terribly wrong.

They entered a small office occupied by lounging guards and a marshal who was seated behind a large redwood desk. Approaching him, Chance wasted no time with pleasantries, but got straight to the point.

"Marshal, we were informed that you are holding a prisoner by the name of Daniel Macon here. If so, we would like to see him for a few moments."

The marshal glanced up from his paperwork and his bright blue gaze slid past Chance to rest on Reanna, warmly admiring her lovely features and the way that her cream-colored satin gown hugged her lush curves. He turned a level look to Chance and spoke slowly. "He's here, but it is highly unusual for a woman of such obvious quality to visit a prisoner. I must inform you that we require a search of anyone entering the cell area, with no exceptions."

Chance was incredulous and retorted in anger, "Really, I see no reason to subject -"

Reanna stepped forward, resting her hand firmly upon Chance's arm as she interrupted, "It is best just to get it over with, Chance. I will be fine, really." She turned to the marshal, "I would ask only that you allow me to endure it privately, not in front of all your men."

Reanna's face had turned a deep shade of pink, and Chance eyed her doubtfully, but realized the futility of arguing with her. She stood her ground, her chin raised stubbornly as she met the marshal's gaze with an unwavering regard.

The marshal nodded to his men, and they escorted Chance and Billy outside. When he returned his attention to Reanna, she immediately bent, bringing forth a small pistol from her boot, which she laid unhesitatingly upon his desk.

"My gun sir, be assured, it is the only weapon I carry."

The marshal contemplated her silently for a moment, then pushed back his chair and rose to his full towering height, advancing slowly around the desk to stand before her. He leaned his blond head toward her and said softly, "Unfortunately, Miss, it is not that easy. I am still bound to search you, and I take my job very seriously. Let's get on with it, shall we?" it was almost as an afterthought that he added, "Allow me to introduce myself, Marshall Mat Magellan, at your service."

He was not looking her in the eyes, but ogled instead the generous swell of her bosom, his gaze growing heated as he reached for her with eager hands. All pretense of being a gentleman vanished, and he rubbed his large palms over her breasts slowly, then down her midriff to her slender waist.

Reanna started at his touch, wanting to run from him in fright, but knowing that she must endure his thinly veiled advances in order to see Daniel, she grit her teeth instead and stood stock still, staring straight ahead, disassociating herself from the proceedings as best as she was able.

Marshal Magellan moved his hands lower, over her buttocks and down the length of her thigh, his breathing becoming more rapid as he lifted her skirts to massage the smooth skin beneath them. Almost imperceptibly his roaming fingers moved upward, one large hand on each of her legs, until she could no longer control the trembling of fear that rippled through her limbs.

Mindful that she was fighting the urge to scream, the marshal let her skirt drop, removing his hands without a word. When she finally dared to meet his eyes, the bright blue gaze was intent, and he was smiling down at her, but his blond good looks only sent a chill up her spine.

He spoke abruptly, turning to pick up her small derringer from his desk. "Tell me Miss, why is it that you find it necessary to carry a gun while in the company of Chance Nolton? Surely, he is more than adequate protection."

Shocked that the marshal should know Chance's name, she glanced at him sharply. "I have my reasons," she replied, "How is it that you know Chance? He did not seem to recognize you."

"Most people around here know him, or of him. He's made quite a name for himself, fast gun, and more money than he will ever be able to spend. He owns property all the way from Monterey up the coast to Sonoma, and also has sizable holdings near Sacramento. The man seems to be a walking goldmine, even owns interests in a few of those, too. He never loses a card game, and owns his own trading ship outright, which very few people can lay claim to."

Reanna was again momentarily taken aback by the venom in the marshal's voice, but she did not pause to dwell on it, for she was busy digesting this new information about

Chance. He had told her that he was wealthy, but not to this vast extent.

A discreet knock sounded on the door and a guard stuck his head in. "You about done in here Mat?

"Bring them in and leave their weapons on my desk. Then show them what they came here to see." Dismissing Reanna without further words, he turned his back to her and strode to the other end of the room, where he stood considering a large map that hung on the wall.

They were shown through two sets of locked doors and down a long corridor lined on both sides with small, iron barred cells, every other one with a rectangular, iron barred window set high in the brick outer walls. This permitted a small flow of fresh air and meager light into the cells, and Reanna scanned the dimly lit cubicles ahead of them until the guard halted at one near the end.

She called lightly, "Daniel? Daniel, where ...?"

The man that stepped forward at Reanna's request caused her to think that there was some mistake. This was not the Daniel she remembered, this was some shaggy, unkempt soul, but then he spoke, sealing his identity as bitter-sweet memories rushed in upon her.

"Reanna! What the hell are you doing here?"

She stepped toward the cold bars separating them, despite the angry tone she heard in his voice. Tears welled in her eyes as she spoke quietly to him. "Daniel, please, I just want to help you."

"Then get out." He said flatly, but Reanna persisted, grasping the iron bars tightly as she leaned closer to the man within. "Everyone thought you were dead, Daniel. You at least owe me an explanation. What happened? Talk to me, tell me, please!"

A small sob escaped her, and Daniel stepped closer to the bars. "You want to know? Very well, I'll tell you. I was brought in for running a large theft ring, cattle, jewelry, and banks, anything that would bring me in fast money. I even killed a few men; it was easy after what I saw in battle against those red heathens that you're so fond of. But I left the fighting and came out here to get rich quick, to save money to marry you. When I got caught, I sent a man to Carson City with news of my death, so that you would never know of the terrible things I had done. I did it all just to be able to have the perfect Miss Dublin as my wife."

Chance started forward at the nasty inflection of Daniel's last words, but Billy stayed him. Reanna may as well know everything now that she had heard this.

"Daniel, how could you?" Reanna asked softly. "How could you have thought that I would care if you had money? And to think of coming to me with blood money, taken from honest people …"

"Oh, the guilt from that was eating me up at first, and I swore that you would never know, but now, I really don't care. I'm either going to hang or rot in this dark hellhole, and I find that I don't much care one way or another about that, either. Or about you, so you can get out now that you've eased your pretty conscience and visited the doomed man."

Misery was etched plainly on Reanna's features, and she made one last attempt to reach the old Daniel, the bright young man whom she once was to wed. "Daniel, I will go if that is what you really wish, but I want you to know that you are not alone. I still care deeply for you."

"And it was love for you that drove me to crime, and perhaps to death! I suffocated with it until it drove me crazy, can't you see that? I could not live up to your kind of love! You love too much, too intensely, until it smothers. You drove me to madness …"

Daniel's hard, cruel words wounded Reanna deeply. Tears streamed unheeded from her eyes, and she shook her head in an impassioned denial.

Chance, no longer able to hold his anger in check, lunged forward to grab the front of Daniel's shirt, hauling him roughly against the bars as he growled over his shoulder, "Get her out of her Billy!"

But Reanna wriggled from Billy's gentle grasp and cried, "Chance, please, leave him be, come away with me. Please don't hurt him; it would serve no purpose now. Please …"

Her words halted as she burst into a fresh round of tears, and Chance felt his anger dissipate in the face of her distress. In distaste he shoved Daniel from him and grabbed Reanna's arm to lead her out of the cell area and back into the front office, where he and Billy collected their weapons and turned to leave.

Reanna was about to accompany them, leaving her own gun, for she did not want to risk spending even another moment alone with the marshal, and would not have Chance know she carried a gun, thinking it would upset him.

"Miss, it seems you are forgetting something. Your derringer, or don't you want it anymore?"

Chance stopped in his tracks and sent Reanna a sharp, considering glance before he retraced his steps and collected the small gun, handing it to her as they left the building. When she offered no explanation for the firearm, he prompted her.

"Care to enlighten me madam, as to where the marshal found the gun, and why you did not mention that you were carrying a weapon? Do you even have the faintest idea how to use it?"

"He did not find it; I gave it to him. I keep it here." She bent down to tuck the gun back into the strap inside of her boot and mounted her horse. "I don't wish to discuss it now

Chance, please. My head is splitting, my heart is aching, and I think I could use a good strong drink."

Billy and Chance mounted, and they started toward the hotel – saloon. "All right, Rea, but I do intend to get to the bottom of this," Chance agreed readily. Of course, he knew that she blamed herself for what Daniel had done. She would not see that it had only been an easy way out for a weak man. Well, in time she would come to understand, he was sure of it.

Suddenly Reanna kicked her horse into a gallop, swiftly covering the distance back to the hotel. Chance never did get to the bottom of anything that night, with the exception of a bottle, for he, Billy and Reanna sat and drank in the saloon until Reanna could no longer keep her eyes open. Chance carried her up to her room and as he gently removed her boots and tucked her into bed, she looked up at him, trying very hard to focus.

"Chance Nolton … ssscoundrel …. Rogue … my anggggell …" Then she closed her eyes.

Chance laughed heartily and went to find his own bed. He knew that they would all wake up with aching heads, but he also knew Reanna had needed to try and drown out her pain with the wine. He knew her pain as if it were his own but knew not how to help her. All he could hope to do was to give her all his love and support and try to help her through the shock of seeing the man she once loved as a mad man.

"Wake up lazybones, or do you plan to sleep all day?"

Chance opened his eyes to Reanna's dazzling smile and sat up in surprise. He had expected her to be downcast, full of self-blame, but her clear, shining eyes held no shadows this morning. She appeared happy and carefree.

He smiled rakishly and gently teased, "Surely, Milady, you must realize the dangers of coming so close to this sorely starving man's bed? And it's not breakfast that I'm hungry for." His dark eyes emphasized the meaning of his words as his gaze longingly roamed her body.

Reanna moved enticingly closer, bending over him. "I am fully aware of the danger, Sir Rogue knight, but I do not worry for my virtue, for I know that I am safe with you."

Chance grimaced at the pain that her close proximity brought; he longed to pull her down into bed with him. "Just don't push my patience too far, my love, for I am fast losing it. Every man has his limitations, Reanna."

He chuckled as Reanna straightened and moved away from him in haste. "No need to fret, love, I have not completely lost control yet. Now, if you wish to see that seashore today, perhaps you had better leave so that I don't embarrass you further when I rise."

At her questioning look he raised a dark brow, explaining mildly, "I sleep in the raw, my dear."

"Oh, you scoundrel … you … you devil!" Reanna fumed, and flounced from the room, slamming the door behind her.

Chance chuckled again, directing his comment loudly, toward the closed portal. "And just last night you called me an angel."

When Chance joined Billy and Reanna downstairs for coffee, however, she could not help but return his wide, secretive grin, her previous anger forgotten.

They rode together to the shore, opting to take the horses just for the sheer joy of an early morning ride on the sand, even though they did not have far to go. Picking their way carefully down the steep, rocky decline, Reanna could hear the pounding surf long before they pulled their horses up and she exclaimed in awe as her eyes were finally able to drink in the mixed beauty of the waves as they curled to crash upon the shore, but calmly meeting the blue of the sky as they stretched along the horizon. As far as the eye could see the water spread its magnificent, glistening, ever-changing surface before her.

"Oh, Chance, how beautiful it is," Reanna breathed and kicked her mare into a run, galloping along the breaking waters, sending the wet sand flying in small clumps as hooves churned the smooth, soft surface, leaving deep impressions.

Chance smiled widely at her unbridled enthusiasm, thinking that he would not have missed her first time here for the world, and sent Lancelot in a swift leap after her.

Billy watched as they sped away, their figures growing smaller as they reached down the beach, and turned his horse in the other direction, intending to explore further up the sandy expanse and rocky outcroppings, giving the couple time to spend alone, now that they had been reunited.

They slowed their horses to a walk and dismounted. Reanna's green eyes sparkled with pleasure as she unabashedly raised her skirt and drew off her boots and stockings to sink her bare feet into the warm sand, wiggling her toes to bury them beneath the tiny grains before she ran to the water, giggling as she splashed about in the incoming waves.

Chance could not help but laugh as Reanna spun round and round, her arms outstretched as if she would like to reach the freewheeling gulls that circled above them, and he ran to her, catching her up in his arms to lift her high above him, spinning around as they both now laughed in carefree abandon. Slowly they sank to the soft sand together, the love and joy they felt for each other overwhelming them, intermingling until their hearts were as one. They lay where they had fallen; gazing into each other's souls, but then, after a time, reality intruded, and Reanna was flooded with guilt for forgetting Billy. She began to rise, but Chance held her back, accurately divining her thoughts as he searched the beach with his keen gaze.

"Billy is far down the beach, Reanna, so you need not worry about him. What I want is for you to talk to me, tell me your feelings about Daniel, about how you feel after discovering that he is alive, and what he has become."

Reanna took a deep breath, groping for the right words, searching her heart. "Oh, Chance, I feel … terrible about what has happened to him. When I first heard that he was alive, I was overjoyed. All I could think of was to get here as quickly as possible, to offer him my help and support. I once thought that I loved him, and we were engaged to marry, so I grieved very deeply when I heard that he had died. But now, well, I may have been better off believing him dead. I have realized for some time that what I felt for him was not really love, but now I am filled with remorse and pity, not for what might have been, but for a gentle man that has chosen to deny the morals he was raised with. I was not worth it to him, not worth the effort of honest work, however hard, so I suppose that his love for me was not what it should have been either. What matters is that I can put that part of my life to rest now, for Daniel frightens me by what he has become."

"I'm glad to hear that, for I do not particularly relish hearing the woman I love murmur someone else's name in her sleep."

"What! When did I ever?" Reanna, aghast, turned a decided shade of red, wondering what else Chance may have heard, and when he had had the opportunity to do so, but he merely smiled devilishly and raised a dark brow.

"That is for me to know, and you to never find out."

Chuckling at the fulminating look she sent his way, he jumped to his feet, turning to help Reanna up before sauntering off towards Billy, who was riding back their way.

Reanna turned and grasped the reins of the horses, then turned abruptly back as she heard a distinctly unfriendly male voice call out, "Say your prayers, Nolton!"

It was in slow motion that she saw Chance turn toward the voice as a large boned, sandy haired man stepped from behind a rock with gun drawn. The shot that rent the air rang in her mind for hours afterward, and then another shot shattered her shock. She saw Chance stagger, clutching at his chest as a bright crimson stain spread outward from his hand, and the other man pitched forward lying face down in death even as Chance sank slowly to his knees, then crumpled to the sand himself.

It seemed to take Reanna hours to reach Chance's side, to run the few feet to his still form and it seemed to her to be someone else's voice that screamed in denial over and over, until she knelt in the bloodied sand beside him, weeping as she watched in horror his efforts to draw breath.

Agony such as she had never known before shot through her, and she cried out, "Chance, no Chance, please don't leave me!"

Chance opened his eyes slowly, even that small movement a struggle, and spoke so softly that Reanna had to strain to catch his words.

Reanna … love you …thank Billy for," he grimaced painfully, then swallowed tightly, "dropping him." He finished with the last of his strength, slipping into unconsciousness, the effort too much for him.

"Reanna, pull yourself together, we have to get him on a horse and to a doctor, and quickly, if we are to save his life!"

The sense of urgency in Billy's voice penetrated Reanna's stricken weeping. Dashing her hands to her eyes, she wiped away her tears and tore a length of cloth from her petticoat, with which she and Billy managed to bind the wound, and then together they hefted his still form across Lancelot's saddle. Reanna grasped the great horses' reins to lead him back the way they had come.

"There is a good chance that he will not pull through," the doctor stated grimly, "It is out of our hands now."

"No, it isn't," Reanna countered emphatically, stroking his thick, black hair, "I will not let him die!" Kneeling by his bedside, she pleaded desperately with him, "My love, my heart, you cannot leave me, I will not let you go. I need you Chance, you are my very life, and you must come back to me."

Reanna refused to leave his side, even sleeping on a pallet on the floor next to his bed. Billy brought her food, insisting that she eat every bite, his concern for her almost as great as it was for Chance.

Other than Billy, she saw no one but the doctor, who came daily to change Chance's bandage and check on his condition. After two days he developed a raging fever, and woken by his delirious ravings often, Reanna would bathe him with cool water, and then cry herself back to sleep.

Into her nightmares crept another terror, as she witnessed her beloved floating up to the heavens like the golden eagle in her song, leaving her very much alone in a cold, cruel world, where the sun no longer shone, and she would wake, silently screaming her rage to God. "No! No, you cannot have him!"

Billy continued to see that she ate her meals, and it was he who wired Raymond Dublin, explaining the reason for their long absence. He also made it a point to visit with Reanna for a couple of hours each day, bringing her news of the outside world and of the daily happenings around the town, for she still insisted on staying by Chance's side, leaving him in Billy's care only long enough to return to her room to bathe and change her clothing.

The marshal came to see them, he needed their statements about the shootings, but it was with a decidedly cold attitude that he interrogated them, and he seemed not to care if Chance lived or died. The cool, calculating look in his eyes sent a shiver of revulsion through Reanna as he towered over her in a distinctly threatening mien, but she had no time to dwell on the cause, so wrapped up was she in her concern for Chances welfare.

One night when she reached her most remote level of fear and hopelessness, her inner horror and despair bringing her down into the blackest doom, she began to scream, but then she felt Chance's heart softly whispering to her own. She stopped, straining her ears to catch the gentlest phrase … there it was again … from Chance's hoarse, dry throat, a rasping whisper:

"Reanna, Rea, my love …"

Reanna was instantly wide awake, and she flew to his side. "Chance! Oh, Chance! I hear you, my love, I am here for you." She covered his lean, familiar face with tender kisses of joy as tears of relief rained unnoticed down her face.

"Water," he managed with effort to rasp, and Reanna brought him a glass, assisting him as he drank, and then bathed his brow and darkly handsome features once more with a cool cloth while she whispered sweetly her joy.

"Oh Chance, I knew that you would come back, that you would not leave me. I love you so much, my darling, more than life itself. I could not let you …"

Her words stopped abruptly as she had a sudden vision of Daniel in his cell, bitter, hard and uncaring … because of her love, he had said, and it was as if the memory plunged a dagger into her breast. The pain hit her with force, and for a time she could not draw breath, not until she realized that it was, indeed, this love she had for Chance that had pulled him through, back from the brink of death. She had held him from it for hours at a time as she grasped his hand and prayed aloud, she had not done him harm. This was the truth, inescapable, eternal; the special bond of love that they shared. There was nowhere to run from it, no place to hide, and she wept once again with the joyful knowledge.

Chance improved steadily under Reanna's constant care, and since he was confined to bed, she stayed with him every minute, reading to him, speaking of the things in her heart, soul and mind, and Chance felt that he was beginning to know her better than he knew himself.

He, in turn, when he was well enough, opened himself to her as he never had to another human being, allowing feelings that he had thought long drowned to surface. The only thing he refused her knowledge of was his family, even though he spoke openly to her of his past. All he would volunteer was that he had left home at the early age of thirteen and made his own way in the world, asking nothing, and expecting less, of anyone. He did say that he had named his ship, the Ellen Dorothy, for his mother, but when Reanna would press him for further information of this unknown piece of his history, he would simply smile and gather her into his arms, stating, "You are my family now, my love, for always and forevermore."

At night now when Reanna would wake screaming in the grip of a nightmare, Chance would call to her and she would make her way into his arms, there to be warmed and comforted until she slipped back into peaceful slumber. Then she woke each morning in this manner, cradled within his strong arms, the comfort was bittersweet, the emotion of deep love she felt for him conflicting with her persistent inability to show him that love in any physical way. She would manage to slip quietly from his embrace, ever conscious of his wound, and try not to wake him, but he always knew the moment she left him and their eyes would meet, plainly sharing their pain without the benefit of words.

When Billy shared his knowledge of the shooting and divulged the man's name, Chance informed them that he must have wanted revenge. Chance had hunted his brother, who had brutally murdered an entire family, and it had been necessary to kill him. His brother had evidently wanted to even the score. But how had he known that Chance was here, especially since he had been in Nevada for so long now?

Reanna, not paying attention to the beginning of their conversation and having been so distracted when the marshal questioned her, never did learn the identity of the would-be assassin.

Luckily, Billy had seen the man and, acting on impulse, had drawn his gun and fired. By killing him, he had saved Chance from a second and most certainly fatal bullet. Chance had done something he had not done in years; he had dared to drop his guard, and so had failed to realize that they were being followed. He was indebted to Billy now for his life, as well as Reanna's, and it was driven home to him once more that he could never, ever, let anything sway him from his carefully honed instincts again, not if he were to survive for long in the world he had been forced to make for himself. He could pretend to be a part of Reanna's world, but the ghosts of his would keep him ever vigilant.

Chance would be well enough for travel in a few more days, and upon noting Reanna's pallor, he bid her take a long walk on the beach with Billy. She had spent too much of her time locked away in this room, caring for him, and there were dark circles beneath her eyes, which had lost their customary luster.

"Go, I want you out in the fresh air and sun," he ordered her, "and don't come back with your skirts dry."

With a smile of gratitude, she left him, seeking the solace of nature: the sound of the breakers on the rocks, the feel of the wet, salty spray on her face, the warm, rainy texture of the sand between her toes. How she longed to come back again someday!

When she returned there was a softer, healthier look to Reanna's pale skin, the sparkle had returned to her lovely eyes, mirroring her intrigue with the endless, sparkling water that they now had to leave. It was almost too late to be traveling through the mountains; there was always the danger of early winter snow at their high altitudes.

The first night of their return trip home, Reanna awoke from yet another of her nightmares, screaming her terror. Chance went to her and drew her close, but when she would not cease her tears, he became annoyed.

"Reanna, why? Why can't you put it behind you now, let it rest? It is over, you are safe now. I am here with you, and I will never leave you again. Stop … Stop it!"

As Chance shouted his last words, Reanna looked up at him with fear showing plainly in her large, luminous eyes, and he quickly regretted his flaring anger. He clutched her tightly to his chest, apologizing over and over, and pulled her down to lay with him.

Reanna, finally able to accept his comfort, slept peacefully, and from that night on when they slept, Reanna would be held in Chance's arms, and when she woke, it was not to scream and sob, but to reach out for the comfort of her beloved's embrace.

They reached home without further incident, and were celebrating their safe arrival, and Chance's narrow escape from death, in Raymond Dublin's parlor.

Taking a tentative sip of her sherry, Reanna stood and began to cross the room, intending to play her guitar which was lying on top of the piano.

Chance's dark gaze, as usual, followed her gracefully swaying hips, and when she suddenly swooned, he found it difficult to believe. Reanna had passed out cold.

Billy raced to town for Dr. Farley while Chance carried her inert form up to her bed. Carmelita was there, fussing and fretting over her while they all anxiously awaited the doctor's arrival, who, upon completing his examination, announced his findings in a grave voice.

"Reanna, you are with child."

Chapter 8

Reanna felt the fiery walls of Hell closing in on her, searing her mind, scorching her soul, the source of the combustion emanating from the darkest depths of her inner being. Her mind recoiled from what she knew was the terrible truth, screaming as if in burning pain, "No! No ... It cannot be! I will not let it be true!"

She began to pummel her abdomen, then to claw at it in a desperate attempt to rid herself of this hideous invasion while Dr. Farley made every effort to restrain her from self-hurt. She would stop it from being true! She would kill it!

Oblivious to all else, her screams of denial went on as her struggles gradually lessened, for strong arms now held her gently down, her strength was waning. Chance, assisting the doctor in response to Reanna's screams, continued to hold her down in a vise-like grip until, realizing the futility of her struggles, she gave up, exhaustion finally claiming her. She lay with her eyes tightly closed, attempting to shut out the image of Chance, who was watching her with fearful eyes.

She obediently swallowed the warm liquid pressed to her lips and Chance's concerned visage grew blurry, and then faded to darkness as the laudanum helped her to find surcease in deep, dreamless slumber.

Completely stunned by what he had just witnessed, Chance turned an accusing glare to the doctor. "What the hell was that all about?"

Raymond, Carmelita, and Billy all waiting in the upstairs hall, having been brought by Reanna's screams as well, wondered the same thing.

"Doctor?" Prompted Raymond; his haggard appearance suggesting that he would rather not be apprised of the reasons for his daughter's furious reaction.

Leading Chance through the doorway to the others, the doctor gave them the grim news, his seasoned heart aching for the plight of the beautiful young woman now resting beyond.

He took a deep, quavering breath and related his findings. "Reanna became pregnant during her abduction. I'm sorry Ray," he finished, looking at his old friend in anguish.

His words hung leaden in the stillness. No one spoke, and the moment seemed to stretch for an eternity, until Dr. Farley's voice broke the silence. "You have all got to hold yourselves together, now more than ever, for Reanna will need all of your strength and support, every bit you can give. This child, the burden she carries, is too much for her to bear alone. I will leave this medicine to help her sleep; she will have need of it again. Do not leave her alone. Have someone with her at all times to prevent her from harming herself."

Chance's hard, lean features paled, to be replaced by raw, unleashed anger as he stormed past them without a word. The others made their way downstairs more slowly, reaching the back door just as Chance, upon Lancelot, careened wildly away.

Dr. Farley patted Raymond's shoulder in commiseration, the sadness that lurked in his eyes saying all that had to be said between them.

Carmelita was attempting to stem the flow of her tears. Billy left the house quietly, with drooping shoulders, and Raymond made his way, in shock, back to Reanna's side to wait out the night.

Reanna fought off the last vestiges of sleep near dawn the next morning as Chance's garbled, off-key singing penetrated her dreamless repose.

Opening her eyes slowly, she whispered his name, sitting up to meet his red-rimmed eyes. He stared mutely at her, startled that she had awakened, and was not able to offer her a word of comfort. He could think of none in his befuddled state and was not sure that he should even try.

The pain of knowledge returned, cutting her keenly, and she sobbed, "Oh, Chance, there is no hope for us, no hope at all now."

Realizing that she did, indeed, need his comfort, he sat on the edge of her bed, pulling her into his arms. It took him by surprise when she pulled violently away.

"No! Don't touch me! Not while I carry this vile proof of their abuse. Not until I have rid myself of this burden -"

Chance grabbed her shoulders, shaking her so that her head dipped back and forth. "Reanna, stop it! Stop it, you hear?"

Realizing what he was doing, he loosened his grip to run a trembling hand through his dark, tussled hair. He reached into his coat pocket and pulled out a bottle, raising it to his lips, before offering it to her. "Here," he said in a flat, dead voice, "drink this, it might help. Done wonders for me."

Before he could raise the bottle to her lips, Reanna caught the odor of whiskey on his breath, shuddering in revulsion. "Whiskey!" she screamed as she grabbed the bottle from his hand, hurling it across the room to send shards of glass flying everywhere as it smashed against the far wall.

Fighting back the nausea that threatened to envelope her, she pummeled at his hard chest, screaming at him, "How dare you! How dare you bring that stinking poison to me! I cannot stand the smell of you! Get out!"

Chance backed away from her fury, mortified by her actions, at a loss as to just what it was that he had done, other than to have imbibed a bit too much. Had she gone completely mad?

She leaped from the bed, her hair swirling wildly about her, and began to distractedly pull on her clothes, heedless of

Chance's presence. While he would have welcomed the sight of her soft curves clad only in the sheerest of underclothing any other time, it now served only to heighten his fear that something was drastically wrong with her.

She bolted to the door, but Chance was ready for her. He instantly jumped for the portal, arriving just before she did to block her path of escape. He grasped her shoulders, his fingers sinking into her tender flesh as she struggled against him.

"Reanna, where do you think you are going? What has gotten into you?" Chance shouted.

"Let go of me, just let me go!" Reanna screamed, on the brink of hysteria, but Chance held her fast, suggesting in a calmer mien, "The doctor left medicine, Reanna, perhaps you should take some."

"I will not. I do not need to sleep; I just wish to be alone for a while." She drew a deep breath, calming herself. "Let go of me, please, Chance," she implored.

His indecision lasted only seconds, and he relented, releasing her shoulders, and stepping aside to let her pass. "Go then, but remember that my love goes with you," he whispered. She lurched through the door, down the stairs, and out to the barn where she bridled a mare, not bothering with a saddle. She kicked the beast into a swift gallop, hoping to rid herself of her unwanted burden, leaving Pier to stare mutely after her, the overwhelming sadness he felt plainly showing in his dark eyes. It was with great relief that he welcomed Chance to the barn a few minutes later, the bounty hunter having decided it would be in Reanna's best interest to follow her, which was just what he intended to do. Reanna slowed the mare only when the terrain became too rocky and steep for the safety of the horse. She may not care for herself, but she would never willingly bring injury on her mount. As they climbed toward her destination, that secret place she had always gone to be alone, the scenery became ever wilder and more beautiful.

High atop the rocky overlook, she reined in and dismounted. Walking to the edge of the precipice, she gazed out over the cliff, uncaring that just a step away it plunged sharply to oblivion somewhere far below. As the wind whistled through the great pines, she stood, simply staring out at the raw beauty sweeping endlessly before her without really seeing it.

Dashing the unbidden tears from her eyes, she tried to imagine a way out of her dilemma. Hating every alternative, suddenly hating all of life, which, it seemed, was grossly unfair, a low moan rose from her tightened throat. Here was the place, she decided, to end it all. She swayed toward the edge, the weight of her burdens carrying her forward, when suddenly her shoulders were clasped from behind and she was pulled roughly backward, away from certain death.

Gasping in surprise, she whirled to face Chance's dark, forbidding expression and opened her mouth to speak, but Chance hushed her with harsh accusation as he reprimanded her.

"Just what the hell were you thinking, Reanna? Trying to pull a stunt like that?"

He pulled her up against his chest, leaning his chin on the top of her fragrant copper hair, and ground out, "Marry me, Reanna. Marry me and give your child a father, for he is innocent of any wrong. My love for you has not changed; do not let their sins ruin your life. As I love you, so shall I love any child that you bear. Say that you will marry me."

The pain in Reanna's sea green eyes showed so deeply that it cut him like a knife, and she felt only a well of grieving emptiness for both of them.

"How can you Chance? How can you want me now, with this terrible sin that I carry? It is pity, not love that speaks for you now I think, and I will not rest until I am rid of this tangible evidence of my shame. Now let me be!"

She pulled from his embrace, swiftly mounting her mare once again to careen back down the path she had taken, with Chance following right behind her on Lancelot. It did not take the much larger horse long to overtake the small mare; as they ran astride on a wider stretch of the trail, he reached over and yanked Reanna from her horse, holding her wriggling form firmly against him, finally reining to a stop.

"Reanna, don't! Do not let them win! Don't let their evil take the love that we have found and kill it. I need you, Rea. I need your warmth, your goodness; I need to drink in your beauty, to live with your grace, for without it I am nothing but an empty shell, as I was before I found you. Our love will triumph over the hatred that would snuff it out."

Reanna sobbed against him, "Why Chance? Why does it always seem as if there is something trying to tear us apart? Why is there always something else to remind me of those horrible men and the atrocities they forced me to endure? If not the scars on my body, or the sickening stench of tobacco and whiskey, then it is the endless, horror filled nightmares I yet entertain, and now this! This evil thing growing within me! When will it ever stop?"

She was close to hysteria once more, and Chance could not blame her. He merely held her tightly, knowing with sudden clarity the reasons for her reactions earlier when he had so thoughtlessly offered her a drink of whiskey.

When her sobs finally abated, Chance led her to a large pine, sitting beneath it to lean against its great trunk, pulling Reanna down onto his lap. Rocking her in his arms, he whispered into her ear all the words of love and comfort that he could find in his heart, which swelled with a love for her that he had never known before. She finally lifted her lovely countenance to his deep brown gaze and whispered, "Take me home now, Chance. I want to go home."

For the next few days Reanna wandered aimlessly over the ranch with her pups at her heels, seeking to sort out her conflicting emotions, to quell the tide of angry, hateful thoughts that had replaced her gentle dignity.

Raymond saw to it that she was never really alone, however, having posted one or more of his men to follow her everywhere, but discreetly, without her knowledge. He would be damned if he was going to let his only child take her own life. After Chance had informed him of the one attempt, he was determined that there be no chance of another.

She relived Chance's words over and over in her mind, and although she knew him to be right, she could not rid herself of her revulsion, could not change the way she felt. Reanna simply did not want to give birth to this child and spent most of her time seeking a way to end her pregnancy.

Having finally decided upon what, to her way of thinking, was the wisest course of action, she was determined to act upon it, and was saddling her mare in the barn when Chance came up behind her. Placing a warm kiss on her neck, he murmured, "Reanna, you are driving me to madness, moping around as if you wish you were dead. Marry me, Rea. I will never give up until you finally relent."

Afraid that he would guess her intent, she retorted sharply, "Will you please stop badgering me? I need time to think."

She was going into town to visit Aggie, for she was certain the saloon girl would know of someone that could help her, much as she hated being indebted to the woman. As she saw it, abortion was her only way out. But Chance could never know of what she planned, for she was certain that he would put a stop to her intended actions. So, she turned a withering look his way, and in an icy tone continued, "Now, if you will excuse me, I am going riding."

She mounted her mare and haughtily turned from Chance, urging the beast toward town slowly, so that his suspicions should not be aroused, plunging into a gallop only when she was beyond his vision.

It was not long however, before she became aware of hoof beats behind her. Casting a glance over her shoulder, she saw that she was pursued by Chance on Lancelot. Knowing it to be a useless endeavor, she urged her mare to a faster speed, but the huge stallion was soon stretching his long legs beside her mare, and Chance leaned over, grabbing the reins from her hands to bring both the horses to a standstill, the mare with flanks quivering, flecked with foam.

Chance clenched his fists, the muscle in his cheek twitched slightly, the only outward, visible signs of his great anger, but Reanna, furious that he had followed her once again, failed to heed these warnings. She attempted to wrest the reins of her mare from his grip, without success.

"Damn you, Chance Nolton! Just who do you think you are, following me about, interfering with my plans?" Reanna screeched.

"Plans?" Chance questioned, his voice tightly controlled, a brow raised speculatively. "And just what plans might those be?"

Reanna stared at him mutinously for a moment, seething with fury, before she slid from the mare, running to her fullest extent in order to escape him. It was another act of futility, for Chance was off Lancelot, overtaking her before she had run more than a few yards. He reached out to grab her shoulder from behind, intending only to halt her forward flight, but the backward jerk caused her to lose her balance, and she tumbled toward the ground.

Chance acted immediately, falling with her, and rolling to absorb the brunt of the impact, his breath escaping sharply as they hit.

Reanna attempted to rise, struggling violently against him, kicking, and flailing with all her strength. "Let me go, damn you! Let me go!"

Chance was no longer able to control his fierce anger, her words serving to spur it on, and he slapped her face soundly, seeking to halt her hysteria, before grabbing a handful of her long-tumbled locks to yank her head back. Rage, a fiery red glow, burned in his dark eyes as he met her gaze, her green eyes smarting with tears of pain.

"Let them win then, Reanna! Let the hate fill you until you smother under the weight. Let our love burn in hell, and all life with it!" He shoved her away from him, rising to turn away, his voice defeated. "I'll not beg you anymore. I'm through with it."

The finality in his voice broke through her anger, and as he walked from her, it was her entire life that walked with him. If he had ripped out her heart to carry with him, it would have been no more painful. An intense, lonely emptiness surrounded her, and she sprang to her feet, running after his retreating form, pleading, "Chance, please, don't hate me. Just don't hate me, for I could not endure it. Please …"

Chance stopped, turning very slowly to face her. "No, Rea, I could never hate you, never that. I only hate the evil you are allowing to seep into the gentle heart that you once owned, destroying our love, everything. Where is all the love you once held so dear? Where is the gentle spirit I fell in love with? Why can't you feel it now, and use it to triumph over your hate? I would help you, yet you constantly refuse me and reject the love that I would offer you. I cannot remain here to watch you destroy yourself, Reanna."

With sudden clarity, Reanna suddenly saw just how irresponsible her actions must seem to Chance, and she clutched his arm, tears making her eyes bright as she sent him a beseeching look. "No ... Wait Chance, please ... Don't leave ... I need you. You have my love, you have my very soul, and if you go you shall take everything, and I would be left empty."

He took a deep breath, his anger dissipating in the face of her heartfelt plea, and Chance enfolded her in his strong embrace, softly stroking the silken mantle of her hair.

"Let me help you then," he said tenderly. "You saw what bitterness did to Daniel ... it ate away at him until nothing was left. Do not make the same mistake Reanna; don't let it happen to you. Let the warmth and beauty of love heal you. I do love you, Rea, more than my own life. Just love me back. Don't shut me out, don't reject me. Love me, Reanna."

"I do love you Chance, with all my heart. I cannot see, though, how you can still love me, still want to marry me, when I carry another man's child. Will you still want me months from now when I grow large with the life of this baby? Every day would but serve as a reminder to you of my shame, and the sight of me would eventually repulse you."

"My God Reanna! Why can't you understand that I love you, that I cannot help but love your child, for it will be part of you, and I could never hate anything that is part of yourself."

Reanna looked deeply into his dark eyes, realizing that he spoke the truth, her own mirroring the awe dawning within her. She spoke softly, "Under your hard, stern looks Chance Nolton, lies one of the most tender human beings that I have ever had the good fortune to know. But ... what if this child carries their looks ... or their temperament?"

"She will look like her mother and will possess her mother's gentle soul."

Chance smiled down at her tenderly, and she could not help but smile in return, her arguments stilled by his faith in their future.

Suddenly a shrill cry pierced the stillness, and they looked up to see a golden eagle plying the air currents on great, outstretched wings, its timely appearance bringing to their minds the meaning of the song about the majestic bird. Understanding began to replace the pain in Reanna's shimmering green eyes, and Chance, never hesitant, seized upon his first opportunity.

"Now, Rea … say you will marry me. Now." He prompted gently, and Reanna, gazing into the dark depths of his eyes and finding only love there, answered, "Yes, my love, if you truly want me, then I will be yours."

Elated by his victory, Chance felt his heart leap within his chest. Lifting her in his strong arms, he threw his head back in joyful laughter and hugged her tightly. Reanna was finally able to laugh with him, but deep within her heart she felt a chill of foreboding for their future.

Reanna became more curious as the days went by and no mention was ever made of Chance's family. She was working on the guest list for their wedding day, yet whenever she questioned him about inviting them he would instantly change the subject, and she began to feel that something was dreadfully wrong. If Chance did have family, they should be present at his wedding. He had spoken of his mother, perhaps she was the only family he had? Why then not send for her? She simply had to know, and so decided, since other more artful tactics had failed, to be perfectly blunt.

She approached him in the barn where he was currying Lancelot and hearing the soft rustle of her skirts he turned, a smile of approval on his lips as he gazed at her soft curves.

Taking a deep breath for courage, Reanna plunged in. "Chance, why do you constantly refuse to discuss your family? Are you … I mean … was your mother … were you fatherless?" She finished quickly, finding it difficult to meet his eyes.

A loud guffaw came from the neighboring stall, and Pier raised his head over the partition, smiling broadly. A level gaze from Chance however, sent the little Mexican ducking immediately back to work.

Chance then turned back to Reanna. Leaning against his huge stallion, he raised a sardonic brow, but was not inclined to answer her just yet.

She had hit a sore spot, Reanna realized with a sinking feeling in the pit of her stomach and wondered if she had committed a grave error in asking, but he suddenly threw his head back, roaring in laughter. The sudden loud noise frightened Lancelot, who sidestepped suddenly, causing Chance to lose his balance, and he toppled backward into a pile of dirty straw and manure.

As he looked up in disbelief, Reanna's hand flew to her mouth to cover a startled gasp, and laughter surrounded them as they both turned to see Pier at the entrance to the stall, doubled over in mirth.

Reanna was just wondering whether she should gracefully depart the scene of the crime when Chance became convulsed with fits of laughter himself, until, gazing up at her, he remembered the cause of his predicament and answered her soberly.

"Reanna, I do not think it possible to be fatherless, do you? But if you are asking if I am a bastard, then let me set your mind at ease. I have a mother and a father, four brothers, and another sibling of whose gender I am unaware, since I left home just before my mother was due to give birth. We lived on a run-down farm, not much more than a shack, in the hills of Tennessee. I am not overly proud of my background Reanna, thus my reluctance to speak of it."

"Oh Chance," cried Reanna, hurrying to kneel by his side. "How can you say that? They are your family, no matter where they live, or the work they do. If you are one of those who has started with nothing in life and turned opportunities to your advantage, to become what you are today, then you should take pride in your achievements, and in the place where it all began. Chance, it would make me so happy to meet your family! I had hoped that they could attend our wedding, but two weeks is certainly not time enough to have them all here. Still, perhaps we could …"

"No Reanna!" Chance firmly cut in with finality to his voice that ordinarily would have brooked no argument. "I left my family long ago and have never gone back. I have not the slightest desire to set eyes on them now, or ever."

Shocked by his flat refusal and the unmistakable bitterness in his tone, Reanna attempted to reason with him despite the hard, closed look on his face that clearly warned against such folly.

"Please, at least invite them Chance, or let me write them. It would mean so much to your mother, I'm sure, and so very much to me."

Chance's brow furrowed in anger, but Reanna, ignoring the warning, threw herself completely into convincing him to at least let his family know of their upcoming nuptials.

"Chance, your mother has a right to know that you are getting married and will soon be a father. And what of your own father, you are his son; surely, he would desire to know all that you have accomplished during all the years of your absence."

Chance rose abruptly, his muscles taut, his facial features rigid in a black fury. "Enough!" he bellowed, his voice thundering in Reanna's ears as he turned to swiftly saddle Lancelot. She shrunk from his wrath, but daring one last effort, she plead, "Chance, won't you please listen to me …"

Chance did not bother to answer as he mounted the huge black stallion. Sending her a fulminating glare, he nudged Lancelot into action and rode from the barn.

Reanna was stunned by his vehement reaction and turned hurt, bewildered eyes to Pier, who had by now, smoothed his shocked features over with an outwardly calm countenance. Gently placing his hands upon her shoulders, he reassured her, "Reanna, I am sure that he did not mean to hurt you by his angry words. I'm sure that there must be some deeply rooted hurt in his past, something that even he does not want to face."

"Yes, Pier, I believe you're right." She decided then and there to follow Chance in the belief that once he had some time to cool his temper, he might wish to talk after all.

Chance strode angrily into the Horseshoe and ordered a beer at the bar, his tone menacing. Downing it in rapid gulps, he slammed the empty glass onto the counter, ordering another.

Billy and Bob, lunching at a corner table, exchanged glances until Bob had a sudden idea occur to him. He turned to Billy with a knowing grin.

"Premarital jitters, perhaps?"

Billy returned his grin with a mischievous one of his own. "Maybe he just needs some friendly advice or could be he yearns for the company of another understanding male."

They stood; their meal finished, and slowly ambled across the room to stand beside Chance, only to sniff suspiciously as soon as they came near.

Bob, taking the initiative, cautiously suggested to the bounty hunter, "Chance, whatever reason for the questionable odor that clings to you, perhaps a change of clothes may be appropriate?"

Chance sent a baleful glare their way, then, recalling his fall in the barn, became even more furious, silently cursing both the female race, and a certain black stallion that just might find himself in possession of a new owner before long.

How the hell had he forgotten something as noticeable as the distinct aroma that clung to him? A certain red-haired female, that was how. Well, there was nothing to be done about it now but endure the smell, and the stares, until he could withdraw from his present company with some semblance of dignity, but how that was to be accomplished he hadn't a clue.

"Chance, is there something you wish to discuss?" Billy questioned tentatively, but his dubious smile faded quickly as he became the object of a dark, ominous look.

Chance's voice was coldly controlled. "No, thank you Billy, I have nothing that requires anyone's attention." He glared at Billy a moment, and then asked, "Was there something else?"

"I – I guess not," Billy stammered, and backing away, suggested, "Bob, I think that we best leave Chance to his own company."

"I agree," Bob answered, holding his nose as they turned to leave, and noticed that Reanna's shadow darkened the doorway.

Sending her a look of commiseration, both men left her to her less than happy gunman, who now glared at her hesitant approach with clenched jaw.

Reanna, garbed in a softly flowing green gown, with the warm afternoon sunlight streaming in the door highlighting her halo of darkly burnished, fiery curls, presented such a fetching sight that Chance immediately felt his anger draining away.

Taking a deep, fortifying breath, she once again dared to broach the subject that had her curiosity completely piqued.

"Chance, why? What is it about them that bothers you so? Do you think that I would not understand whatever it is?"

Chance, his gaze softening as he peered closely at her, turned and stared for a moment into the liquid in his glass as he casually swirled it around, glancing up once again to meet her eyes, considering his answer.

"It is not something that I am able to discuss, Rea, not even with you. I am sorry, I truly am, but I just … cannot." He dipped his head, once more gazing into his glass, and Reanna moved close, placing her hand gently on his arm. "I am sorry Chance; I should not have … obviously your past holds painful memories for you. Perhaps someday you will wish to speak of it, but for now, well, I have been most insensitive, and I apologize for that. Please, let's forget it for now."

Their eyes met once again, the love they felt for each other flowing freely between them, ever giving, gaining strength from the other. Their lips, of their own accord it seemed, drew slowly closer and met with an intensity that sent waves of a deeply rooted yearning through Reanna's body before Chance unwillingly lifted his mouth from hers.

"Chance, oh Chance …" Reanna murmured, then, recalling suddenly their surroundings, blushed profusely and moved a step back from his disturbing warmth. Seeing her discomfort, he searched for a safer topic of discussion. "I suddenly remember that I had someone I desired for you to meet. I would like to take you there now, if you are up to it."

Chance lost the last vestiges of anger as he leaned toward her, inhaling her sweet fragrance, and was dazzled by the wide smile she turned upon him, when she answered, "Yes Chance, by all means, let's go now."

Crooking his arm for her to take, he said, "As you wish, milady. Please accompany me to our humble home to be."

Arriving at the ranch, they started toward the door, but Reanna hesitated and, turning wide, innocent eyes to him, dared to venture, "Kind sir, I believe that this meeting would be much more pleasant if you would only bathe and change your clothing while inside."

Chance smiled wolfishly as a vision of Reanna's delicate hands sponging his back, and other places, came immediately to mind …

"Your wish is my command, Milady."

He led Reanna into the kitchen, calling out in his deep voice a summons that brought forth, with a soft step, the most beautiful Indian woman Reanna had ever seen.

"Reanna, this is Lada, who I have retained as a cook and housekeeper. I was lucky enough to meet her in Reno, for she has already proven her worth by feeding me like a king when I am here, and if you look around, her talent for keeping house speaks for itself."

Right now, Reanna had eyes only for Lada, and as they appraised each other there flowed between them an instant mutual admiration.

When Reanna did finally look about her, it was with astonishment that she noted the vast differences from her last visit. Everything sparkled with cleanliness, the woodwork gleamed with a soft luster, and a pot of herbs simmering on the back burner of the newly blackened stove lent a subtle, spicy fragrance to the air.

Her pleasure showing clearly in her eyes, Reanna smiled warmly and extended her hand to Lada. "Lada, I am pleased to meet you. I am Reanna Dublin, soon to be Nolton, and I feel very fortunate that you will be living here with us. The thought of working the ranch, plus trying to cook, which I am not much good at by the way, and clean, was frankly, quite overwhelming."

The two women quickly became immersed in conversation, and Chance, realizing that his hopes of Reanna helping him bathe was not to be, excused himself to do his own washing with a heartfelt sigh of disappointment.

Lada and Reanna shared a pleasant afternoon, Lada finally daring to share her sad story with someone who would not judge her but offer sympathy and support.

When Chance rejoined the women, the three of them enjoyed a late afternoon snack of light, flaky biscuits spread with sweet honey that Lada had prepared while conversing. It was, all too soon it seemed, time to leave.

Reanna impulsively hugged Lada, saying, "I am so glad that we met, and I know that we will become great friends."

"I feel much the same," Lada shyly answered.

Reanna could not help grinning on the way back to High Ridge, and Chance, noting her happy, carefree smile, could not resist teasing her. "Just what do you find so amusing, my love? Is it possible that you are dreaming of our wedding night, and that the thought of such sheer bliss brings that lovely smile to your adorable lips?"

Reanna's eyes widened in mock astonishment as she quipped, "Chance Nolton, you really are a scoundrel!" She then continued in a more serious tone, "Actually, I was thinking about the warm, loving man that lurks beneath your hardened exterior, about the happy life that I am certain we will have in our new home, and Lada, with whom I am very impressed. I just know that we will become very good friends; I felt it as soon as I saw her. She is wonderful Chance, and so are you."

Chance, smiling widely at her enthusiasm, decided to press the issue that was uppermost in his thoughts. "I knew that you would like her, my love … and I will show you just how warm and loving I really can be once we have spoken our wedding vows and I have carried you to my bed, and -"

"Stop! You mischievous rogue!" Reanna cried, and kicked her horse into a gallop, racing Chance all the way back to the ranch, their joyous laughter carrying on the wind.

Parting that evening, when Reanna raised her lips to his, Chance kissed her hand, lingering to savor her sweetness, and she suddenly found herself wishing that tonight was their wedding night. As he gently pulled away, his eyes held her in a gaze of such naked hunger that it burned her very soul. She felt almost overwhelming stirrings of desire, but this time there was no fear at all in the look she returned, only an intense longing burned in the depths of her own eyes.

Her strong feelings found no reprieve, until two days before the wedding, when Reanna found that she was once more besieged by self-doubt. What if the wedding night that Chance teased her about did prove to be a disaster? What if she froze, gripped in the bonds of fear, and was repulsed by his advances? Would he, once he felt the slight bulge of her stomach stretching with the growing child within, lose his desire for her?

These fears, once they had crept into her thoughts, took firm hold, whispering their ominous threats, spreading their clinging tendrils to choke out her new-found happiness and effectively quell her impatience for marriage.

She must find out. What would her reaction be to Chance's overtures when the time came? He was, after all, a virile, and she was certain, demanding lover. She had to know now, before the wedding … before it was too late and Chance was tied to her for the rest of his life, unable to share the physical love of his wife. It would most assuredly bring ruin to both of their lives.

Pacing back and forth, Reanna came to the realization that she must do something, but what? It was then that the seed of an idea took hold, and as it grew, a glint of determination appeared in her eyes. But how would she find the opportunity to catch Chance alone tonight? Would she be able to carry her determination that far?

"I must!" She muttered urgently, and stood in thought, nibbling her fingernail, until a knock at the front door interrupted her musing, and she moved to answer it. "Why, hello!" Reanna greeted, smiling down into the freckled face of the little Grady boy from town.

Awed by her beauty, he swallowed and took a deep breath, barely able to force the words from his constricted throat. Why, she must be the most beautiful lady in the whole world! "M-M-Miss Dublin, I have a message her for you f-from Mr. Nolton ... and he paid me a whole gold coin to deliver it," the boy finished proudly.

"Thank you ... Lee, isn't it? Be sure to give your mother my regards," Reanna said kindly.

The boy smiled, gulped again, and turned, high tailing it to his pony, able once more to breathe normally when he put some distance between himself and the beautiful mistress of High Ridge ranch.

Reanna eagerly tore open the envelope and pulled out the folded message from Chance. As she began to read, a smile of satisfaction curved her lips, and then shone from her eyes as she regarded the note. Here, in her hand, was the answer to her dilemma.

Chance would pick her up tonight at seven thirty and bring her to his new ranch. He had a surprise for her and wanted them to be alone when he presented the gift to her. It was perfect! Almost as if he had read her mind. Casting a quick glance at the clock on the mantle, she realized that she had better hurry.

Dashing into the kitchen, she grasped Carmelita's plump arm, crying, "Oh, Carmelita, could you leave your stew and help me please? I must bathe again, and quickly, before Chance arrives to pick me up!"

Studying Reanna's eyes, shining with true happiness as they had not in so long a time, Carmelita could refuse her nothing. "Of course, my child; I'll put water on to warm while we lay out your clothes. I can see that you are very excited about something, and it has to do with your young man I'll wager."

"Oh, you're a dear." Reanna impulsively hugged the older woman before she fairly flew out to the well. Carmelita, chuckling, followed more slowly. They dumped their buckets into the large pots used to heat water, she needed only to have it pleasantly warm and retreated to her bedroom to choose the outfit she would wear that evening, taking particular care in her choice.

The thin white blouse was shot with threads of smooth satin, lending it a silky luster, and yes; she would daringly leave the tiny pearl buttons undone as far as, no, a little further, than decorum allowed. The skirt she decided upon was of the softest suede which glittered with tiny black beads, strewn in random as the full gathers fell from the waistline, giving the creation a sparkling effect as she moved.

Carmelita came in lugging two buckets of warm water, and Reanna dashed to the door intending to bring up more, but Carmelita stopped her.

"Your help is not necessary, child. Pier is on his way with the rest."

Reanna flashed Carmelita a wide smile and noting only happiness in her only charges beautiful green eyes, together with the clothing laid out carefully on the bed, made her own astute suppositions. "I see that you have planned well, Chica, and I wish you luck." She gave Reanna a long look, causing her to blush profusely.

"Thank you, Carmelita," was all that she could think to answer as the rest of the water was delivered.

"You have a good time tonight," Pier wished her, adding the rest of the water to her tub, and Reanna's full lips curved in a saucy smile. "Yes, I think that I will."

Alone at last, Reanna added rose oil to her bath water, disrobed, and slid into the warm, fragrant water, a sigh of pure bliss escaping her softly parted lips. As the heat relaxed her muscles, her tensions too, began to drain away, and she felt nothing but the smooth liquid caressing her silken skin.

Reanna stood, rising from the tub on long, shapely legs, and stepped from the rapidly cooling water and dressed carefully, examining her reflection closely in the mirror. She brushed her long hair until it gleamed; the soft, shining locks alight with red fire that danced along the crest of the curly waves. Then, gathering up the heavy mass, she pinned it atop her head, securing the length with a carved ivory comb.

Her blouse she left unbuttoned just far enough, daring to reveal a hint of her smoot, creamy breasts, the silky, thin fabric hugging what remained clothed so closely that Chance would be sure to take an interest, although she was sure that he would need very little encouragement in that area.

Satisfied with her appearance, she met her father in the parlor to await Chance's arrival. He raised a speculative brow at her attire, and the bewitching sight she presented, but elected to refrain from any censuring comments after all she had been through. She was, after all, to be married shortly.

He glanced down to the floor, taking note of the heavy leather boots she wore, and questioned, "You feel the need to carry your gun tonight, Rea? Carmelita told me that the two of you were to spend a quiet evening together at his ranch. I hardly think you will have need -"

She cut him off, stating bluntly, "I will not be without a gun ever again, Papa."

Raymond merely grunted, conceding the point, for the unsettling image of Cal McPherson's cruel face suddenly came to mind. He wished that he had some inkling of Cal's whereabouts, for surely the devil had some twisted idea of revenge, if he still lived.

A carriage approached; the sound cutting into his thoughts as it drew alongside the front porch. Reanna kissed her father's weathered cheek. "That will be Chance, Papa. I must go now." As an afterthought, she informed him, "I may be late, so please don't wait up."

With a nod of acceptance, Raymond sent his daughter out into Chance's waiting arms, after placing a warm shawl over her shoulder.

Reanna was abnormally silent on the drive to what, in a short space of time, was to be her new home, causing Chance to glance keenly sideways at her stiff profile more than once. It was very tentatively that she extended her arm for him to help her from the carriage once they arrived. He suppressed a groan of dismay; surely, she was not having second thoughts about marrying now that the day was nearly here? He would definitely not accept such news with anything close to good grace.

He drew the shawl off her shoulders when they entered the house, inhaling the fresh, soft scent that clung to her, and then paused to admire the striking beauty that stood before him. There was something different about her tonight. Was there an alluring curve to her lips, a promise in the way she stood? No, he was merely imagining that which he so hoped could be true.

Extending his arm, he said in a carefully neutral voice, "Allow me to escort you into dinner, Milady."

Reanna hesitantly took his arm, allowing him to lead her into the parlor, a blush still staining her cheeks from his close perusal of a moment ago. She had resolutely pushed her fear aside on the ride over, reminding herself time and again that she must find out, before it was too late, if she could be a wife to Chance in every way, or if she would have to refuse to marry him. She closed her eyes and breathed deeply in an attempt to steady the erratic beating of her heart.

She opened her eyes to find herself standing in front of the large stone fireplace, alight with a bright, crackling fire that lit the room, reflecting in the highlights of several tables, exquisitely carved of heavy mahogany, the legs twisting round various exotic birds which were delicately carved into the sturdy, but lovely furniture. A bottle of fine wine stood on a table in front of the settee, which was covered in a tapestry fabric, alive with more of the birds on wing and half hidden in strange foliage. It presented an unusual, but totally lovely setting, the crystal glasses and delicate china lending an elegant yet cozy atmosphere.

A sudden thought occurred to Reanna. Had Chance read her mind? Had he planned this intimate, romantic setting with certain knowledge? She felt her face flush with heat again, he stood so close that she could feel his warmth with every fiber of her being, and he ravished her with his gaze as his eyes raked the length of her, as if he wanted to devour every inch of her.

His voice was low and husky as he sought Reanna's approval. "What do you think of our home now, Milady?"

Reanna found it difficult to focus on his words, so overcome was she by his obvious burning, raw hunger. "I – I think…"

"Wait, there is more," Chance promised softly, gently taking her arm to lead her to the settee. "Sit and enjoy the wine, I have something special for you."

As they seated themselves, he reached around the far end of the settee, and Reanna gasped as he drew forth the most beautifully fashioned guitar she had ever seen. The entire neck was inlaid with mother of pearl, set into highly polished olive wood. The base, sprinkled with iridescent lily of the valley blossoms, was the same inlaid mother of pearl.

She reverently took the proffered gift, running her fingers lightly over the strings as she gazed with awe upon its beauty.

Chance's voice near her ear was low. "Well?"

She glanced up at him, incredulous at this precious gift. When she finally found her voice, she whispered, "Chance, how? Where did this all come from?" She indicated the contents of the parlor with a sweep of her arm, and then stroked the guitar lovingly, adding, "I have never seen anything so beautiful!"

"I own a trading vessel, remember? That certain piece comes from Italy, it is to be part of your wedding gift. You are not disappointed, I take it?"

His nearness sent waves of pleasure through her; she felt tears of joy prick her eyes as she answered. "Disappointed? Oh, Chance, I hardly feel worthy of such a gift. I have never seen anything so lovely, not in my entire life."

Chuckling at her heartfelt pleasure, he demanded in a husky tone, "Play it for me, Rea."

She found it hard to tear her eyes from his compelling dark gaze, but she managed to lift the guitar, lightly testing the sound as she tried the strings, and soon the haunting melody of a love ballad filled the room, the soft words touching both their hearts, reminding each of them of the great love shared between them.

Finished, she laid the guitar aside and turned to face Chance. "Where is Lada?" she whispered softly.

He answered slowly, "She will not disturb us Rea, nor will she hear our words."

She leaned very close, her words no more than the merest whisper of sound. "It is not words that I am thinking of." She placed a light, delicate kiss upon his lips, her invitation obvious.

The sweetness of her softly parted lips served to intoxicate, and Chance gently took her head between his large hands, sinking his fingers into the silken soft mass of her hair. He pressed his mouth firmly to hers in a searing invasion of fiery passion, and when he finally released her to draw back, breathless, she could see the fire plainly in his dark eyes, for their glowing red depths reflected his raw desire.

Reanna caught her breath, so mesmerized was she by his gaze, and then his mouth was plundering hers once again, chasing away any doubts she may have had of this night. He covered her face with hot, urgent kisses, returning again to the sweet warmth of her mouth before blazing a hot trail down the slender column of her neck to the deep opening of her blouse.

Groaning as he tasted the softness of her breast, he suddenly jerked away, staggering to his feet with an effort. His breathing was harsh and labored. "Reanna, I think it is time we called a halt to this evening." His voice was ragged, as if he were in great pain.

Reanna rose slowly, her gaze wide and luminous in the firelight, and moved to stand in front of him. Deliberately placing her hands upon his shirt, she began to undo the buttons, sliding her hands beneath the fabric to gently caress his muscular chest, hoping that he would not notice their trembling.

Chance caught her roughly by the shoulders, and she winced slightly as he grated out, "Stop it, Reanna! Don't you know yet what you do to me? Be fairly warned Milady, you will send my passions soaring beyond the limits of endurance."

She placed her trembling fingers against his lips. "Let us soar together then, Chance, soar high like the golden eagle. I wish to prove my love for you, and would know that you can love me, soiled as I am by others."

Chance grated his teeth. So, they were back to that again? "You little fool," he ground out, in the same instant lifting her easily to lay her before the flames of the hearth, placing her upon a thick, hooked rug. He looked steadily into her luminescent green eyes and seeing nothing but a reflection of his own raging desires, he forged ahead with deliberate intention, covering her face and neck with hot, passionate kisses until she could breathe only with heavy sighs of aching pleasure.

Slowly, sensuously, he removed each article of her clothing, his burning eyes sweeping every revealed part of her with hot desire, his searing tongue trailing over the same path blazed by his gaze.

He paid homage to the creamy globes of her breasts, licking the peaks of her nipples to hard points of desire, and then moved down the still slender length of her abdomen to her long, beautifully proportioned legs, pausing to massage her feet and taste each toe, before working his way back up her legs, stopping just short of their juncture.

A groan of painful desire escaped her softly parted lips, and Reanna opened her eyes, wondering at the cessation of this purely primitive pleasure, her newly awakened yearning evident in her large eyes.

Chance had begun to remove his own clothing, and Reanna, with much effort, so drowsy was she with passion, sat up and took the chore from him, softly caressing the hard planes of his chest, covered with a dark sprinkling of softly curling hair, moving on as his male beauty was revealed to her. He helped to remove his pants, and she found herself averting her gaze from the sight of his lean hips and his manhood, but, gaining courage, reached out to gently touch him there, and was rewarded with his soft groan of pleasure, daring finally to glance at his erect, throbbing member, her eyes widening in surprise, and a little fear, as she noted his large size.

Meanwhile, he watched her reactions intently from beneath hooded lids as the firelight cast her lush body in light and shadow that constantly changed with the flickering light. He dipped his head to her breasts, reveling in her soft moans of pleasure as his tongue circled her thrusting pink nipples, teasing them once more to hard red peaks.

As his hands roved over her smooth, silken skin, Reanna felt with every fiber of her being, oblivious to all else, the burning fires of Chance's unrelenting, demanding passion, his pressing hands, the depths of his eyes, becoming the hot flames of that fire, threatening to devour her as if she were no more than a piece of kindling in his searing path.

Chance had reached the limit of his endurance, and with an intense need to smother the fires that drove him, he positioned himself above her and began to drive his urgent desire home.

She stiffened at that moment, tightening her muscles against his entry. He held himself rigid for a moment, an impassioned, painful moan rising from deep inside of him. She was not ready after all. When he would have pulled away from her, she clung tightly to his broad shoulders, sinking her nails into the bunched muscles of his back, almost tearing at his flesh.

"No!" she whispered. "Finish it Chance … love me …"

She raised her head to kiss his lips, her breasts brushing the fur of his chest softly, and he was lost to all reason.

Consumed as he was in burning flames, his fear of damaging her future enjoyment of their passion lasted only a moment, quickly replaced by the blazing, undeniable need that he had ignored for too long.

He groaned, "Reanna …" before he drove into her silken warmth again and again, swept away on an intense level of pleasure such as he had never known as he soared to the heavens with the golden eagle, crying out his fulfillment as he at last filled her with his seed, and Reanna knew a fierce joy for the pleasure she had given him, for she had bestowed upon him that which she had never given any other man, her total surrender.

She had not reached the heavens as she had fully expected to, offering herself openly and freely to the man she loved with all her heart. A deep sorrow consumed her, bittersweet with the aftermath of their passion. She thought I am too impure. Chance does not mind, but I will forever know the shame of what has gone before, denied the pleasure of total happiness with the man to whom I would gladly give everything. She turned her face from his concerned gaze and stared into the flames of the fire, blinking back the stinging tears of disappointment.

Chance turned and gathered her close in his arms. "You know I love you, Reanna Dublin," he murmured, before they both drifted into a light slumber.

It was much later that they dressed and sat on the floor near the hearth to partake of a light repast, cheese, biscuits with honey, and fresh pears, sliced and chilled, washed down with the wine they had neglected earlier.

As she bent to draw on her boots, Chance nearly choked on his laughter. "Reanna, why did you feel it necessary to wear those, and that hidden gun of yours? Did you think that perhaps you would flee from me if I became too amorous? But yet, that cannot be the reason, for I distinctly remember that it was you, little vixen, who seduced me."

Reanna blushed crimson at his gentle reminder but offered no excuse for carrying her gun.

Slightly vexed by her silence, Chance prompted, "Well, there must be some reason you refuse to be without it, even in my presence. When I found that you had it at the prison, I assumed it was because you were traveling in unfamiliar territory. I am incapable of protecting you, is that it?"

He sat heavily on the settee, pouring himself another glass of wine. Savoring it slowly, he said levelly, "Well, I can't blame you I suppose. It seems that each time you have needed me I have been elsewhere, haven't I?" When he glanced up at her, she could see plainly the self-blame with which he berated himself.

She flew to his side, and perching beside him, wrapped her arms around his neck. "Oh, Chance, never think that! It was you who rescued me, and even saved my life several times. You have not failed me yet my love, not ever. You cannot hold yourself to blame for others actions."

As she passionately spoke these words, she remembered that Chance had told her much the same thing not long ago and it was with a more enlightened tone that she continued, gently explaining her need.

"Sometimes, Chance, when I am not with you, alone on the ranch or riding, or even after you leave me at night, I fear to be alone. When the house is silent, and everyone sleeps, I imagine that I hear things. Please try to understand, Chance, it has nothing to do with any shortcomings on your part."

An image of Cal McPherson, loose somewhere in the night, suddenly flashed through Chance's mind, along with Raymond's words, "His body has never been found," and cold fear clutched at his innards.

"Yes, I see your need for the gun, Rea," he said softly, "and I agree with you. In fact, make sure that you are never without it again, my love."

Surprised at his easy capitulation, Reanna thanked him with a tender kiss of gratitude.

Chance bent his head to hers, reaching a hand to softly stroke her cheek. "Would you entice me again, my love?" he whispered hoarsely.

Reanna slowly bent and slipped off her boots ...

Chapter 9

A yellow sun rose to kiss the snow-covered mountain peaks, tinging them with a pink iridescent glow and chasing the shadows of darkness gradually down the mountainsides while rapidly warming the chilly morning air.

Reanna woke gradually, blinking the sleep from her eyes as she breathed in the fresh, crisp air that fluttered her window curtain. She leisurely yawned, and then stretched contentedly. What a perfect day for a wedding.

Her wedding! She gasped and sat up, rubbing the sleep from her eyes. Her heart skipped a beat – she had better hurry. There was much to be done! Quickly snatching up her robe, she hastily tied it at the waist and was ready to dash down the stairs when Carmelita entered, laden with a tray full of tempting dishes for her breakfast. Bacon, eggs, warm toasted bread with apple jelly, custard, fresh applesauce, and coffee, all lent their distinctive aromas to the room, reminding Reanna just how ravenous she was.

"Carmelita, you shouldn't have!" she exclaimed. "Especially with all the wedding preparations that you must certainly be in the midst of."

"Do not worry yourself," Carmelita hastened to reassure her. "I have several girls from town here helping already. Besides, it is your last breakfast in your father's home. I will miss you, Reanna. It will not be the same with only that old bear, your father, to care for."

Reanna giggled as she dug into her breakfast, watching Carmelita's large, familiar form bustle around the room, straightening clothing, flicking her dust cloth lightly here and there, and plumping the pillows on her bed.

"Carmelita, you know that you love nothing more than telling that old bear what to do, scolding him for not eating enough, or forgetting to wipe his feet, you live for it."

"That may be so, Chica, but this morning he has been worse than a rampaging bull. He has most of the men busy setting up for the wedding, but is he satisfied with that? No. He is constantly changing the arrangement of the tables, fretting over the barbecuing steer, he has even invaded the kitchen once! And now … now he is out there with Pier, the two of them trying to string Japanese lanterns in the trees for later tonight. I don't think that they will get too far. You would think that it was they who were getting married, they are so nervous."

Reanna finished eating and rose to lean out her window, spying her father and Pier and a few of her father's men working out back among the extensive gardens. Her father was gazing distractedly around, rumpling his hair with his hand, and then walked to a tall pine, slowly circling it while he eyed the branches above him, his hands on his hips.

Carmelita moved to stand beside her, saying, "Humph, I had better get back to that kitchen, before he decides to invade it again and drives everyone crazy!" she gathered up the tray and hastened down the stairs, leaving Reanna to don a simple cotton dress sprigged with bright yellow violets against a dove gray background. She left her hair unbound, and it hung loose to her waist in shimmering waves of dark red curls.

Nimbly descending the stairs, she made her way through the busy kitchen, calling greetings along the way, and stole a look out the backdoor before venturing out. Pier was just handing her father, who was balanced precariously on a ladder beneath the tree he had been inspecting earlier, a brightly colored lantern.

Preoccupied with how the total effect looked thus far, Raymond reached up to hold the lantern in position before tying it to the branch above him, asking anxiously, "Pier, are you sure this should go here? Are they spaced far enough apart? I don't want them to be too thinly spread though. Do they hang low enough do you think? Damn! Son of a ..."

Pier raced forward to support the toppling ladder before Raymond could fall, admonishing, "See what you have done again boss? Put that ladder up in such a hurry that you almost broke your neck! We need you in one piece to give the bride away. Will you please let Sean see to these now?"

"I agree Papa." Reanna came to stand beside him, relief at his close call, making her knees feel weak.

Smiling indulgently at her, Raymond felt a need to defend his actions. "It's not every day that a father's only daughter gets married, now, is it? But very well, I will leave this to the men, for at the rate I am proceeding we won't finish these until a week after the wedding. And I want you to gather the flowers and decorate the way you like, Rea, then try and get some rest. This promises to be a very tiring day, and I would not have you unable to attend your own wedding."

"Oh Papa," Reanna smiled happily; "nothing could keep me from marrying Chance today but promise me that you will do nothing to keep yourself from attending, as well."

"Very well," Raymond relented, his hands in the air. "I will do nothing but supervise this grand event, you have my word."

"Thank you, Papa." She brushed a tender kiss to his bronzed cheek before taking up the basket and shears she had brought out with her and began to wander among the gardens, snipping the best of the late blooming roses that were, as yet, undamaged by frost. She was also able to find several clumps of sheltered black-eyed Susan and Asters, cutting them along with fragrant pine boughs to fashion into garlands for the mantle and doorways, humming softly as she worked, a lilting serene sound that floated with the slight breeze stirring the evergreens that shimmered in the morning light.

There were more than a few of the men, hearing her happy tune, who wished that she weren't quite so content in her choice of a husband, but Reanna did not notice their yearning looks, returning to the house with her fragrant burden swinging from her arm. She had much work to do.

She sat for the rest of the morning weaving garlands of pine, attaching large white ribbon bows every so often and draped them on the fireplace mantle and doorways of the parlor. She placed vases of roses and other flowers wherever there was space on the polished tables and the mantle, the roses a mixture of whites, yellows, pinks, and varying shades of red, filling the house with their fragrant perfumes.

She then gathered what was left of the pink roses, tying them with a large white ribbon with trailing streamers. This would be the bouquet she would carry to marry Chance.

Carmelita rushed in from the kitchen, wiping her hands on a towel as she inhaled the floral scents. "Mmm, it smells as nice as it looks in here. You have done an excellent job Rea, but you must hurry now. Your bath water awaits you, and then you must rest for a while before you begin to dress. It would not do to have you looking peaked for your wedding."

"Thank you, Carmelita, I am a little tired. Oh, I will miss you so after today."

"You will visit Chica," Carmelita assured her, patting Reanna's hand. "Now on up to your bath."

As Reanna turned to mount the stairs, Carmelita hugged her to her bosom, whispering, "I will miss you, also, my child. Now go, for I have many more things to do before the guests arrive."

Reanna was just emerging from the fragrant water when there was a knock on her door. Reaching swiftly for a towel, she called, "Yes?" as she began to pat herself dry.

Carmelita stuck her head in around the partially opened door. "I thought it necessary that we speak before you lay down to rest, Reanna."

"Please, come in Carmelita." Reanna invited her, looking at the older woman curiously as she slipped her robe on.

Carmelita sat heavily on the bed and beckoned Reanna to do the same, patting the place next to her. "Sit with me."

Reanna obeyed, asking, "What is it, Carmelita?"

"Reanna, I do not want you to get the wrong impression about what I am going to say, for I have grown very fond of Chance. I just want you to realize a few things. You have, I know, always seen Chance as a gentleman, a knight in shining armor, and he has always treated you with kindness and respect, but he is a gunman. He can be harsh and cold as a winter wind, ruthless and unforgiving if it is necessary, as a second nature, and you will not always find it easy to live with such a man. Your very sweetness has tempered some of his steel, but at times it will take all the inner strength that you possess to forge a life together. You have captured his heart, which can whisper as softly as the breezes of spring, and you hold it in the palm of your hand. He has proven beyond a doubt his love for you these past months, so guard it well, and never forget the man beneath the civilized veneer. If you remember these things, you will have a happy future with this man of your choice, and I wish you a long life together ... now, get some rest if you can my child, before this afternoon."

Reanna tenderly placed a kiss on the older woman's cheek, saying, "I'm sure that Chance and I will be very happy." She smiled softly as Carmelita left the room, closing the door quietly behind her.

She laid back on her familiar, comfortable bed and sighed. This would be the last time she ever would sleep in this room, where she had grown up, she thought, and drifted into a light sleep.

It seemed she had slept no time at all before Carmelita was back, shaking her from her slumber. "Wake up, Rea. It is time for you to dress now."

Reanna yawned and rubbed the sleep from her eyes, then threw back her covers and disrobed, slipping quickly into soft silk undergarments and widely ruffled petticoats, stiffened to make the skirt of her wedding gown bell profusely out from the waist.

Reanna adored her dress, which her father had ordered long ago from France, in hopes that his daughter would marry, and he was finally getting his wish, she thought with a sentimental smile.

Carmelita helped her into her dress, a lovely creation of white satin with a very full skirt, softened by yards of frothy lace ruffles around the décolletage and hemline, and below the elbow down her arm to her wrist, forming the loose lower portions of the puffed white satin sleeves. She turned so that the pearl buttons that ran down the back of the dress could be fastened and smoothed the bell of her skirt. On her feet went the special white boots that Molly, Kenny, and Billy had given her as a wedding gift, pleasing Reanna beyond words. Now she could feel at ease with the cold comfort of her derringer tucked inside, the need for its security strong even on this, her wedding day.

She checked her appearance in the mirror, studying her reflection carefully, and was pleased with the image that peered back at her. The boots went well with her graceful dress, surprisingly, for the soft suede glimmered with delicate beadwork which sparkled from beneath her gown when she moved.

Carmelita pulled back only the sides of her hair, gathering the silken waves softly from her temples to the back of her head, and then braiding it with a satin ribbon to hang down her back against the cascading copper waves of her waist-length hair. Over her long tresses they then draped the simple piece of white lace that her mother had made and worn on her wedding day, securing it on each side of her darkly burnished head with iridescent mother-of-pearl combs.

As she scrutinized her reflection in the mirror yet again, Reanna decided that some sort of necklace was needed, but which of her pieces should she wear? It was just then that Belinda bustled into the room, excitement glittering in her large blue eyes, and announced, in her matter-of-fact way, "Oh, Honey, just wait until you open this! It is a wedding gift from your amorous groom, and he would like you to wear it today."

Reanna took the leather encased box from Belinda's outstretched hand and opened it, then drew her breath in sharply as she spied the contents, a necklace of fine gold chain bearing a single, large, teardrop shaped pearl. All the more beautiful for its unadorned simplicity, Belinda moved to fasten the luminous piece about Reanna's neck, the large pearl nestled enticing against her creamy cleavage.

"You look perfect, just beautiful!" gasped Belinda, then almost shyly held out another, smaller box. "This is my gift to you, Rea."

Reanna took the second box and exclaimed, "Oh, Belinda, it's lovely!" as she lifted the cover. It was a simple gold bracelet made of interlocking circles, and Reanna immediately clasped it onto her wrist, saying, "You shouldn't have Belinda, this is too fine a gift by far, but I do thank you." She hugged her friend warmly.

"Oh pooh, since you are really my only good friend, it was the least I could do, for I value that friendship greatly, and besides, who else do I have to spend money on, other than myself?"

That was Belinda, Reanna thought fondly, trying to make light of any situation, inept at accepting thanks, and she kissed her friend's cheek. This caused Belinda once again to launch into speech as she made herself comfortable on the edge of Reanna's bed.

"Well, Honey, this is it. Everything downstairs seems to be ready. The steer smells heavenly roasting, and all the guests have arrived, including your groom. And he is, from what I can see, awaiting you eagerly, like a hungry stallion chafing at the bit."

Reanna's eyes widened at Belinda's suggestive remark, and she gasped, "Really Belinda!" but her friend merely grinned at her embarrassment and noted, "Seriously, though, Reanna, it is time for the ceremony, then you will forever more be his. And I know that the two of you will be very happy together, so you don't need good luck, but I will wish you both long lives in which to share your love."

Reanna pressed another kiss to Belinda's cheek, tears welling in her large expressive eyes as a small smile played about her generous lips.

Belinda reached out to tenderly brush the tears from Reanna's cheeks, saying, "Brace up now Honey, it is time to meet your father downstairs." She took her friends' hand, both descending gracefully the length of the staircase to Raymond, who was anxiously waiting at the bottom.

As Reanna's eyes met the steady gray of her father's, she immediately noted the mixture of great joy, and sorrow, held within their depths. Sorrow that his daughter would be leaving the home he had kept for her all her life, and joy in knowing that she was happy in her choice of a husband, someone strong to protect her from harm.

He smiled soberly, chiding gently, "I thought today was to be a festive occasion, yet it seems that all I have seen today is women's tears." He threw up his arms in mock exasperation, and Reanna rushed into them, sobbing, as Raymond held her tightly to him, incapable of further speech himself.

After some minutes Reanna pulled away, brushing the nervous tears from her cheeks, and taking a deep breath, she slid her arm through her fathers, and they slowly made their way out into the warm sunlight down the path strewn with rose petals into the garden to stand before the minister. Chance was waiting with Kenny in his wheelchair, and to his left stood Molly as Reanna's matron of honor. The guests were lined up on either side of the wedding party straining to get a glimpse of the lovely bride on her father's arm.

Chance caught his breath at the beauteous vision of Reanna coming toward him. His gaze swept the length of her, drinking in the beauty of her dress and the lovely countenance of her face, her cheeks stained with the slight hint of blush, then losing himself in the glittering depths of her bright sea green eyes, which sparkled like sunlight on ocean waves. His heart beat faster at this discovery, and he flashed her a wide, welcoming smile, more sure now than ever that this day would bring him all that he could ever want in his life.

Reanna's eyes, meanwhile, admired the picture Chance presented as he stood in the sunlight, his hair gleaming blue-black, tall, and masculine in his formal attire. He wore an elegantly cut double breasted coat and tight-fitting pants all in black, a white silk shirt, and boots in black of the finest leather gleaming with the deep luster of polishing, and a narrow black silk tie was knotted at his neck.

Reanna felt a peculiar flutter in her heart as she met the knowing look in his deep brown eyes, and then she reached his side.

She turned a dazzling smile upon him, and they gazed deeply into each other's eyes, love flowing freely between the two of them, filling them with expectant warmth, and then the minister cut into their private world as he began to intone the words of their union. Yet, their gazes wavered not through the entire ceremony, each claiming the other's life and love, until death do them part, nay, through all eternity.

When the last words binding them had died, Reanna raised her face to accept Chance's kiss, only this was no chaste endearment as she had expected, but a hot, consuming demand that seemed never to end, drawing every ounce of breath from her body.

He reluctantly withdrew his lips with a deep throated chuckle, and Reanna blushed crimson as hearty applause engulfed them from the assembled guests, but she had to smile.

"Chance, you scoundrel! You irrepressible rogue!"

"Let us not forget angel, sweetheart," he replied easily, not at all concerned with her chastising tone, and then they were surrounded by friends and well-wishers congratulating them repeatedly. When Billy pushed his way to them, he stood gazing at Reanna in open, rapt admiration, speechless until Chance cleared his throat noisily, recalling him to his manners.

"I – I'm so glad for the both of you, and I wish you much happiness," Billy offered shyly, then could think of nothing else to say, so he stood once again in mute admiration of the bride before she hugged him tightly, pressing a soft kiss to his cheek. She smiled as she noted the familiar blush color his face.

Later, Chance teased her, saying, "Milady seems to be but a vixen in disguise, besotting poor Billy with her many admirable charms."

Reanna laughed and questioned in lighthearted humor, "Do I detect a proprietary note of jealousy in your voice, Sir Knight?"

Chance slipped his arm around her creamy shoulders, answering softly, "My jealousy could be easily aroused where you are concerned, my love, never doubt that. But I know that Billy is like a brother to you, and so do not mind if you wish to practice your wiles upon him." He stopped and smiled wolfishly down at her, then continued, "As long, that is, as you promise to really use them on me later tonight."

With a great pretense at shock over his words, Reanna widened her eyes. "Oh, you cad!" she gasped as she playfully tapped his broad shoulder with her hand. "Rogue!"

They both laughed merrily, and Chance took her arm as they began to mingle with their guests, propriety demanding that they dance with many others as the music began, but they constantly sought each other out with their eyes, which shone with happiness and already obvious devotion.

When the music changed to a slow, sensuous rhythm, Chance eagerly sought out his new bride. Gathering her into his arms, he leaned close, his penetrating brown eyes impaling her so that it was impossible for her to glance away.

"I believe this is our dance," he stated, his husky voice softly caressing her soul, leaving her without the strength for words. She merely clung to him, to his broad muscular form, enjoying the warmth and tingling excitement of his strong arms wrapped gently around her.

She suddenly had the heady desire to leave all these people, family, and friends, to be alone with the man she loved. As she gazed raptly into his eyes, she saw that he felt the same, for his eyelids had grown heavy, over the red fires blazing now in the brown depths.

Her breath caught in her throat, and she felt it being drawn steadily from her when Chance leaned slowly forward and pressed his mouth tenderly to hers. Her knees buckled, but his strong arms supported her, the only thing keeping her from sinking to the ground. She was consumed by a raging desire such as she had never before known.

"Reanna, what is it? Are you feeling unwell?" Chance questioned her, but deep within his eyes she saw that he knew her hidden thoughts, and although her head was beginning to spin, she managed to find a thin thread of her voice, whispering with effort, "I think that I must sit a minute, that is all. It must be all the … excitement."

He smiled in his knowing way and lifted his hand to trace the full softness of her lips, then wordlessly lifted her and, ignoring the inquisitive looks cast their way, carried her easily to one of the chairs at a refreshment table, sitting her down and handing her a large, cool glass of lemonade.

"Perhaps you should lie down for a while Reanna," he suggested softly, but she demurred.

"No Chance, I really am feeling much better already. It has been such an emotional day, but I will be fine as soon as I catch my breath, and perhaps try one of those delicious looking pastries over there."

She glanced up at him entreatingly, and Chance chuckled, amazed at how much her appetite had increased in just the past several days, but gladly went off to do her bidding, returning with three of the sugary confections, which she promptly hastened to devour.

Chance could not resist the urge to tease her. "I can see that you are well on your way to eating your father out of house and home before you leave, my little mother to be. It is most fortunate for you that I am a rich man."

They both laughed playfully at his easy banter, but deep inside Reanna felt the familiar clutch of fear twist her innards, if only for a moment. She had become adept at pushing this unwanted child from her thoughts.

It was then that Reanna chanced to glance up, and her face was immediately awash with pleasure, causing Chance to curiously follow the direction of her gaze.

He tensed, automatically reaching for the butt of his pistol, then belatedly recalled that he had declined to wear them for his marriage ceremony, and so was powerless to stop the approach of the four Indians riding nonchalantly toward them on sinewy chestnut horses, led by one large warrior, slightly ahead of the others, on a huge, golden palomino stallion. Dressed in elaborately beaded and fringed buckskins that winked in the sunlight, the men wore fringed leggings and the lone woman with them, a long-beaded skirt and soft doeskin boots.

Reanna sprang to her feet, rushing headlong toward the oncoming group, leaving Chance with no choice but to follow Billy, who had appeared at his side, armed, in case the need arose.

The group dismounted, waiting silently as Reanna stopped in front of them, gazing lovingly into the eyes of the most incredibly handsome Indian warrior that Chance had ever seen. His eyes narrowed in suspicion as he continued to size up the warrior so seemingly favored by his bride.

The man's long, silky hair was worn loose and hung just below his shoulders, with a braid hanging on either side of his temples. His eyes, dark and fierce, black in a bronzed face, glittered with intelligence and life. Chance was not at all certain that he approved of the way those eyes were hungrily drinking in Reanna's beauty. The man exuded a very powerful, earthy sensuality, and caused the groom his first real pangs of jealousy he had ever known in his life. His eyes narrowed even further when his wife spoke, for there was a certain breathless quality to her voice. "Mansunama! I cannot believe that you are here. How did you know?"

"Reanna, how could I fail to know? On this your wedding day, I have come to wish you the love and strength of the earth, the happiness of a lighthearted wind, and all the pleasures of the abundant sea. Although I have lost my own heart's desire, I know that you have chosen wisely on your path in life. Will you open your heart to receive my blessings?"

Because the Indian spoke in his native Paiute tongue, Chance had not understood his words, and his muscles tightened in anger as Reanna threw herself into the warrior's arms, but halted his forward stride, astonished as she began to answer in the same language. Just when the hell had she learned Paiute anyway?

"Mansunama, I am ever so grateful that you have come to offer me your blessing. It means more to me than you will ever know. Now I will never need to doubt the success of my union with Chance, as we have the gift of your powerful magic helping to bind us ... I have missed you sorely these past years, my friend. I hope you can be happy for me."

She turned her attention to the tall woman standing just slightly behind Mansunama, and with an elaborate gesture of her hands, welcomed the sister of her best friend.

"Talohan, I am pleased to see you also, my friend. May we offer you refreshments? You have come a long way."

Reanna smiled softly at the Indian woman, sister to Mansunama, and Talohan returned her fond grin. She answered in a deep, husky voice. "We would like that, my friend, for we would share with you the joy of this day."

Suddenly remembering that Chance stood by her side and had probably not understood a word of their conversation, Reanna blushed profusely, ashamed of her bad manners. She turned to take his arm, but halted briefly as she was greeted by the harsh expression on his face.

Hesitantly, she began her belated introductions. "Chance … these are my … my friends of many years," she gestured with her hand toward the tall warrior, who obviously led the small group. "Mansunama, the revered medicine man, shaman, of the Paiutes' Red Thistle tribe, and his sister, Talohan. The other two warriors are Running Wood and Tutonqua."

As Chance's angry astounded gaze turned to one of speculation, he could not help but notice the serene beauty of the young Indian woman, who, like her brother, stood with quiet dignity, taller than the two others of the group. Her mischievous black eyes full of humor, gazed back unabashedly from beneath upswept brows, her dark, smooth skin was unblemished, and her waist length black hair shone brightly in the sunlight, as soft as watered silk, Chance guessed. His perusal was cut short however, as Reanna once again spoke to Mansunama in his native language.

"My friend, this is Chance Nolton, great friend and love of my heart, my husband."

She stumbled slightly over the word husband, finding it yet too unfamiliar a term, but her smile widened at the knowledge that she was, indeed, Mrs. Chance Nolton, as her husband stepped forward to take Mansunama's hand in greeting. The two men, their gazes locked, studied one another, each of them swiftly measuring the other's worth, garnering an instant respect for each other, while realizing at the same time that they would never become fast friends. They were tied together, though, by the love of the woman who stood at Chance's side.

Even Chance, hardened though he was, was moved by the great power that seemed to surround Mansunama. Strength and bravery, raw earthy knowledge, and sharp spiritual

270

insight were worn with a calm acceptance that would have crushed a weaker man.

Mansunama turned to Reanna, speaking again in his own language. "You have chosen well, my friend, for this Chance Nolton is a man without weakness of spirit. He would make a great warrior."

Reanna smiled widely, her pleasure sparkling in her eyes with the knowledge that these two important men in her life accepted and respected each other. She turned to her husband and grasped his hand softly, "Chance, Mansunama has given you a great compliment. He senses that you would make a true warrior, and only those that are strong and fear nothing are honored with that distinction."

Chance peered at Mansunama once again, closely, and then inclined his head slightly in the tall Indians direction to acknowledge his words of praise, then offered him their hospitality, whether the shaman could understand his words or not.

"You seem to be a great friend to my bride, so I would extend to all of you the offer of rest and refreshment."

"We would be pleasured, Chance Nolton." Mansunama replied in perfect English, which momentarily startled the bounty hunter, but he recovered quickly and motioned them to follow him, wending their way through groups of curious onlookers toward the food laden tables.

"Oh, Billy!" Reanna suddenly exclaimed. "I am sorry; I forgot to introduce you to my friends. This is Mansunama and his sister Talohan, Running Wood and Tutonqua."

The Indians gravely acknowledged the introduction, and Billy bound himself highly impressed with the civility of these people, whom he had been taught to hate as savages and masters of cruelty. Of course, that had been his father and brothers talking, and he should not be surprised that their words were proven to be untrue, he thought.

"Let's help ourselves to some lemonade, and then find a place to sit." Chance suggested, "Billy, why don't we gather some chairs and set them under the tree in the side yard."

The Indians sat cross legged on the ground while the others settled themselves comfortably in the chairs, and Reanna turned to Chance and Billy.

"Would you like to hear the story of how Mansunama and I first met?" she queried, and Chance leaned forward, raising a sardonic brow.

"To tell the truth my love, I await the tale with bated breath. Please, enlighten me, if it is not too much trouble."

Reanna began. "I was ten years old and fond of riding by myself to a lovely meadow where I could play my guitar and think about my mother. I did not want to burden my father, who brooded often enough at her loss. It was very quiet there except for the birds. The breezes carried the scent of wildflowers, and I would sit with my back against a certain large boulder, soaking up the heat of the sun. One day I had dozed off, and was awakened by a deep, ferocious growling. I froze in panic as I spotted a brown bear lumbering directly toward me. I forced myself to stand, thinking to inch my way around the boulder. It was not much of a chance, but it was the only one I had. It was a futile effort, for the bear was almost on top of me. I could see the sun glinting on his huge white teeth, his mouth open and ready, when suddenly the beast faltered in his tracks, an arrow found its mark, piercing the bear's belly. He dropped in his tracks, and I felt as if I might do the same, but someone came from behind to support me, a young Indian man. He gestured for me to go with him. We climbed to safety among some high rocks, afraid that the bear would not be truly dead, and while I struggled to catch my breath, we really looked at each other for the first time, each of us feeling an instant friendship."

Reanna met Mansunama's black gaze, their mutual devotion showing plainly, the shaman letting his feelings show but briefly before hiding them. He remembered well the first moment he had laid eyes on Reanna. It was not exactly the way she recited the story, for he had loved her totally at first sight, and he recalled with fondness his first glimpse of her startling green eyes. But she did not know that, and when he spoke, he betrayed nothing of this private passion.

"Yes, and she tried very hard to thank me, but we did not speak in each other's tongue. The wild gestures she made with her hands in that attempt caused me to smile and laugh, but then I squatted down and began to scratch pictures in the dirt. She followed my example, and we soon had a way to communicate."

Reanna favored Mansunama with a dazzling smile, but his lean warrior's face remained impassive, guarding his emotions well, and she continued the story.

"That was the beginning of our friendship, which was held steady through the years. Mansunama and I, and often Talohan, would meet in what we came to call Bear Meadow as often as possible. I taught them English and music, and they in turn shared with me their own language and many of their musical ballads, such as the one about the golden eagle that I sang for you Chance."

She did not add the heartbreak she had felt when, three years ago when she was sixteen, Mansunama had to cease his visits to the meadow. She had not seen him in those three years at all, although he had remembered her birthday each year, sending her exquisite gifts. She was truly honored by his appearance here today.

Realizing that they were neglecting their other guests, Reanna invited Mansunama to play her guitar after she introduced him to several of her friends, including Lada, who was quite timid in the tall warrior's presence until he placed a hand upon her shoulder and smiled warmly, thus calming her fears of rejection by others of her race.

It was Billy though, that showed a keen interest in Lada from their first introduction, dancing attendance upon her through the afternoon, but she kept an established distance between them, fearing the duplicity of a white man's motives after her treatment at their hands.

A hush fell over the assembled guests as the first strains of Mansunama's song wove its magic, his earthy voice softly canting in the rhythmic music of his own tongue. Everyone was spellbound, even though most could not understand its meaning. As the last notes drifted away, he began another song, this one in clear English, an old Paiute ballad of blessed love.

Realizing that this song was a gift to their joining, a blessing, Chance and Reanna exchanged a melting look which spoke the volumes of their deep love for each other. Mansunama did not miss the look, and it caused his heart a sharp pain even as he felt elated for Reanna's obvious happiness.

As the afternoon waned to an early dusk, the newlyweds bid goodbye to their friends, and Reanna hugged her father tightly, tears smarting her eyes now that the time had come to leave her childhood home, to begin a new life.

"Be happy Rea," Raymond whispered, his voice harsh with emotion, and his daughter straightened her shoulders and turned to her husband but was caught speechless by the sight that met her eyes.

Pier stood with their mounts ready, Chance's huge black Lancelot and next to him, a small Arabian mare, pure white, with the characteristic dished face and intelligent deep brown eyes. Her ears pricked forward, taking an interest in the throng of people who danced in the gathering darkness.

Reanna was unable to move, her feet rooted firmly to the ground, until Chance grasped her arm and led her closer to the two horses, and at her bewildered look, Chance explained. "A wedding gift, Milady. Do you like her?"

"Oh yes," gasped Reanna, running her hand over the mare's silken muzzle. "She is beautiful, Chance!"

"No more beautiful than the lady who will ride her," he whispered, raising a hand to gently stroke her smooth cheek, his eyes speaking volumes as they deeply probed hers.

"But you have already given me so much," Reanna objected, tears smarting her eyes once again.

"Reanna, my love, my heart, I have never known such happiness as this day has given me. It seems as though I have been waiting forever to bring you home. To our home, to fall asleep in your tender embrace, to wake in the morning with your beautiful green eyes before me. There is not enough in this world to express my thanks for your love, not nearly enough. Now let's go home Reanna, to the first real home I've ever had."

"To wake in the morning with you beside me is all that I ask," she said softly. "All I will ever ask."

They picked their way homeward through the darkness, each silent with their own thoughts, relying on the horse's keener senses not to stumble on the rutted dirt road.

Chance's heart was filled with pleasure at Reanna's last words, to hear that she wanted to sleep with him, to live with him in their own home, was pure bliss to his hardened soul. All the years of solitary wandering were finally at an end. He now had a wife any man would desire, a large ranch they could call their own, and they would soon have a child, the first of many, he hoped. To Chance Nolton, gunman and rogue, this would be the family that he could finally love and cherish; this was the longed-for peace that his heart had been seeking.

He heard the sudden giggle of his bride, and turned toward her, the white of her horse and her wedding dress, making her easily discernable in the darkness.

"And just what is it that you find so funny, Milady?" he queried.

"I was just thinking, Sir Rogue Knight, that I have had many surprises of late, and wondering if you have any in store for me in our marriage bed. I find the thought provoking … I am anxious to be there."

Chance laughed deeply, like the true scoundrel that he was. "And you, Milady, have thrown many surprises of your own my way, denting my knightly armor in many a place." He continued, but in a more serious vein, "But the most shocking had to be your Indian friends, and their timely arrival. How did he know that you were to be married today? Your father was just as surprised as you when he showed up."

Reanna regarded her husband intently under the cover of darkness, hoping that she had only imagined the tone of resentment that colored his voice. She answered slowly, wondering just how much she should say, how much he would scoff at in disbelief.

"Yes Chance, I can enlighten you somewhat. Mansunama is very … special. He listens to and understands the voice of the wind and is a master at interpreting dreams or visions. He comes from a long line of shaman, his power derived from them, since their people first walked the earth. You may be skeptical, but that is how he knew of our wedding, how he came to Bear Meadow at just the right moment the first time we met. I know that he was aware of my kidnapping, though he has said nothing on the subject, and I also know the reason he did not come to aid himself. But it is not my place to tell you all of that. You will come to know it someday, as I do. You will feel it in your heart, just as Mansunama surely does."

Chance had listened incredulously to Reanna's words, schooling his features to show none of his disbelief even though the night hid his expressions. Then he remembered the wrenching feelings in his gut when he had run from his heart, from her the night of the kidnapping, of something telling him to turn back, that Reanna was in great danger, but he had kept running, had failed to listen to that voice that had reached out to him, had not listened to his heart. Perhaps there was some truth to her words, after all, but he kept his voice carefully neutral when he spoke.

"It does not make a lot of sense to me right now Rea. I suppose it could be true, for there is something ... different about him, but it might all be coincidental. However, I am not inclined to sort it all out at the moment. I would much rather think about my lovely new wife, and the pleasures that await me in our bedchamber."

Having no rejoinder for that, Reanna lapsed into thoughtful silence, although she felt the rush of color stain her cheeks. Chance, sensing her unease, respected her need for private musings, offering no other comment for the rest of the ride home.

As Chance helped her down from her mare, he allowed his arms to linger about her waist, and she put her fears to rest. She now was aware of what to expect from their loving union and was certain that she could give herself to him without any reservations. If she did not find the fulfillment she sought, she still took delight in giving Chance pleasure through her body. She stood waiting while he unsaddled the horses and turned them into the corral, watching the smooth, delicate movements of her new mare.

"Chance, I have the perfect name for her! She is a lovely lady, and I shall call her Guinevere, to go with your Lancelot. What do you think?"

"You're right, it is perfect Rea," he whispered, coming close to her. "Now about that wedding night ..."

Alone in their bedroom, Reanna turned so that Chance could unbutton her gown, which he accomplished slowly and expertly, following his fingers with soft kisses down her back, then finally sliding it from her shoulders and over her breasts to lie in a shimmering pool of satin at her feet. He then, with the utmost care, removed the combs, lace, and ribbon from her hair, unpinning the dark, shining mass to fall in a molten cascade about her shoulders and hips in delightful freedom.

Reanna felt his burning desire in the touch of his hands as he pushed aside her hair to unclasp her necklace, and when he turned her to face him, she met his eyes, gazing into the driving raw passion of their red depths which he was attempting valiantly to hold in check. Her breathing ceased, and Chance drew his own breath in sharply as he looked into her eyes, into the promise that sparkled and swirled in their deep-sea green depths. The scent of roses that clung to and drifted warmly about her served to tease and delight his senses with the thoughts of touching her silken skin. God help him, he would need every ounce of strength and self-control that he possessed to proceed with what he knew he would have to do, and the thought gave him no pleasure, but brought instead wrenching pain.

While their gazes remained locked, Reanna raised her hands tremulously to the buttons of Chance's shirt, slowly releasing them, and then sliding the silk off his broad shoulders. She slid her hands down his bare, muscular chest to his trousers, and Chance held his breath as she paused, but unable to go on, she turned from him, bending to remove her boots and stockings.

Chance eyed the enticing view appreciatively, unable to turn away, and when she turned and encountered the fire in his gaze, her glowing skin turned pink, aware as she was now of his open perusal. Suddenly overcome with an unreasonable shyness, she nervously requested, "Chance, the lamp ... could you turn it down please?"

He made no move to do so right away. Instead, his heated gaze slowly, carefully caressed her entire body. He had no desire to turn down the lamp until he had clearly seen every bit of her, including that which lay hidden beneath the chemise she wore. He sighed regretfully, reminding himself that this was still very new to her, and moved to turn the lamp to its lowest setting, proceeding to do his own disrobing.

When he turned back, he saw that she had slipped quickly into bed, still wearing her chemise, which brought an amused smile to his lips. He slid into bed beside her and, wrapping his strong arms around her body, enfolded her in his love. He slipped the chemise from her, and then his mouth covered hers, plundering her sweetness while searing hot flames of desire spread through her body with rapid speed, burning them both with intense heat. He moved his mouth slowly, enticingly over her entire body, leaving none of it untouched, seeking, searching, finding, and finally melting her very soul.

Reanna, aghast, heard her own voice begin to beg, to plead with Chance to take her, now, and it was then that he chose to enact his painful plan.

He whispered hoarsely, "No, my love, I will not. It is your turn ... you who must take me. Prove to me that you can ... that you are truly ready to make love with me."

Her eyes widened in astonishment, and she lifted herself to one elbow, seeking out his eyes. "But did I not do that, just two nights ago?"

"Nay, precious Reanna, you did not. You allowed me to make love to you. You offered yourself as a sacrificial lamb, and, sweetheart, I will admit that I enjoyed it immensely, but I want more. I want you to prove to me ... and yourself, that you can love me back ... without reservation."

He whispered pleadingly, "Love me, Reanna," and lifted her to lay on the broad expanse of his chest, the crisp mat of his hair delicately brushing against the lush fullness of her breasts.

She realized, suddenly, that he was aware of the fact that there had been no rapture for her in their first union and was helping her to find that pleasure by allowing her mastery of the situation, to shed all her reservations and shame.

Still, she froze as she lay on him, unable to do as he asked. His words came, soft and warm, brushing her ear.

"Reanna, my love, you must, for both of us. You have nothing to fear now."

She began to move, slowly, easing her body ever lower until she could feel the hard shaft of his manhood pressing eagerly against her moistness, seeking to enter, but waiting for her to do the conquering.

Fevered, desperate yearnings coursed through her, but with those feelings came the shame, the memories of her active participation and cries of a drug induced joy, but there nonetheless, the last night of her kidnapping, and she froze, unable to consummate their act of love. Degradation brought the sting of tears to her eyes as she swallowed past the painful lump in her throat.

"No!" she cried in frustrated rage, weakly pummeling his chest, "I can't, damn you! You know I love you. You know I want to give myself to you. Please, Chance, make love to me!"

Chance grabbed her arms in a steely grip and lifted her off him, roughly rolling her over, pinning her down. Tears traced wet tracks down her cheeks, but he paid them no heed, his words grated harshly in her ears.

"All right, Reanna, all right! You don't have to continue, but I will not take you, not until you are ready to act like a real woman!"

With all the inner strength that he possessed, he turned away from her, wincing in pain and attempting to still his labored breathing as he presented his back to her, while through bitter tears Reanna moaned brokenly, "Bastard!" and turned from her husband to sob desperately into her pillow. And chance cursed himself for being every kind of fool.

Through the swirling mists, hard fingers grasped her to the ground. There was a rending noise, the sound of her clothes being torn from her, and the onerous stench of whiskey laden breath threatened her.

"No!" she screamed, struggling against her captor with all her might, and continued screaming …

Chance held her tightly, gently rocking her in his arms as he murmured words of comfort and love. A deep regret welled in his chest for his earlier actions, as he felt responsible in part for her nightmare. He continued to hold her as she sobbed and trembled in fear, pressing soft kisses against the silk of her hair until she quieted. She had been through so much. His words echoed the depth of his regret.

"I'm sorry, sweetheart. I am so very sorry if I hurt you. Forgive me, my love."

She wrapped her arms tightly about his neck and attempted to ease his guilt. "No, my love, you are not to blame. I understand what you were trying to do and realize what it cost you. But please, I beg of you, understand my need for your patience; for I still carry many scars that cannot easily be wiped away, just because we wish it so. I still need time to heal."

As he peered into her eyes, he saw the depth of her anguish mirrored there with her love for him, and felt his chest constrict with the intensity of the love that he returned in kind. They clung together tightly for the rest of the night, each realizing in their own heart that they would indeed overcome their past scars and present weaknesses, despite any hardships experienced along the way.

The next morning, with renewed spirits, the young couple began the ride to Lake Tahoe, where they planned to spend the next few days by themselves. They stopped to share an early breakfast at High Ridge with Raymond on the way. Chatting happily, they enjoyed the repast, then Reanna embraced her father, and he and Chance shook hands, Raymond secure in the knowledge of his daughter's happiness.

They met Mansunama as they neared their destination, the shaman sitting tall and proud upon his golden stallion in the morning light. At the fore of the small group of Paiutes, he waited silently as they approached. The Indians would have been gone hours ago, but they had stayed on to hunt this morning, or so they said. And it was true, they did carry several rabbits and ducks among them, but somehow, Chance sensed, this meeting had been contrived, in the guise of innocence, by Mansunama. It was there in the man's eyes as they deeply probed Reanna's, searching for her feelings of their wedding night.

Mansunama did feel Reanna's pain, the doubtfulness of her self-worth, and the magic strength of his spirit enveloped hers, bringing an elated glow to her features and a sharp pang of resentment sweeping through Chance.

In taking their leave, Chance finally admitted something else. Mansunama was deeply in love with Reanna. It was there in the Indian's fierce black eyes, carefully hidden, but Chance was an expert at reading people. At first, anger gripped him, for he could find no merit in having the shaman look upon his wife with the longing of one who is deeply, irrevocably in love, but then a sadness for the man settled in his heart, for he could not help but admire Mansunama. Now he understood that some of the heavy burden he endured came not from the weight of his responsibilities, but from a lifelong unrequited love.

Once they arrived at the lake however, Chance forgot all thoughts of Mansunama as he watched the rugged beauty of the landscape soften Reanna's features with pure pleasure. He could easily forget that anyone else even existed beyond themselves, and the paradise that engulfed them.

They spent most of that day in little conversation, needing no words between them, reluctant to shatter the peaceful tranquility of nature with human voices. Instead, they wandered aimlessly through the vast woodland, enjoying the musky scent of the damp earth and watching contentedly as the thin rays of sunlight, breaking through the green canopy above, danced upon fluttering leaves and bowed down now and then to honor the dark floor from which they sprang with a bright iridescence.

Exiting the dark peacefulness of the trees, they burst into the brightly lit meadow beyond that swept to the lake, encountering the late afternoon drone of late season crickets, and a few remaining blooming wildflowers, while birds called as they dipped and swooped among the tall grasses, singing their varied melodies. Reanna sighed as she gazed up at the majestic mountains, for even in the clinging warmth of this afternoon the scent of autumn lingered in the air. Already some of the trees were turning a bright color, and she knew then that the snow, always present on the mountain peaks, reflected in the water of the lake, would creep steadily down to blanket the world in white.

A low whine broke the stillness, and Reanna glanced fondly down at Modoc and Tasha, who had followed them obediently everywhere. She had refused to leave them at home, knowing how much they would enjoy this trip. Now they gazed up at her, their friendly brown eyes expectant, and Reanna gave them the sign that they were free to run. Happily, they raced swiftly to the water, bursting into the calm stillness frolicking and swimming, sending spews of water droplets up to catch the sunshine, sparkling like many diamonds as they rained back down. Watching them, she could not resist the urge to join in their sport, and shedding all but her chemise, dove into the icy cold water.

Chance was surprised at her impulsive whim and hungered to run his hands over her shapely body, revealed openly in the sunlight, but decided that for now, he could but touch her with his eyes. He had to exercise patience and wait for her to come to him on her own. Dear God, he prayed fervently that it would be soon!

He slowly removed his own clothing, joining her in the water, but he did not touch her, nor did they speak, each merely enjoying the sight of the other gliding effortlessly just beneath the smooth surface, supple and young, in harmony with nature.

Finally, Chance waded from the water to collect some blankets for them, and when Reanna followed, he wrapped one around her, tucking it snugly to ward off the chill that had crept into the waning daylight. Toweling himself dry, he dressed and went about setting up their meal, thoughtfully provided by Carmelita, which included a bottle of sherry.

The food was delicious, much of it leftover fares from their wedding, and sated they sat in the swiftly gathering shadows of the coming night, content and quiet.

By the time Chance stood to ready their bed, Reanna had consumed three small cups of the sherry, and felt a delicious warmth spreading through her. As Chance laid out the blankets over fragrant pine needles, he turned to find her right behind him. Holding his gaze, she carefully let the blanket fall from her shoulders, then, catching the straps of her chemise, she slowly allowed them to slip down her arms, letting the garment fall in a gossamer pool at her feet, atop the blanket.

His breath caught sharply in his throat, and he felt an instant burning fire in his loins, but he dared not move.

She had been healed by the earth, water, and tranquility of their secluded mountain retreat, all the powers that Mansunama had used to wrap her in his magic. It was time to put her shame to rest. If she could not show her husband the love that was in her heart, then their vows had been spoken in vain. She had finally reached deep within herself to find a hidden well of strength, and she decided now was the time to put it to good use.

She reached out, enfolding Chance in a light embrace, raising her lips tentatively to his in a delicate, exploring kiss, and he responded in kind, deliberately keeping his embrace and answering kiss light and easy. He intended to let Reanna do all the leading tonight, though it was no easy task to force his raging passions into control as her hands, as light as the touch of a butterfly's wings, danced over his body, slowly, gently removing his clothing, this time never hesitating to remove every last stitch.

Slowly Reanna lowered herself to lie upon the bed he had made, her eyes full of invitation, never leaving his, and he followed her, their bodies lying close, but barely touching, for he would still take no liberties.

Her soft hands and moist lips covered him in a fevered searching, always light and delicate, but with the power to burn his flesh, bringing the blood that flowed through his veins to a boil. He was no longer able to keep his hands and mouth from seeking their own delights as with a low moan he began to return her passion, holding back slightly to encourage her delicate lead.

Raising her leg along his lean, powerful thigh, Reanna threw the long, shapely limb over him, drawing herself up to sit astride his throbbing loins, and a hoarse groan of pent-up release escaped him as she slowly lowered herself onto his erect manhood, taking him into her warm depths, quickly establishing an easy rhythm between them, smooth and sensuous, causing her to gasp in pure delight as waves of pleasure washed over her. Thus, they swayed for a blissful eternity, until the magic of the love they shared lifted them to the starry sky, and Reanna finally experienced the joy of fulfillment with the man she loved, crying out in sheer abandon as Chance shuddered below her.

Later as they lay entwined in the afterglow of their passion, Reanna mused upon the pleasures that she had just discovered. She had flown to the tops of the trees, and the remaining two days at the lake were spent seeking pleasure in an eternally loving union. They returned home sated and content.

*   *   *   *   *   *

The next months were filled with the constant demands of establishing a working ranch. Chance had purchased the lot of the Beckett's horses, for they had decided to move back to town, where it would be much more convenient for

Kenny. The horses had all been bred from the wild herds of the plains; strong, healthy, spirited animals in constant demand as cow ponies by drovers for herding their vast holding of cattle.

They had started a large flock of chickens, and Raymond Dublin was holding a select herd of cattle for them as a wedding gift until such time as they were ready to accommodate them.

Although the house was in good condition, many of the outbuildings were in need of repair, corral fences needed mending, and ground was broken for large productive gardens to be planted in spring.

Working side by side through the chilly winter rains, and even during periods of snow inside the sheds and barns, Reanna proved on more than one occasion that she was a capable working partner. Chance tried to get her to relax, insisting that she should not work so hard when she was with child, but Reanna refused, determined to be as much a part of making this ranch work as Chance was. Through their daily efforts they developed a strong sense of pride in their work, their goals, and in their love for each other.

At night in bed together they derived immense pleasure as they sensuously made love at their leisure. Neither Reanna nor Chance had ever known such intense happiness, although Reanna still occasionally felt stabs of fear cut through her heart when she thought of the life growing within her. She would then turn her attention to Chance and let his love chase away her worries. There were still many nights when she would wake sobbing or struggling from her persistent nightmares, and Chance feared that she would forever be burdened with the horrible memories of her abduction. He offered her the solace of his arms, and softly murmured words of reassurance, but he could not completely banish her fears. With Chance beside her to hold onto, though she would still wake with tears or struggles, she no longer screamed in terror, which was an encouraging sign.

Their social life was full and busy as well. Billy had moved in with them after Molly and Kenny moved, taking a bedroom two doors down the hall from the master bedroom.

Billy felt immediate happiness at becoming part of a family he could admire. He was also becoming more enamored with Lada, taking to helping her around the house whenever he could, including kitchen work, even going so far as to rise early to make coffee for everyone in the morning.

He asked Lada to go dancing several times, but each offer was gently refused. Lada wanted to keep their relationship on the level of a polite friendship.

Lada and Reanna had become fast friends in the past months, enjoying a light easy feeling of comradeship as they gossiped and laughed over many of the little everyday events around them. Lada consulted her about meals and running the household, but Reanna in the end let Lada herself make many of the decisions, wanting her to feel as if she were part of the family.

Raymond Dublin called on them twice weekly, sometimes sharing a meal, after which Reanna would play the music that he held so dear. He had sent the piano to his daughter's new home, to Reanna's joy, and now almost every night she played either the piano or the guitar that Chance had given her.

Once a week Chance would accompany Reanna to town to renew supplies for their household, after which they would stop to visit with Kenny and Molly, who seemed much happier since their move. Reanna talked excitedly about the progress of the horses, which pleased Kenny immensely, since he still held them dear.

Belinda visited about every two weeks, never staying longer than a cup of coffee, explaining that she was a very busy person and was just there to check on Reanna, to see that Chance was taking good care of her best friend. This, in time, became a joke between Chance and Reanna, for they suspected that the real reason she came was to see Billy since he no longer worked at the saloon. They could see plainly that Belinda was in love with him, but it seemed that Billy had eyes only for Lada.

It saddened Reanna that her friends could not find the love they desired and deserved, but Chance assured her that these things had a way of working themselves out for the good of all involved, and Reanna prayed fervently that he was right.

Michael and Jared Dublin visited often also, many times with Uncle Bob and Aunt Martha. Chance teased Reanna because so many people sought out her music.

"Soon Rea, we will need to open a dance hall, for our parlor barely holds all of those who come to hear you play. Just think of all the profit we could make from such an endeavor. All I have to do is stand back and reap the rewards while you do all the work."

They laughed and Reanna felt a sense of pride that so many enjoyed her music, Chance most of all. His eyes never strayed from her as she played, the dark brown orbs taking on that familiar red gleam, and his smile became a sensual invitation. She would then feign exhaustion so the guests would bid them good night, and the two lovers could retire to their room, quickly becoming consumed with the burning fire that seemed to engulf them at a mere look or the slightest touch.

As Reanna's pregnancy progressed and her middle grew large with the child within, she began to feel very uncomfortable, the simplest function became difficult, her movements slowed and her temper shortened, especially as she had to give up working with Chance. She would not have stopped, but one day Chance declared that he was at the end of his patience with her and picked her up to carry her into the house, where he settled her into a chair and ordered her to stay put, before she hurt herself or the baby.

Now, with barely a month and a half of waiting to endure, she stayed inside, going out only to feed and play gently with Tasha and Modoc. At least her dogs did not order her to sit still.

It was also at this time that Chance cooled his passions toward Reanna. The first night that it happened, she had given him a feathery kiss, whispering, "I seek our bed, Sir Knight, and I do not wish to find it alone."

Starting for the stairs, she expected Chance to follow, but instead he called, "Billy and I have some business Rea, I may be awhile."

She fell asleep waiting for him, and when she awoke from her usual nightmare, there were no strong arms to comfort her. She shakily slipped out of bed and padded downstairs to discover Chance sleeping in a chair, the smell of brandy strong. She left him there; hurt by his preference for a bottle over their bed, but by morning she had excused it as an unintended overindulgence.

The next night they retired to their room together, but when they got into bed, Chance simply gave her a chaste kiss on the cheek, murmured good night and rolled over, presenting his back to her.

On the third night he would have done the same, but Reanna stopped him, sinking her nails into the flesh of his arm to prevent him from turning away.

"Jesus, Rea! What the hell is that for?"

"You tell me what it is you think you are doing, Chance Nolton, turning away from me every night! I knew this would happen. I knew that you would cease to want me when …" she suddenly broke into wrenching sobs, choking off her words.

Chance sat up, surprise registering on his features, and he embraced her tightly in his arms, attempting to sooth her foolish fears. "No, my love, no. it is not what you think. Dry your eyes and let me explain."

When she quieted, Chance tenderly wiped the remaining tears from her cheeks, kissing them warmly, soothing her with his words. "Rea, my love, my foolish love, it's not that I don't want you. My body refuses to give me peace from the desire you stir in my blood. Even now, when I know that it would be wrong to take you, my passion rushes hot at the very sight of you. I burn for you, and it is torture, for I may not seek release from the flames…"

She covered his mouth with her fingers, cutting off his words. She began to laugh, and Chance peered suspiciously at her through narrowed eyes, wondering what the joke was, until, still giggling, she explained, "It is you who are foolish Sir Knight, for your fears are groundless."

She became serious, murmuring softly, "You will not hurt the babe, nor me with your love. And even now my own blood rushes elatedly through me …" She pressed her mouth to his and again Chance felt the fire of her touch burning him to his very soul as she continued, caressing his body with her hands and mouth, touching, teasing, everywhere, until he returned her fiery passions with his own, driving her to cry out in her need of him.

As he entered her with his throbbing shaft, he murmured, "You bewitch me, vixen, with your passionate love."

Her answer was a whisper, "Yes, my rogue, I bewitch you. I only hope that I always will."

Chapter 10

Reanna was due any day, and she was large and cumbersome; so heavy with child that it often seemed she could barely move. The constant ache in her back was a nagging reminder of the pain she had gone through when the child was conceived. She could not wait to be delivered of her burden. This was how she thought of the child. There was no joy, no desperate yearning to hold the child in her arms.

Maliciously, her painful memories closed in upon her to torture her daylight hours, and nightmares encroached upon her sleep. Terrible dreams of holding her baby, who laughed evilly up at her from a face which was the exact replica of Cal or Larry McPherson.

Her fears closed in, poisoning her mind, until she could think of little else. Much to her husband's dismay, the lilting notes of her music ceased to entertain his evenings, and she could not bring herself to eat her meals, even with his constant urgings.

Helplessly Chance watched as, after only a brief period of this self-abuse, she began to look quite ill. Dark circles ringed her eyes, and the shining light in their depths became muted as she lost interest in her surroundings. Her bright copper locks framed her pale face, hanging in unkempt disarray, and her complete lack of energy had Chance frantic with worry.

One morning as they sat at the breakfast table, he decided that he had had enough. "Rea, I am going to take you to the doctor's today. You cannot continue on as you have with this self-destructive behavior."

She focused on him, his words penetrating her cloak of lethargy. "There is nothing that the doctor can do for my tortured thoughts and heinous dreams, save slit my throat and put them all to rest, which I find I wish for overmuch of late!" she snapped.

At his look of horror, she smiled mirthlessly, and a chilling laugh escaped her. "Yes, my words shock you, Chance. But that is truly how I feel. This burden that I carry is proving too heavy for my soul, and there is nothing I can do but suffer with it until it is finished and pray then that I shall know some peace. Now ..." she closed her eyes, and a long sigh escaped her tightened lips, "leave me be. I am sure you have plenty of work that you could be doing, instead of sitting here annoying me!"

Chance grew livid as her harsh words seared him, sending a wrenching pain through his soul. His jaw tightened, a muscle ticking in anger. Furiously he stared at her in mute accusation, not trusting himself to speak.

Lada, who had come into the kitchen in time to hear Reanna's ugly words, stepped behind her, placing her hands gently upon her friend's shoulders, her warm brown eyes telling Chance that she would look after his wife.

He swiftly stood, deliberately sending his chair smashing to the floor. Coldly noting where Lada's hands rested, he found that he had the overpowering urge to see his own hands on those smooth shoulders, shaking some sense into her. But knowing that this would do no good, he silently turned and strode from the house, joining Jared and Michael, whom he had recently hired, to ride swiftly into the farthest fields. There were many sections in need of inspection, having fallen prey to long periods of the spring rains.

Once they were alone, Lada attempted to cheer Reanna with light chatter, and even went so far as to venture a joke or two. Knowing that this was an extremely rare pastime for the gentle Indian woman, Reanna responded with a tremulous smile.

"Thank you for trying to ease my mind Lada. You have helped, but I find that I am weary, so I will go and rest for a while. Perhaps I will be in a better frame of mind by the noon meal."

She pushed herself from her chair to make her cumbersome way up the stairs. Collapsing on the bed, she stared blankly up at the ceiling, and slowly she dissolved into silent tears. She wept bitterly at the unfairness of life, and for the burden she was forced to bear, but mostly she wept for Chance, who bore her burdens with her with no complaint, yet she had deliberately berated and hurt him, turning him from her.

Her sobs subsiding, she finally ceased, dashing the tears from her eyes and wiping her cheeks with her slender hands. Taking a deep breath, she resolved to make her peace with Chance when he returned at noon. If he returned, she thought wryly.

Heaving herself from the bed, she gained her feet. Feeling as if somehow her load had been lightened, she sighed with relief. She decided that she would go feed and visit with her dogs, having neglected them for some days now, leaving their care to others. She felt a prickle of shame at this realization and determined that she would have to make it up to them.

She quietly descended to the kitchen, hearing Lada's melodic humming drifting through the house as she busied herself straightening up. Finding the dogs dishes sitting ready on the table, she gathered them up, and leaving the back door ajar, carefully made her way across the short cleared area to where the dogs pens were nestled under the protective branches of tall, stately pines, which provided shade in the summers dry heat, and an effective wind break when the cold blast of winter wind howled heartlessly down from snow peaked mountains.

As she walked, she idly wondered where Billy had gone. He had begun repairing the stonework around the well early this morning, and his work stood unfinished, something Billy had never been known to do. Absently deciding that he must be in the barn, she gave the matter little more thought.

She opened the pens after setting down the bowls laden with fresh meat and table scraps, smiling with genuine warmth for the first time in days as two large, dark heads pushed their way beneath the palms of her hands, greeting their beloved mistress. Petting them fondly, Reanna murmured, "Modoc, Tasha, I am sorry that I've been neglecting you. Do you think that you can ever forgive me?"

They both quivered in excitement as they eagerly whined their assent, their love for her shining from their dark, intelligent eyes before they lowered their heads to hastily consume their meal. Then, with a deep bark of joy, Modoc lead the way as he and Tasha dashed to and fro, darting in and out as they playfully nipped each other in mock battle. Soon they were out of sight, running free as they were allowed to do each day, being penned only at night.

She stood and watched as they disappeared from sight, a fond smile lighting her features. The sudden snap of a twig drew her attention and she turned to peer intently into the deep shade beneath the near pines, "Billy?" she ventured, "is that you?"

A prickling sensation raced down her spine as silence greeted her inquiry. As she waited with bated breath, the silence seemed to grow somehow menacing, and she swallowed convulsively as she turned to hurry back to the house, greatly impeded by her large stomach, heavy with unborn child.

The scream of terror died in her throat as she was suddenly grabbed from behind, her neck cruelly jerked backward as a sharp, thin blade of steel pressed against the slender column of her throat, and her arms were caught and roughly pulled behind her back.

A voice, hard and cruel, rasped in her ear. "One sound from you, little bitch, and I will slit this lovely throat of yours, quick as anything. You got a lot to pay for, you and Billy, that traitor to the McPherson name!"

Cal! Waves of sheer terror rippled through Reanna's body as she recognized his voice, and nausea rose in her throat as the repugnant odor of cheap whisky and stale tobacco assailed her nostrils, bringing back to her in sharp detail all those memories she had sought to forget. But how could this be? Cal was dead. He was dead! She had seen him, lying lifeless as his blood pooled around him the day she had been rescued. Shaking with fear, she dared to turn her head slightly to view her assailant from the corner of her eye. It was Cal!

She gasped in pain as he brutally jerked on her arms, forcing her to stumble against him as he pulled her backwards with him to the concealing cloak of the trees. She began to struggle, but he only chuckled evilly as he continued to half drag her through the trees.

Having reached what he considered a safe distance from the house, he grated, "No one will here you if you scream but I am in no mood for it, so keep your hysterics to yourself." He tightened the pressure of his arm, pressing the knife further into her exposed neck, drawing a thin line of blood. "Understand?"

At her faint nod, he released his strangling hold, and she drew a deep breath, shaking with fear and shock. She squeezed her eyes shut on the tears that threatened to fall. They would do her no good.

Letting her hands go, he stepped around in front of her. There was no way she could hope to escape him in her condition, and he knew it.

He smiled a cold, nasty smile that did not reach his calculating blue eyes. "I see that Larry's seed has found its mark, judging by the size of you."

She had been backing away from him as he spoke, but he followed closely, and now her retreat was halted by a tree at her back. Laughing he mocked her, "You cannot hope to get away this time. I got Billy all trussed up in the ol' shed up the hill. Even sliced him up a bit. But not enough to die, mind you. You an' him, you're gonna suffer afore ya die, jus' like I suffered when ya'all left me there to die that day."

"B – but you were shot," Reanna stammered.

"Yes, you bitch, I was shot, but only wounded," he spat. "It took me a long time to mend, an all that time, I thought and planned for this day. I waited, and now I'll have my revenge on all of ya! I'm gonna have you right in front of that little brother a mine..." He paused, smiling thinly, "After I carve that soft, silky body a yours up a bit. Then I'm gonna kill ya both, and when that gunslinger a yours finds your bodies, my revenge 'll be complete. I hear..." he ran his finger roughly down the side of her face. "That he loves ya very much. He will suffer, knowin' what happened to you. He'll suffer awhile, then I'll kill him. I'll kill em all, everyone who shot me up an killed my brothers that day."

"Please," Reanna begged, "Please, would you bed a woman heavy with child? A child that may be yours? You would risk harming your own child?" she was grasping at any excuse to alter his plans.

He reached out, placing a dirty hand upon her stomach, the fetid smell of his breath reaching her nostrils as he leaned close to her. "I would bed any woman that strikes my fancy, any time I want. So you can quit tryin to hide behind this..." he slowly began to stroke her belly as he softly continued, "an try bein real nice to me."

If only she could reach her gun. She had continued to wear it strapped inside her boot, but now it was too awkward, indeed, impossible, to bend and reach it.

Her senses recoiled as his mouth crushed hers in a brutal, punishing assault. She began to struggle wildly as he pressed her back against the rough bark of the tree, but her attempts were futile. His arms came up on each side of her, imprisoning her further.

Failing to escape his savage embrace, she bit down hard on his plundering tongue, tasting his blood as he jerked away in surprise, a bellow of pain and rage escaping him.

As she bent to reach her gun, Cal drew his arm back and swiftly smashed her in the side of her face, knocking her to the ground. Unbearable pain shot through her belly as she clutched at it, writhing and moaning in agony.

Barely able to think, so great was her terror, she again tried to reach her gun. But Cal was upon her immediately, eagerly parting the bodice of her gown as he carelessly settled his great weight fully upon her, causing her to cry out as fresh waves of pain wracked her body. As his wet mouth found her heavy breast, Reanna heard a low, warning growl through the misty haze of horror that surrounded her.

Tasha wasted no time springing to the defense of her mistress. Fangs bared; she closed her jaws on Cal's arm with a powerful grip. Howling in pain, he could not shake the angry dog from him, and Reanna saw the flash of his knife as it arched above her to sink deep into Tasha's side. He rose up and threw her from him as with a yelp of pain, she released his arm.

Reanna saw Tasha's beautiful dark coat stained crimson as Cal withdrew the blood-covered knife. Swiftly she bent her knee toward her; bringing her gun within reach, and as Cal turned back to her, she brought the derringer up in a firm grip to his side.

Cal's emotions registered plainly on his face as she squeezed the trigger, sending a bullet into his flesh. Shock turned to rage, and he brought the lethal knife high as if to plunge it into her breast. She quickly raised the gun and shot him in the chest. The impact of the bullet raised him as he fell to the side, rolling off of her as his life blood stained the front of his shirt. He finally lay still, death claiming his black soul at last.

Using the last of her failing strength, she pushed herself up to stand on shaking limbs. Swaying treacherously, she leaned against the tree that had held her before, and, leveling the gun, emptied it of another bullet, firing into Cal's now still body. Sobbing hysterically, she pulled the trigger again, then someone was clutching her shoulders, but she fired yet again, unable to stop, killing him over and over again, with no will or desire to stop. Someone was violently shaking her, getting in her way, but she found a way to get her last shot around the intruder and into her demon enemy.

$*$ $*$ $*$ $*$ $*$ $*$

Chance, astride his great black stallion, was slowly riding back to the house with Jared and Michael. Reviewing this morning's events, and Reanna's behavior, he certainly was in no hurry to face her again, his anger rising anew as he remembered her words. Sighing, he supposed that she had a right to her anger after all she had been through. He drew a deep, calming breath. She would probably only toy with her food, picking at it before pushing it aside, as she had done all week.

His next thought hit him like a physical blow. What if she really could not accept the baby after it was born? What if it did look like the McPhersons, reminding her daily of the horrors she had experienced at their hands? Hell, for that matter, reminding him. Could he live with it? Could he ask her to?

As he neared the house, his black thoughts were abruptly shattered when the sound of a gunshot echoed in the stillness. Kicking Lancelot into a rapid gallop, he headed in the direction of the sound, his heart in his throat, with Jared and Michael right behind him. He heard yet another ring out, closer this time. A sure sense of dread gripping him, he urged the laboring horse to even greater speed. The great steed responded, and Chance fairly flew as Lancelot covered the distance in ground eating strides. The scene unfolded before his eyes with cutting clarity. He was off his horse and running to Reanna as he saw it was her who was firing the gun, over and over…

Waves of pain suffused Reanna's body, but she managed to pull away from Chance's tight grip when through the red haze of anger and hurt, she heard Tasha's pitiful cries. Dropping the empty gun and wavering unsteadily, she staggered to her dog, kneeling close as Tasha lay whimpering where she had been flung. Seeing to comfort the injured animal, she slowly, gently ran her shaking hand across the dog's head.

"God no! Tasha!" she wept, her mind reeling in shock and confusion as she watched helplessly the bright crimson stain slowly spreading over the glossy fur, the life of the dog steadily slipping away.

Suddenly she was grasped from behind and turned as she clumsily rose to meet her assailant; only to be embraced by Chance's strong, loving arms.

As she wept uncontrollably, Chance's discerning eyes took in the carnage, correctly assessing the situation at a glance. A black, towering rage filled him. How had Cal escaped his doom that day at the cabin? How could the ruthless bounty hunter have been so careless in dispensing his justice?

Reanna suddenly pushed herself from his broad, comforting chest. "Billy!" she wailed. "Oh Chance, he has hurt Billy. He may be dying! He us up … Ah!" she gasped as a terrible pain gripped the entire middle portion of her body. She clutched her stomach, trying to catch her breath, as she ground out, "Up the hill … old shed!" She bent over double, her face reflecting the agony she felt.

With ashen face, Chance bent and swept her up into his arms, seething in anger as he gazed down at her beautiful face, swollen and bruised along one side where Cal had struck her.

Just as he emerged from the concealing forest, Jared and Michael jerked their mounts to a stop in front of Chance. Clasping Reanna close to shield the gaping bodice of her gown, Chance barked, "Jared, go for the doctor, fast! Michael, Tasha is over through those trees. Do what you must but be quick about it. We have to find Billy. He is hurt and I am not sure how badly. I will bring Reanna to Lada. She is going to have the baby!"

Having heard the gunfire, Lada met Chance at the back door, hurrying in his wake as he climbed the stairs, tenderly depositing his precious burden safely in their bed.

"Lada, see to her. We have to find Billy." At her quick nod of assent, he was gone.

Reanna lay sobbing against her pain as Lada efficiently helped her out of her soiled and torn gown. Hurrying downstairs, she returned with warm water and a cloth, gently bathing Reanna's bruised and battered body as the laboring woman struggled for breath.

Lada sat by her bedside, holding Reanna's cold hand within her warm ones as she softly spoke, instructing her to breathe evenly and deeply. Finally, Lada's quiet words penetrated, and Reanna calmed, her breath coming more easily. She did not notice the worried frown on Lada's pretty features, or the silent prayers that she sent heavenward.

Chance motioned Michael to silence as he crept cautiously to the door, opening it slowly, every sense keenly alert, unsure if Cal had recruited others of his like to help in his cruel games.

Billy was tied upright to a large center beam that rose from floor to ceiling. He had been gagged with a filthy rag, and his chin hung limply against his chest. His clothes hung in tatters, his body covered in bloody welts where Cal's knife had pierced the skin. His face was a bloody, swollen mass of bruises.

"Jesus! His own brother." Chance muttered as he turned to the door sickened at the thought of what would have been in store for Reanna if Cal had succeeded in his vengeful plot.

Calling Michael in, they loosened Billy's bonds and gently lowered him to the floor. He moaned in pain, and Chance swore softly as he quickly stripped his shirt off, tearing it in strips to bind the worst of Billy's wounds. There was a particularly deep one under the rib cage that had Chance worried.

Carefully they carried Billy's unconscious form to the waiting horses, and gently levered him over Lancelot's shoulders, taking great care as they made their way back to the house. There they laid Billy on the settee in the parlor and Chance covered him with a blanket, making him as comfortable as possible until the doctor arrived. Instructing Michael to stay with Billy, Chance swiftly bounded up the stairs, startling Lada as he burst through the doorway.

"How is she?" he demanded, noting Reanna's pale, frightened face. She did not even raise her head to look at him.

Lada answered truthfully, wishing she could reassure the frightened man standing before her. "I do not know for certain, but I think that it will be a long time before this child is born, and she is already weakened and tired. The only thing we can do is to keep her calm and wait for Doctor Farley." Lada paused, almost afraid to ask, "How is Billy?" She never doubted for an instant that Chance had found him.

Chance ran a shaking hand through his dark hair, sighing heavily. "I think he will live, but he is pretty badly cut up and beaten. Michael is with him in the parlor. He can help you dress the majority of Billy's wounds, and the Doc can take a look at that deep one when he gets here. I will sit with Rea now, Lada, and ... thank you."

Lada nodded and silently turned to make her way down the stairs, trying to hold her worried thoughts at bay as she hastened to the parlor.

Chance moved to the side of the bed, taking Reanna's fragile hand within his own as he sat beside her. She turned to look at him, speaking in a strained voice. "Chance, I am so frightened ... don't leave me. Please promise me ... I need you with me." Her large eyes brimmed with tears, pleading her cause, as her nails dug almost painfully into the flesh of his hand.

Chance, as frightened as she, strained to keep his voice from wavering. "It is all right, love. I am here, and I will not leave you. You have my undivided attention for as long as you like."

She smiled her thanks, asking in a weak voice, "What happened to Billy?"

"He is going to be fine. Michael and I found him up in the old shed. He is cut up some, but he should mend nicely."

"That is good," she sighed, but suddenly rose up on her elbows. "Tasha!" she gasped as another pain tightened her innards.

Chance eased her back to the pillows, stroking her rich copper hair as he hastened to reassure her, deliberately avoiding her query. "Hush, my love, you have nothing to fear now. I will stay by your side, and everything will be fine." And he hoped to God it would be so.

Reanna thrashed about, dislodging her covers as she rolled her head from side to side, seeking to escape the almost constant pains that clasped every part of her in a cruel embrace. Chance paced restlessly around the room, the contained energy of a caged panther surrounding him, unable to aid his suffering mate.

Dr. Farley rushed in, followed by Jared, as Billy lay groaning in pain and Reanna moaned loudly from above. The doctor grabbed up his black bag with all due haste and quickly set about checking Billy's wounds. As another louder cry issued forth from upstairs, Jared's face turned completely white, and he stammered, "Well if y – you don't n – need me, I can go help M – Michael outside."

At Dr. Farley's brisk nod, he thankfully left the house to help Michael who had carried Tasha back and was treating her wound, stubbornly refusing to take her life without a fight.

Dr. Farley cleared his throat, questioning Lada as he deftly set to work, inspecting Billy's injuries. "You have done just fine Lada, but this deep one here needs stitching. If you would assist me!"

When he was finished, Lada placed her hand on the doctor's arm. "Please Doctor, if you have no objections, I will make a poultice for his wounds that will help them heal more quickly." She took a deep breath, "I think that Reanna and Chance need you more now that Billy is taken care of."

"Lada, I would not shrug off the judgement of others who are trained in healing, even if their training differs from mine." He smiled kindly at Lada. "I will leave my patient in your very capable hands."

Entering the bedroom, Doctor Farley was immediately struck by the changed appearance of an agonized Chance, whose eyes were red rimmed with fatigued worry and whose once steady hands were shaking in undisguised emotion. He half rose, and then sat back down again as Reanna was wracked by yet another hard contraction.

His voice hoarse and thin with worry, Chance whispered loudly. "Doc, you must do something!"

"Right now, I have to examine her Chance, to see how far along she is. Unfortunately, there is usually little we men can do but wait and try to lend comfort where we can. Would you care to wait downstairs while I examine her?"

Reanna heard the doctor's words and frantically gripped Chance's arm. "No Chance, do not leave me!"

He placed his fingers gently on her soft lips, stilling her fears. "Don't worry, my love, I will not leave you. Try and stay calm. I will be right here."

He spoke to the doctor, even though his eyes remained locked with his wife's frightened gaze. "I have promised Reanna that I would stay, I will not leave her."

Dr. Farley sputtered; "Chance, I really do not think it wise …" He stopped as he met the cold, determined glance directed his way. Resignedly, he continued, "Yes, well, let's get on with it then. I have to check her to see how far the baby has dropped."

Completing his examination, Dr. Farley sympathetically patted Reanna's hand. "It will be a while yet, my dear. There is nothing more I can do for now. All we can do is wait."

"Doctor, how long do we have to wait? Surely you can tell us more than you have!" Then, struck by the alarming thought that there must be something dreadfully wrong, Chance continued, forcing the words through his tight throat. "What is it that you are not telling us? Surely there is a reason for your vague diagnosis! I want to know just how long she must suffer this way!"

The doctor managed somehow to conceal his humor from the nervous, first time father standing before him, showing Chance only a tight-lipped smile. "There is no way of telling, Chance. You must believe me. Now, if you are going to stay here, then please try to remain calm, for Reanna's sake. I am going down to check on Billy, but I will be back in a while. Now please, try not to worry."

Chance waited, placing cool cloths on Reanna's brow and murmuring words of comfort as she fought against the terrible pains of her labor, and the ghosts of Cal's evil treatment. In her mind she saw him fall again and again as she fired the gun.

Hours later, Chance was frantic. He could do nothing to help her, and his heart ached as she moaned and dug her nails into his calloused palm. She began to twist and turn, trying to escape the pain that was now unrelentingly wracking her midsection.

Through the sheen of unshed tears Chance pried Reanna's fingers from their grip, rubbing his eyes as he moved swiftly through the doorway to the top of the stairs, calling the doctor in a booming voice edged with panic.

The doctor glanced up from reassuring a now conscious Billy, and with a sigh turned to Lada. "I leave him in your hands dear."

Lada, assured that Billy would be fine, smiled her gratitude and nodded.

Chance paced the width of the room, his smooth strides belied by the tightly clasped hands at his back as the doctor knelt and examined Reanna, then stopped in agitation as the doctor drew him aside and softly told him, "It will be a difficult birth Chance, I will not lie to you. Her birth passage is very small. If however, it becomes necessary, I can open her and take the baby, which will be risky. All we can do now is wait, hope and pray."

"I cannot stand to see her suffering such pain, doctor, and I am also concerned about her state of mind. She does not want to have this baby at all and ..." he paused to splash a healthy portion of brandy into a glass and toss it down his throat. The muscles of his jaw clenched as he looked the doctor deliberately in the eye, "I'm not sure now that I do either. Damn them! Damn them all to hell!" He raised his arm and pitched the glass into the corner of the room, where it shattered into brightly lit shards that reflected the late sunlight streaming through the window, tinkling softly in the silent room as they fell to the floor. Chance ran shaking hands through his dark hair as he gazed down at his wife, who had slipped into an exhausted slumber. He hadn't felt so helpless since he was a boy, and he did not like the feeling at all. He had been hardened by life, gaining lightning reflexes and a sharp wit, but now he was powerless to help the woman he loved more than life itself.

Suddenly her eyes opened, wide with fear, unfocused in the grip of a horrible nightmare. "No! Please, don't ... don't hurt me. No! ... Not again! Larry ... knife ... not my blood ..."

Chance swallowed past the lump in his throat, wishing that he did not have to listen as she shuddered and seemed to focus on him.

"Chance! Help me ..."

He grasped her firmly by the shoulders, shaking her gently as he hoarsely, urgently called to her, "Rea, Reanna, wake up!"

She blinked a few times and recognizing Chance, broke into wrenching sobs as she clutched him to her with sudden strength. "Chance, oh Chance. I'm so frightened. Hold me please. I don't want this baby, God help me, but I don't!"

She closed her eyes; pain etched her lovely features as another spasm wracked her body, opening them to mirror the misery and hate that she carried inside. "I don't want it Chance. I hate it! It's one of them! Will they never cease hurting me? Will I ever be free of their evil? AH!" She clutched her abdomen as pain once again seized her.

Chance knew that there was nothing he could say or do to change what was in her heart. If she could not accept the child, so be it. It was her right, and he could see that she would wrap herself with that cloak of hate no matter what any one of them said or did. Yet, even as he accepted this, his heart bled for the bitterness that had replaced the love and laughter of the spirited girl he had fallen in love with.

He raised his head and met the anguished gaze of Dr. Farley. There was nothing he, nor anyone else, could do. They sat in silence, wiping her brow with cool cloths as she tossed upon her bed, panting and straining in her efforts to bring forth her unwelcome burden.

More hours passed and she grew weaker with her labor. Her damp hair was matted around her face, and her body was bathed in sweat.

She whispered softly through parched lips. "Chance … Chance, I am dying. I do not want to leave you. Oh Chance, help me, please." Her voice trailed off as she closed her eyes in total exhaustion, too weak to go on.

Dr. Farley had dozed off in his chair, but jumped up quickly at Chance's shout, sending the chair crashing back against the wall.

"Damn it man! Take the child! I'll not watch her suffer more." As he stormed from the room, slamming the door in his wake, the doctor hurried to Reanna's side.

Downstairs, Chance locked himself in his study and proceeded to empty a bottle of brandy, welcoming the burning sensation as his nerves gradually calmed and his hands steadied.

He stood slowly and, taking a deep breath, went to check on Billy's condition. He realized that he had not even thought about him in the past hours, so worried was he about Reanna.

He entered the living room to find Lada kneeling by Billy's side as he lay on the settee, a tender look in her dark eyes, and Chance smiled sadly, wondering if Reanna would ever be able to smile with that warm light in her eyes again. She might not even be alive tomorrow, and at that thought he felt the muscles of his abdomen clench in terror. He crossed the room to where Billy lay and spoke softly, "Billy, how are you?"

As he looked up into Chance's carefully controlled features, Billy could sense the agony lying right beneath the surface. "I will be fine, Chance, just a little weak for a while. Again, you and Reanna have suffered at the hands of my family, and I am deeply sorry that I could not prevent Cal from further harming Reanna. How is she?"

"The birth is a difficult one. I ... truly," he wiped a shaking hand across his face, and turned to stare out the window. "I do not know if she will make it."

Lada and Billy exchanged glances, their misery at Chance's words clearly apparent.

"Chance," Lada whispered, "Reanna's father and Uncle are in the kitchen, waiting to see how she is. I have given them coffee. Jared rode to tell them after he got the doctor."

Chance sighed heavily. "I cannot face her father right now, Lada. Tell the Dublin's I'll ... I'll let them know soon."

Then Chance was across the room and rapidly mounting the stairs, each step bringing him closer to that which he feared. They had all heard it, the faint cry of an infant.

Chance pushed the door open to find Reanna pale and still, while the doctor bent over the cradle beside the bed. His heart slammed in his chest, and he rasped, "Doctor, is she ...?" He could not continue.

Dr. Farley turned, a tired smile lighting his face. "She is fine, Chance. She will probably sleep for quite a while. She finally birthed the babe herself and is bound to be weak for a couple of weeks, but she will be good as new before you know it."

Chance glanced over to the cradle. "The child ... does it live?"

The doctor motioned Chance closer, pulling the blanket down to give him his first view of the baby. "Alive and well Chance and I might add, quite a pretty sight."

As Chance gazed down at the baby, an expression of wondrous awe dawning on his face, the doctor could not help but laugh. "She is one of the prettiest babies I have ever seen, and I've seen plenty. How do you like your new girl?"

Chance was speechless. As the child seemed to gaze steadily at him, Chance knew that he would love this tiny girl forever, just as if she were his very own. He was amazed at the feeling of fierce protectiveness that rose in him. He knew great relief, and happy pleasure, for he gazed down at a perfect miniature replica of his beloved Reanna.

Later, Lada paced the floor, crooning to the baby, rocking her ceaselessly, but her efforts were in vain, for the infant squalled loudly in hunger. Reanna was still sleeping soundly, the commotion not making the least impression on her, and Chance decided that he better wake her.

He shook her gently, calling her name, and after some effort she finally opened her eyes, heavy lidded with sleep. Perplexed, she glanced around to find the source of all the commotion. She attempted to sit up, and Chance solicitously bent and fluffed the pillows behind her back, making her comfortable.

He chose his words with care, fearing her rejection to the baby. "Rea, my love, we have a babe, a beautiful baby girl. She looks just like her mother, Reanna Dublin Nolton, with no resemblance to anyone else. She is such a small, helpless little thing, and needs you now. Will you hold her, feed her?"

She turned to him, the wide, deep green pools of her eyes filled with fear and indecision, her soft lips trembling. "Chance ... I ..."

Lada came and laid the baby on the bed beside its mother, leaving them to get acquainted. Reanna did not glance at the child but kept her frightened gaze on Chance. He knelt close to the bed and reaching over her, pulled the blanket down to further expose the child. He commanded, "Rea, look upon the babe. She is beautiful."

She held his gaze a moment longer, then slowly turned to look at the baby, who had quieted to catch her breath. "She is lovely Chance. Strange, she does not look at all like ... she looks ... like me."

This was a promising beginning, but Chance was not totally satisfied, for Reanna had made no move to hold the child, and he silently prayed that she would accept the tiny life that lay next to her.

"Rea, love, she is hungry. You must feed her; you are the only one here equipped to do so. Will you ignore her pleas? She cries for the comfort of her mother."

"I don't think ..." Greatly pained, she burst into tears. "Oh, Chance, I don't think that I can take the child to my breast. I fear … I just …" Her shoulders shook as she buried her face in her hands, sobbing in misery.

Chance leaned over, enclosing her in his warm embrace. He rocked her gently as he placed a light, warm kiss atop her head, giving her comfort even as he felt her anguish within herself. He said nothing until she was quiet again, then holding her away, he looked into her deep green eyes, his dark brown gaze mirroring the frustration and impatience that churned within his soul.

"Reanna," he pleaded urgently, "my dear, sweet Rea. Can you simply allow the child to die? Listen to her cry for love! Hear it in your heart! You must try my love, for I think if you do choose the course of neglect, you and I would sorely regret it the rest of our days. You, for turning your back on your own helpless child, and me for allowing it."

His words touched her more than the cries of her child. She wanted to pick up her baby, to give her the nourishment that she needed, but could make no move to do so.

She slowly began to speak. "Chance, I am helpless to do that which my mind tells me is right. Somehow my heart has not yet received the message, though I truly desire no harm to come to the babe. Perhaps, Chance, if you help me."

Chance noted the rising desperation in her voice, and caught her to him, tenderly kissing her before reaching over her to gently scoop up the tiny bundle. Looking down at the little features, he felt his heart contract. Even now, when she was red as a beet from crying so, she was still very beautiful. The dark, copper color of Reanna's hair, the long thick lashes shading sea green eyes, her mouth of the same shape and fullness. Smiling wistfully, he brought the baby close to Reanna, resting his arm on her lap. Locking his gaze with hers, he slowly, deliberately freed one hand, and reaching up, lightly caressed her pale, smooth shoulder before he purposely tugged on the neckline of her gown, exposing her swollen breast. Then he turned the baby so that her little mouth could find that which she so eagerly sought.

At Reanna's gasp of surprise, he looked up to find her watching the child in mild interest. When the babe had suckled for a few minutes, Reanna brought her arm up to hold the child on her own as she gently pushed Chance's arm away.

"I can do it now."

But there was no smile, no sparkle of her eyes, and Chance could see only coolness in her attitude, certainly not the burst of motherly love he had hoped for.

Reanna did not feel cold, but neither could she feel the joy that she knew she should. As the babe had begun to suckle, she had felt a surge of warmth, a tugging in her heart, and so was not repelled by the act. Something inside however, prevented her from feeling any real maternal love. She was not able to forget that this was not Chance's baby she held in her arms, not Chance's offspring that nursed at her breast, and she sorely wanted only his children.

Chance knew he could expect no more of Reanna right now. As long as she fed the babe, perhaps in time she would come to love the tiny new life that had already effortlessly stolen his heart.

For the next six days, Chance barely left Reanna's side. He shared his meals with her, and cared for her bruised body, not allowing anyone else that duty except the doctor, when he came to examine her and announced to her worried husband that Reanna was recovering nicely, and the babe was healthy and strong.

Chance sat and talked with his wife or read to her as the soft spring breezes gently billowed the crisp curtains at the window, and bright sunshine and bird song combined to speed the healing of body and mind. At times during these pleasant interludes, Chance would ask Reanna to name the baby, even making suggestions of his own, but leaving the final choice up to her. Reanna demurred, saying that she did not want to think about it yet. So, for now, the child remained nameless.

Raymond had come to stay since the birth, visiting with his daughter and helping Chance out with the chores, so that he had more time to devote to Reanna. He was quite taken with his granddaughter, proclaiming her to be another Reanna all over again, and boasting to anyone who would listen of her every sound and gesture.

Bob and Martha, Jared and Michael, all came to view the child, making claims very similar to Raymond's, and exclaiming at the remarkable beauty of the baby. They were all eager to help Lada as she lovingly bathed and cared for the infant.

Reanna was concerned for Tasha and asked after her welfare daily. Chance thought this ironic, for she showed more concern for her dog than she did for her own child.

Not satisfied with Chance's assurance of the dog's health, she insisted that he bring both her pets to her. Finally, Tasha recovered enough, and the morning came when the dogs bounded exuberantly into her room, nudging her arms with their large heads, and whining in pleasure at the sight of their mistress. She laughed, a musical, happy sound, as she scratched their heads in affection. It gladdened the heart of her husband for she had not laughed in so long a time.

Belinda, Molly and Avis all came to visit Reanna and the baby, bringing gifts of small, pretty gowns they had fashioned and embroidered themselves.

Reanna gradually responded to the loving concern of all her family and friends. She began to smile gaily once again, and to take an interest in the happenings of the ranch and the small town.

Billy was the only person who had not come to visit with her, or to see the baby. She began to ask for him, but he never set foot in her room. Belatedly, she realized that it was the babe that prevented his coming. He did not want to face the proof of his brother's sins all over again. His burden was, for him, just as great as hers. She knew that she should go to him, but was still too weak to make the effort, and so remained safe within the confines of her room, her only responsibilities being to feed the baby and be entertained by those who loved her.

It was on the baby's seventh day of life that Reanna received a visitor who would, forever after, be known to Chance and Reanna as their child's savior. Indeed, savior to all those who were part of the child's life.

Chance had gone to inspect some fencing with Reanna's father, and Lada was busy downstairs, leaving Reanna alone with the child, who was nursing greedily at her breast. Suddenly she was filled with a sense of peaceful contentment, and the knowledge that she was not alone. As she glanced up, her eyes locked on the black, smoldering gaze of Mansunama. He filled her with his earthy presence, and so intense was his gaze as he silently moved toward her that she felt the stab of fiery heat in her very heart. He came to stand beside her, a bouquet of purple windflowers and yellow violets clutched in his large hand, which he slowly held out to her. She found it difficult to envision the great medicine man stooping to pick the fragile blooms, or even to think of offering them as a gift. She smiled at the notion, saying softly, "Thank you, Mansunama. They are quite beautiful."

As if knowing her thoughts, he smiled in return, "I have brought you these to lighten your heart, for I know that the birth of your little one has weighed heavily upon it."

"How did you get in?" Reanna queried. "Lada should have warned me that you had come."

"She does not know, and I have brought Talohan with me to insure our privacy. She will keep Lada busy visiting and gossiping, as you women are so fond of doing."

He smiled again at the look of outrage that crossed her pretty features, then, realizing that he was jesting; she gave a sigh of resignation. He was not going to tell her how he had gotten into her room without anyone's knowledge. He had also somehow known that Chance and her father would be gone today. She looked up at him again as he moved to lay the flowers on the table beside her bed and noticed the twinkle of true pleasure that danced in his dark eyes as he turned to her. He reached his arms out to hold the child, and she silently handed the bundled babe over to his waiting arms, noting as she did so the way his hungry gaze lingered appreciatively on her full breast.

Strangely unashamed, Reanna reached to pull her gown back up, effectively blocking his view. She moved lethargically, strangely filled with Mansunama's aura of the earth and woods; of the centuries of knowledge and mysticism that enveloped him.

She grew sleepier as she watched Mansunama. His handsome face softened as he looked at the tiny baby in his arms, and he slowly began to chant. His eyes closed, and there was not a sound but for the deep, rhythmic singsong of Mansunama's voice, lulling her into a peaceful slumber.

The golden eagle flew high, the echoes of her harsh cry reverberating in the brilliant sunlight off the towering mountain peaks. Riding the ever-changing currents of air, the eagle soared higher, coming to rest on a large nest made of branches and twigs, and the bird's heart wrenched painfully in her breast. Her offering of fresh meat lay uneaten, her fledgling immobile beside it. She stretched out her neck, nudging the limp form gently with her powerful beak, but her only chick remained still.

For two days the eagle kept her lonely vigil, her mate having died a month ago when he was shot hunting the farmer's downy yellow domestic chicks which he had found to be such easy prey. The arduous task of raising their four chicks had been left for her to bear alone, and one by one they had met with death, until only the one chick remained.

The eagle was filled with pain, her heart ached with the burden of life, and she opened her great, curved beak, screaming her anguish to the heavens. As the cry of the eagle floated on the wind, she plummeted down to the rocks below, breaking her neck as she landed, to lay lifeless and twisted, the agony of her grief too great to bear. The eagle was forever still, the only movement the ruffling of her feathers as the wind carried her death dirge to the silent mountain peaks.

Reanna's eyes flew open as she suddenly woke, bathed in perspiration. Mansunama knelt by her side and whispered her name, and she knew the pain of the loss of a child. She quickly reached to take the baby, consumed by a burst of maternal love, and raised her surprised gaze to Mansunama, tears of gratitude glistening in her large green eyes. It was in that moment that Reanna knew, just as surely as if he had spoken, of the depth of love he felt for her. A love that could never be.

He spoke, his voice the music of the wind, his words the wisdom of the earth. "The Great Spirit has given you a great gift of life in this child, no matter what has gone before. She is filled with the spirit of the running waters and will hold all of life dear to her heart. She is, like her mother who gave her birth, all things good and beautiful." He reached for the flowers, laying them on her lap. "As these flowers are the proof of life renewed, so is the child that you hold to your breast."

"Oh, Mansunama …" The words caught in her throat as she closed her eyes, tears of relief streaming down her face. She felt as if she had been freed from a great weight, and the heavy burden of guilt she had felt because she could not love her child was gone.

When she opened her eyes, she was alone. Mansunama, with his powerful presence, was gone, and though he had brought her much happiness, a part of her ached for the man who was filled with such love for a woman who would always love another.

Lada stopped in surprise as she entered the bedroom to ask Reanna what she would like for the noon meal. Humming softly, Reanna was just putting the finishing touches to her lustrous hair, which she had brushed to a fiery gleam and pulled back, tying it with a wide yellow ribbon that matched the gown of pale yellow that she wore.

Noticing Lada in the mirror, she turned and smiled widely. "Good morning Lada. It's such a lovely day that I thought I would come downstairs to eat with everyone else. Have the men come back yet? And where is Billy? I must talk to him right away."

"Your father and Chance are still out, and Billy is out back washing up. He should be in at any moment."

Wondering at the abrupt change that had come over Reanna, Lada looked at her closely and slowly said, "I had a visit from Talohan this morning, and it seemed odd but she did not want me to come up here to get the baby so she could see it. She said you needed time alone with your child. But you were not alone, I think."

"You are right Lada. Mansunama was here, and he brought me this lovely bouquet." She turned and picked up the flowers, handing them to Lada.

At Lada's look of disbelief, she chuckled warmly. "I know that it sounds preposterous, but it is true. Then he held the baby and said some words I could not understand. I must have dozed off, because the next thing I remember is waking up, and suddenly feeling warm and wonderful and, more importantly, I found that I love my baby very much. I owe Mansunama much more than I can ever repay."

"Then I am very glad that he came. I am sure everyone will be. But come, Billy is probably in the kitchen waiting to be fed." Lada smiled shyly. "He seems to be very fond of my cooking."

Reanna picked the baby up from the cradle and started down the stairs with Lada. "Lada, it is certainly not only your cooking that he likes, as you know very well."

"We shall see," was all Lada would say.

Billy was in the kitchen when they entered, but at the sight of her holding the baby, he jumped up, his face turning crimson, and muttered, "hello Reanna, how are you? I just remembered something I have to do, if you will excuse me?"

Lada went to place the flowers in water and set them on the table.

"Billy – wait!" Reanna cried.

He stopped at the doorway, his back to her.

"Please, none of this was your fault. I know you blame yourself for what your brothers did, but I do not. Look at the baby – please Billy. I love her very much, and I want you to be her Godfather. It would make me very happy if you would." She finished as Billy slowly turned to face her.

He noticed Reanna's wide smile and glowing countenance and looked down at the sleeping baby in her arms, and gradually, a warm smile lit his face. "I would be honored."

At that moment Chance and Raymond entered, engaged in serious conversation. They stopped dead at the sight of Reanna, radiant and happy standing in the kitchen, the babe cradled lovingly in her arms. Their mouths dropped open in surprise, and Chance finally ventured, "Reanna, what are you doing? Is something wro…?"

Glancing at the flowers on the table, Reanna smiled. "Spring, her name is Spring, Chance."

Chapter 11

Reanna studied her reflection in the mirror more closely, pleased by what she saw. Her body had not changed at all from carrying Spring, with the exception of much fuller breasts, heavy with the milk they now produced for the child.

She had finally been able to shed all the numbing fears that had haunted her for so long. Her nightmares had miraculously disappeared. She wondered if this was because she had killed Cal, or because her fears about her child had been laid to rest. The baby was happy and healthy, and Reanna loved her dearly. Thanks to Mansunama. They owed him more than they could ever repay.

She frowned into the mirror, worrying her bottom lip. There was just one more thing that she wished for. Chance had not yet come near her, not touched her at night when they lay in bed. At first Reanna had not minded, she had been so tired from waking at night to feed the baby. But it had been two months now, and her body was healed, burning as her heart ached for her lover's touch. She felt better than she had in a long time, and she wanted her husband.

Chance had even stopped sleeping with her, staying locked in his study every night until it was time to wash and change in the morning. Then he would eat and be off to work, driving himself mercilessly until nightfall, returning dirty, dusty and bone weary.

She knew very well the reason for his behavior, and so was not hurt by it. She smiled softly and shook her head, wondering at Chance's misunderstanding of the birthing and recovery process of a woman's body. After all, he told her that he came from a large family. Surely, he had learned something about having children from his parents.

She thought about her own mother and how she had died during childbirth. Perhaps, in light of the difficulty of Springs delivery, Chance assumed that it would take longer for her to recover.

Well, today was the day of Uncle Bob's annual party, and Reanna had chosen to wear the same delicate blouse and skirt she had worn the night of their first loving union, thinking that surely this would give Chance more than a subtle hint of her desires. She had worn slippers instead of boots this time though, no longer feeling the need of the comfort of her gun as a constant companion. She knew that there would still be times when she would need to carry a weapon for practicality, but this was not one of those times. It would be a day of pure enjoyment of family and friends.

As she thought of all the good food, music and dancing they would enjoy, she imagined Chance holding her close, gazing down at her, his brown eyes glowing with desire … she did not have to wait long to see that look, in fact.

Chance was waiting at the bottom of the stairway, holding Spring in his arms. He looked up as Reanna silently descended, his gaze raking her hotly. Immediately sensing her purpose, he drew his breath in sharply, narrowed his eyes as she slowly drew closer.

"I'm sorry if I kept you waiting Chance." She murmured.

He groaned as the soft scent of roses assailed his nostrils, closing his eyes to block out the vision of her creamy skin and wide, sparkling eyes. Swallowing painfully, he opened them as she came close to take the baby, their depths glowing with red flames of desire. He leaned down, captured her lush, inviting lips in a fiercely tender kiss and spoke in a low, husky voice, "I have been waiting far too long, my love. You play with fire."

She smiled, "There is no longer need to wait, my gallant knight." Her eyes glittering like the surface of the sea, sparkled with mischievous light, and gave Chance all the reassurance he needed.

He groaned but kept his voice in a teasing tone. "You had to wait and tell me just when we are ready to leave for, of all places, a party that the whole town is invited to. And …" he sighed heavily, "we even have to share our wagon for the ride over."

His eyes narrowed as, suddenly suspicious, he divined her intent. "You are a vixen, Reanna Nolton. You will tease me mercilessly the day through, tormenting me with thoughts of what splendor your love will offer me when darkness falls, and we return." His voice grew increasingly more sensual as he leaned toward her, his breath caressing her mouth before his lips met hers in a heatedly passionate kiss. "A bewitching vixen."

When she was finally able to catch her breath again, she smiled widely. "And you, Chance Nolton, are a devil, and we have kept Billy and Lada waiting long enough." She took the baby and hurried out the door.

Sitting in the hay in the back of the wagon, Reanna found it hard to keep her admiring gaze off her very handsome husband. He wore a white shirt with button down front, oversized sleeves gathered at the wrist, and dark brown pants, gun belt and boots. He wore no spurs or working hat today, and she admired the dark hair hanging to his shoulders, and his immaculately trimmed mustache which she loved the feel of when their lips met. She smiled at this last thought, feeling a quickening stir in her loins as the thought led to others.

Chance saw the way she smiled and noted the look in her eyes and laughed. "If I carried coins with me, I'd gladly give one to know what thoughts put that look upon your face."

She smiled flirtatiously, her eyes glittering with mischief. "Coins are not the payment I would seek for such information."

He raised one brow inquiringly. "Pray tell then, sweet lady, what you would ask for such a secret?"

"If you would but be patient, Milord, I shall share all my secrets with you, at little cost to your accounts," she giggled.

Chance leaned near and breathed into her ear. "It is such secrets as these that I would demand to know every detail of."

"And I, sir, would demand full payment of the price I ask."

"You have not yet stated what price it is you seek, Milady. Are you so sure then, that I will be able to deliver your price when you demand?"

She gave him a leering smile, "I've no doubt, Milord, as to just what it is that you can deliver."

He laughed appreciatively. "Reanna Nolton, you have become, without a doubt, much more of a woman than I ever dreamed possible when I asked it of you on our wedding night."

"Indeed, Milord? Perhaps that is due to the one who has taught me these last months."

"Or the one who pays so well for the secrets you guard."

"Ah, but they are well tended, Milord, by the one who takes many names and guises."

"Madam, you have sincerely piqued my curiosity. Confide in me, if you will, of this mystery you conceal."

"'Tis simple, Milord, the names include knight, rogue, scoundrel, bounty hunter, husband, teacher, lover…" her voice trailed off as Chance leaned close again and whispered sensuously, "Don't forget … angel."

His mouth claimed hers in warm passion. When they parted, she could see the coals of that passion burning in his dark eyes, and he, the endless glittering green sea in the depths of hers.

For the remainder of the journey, Chance held Reanna and Spring in the warmth of his embrace, finding that words were needless, for they spoke volumes in the silence with their eyes.

Once they arrived at the Dublin's, they were immediately caught up in the fun and gaiety of the festivities.

Chance and Reanna mingled separately among their friends, and Reanna allowed her thoughts to be filled with the joys and sorrows of their friends, focusing mostly on the painful dilemma of Lada, Billy, and Belinda, none of whom had satisfied their hearts desires.

Chance did likewise, though more grudgingly so. His opinions may be much sought, but his eyes kept wandering the crowd, seeking the pleasures that a glimpse of his wife's beauty could bring.

When dinnertime approached, Chance thought that this would be the perfect time to finally visit with his wife, and he eagerly sought a seat near her, only to know frustration for his effort, as she was surrounded by friends and family acquainting themselves with little Spring.

He watched the scene with a growing sense of tenderness in his heart. Spring truly was a beautiful child, and always happy, and her eyes showed a hint of the sea that he saw so often in Reanna's sparkling green depths.

Finally, Reanna excused herself, taking the child and starting toward the house. Noticing her husband, she sent him an inviting look. Noting her smiling eyes, it did not take him long to follow her into the house.

Taking a seat in the deserted kitchen, she turned to Chance. "I dared not offer Spring her dinner among the crowd, my love. Will you sit with us awhile?"

He pulled out a chair and settled in with lithe grace. "A wise decision Reanna, for I would not see you bare your tempting fruits before other men's hungry eyes." His own eyes sparkled with playfulness.

"Chance Nolton, you are a scoundrel! The only hungry eyes I've noticed watching me this day are those of a former bounty hunter, who, I think, has taken up a new hunt."

His voice was smooth as he answered, "Ah, but the pleasures that this hunt affords far outweigh any other, and the bounty it pays is pure delight."

Her eyes mirrored her pleasure at his words, yet her voice reflected the serious path that her thoughts now took. "There will be enough time for seeking that which you speak of later, my love. Right now, I am bothered by the troubled hearts of our friends. Oh Chance," she sighed, "did you notice that Lada has remained behind that table all day serving drinks, as if she is afraid to have an idle moment, that her love for Billy would be obvious for all to see? And that Billy is finding it impossible to stray any distance from that same table, or to ignore Lada? And poor Belinda is pining quite obviously for Billy, wearing her heart in her eyes. What will come of it all I wonder? I wish there was something we could do to help, though it does seem an impossible situation. One of them will doubtlessly end up with a broken heart. I was hoping … that is … do you have any suggestions?"

Chance rose and walked to her, lifting her chin with his hand. Softly he said, "Only this, that you stop worrying about a situation that you cannot change. And that in time will work itself out. And if one of them is left with a broken heart, well …" he shrugged. "Time will take care of that also. We can do nothing, unfortunately, to change their circumstances or feelings. There is however one thing that you can do now that would make everyone here happy, at least for a while. If you would, Milady, take up your guitar and grace us with the magic of your music. I know that you can weave a soothing spell over us all."

She played for nearly two hours, and did, indeed, seem to cast a spell over everyone as they stopped what they were doing to listen as the high, sweet notes rose and dipped, embracing her audience with their purity, for her heart now knew the immense pleasure of true love shared freely and completely.

Later, Chance held Reanna gently in his arms as they shared a dance, and his heated gaze swept the length of her. He glanced up quickly as he noticed her shoes, his amusement evident as he chuckled, "I see that you have found the slippers to match your outfit this time, madam."

She dazzled him as she smiled happily, "Oh Chance, I have found so many of the lovely thing's life has to offer of late. I have never felt so carefree and happy."

He raised a dark brow in inquiry. "Indeed madam? Perhaps that is the reason that I am completely lost when I gaze upon the endless green sea that beckons in your eyes.

His dark, chestnut eyes grew more intense as his lips suddenly tightened and he clasped her closely to him. "Oh God, Rea, I love you! And I share all your feelings of happiness. We are good together my love and we will share a rich life."

She was touched to the point of tears at his words, but she blinked them away as she smiled brightly up into his lean face. "We have truly been blessed in our love, Chance."

His smile returned as he answered. "Yes, we do seem to be, now. We have each other, and a beautiful little daughter. We have a nice home, soon to be a profitable ranch, and we will surely never lack for any material comfort with all my businesses along the coast. The ship alone brings in enough to pay our living expenses. We shall amass a fortune and leave it to our ten children."

Reanna managed, in spite of the laughter that threatened, to look appropriately aghast. "Ten children! I think, sir knight that you had best reconsider. You would have me so busy taking care of children that I would have little time left to lead you on the bounty hunt that you so relish."

He chuckled deeply. "Touché! Consider it reconsidered immediately I shall settle for one more addition to the family." He leaned close, his breath hot in her ear as he whispered, "Let's go hunting."

And later, in the privacy of their room, they did exactly that.

Chance quickly divested himself of clothing, and turning, helped Reanna with her buttons, slowly sliding her blouse down over her creamy shoulders. His hands leisurely followed to gently cup her firm breasts, and she closed her eyes in ecstasy as a soft moan escaped her lips.

The low light of the lamp bathed her skin in golden radiance, and he drew in his breath sharply as he struggled against the urge to swiftly satisfy his hunger for her.

His voice was ragged with desire as he breathed into her ear, "You are lovelier than ever. Your skin fairly glows with your beauty."

She smiled enticingly. "It is only your love, burning from within me Chance." Her breath caught in her throat as she gazed directly into the raw, red desire of his eyes.

"Let us fan the flames then, my love," he growled urgently as he bore her down onto the bed, holding her close to him. Her breasts burned his chest where they crushed against him, and the flames rose high and spread like wildfire, consuming them both as his mouth claimed hers in fierce passion, finally tracing lower to fan the flames over her breasts as they thrust forward to welcome his fevered pursuit. He raised up to pull her skirt over her slim hips and the long length of her legs, his hands caressing her silken flesh as she writhed beneath him, urging him on, lifting to meet him as he buried himself deep within her welcoming warmth.

The flames grew, consuming, searing, fierce with their love and shared passion, until they were drowning in an overwhelming tide of rapture before they were lifted together, high above, to view the stars.

In the aftermath of their intense union, they lay entwined upon the perfect happiness that they had finally found.

"Have I paid your bounty satisfactorily, Milord?" Reanna murmured drowsily, snuggling closer.

"That you have my love, that you have." He kissed the top of her head.

She smiled. They truly shared paradise, she, and her bounty hunter.

These feelings only heightened and expanded with the passage of the next twelve months. It was the most blissfully happy times Chance and Reanna had ever known, the perfection of their days only growing over the course of the year.

They worked hard to get the ranch running smoothly, with Reanna at Chance's side every day no matter what the work involved, spending more of each day outdoors as the demands of feeding Spring lessened. Lada ran the house and looked after the child during the day, and in the evenings, after dinner, Chance, Billy, Reanna, and Lada would gather in the backyard to watch as Modoc and Tasha played with Spring, gently nudging the child, and then laying patiently while Spring climbed enthusiastically over and around them, playfully clutching handfuls of soft brown-black fur in her tiny fist. Reanna had trained them well, and they obeyed her every command, but she had little need to speak to them, for they naturally loved and protected this smaller form of their mistress.

Twice a week when Raymond came to visit, sometimes bringing Bob and Martha along with him, Jared and Michael would stay after working hours and the whole family would gather in the parlor to listen to Reanna play, accompanied by Billy on the harmonica. These were times of soft music, peace and laughter, punctuated by Spring's revelry as she was bounced upon her indulgent grandfather's knee.

About a month after Spring's first birthday, Chance and Reanna decided they would take a trip to their favorite lake site, and so with Spring, Modoc, and an expecting Tasha, spent a week of quiet play and relaxation, enjoying the primal beauty and solitude offered them.

Fulfilled and content, they returned to the house, pausing as they rounded the corner and spied a poor, shabby looking wagon parked in the yard.

Curious, Reanna asked, "Chance, where do you suppose that came from?"

He studied the wagon from his seat, his eyes narrowing as he took in the obvious signs of neglect. That the wagon was unhitched told him whoever owned it planned on staying for more than just a brief visit. "Beats me, but we won't find out if you and Spring don't get down and let me put the horses away. I'll be in as soon as I unpack our wagon."

She took Spring by the hand and slowly, matching Spring's tiny steps, made her way to the back door, unable to explain the feeling of unease that pricked at her conscience. That feeling deepened as she entered the kitchen to find Billy, looking quite put upon, helping Lada with a mountain of dirty dishes. As Lada turned to face her, Reanna noted the exhaustion that was apparent on Lada's face, and her disheveled appearance.

Her question died in her throat as Lada began, nervously, to explain. "Oh Reanna, I am so glad you and Chance are back. Billy would have come for you, but he was afraid to leave me alone. I – I mean ... well, a mess."

She paused, closing her eyes, and drawing a deep breath before proceeding. "It is Chance's family, Reanna. They arrived two days ago and ... Billy and I have tried, but ... Mrs. Nolton has taken sick. She is upstairs in the guest bedroom, but she is not the problem. It is the men. They are the sloppiest ... that is ... they have been very demanding."

Tears threatened to choke Lada as Reanna found her voice, gently coaxing, "Where are they Lada?"

"In the parlor, and the little ones, well ... I just have not been able to keep track of them."

Leaving Spring with Lada and Billy, Reanna hurried to the parlor, but came to an abrupt halt just inside the doorway, her senses swiftly assailed by the stench of tobacco in the smoke-filled room.

Five men lolled indolently about the room, their feet up on her once richly polished mahogany tables, covered now with streaks and scratches and empty whisky bottles.

She inwardly recoiled as the five of them looked her over, assessing her, but she held her ground. They were, after all, her husband's family. Even though they were filthy, reminding her vividly of the McPhersons, she somehow managed to hide her revulsion. There must be some explanation for their unsuitable behavior. They were Chance's family....

Two of the men slowly stood and approached her. The older of the two spoke first, a slow, sneering smile spreading across his face, which was lean and would have been darkly handsome if it had not been for the obvious signs of dissipation around his accusing gray eyes and the unshorn stubble covering his cheeks and chin. As tall as Chance, he loomed over her and spoke sarcastically.

"Well, by God, Chance sure did net himself a real treasure, and got this whole big ranch to boot. You are Mrs. Chance Nolton?"

The words caught in her throat, and she could only nod affirmatively.

The younger man stepped forward, an almost identical copy of the older man, except that his nose was long and narrow, lending his voice a nasal quality. But it was the coldly calculating gleam in his eyes that truly frightened her.

"Names David. Yours is Reanna, ain't it?"

Again, she nodded, her eyes enormous in disbelief.

"Well, little brother certainly has done well for himself. And he thought he was too good to share his money with us. Why, we thought maybe he was dead, that is until you wrote and told us where to find him." He raised his arm to her shoulder, rubbing her hair between his fingers, and she trembled slightly, but held fast.

Sensing her fright, David smiled coldly, leering at the snug fit of her bodice as he softly spoke. "Smooth as silk. You must be a real pleasure between the sheets, little lady."

Acutely aware of the smell of cheap whiskey on his breath, Reanna covered her mouth with her hand and turned to flee. She raced past Chance, who had just come in, and made it to the back yard before retching violently behind a bush.

Chance's narrowed eyes swept the room, coming to rest on his father and brother, his features stiff with fury. But it was his eyes that gave them pause, as they were hard, almost cruel, and the red flames that glowed within came not from loves passion, but fierce anger, surging rapidly through him.

He ground out in a softly threatening tone, "You are not welcome here. Get out. All of you!"

Mr. Nolton spoke up, "We were invited by your wife. She wrote a long letter telling us all about your babe, and nothing would do, what with your ma pinin' away to see the little beggar, that we jes' had to come. 'Sides, we wanted to see what kind of girl you would marry with your high falutin' ways, and what a sight she is. You got plenty enough to share with your lovin' family. And anyways, your ma, she's real sick."

Chance had roughly grasped his father, gathering the front of his shirt into his fist, but at these last words, he loosened his grip.

His father affected a deep sigh, studying the dirty nails of his right hand most intently. "Can't jes' up and leave her, ya know."

"What is wrong with mother?"

"Don't know, can't say."

Chance shoved his father aside in disgust as he let go of his shirt. "I will deal with you scum after I have seen to mother."

Chance retraced his steps, seeking to find Reanna in the kitchen, but she had already gone. Running a hand through his hair, he stopped to speak to Billy and Lada.

"I apologize for any rude behavior you have suffered at their hands." He shook his head grimly. "I had no idea that she had written them. Do you know where she is?"

Lada smiled reassuringly. "Chance, there is no need for your regret. And Reanna said that she was going upstairs. I wanted to make her some tea, but she refused. I think that she just needs some time to calm down."

Reanna had forced herself to recover quickly. Whatever happened was her own fault. What had she done? Why had she not listened to Chance when he warned her about his family? And now ... who knew what kind of sickness his mother may have brought with her.

She entered the bedroom to find it stuffy and hot, the light dimmed by the drawn curtains. She immediately crossed the room to open both the curtains and windows, allowing fresh air to circulate.

She turned, and then stopped in surprise at the sight that met her eyes. The tiny, frail woman in the bed stared at her through large, liquid eyes framed with long black lashes. Her small, heart shaped face was shockingly white, surrounded by a thick crop of yellow hair, liberally streaked with white. Her nose was small and delicate, as was the fragile hand that rested on the covers over her chest.

Brown eyes glowed golden, and the warmth in her voice was unmistakable as she addressed the younger woman. "You must be Reanna. At least I sincerely hope that you are. You are very lovely, and it is easy to see that you have a kind heart as well."

Reanna moved close to the side of the bed and answered softly. "Yes, I am Chance's wife. And you are his mother."

"Yes, my name is Ellen. I want to thank you for writing that letter. You see … well, I had not heard from my son in some years, and I was afraid … that is … I thought the worst. You cannot imagine how happy you have made me."

Ellen moved to sit up, and Reanna leaned down to assist her, fluffing the pillows behind her, thinking that maybe it had been worthwhile, after all, to send for Chance's family. But she could not help wondering how this petite woman with the soft cultured voice had come to marry the obnoxious man she had met downstairs.

"Is Chance here?" Ellen queried as she attempted a tremulous smile.

"He should be up any time now. But tell me, what illness do you have? Have you been seen by a doctor?"

Ellen laughed shortly. "I am afraid that my husband would not hear of wasting coin on a doctor. It is only a weakness of mine dear, that I am afflicted with occasionally, although lately, it seems to come on more often. Have you seen my two younger girls? I am afraid that the men are not particularly watchful of them. And I would love to see my first grandchild if I may."

Reanna doubted that the men downstairs were good for much of anything, but she kept that thought to herself.

"I have not seen them, Ellen. But I will find them when I go downstairs, don't worry yourself. I can bring Spring up later when you have had time to visit with Chance. May I bring you anything, some tea perhaps?"

"No thank you dear. I must rest for a while now."

Ellen leaned her head back with a sigh and closed her eyes. Reanna could see the weariness clearly etched upon the older woman's face and turned quietly to go.

Just then Chance entered the room, and she could see that he was clearly vexed. His lean face was hard and unyielding, and his gaze was cold as it bore into hers before his glance swept past her to rest on his mother. Swiftly crossing the room, he knelt by the bed, taking her fragile hand into his own as he whispered, "Mother."

Ellen opened her eyes, and they warmed with happiness as she searched the beloved features that she thought never to see again.

"Chance, how I have missed you, my son." She raised her hand to lightly stroke his bronzed cheek. "I see that you have chosen a fine wife, Chance. One that I would be proud to call daughter. I have her to thank for this meeting. Why did you never write?"

He looked painfully guilty. "I am sorry Mother. Sorry for all the wasted years, sorry for the extra burden of worry that I have caused you. It is Father and David that I cannot abide. You know how it is with us." He finished lamely.

A shadow of sadness passed over Ellen's face as she answered forlornly. "I know my son. But would you disown your entire family because of your quarrel with them? Your younger brothers and sisters need you, Chance. They need to know that someone cares, that there is another way of life other than that which they have been forced to know."

Reanna noted the muscle twitching in Chance's jaw and the rigid set of his shoulders. Deciding to leave her husband and mother-in-law to settle things between themselves, she excused herself. "Chance, I will be downstairs, and I will send Billy to town for the doctor. Ellen, I am so glad to finally meet you, and try not to worry. I will find your girls."

Ellen smiled, "Thank you, dear. I feel that we will be great friends."

Chance would not look at her, but as she closed the door, she heard the contained fury in his voice as he addressed his mother. "Sisters? You mean to say…"

Taking a deep breath, Reanna began to make her way to the kitchen. At least his mother was kindly, but what she had to face now made her stomach churn.

Billy and Lada prepared dinner in tense silence as David sat at the table with a bottle of whiskey, crudely leering at the pretty Indian woman as she tried her best to ignore his presence. His lustful perusal was quickly drawn to Reanna who forced her words through a dry mouth.

"It has come to my attention that you have two younger siblings which I have yet to meet. I would appreciate your help in finding them."

When Spring saw her mother, she toddled over and clung to her skirts. She gazed up at Reanna and proclaimed loudly, "Mama," which brought a smile to Reanna's face as she bent to pick up her daughter, hugging her tightly. She was suddenly very angry that these men would simply let young children run wild with no thought or care for their safety.

David stood and reached out to touch Spring's hair, and Reanna pulled her daughter back, glaring angrily at him. "Have you no idea where the children are?"

"No ma'am, maybe out in the barn, or with those stinking dogs."

Reanna's temper flared. "I would suggest, sir, that you keep your opinions of my dogs, or anything else in my home, to yourself!" She strode to the door, slamming it soundly on her way out.

She searched the horse barn and scoured the back yard, going to the dog pens and the chicken coop, but could find no sign of them. Finally, she reached the cattle barn, and found the two little girls within, playing and giggling in a pile of hay left from the previous winter. Suddenly noticing Reanna, they froze, and something akin to awe passed over their faces, which were smudged with dirt. Wisps of hay peeked from their tousled hair.

The older one spoke. "Are you … an angel?" she asked in wonder.

Reanna laughed merrily. "No, sweetie, I am not. Whatever made you ask me that?"

"You look like an angel because you are so pretty."

Kneeling beside the girls in the hay, Reanna questioned seriously, "Have you ever seen an angel?"

The girl's brow furrowed in concentration as she thought, then she brightened and glanced up as an answer came to her. "Well, in my dreams I seen – I mean I saw – an angel and she was real pretty, and you are real pretty, so I thought you was – were – an angel come to see me. Besides," she added, "you like babies, and mama says that angels like babies."

Reanna could not help but be drawn to the girl who placed such innocent trust in her. They were studying Spring, who stood silently at her mother's side with her thumb in her mouth.

Reanna reached out to gently stroke the girl's head. "What is your name child? And that of your sister?"

"My name is Holly and that is Beth." She stabbed a grubby finger in the direction of the smaller girl. "Beth is almost four, and I am fourteen."

The girl acted no more than nine or ten, and Reanna was incredulous. "Fourteen! Do you tease me Holly?"

"Oh no, mam. I am almost growed up, that's what Papa says, Mama too," she finished importantly.

"Have you ever been to school or had any teaching?"

"Well, I have never gone to school – Papa says we don't need to read and write – but Mama teaches me things when she's not too tired. She says I must have manners, too. But Papa always tells her it is a waste of time and that I should pull my weight and do chores instead of filling my head with nonsense."

"Now why doesn't that surprise me," Reanna muttered under her breath.

"What?" questioned Holly.

"Nothing precious."

"My name's Holly, remember?"

Reanna laughed and rumpled the girl's hair as she glanced from one to the other. They both looked healthy enough, but they would need a good scrubbing. Their hair was matted and snarled, and they had long ago outgrown the stained, crumpled dresses that were not much better than rags.

Holly had dark, thick hair that hung to her waist, and large blue eyes that peered from beneath thick, dark lashes and finely shaped brows. Her skin was smooth and bronzed, with a rosy blush across her high cheekbones and full mouth. Her classically chiseled nose and strong chin combined with her other features in a pleasing way, to promise beauty and character as she matured.

Beth had her mother's heart shaped face and light skin, and large, luminous brown eyes. Her pert little nose was sprinkled generously with freckles, and she had a tiny pink mouth. All of this was framed by a mass of unruly golden ringlets that bounced at her shoulders when she moved.

"We will talk more about teaching later. Right now, you need a nice warm bath, and I will see if I can get you some clean clothes before dinner. Come along with me now."

She stood, hoisting Spring up onto her hip, and Beth spoke for the first time. "Baby, your Baby?"

Reanna nodded. "Yes, Beth, this is my baby. Her name is Spring."

"Spring," repeated Beth.

Holly looked carefully at the baby. "Spring, what a pretty name. She looks just like you, miss angel."

Amused, Reanna corrected the young girl. "My name is Reanna, Holly. And I am really not an angel. I am married to your brother Chance. Have you ever met him?"

"No mam, but mama speaks of him lots. She cried, but said it was because she was so happy, when papa told her we were going to see him."

"Well, you will meet him soon Holly, and I am sure you will like him. I will tell you a secret," she continued. "He is the one that I call angel."

Reanna entered the kitchen with the three children in tow, to find things had not improved in her absence. Determined to remedy the situation, she began to issue instructions. "Billy, would you mind riding to town to fetch Dr. Farley? I think he should examine Mrs. Nolton. Lada, while you are getting dinner I am going to bathe the children. David, may I ask your help to bring water in to heat?"

David insolently studied her for some seconds before shrugging his shoulders and drawling lazily, "Luggin' waters women's work."

Reanna placed Spring on the floor and set out the large kettles that they would heat the water in, answering smoothly, "Perhaps you would rather fetch wood for the fire then."

She froze. When she felt his hand come to rest on her waist she nearly jumped out of her skin, which set her in motion. Grasping the handle of one of the iron pots she had set upon the stove, she swung it around with all her might, catching David a glancing blow on the side of his head. He stumbled back, a look of shocked surprise on his face that slowly changed to one of anger.

Grabbing the stove poker, Reanna pointed it at David as she stood her ground. Her voice seethed with venom as she hissed, "You will not touch me again, bastard, if you wish to keep drawing breath!" She inhaled deeply, struggling to calm her nerves. In a lower voice she stated, "This is your brother's house, and you will show respect to all those in it, or you will get out! Chance would kill you in a minute for what you just did, brother be damned! If you choose to stay, you will pitch in and help where it is needed. Right now, I need water for the children's bath. Make your decision!"

David looked at her in mute rage but decided that he would let her have the upper hand for now. Eyeing the poker, he relented.

"Put that thing away. I'll fetch your water." He grabbed the pot and strode out the door, slamming it behind him as Reanna had done earlier.

She dropped the poker from numb, trembling fingers. Her knees suddenly felt like jelly, and she unsteadily made her way to a chair, gratefully sinking down with her head in her hands. She was nauseous and dizzy, still able to smell the whiskey that was on David's breath. She did not know whether to scream or cry as memories of the McPherson's obliterated all else in her mind.

Lada brought her back to the present as she gently laid her hand upon Reanna's shoulder. "Reanna are you alright?" she questioned fearfully.

"I will be fine in a minute or two," Reanna answered, raising her head to prove her point.

Lada's voice was low, in deference to the children, who hovered in the corner, the smaller ones behind Holly, but the urgency of her words was not lost.

"We are not safe with them around. They have been treating me that way since they arrived. The others are quiet and seem to be polite enough. It is only David and his father that are lazy and cruel. Billy has not dared leave my side for fear of what those two would do. They kept saying terrible things about Indians and red skinned women. We have had to wait on them hand and foot, and clean up after them, plus take care of Mrs. Nolton, who is a sweet woman, but with our sleepless nights, it has taken much to keep up with their demands."

Reanna studied Lada, taking note of the dark circles under her eyes and the lines of exhaustion in her face. Even her proud, erect carriage dropped dispiritedly.

"Lada, I must apologize. I am sorry it has been so rough on you, and it is my fault that they are here. Chance warned me about them, but I would not listen. I did not think that they could possibly be as bad as he said. If you would be able to stay and see us through tonight's meal, you and Billy can go to my father's, or to town, whichever you prefer, for a few days to rest. Chance and I should be able to handle things for a while. And besides, I think that you are in much more danger than I."

Lada impulsively hugged Reanna tightly before answering. "Thank you, Rea. We will go to your fathers after dinner then."

Reanna watched the relief that flooded Lada's fine features even as icy fingers of dread grasped at her own heart. Lada really was in great danger of ill treatment, especially at David's hands, but she did not think her own position to be that much better, more so now, because she had gotten the best of him just now, which he undoubtedly would not forget.

David came in with the water just then and left to get more. Reanna bustled the wide-eyed girls upstairs to find some clothing they could wear while they waited for the water to warm. Mentally she listed the supply of necessary items they would need from town to properly clothe Chance's younger sisters.

Sensing his presence, Reanna turned to find Chance lounging against the doorframe, his expression inscrutable as he gazed at the roomful of females.

Hesitantly, unsure of his mood, she ventured, "Chance, Billy has gone for the doctor. I …" she stopped at a loss for words.

Chance shifted to stand before her. "First of all, Madame, I warned you not to write them. I will not have those two in my home. And don't look so damned innocent! You know which two I mean. I swear that I should take you over my …" He stammered to a halt as he realized that the two young girls were staring in fright at his harsh tone of voice. "That is," clearing his throat, he continued in a calmer vein, "I do love you for wanting to do something that you thought good and right, but this is not good, Rea, to have those two in our home. I will have to ask them to leave before dark."

Reanna, her eyes wide and probing, beseeched him. "Chance, my love, that is impossible. They have nowhere to go, your mother is ill, and the two youngest need looking after. If you try to send only your father and brother away, they will surely not leave without the rest of the family. There would only be great trouble and hurt if you force them. Please, Chance, wait a while and see what happens. Things may work out better than you think."

Her heart thudded wildly in her chest as she strove to believe the sincerity of her own words, for her husband needed this time to renew his bonds of family love, whether he knew it himself or not.

Chance stood close and stared down into her wide eyes so full of hope. "As you wish," he relented, "Since it means so much to you."

Her smile was dazzling as she answered, "Then, may I have the pleasure of introducing these two young ladies? This is Holly," she indicated the older girl. "And this is Beth."

"How do you do?" Chance asked gravely, but at their timid expressions he hunkered down before them. "I am sorry if I frightened you before. I assure you, I do not bite."

Holly considered him carefully, and finally deciding that he spoke the truth, said, "You are the angel? You look to big to be an angel. I thought you would be smaller, but you are pretty – no, handsome, that is the word. Mama said you were. You are my big brother, aren't you? You are a handsome angel brother."

Chance could not contain his laughter, and Reanna noticed that his face turned a deeper shade of bronze. He lifted Holly in his strong arms and held her up before him. "Yes, I am your brother. My name is Chance, and I am very glad to have a little sister as pretty as you, but usually …" here he paused to look askance at Reanna, "I am not referred to as an angel."

He set Holly down and bent to pick up Beth, sitting her gently on the bed. "Beth … that is a pretty name. How old are you, Beth?"

"Free." Beth held up three fingers.

"Well," Chance smiled at them tenderly, "how would the both of you like to stay here with us for a while?"

"Oh yes!" exclaimed Holly. "It is a big, pretty house and you and Reanna are pretty angels."

Chance stood, his eyes meeting Reanna's smiling gaze, they both showed an obvious fire of love. "Yes, she is a pretty angel, Holly."

"We have bath!" piped in Beth.

"That," said Chance solemnly, "is a good idea."

Bathed and dressed in white linen nightgowns that Reanna had cut down, the girls, with Reanna and Chance, went in to bid Ellen good night, and introduce her to Spring.

Doctor Farley had examined Ellen, proclaiming that all she needs is a period of rest, and proper food, with which she should be as good as new. Having shared their evening meal, the doctor then took his leave, riding part of the way with Billy and Lada. Jared and Michael had gone home earlier, and Chance's brothers had settled on the porch to enjoy the freshening evening breeze, with the exception of David and his father, who had bedded down in the barn, deeply sleeping off their alcohol induced stupor.

"Chance, you have made a wonderful choice in your wife, and in the life you lead. I am very proud of you. Could you, I wonder, teach your brothers, show them that there is a better way of life, than the example that David and your father set?"

Reanna watched as Chance gazed at his mother holding Spring, his love for her clearly evident. "Mother, I would do all that I possibly can for them. That is a promise. But for now, why don't you rest?"

"Yes," she sighed, "I am tired."

They left her, and after tucking the children in, finally joined the three young men on the porch. As they sat and chatted, Chance filled them in on some of his adventures, and on the workings of the ranch. There was an easy comradery between them, as if the years of separation had never been, and as they spoke together, Reanna was able to study them for the first time, as they had eaten out here earlier, instead of with the rest of the family in the dining room.

Nathan, the third oldest, was twenty-five, and almost identical to Chance in looks, but years of difficult, solitary living had hardened Chance's features. It spooked her to see the face of her husband on another, but Nathan's features were somewhat softer, and he did not have that harsh, mocking light in his dark eyes.

Stewart, or Stew as he was called, looked more like Ellen and was, at twenty, a soft spoken rather shy young man who seemed to think things through carefully before venturing an opinion.

Jeremy, the youngest of the brothers, was sixteen, with features like Chance and Nathan. His eyes, however, were a bright blue, shining with good humor and quick intelligence. His hair was the color of Beth's, a light golden mass of curls. Tall and big boned, he was a very handsome man.

Deciding to retire for the evening, Nathan stood and, lifting Reanna's slim hand, he placed a light kiss upon it, his eyes twinkling in amusement as he noted her blush. "Reanna, it has been a pleasure."

She smiled. Not only did he have Chance's good looks, but his charm as well.

"Good night mam," Stewart mumbled softly as he studied his feet and Jeremy, staring in open admiration, wished her good night also, with a wide smile lighting his face.

Chance went up to bed also, but Reanna remained on the porch, sighing as she listened to the soft rustling of the night creatures, watching as the darkness was broken here and there by the tiny bright glow of the first fireflies. As she leaned her head against the high back of the chair, she recalled the tension at dinner.

Chance and Reanna, with the girls and Dr. Farley, had entered the dining room to find David and Luke, Chance's father, already seated at the table. As they were seating themselves, Lada had come in, placing dishes of food on the table.

In a commanding voice Luke ordered, "Squaw, get some whiskey for my cup. By now, I shouldn't have to ask for it!"

Chance, in the process of sitting, stood again. His face was livid with fury, and he looked as though he wanted to kill his father. Reanna was standing next to Chance and placed a restraining hand on his arm, as she could see the muscles of his jawline twitching.

She found her courage quickly. "Mister Nolton," she snapped, "we demand respect be shown to all in this house. Lada – that is her name – is our friend and part of our family. I must insist that you hold your tongue if you cannot speak pleasantly. You may well find yourself in the barn eating with the rest of the animals!"

Not daring to look at Chance, she could sense when his anger abated, turning to amusement as Luke raised his brows in astonishment.

"Well, ain't you a feisty one! No wench ever raised her voice to me before or told me what to do." He chuckled heartily. "But I'll grant ya, ya made yer point, and it's well taken."

He turned to Chance. "You sure did pick yerself a wild filly, son."

Reanna, too, glanced at Chance, and saw the lights dancing in his eyes. He grinned then and raised his brow as he seemed to study his indignant wife. In a low voice he agreed. "Yes, a fine wild filly."

They sat down and ate in silence, and when they were almost through, Chance looked pointedly at his father, then at David. "Since you will be staying here an undetermined amount of time, I think it only fair that you help around this ranch, especially now, with Billy and Lada taking a short vacation. We will decide who will do what in the morning."

"Me and Jeremy can take care of the dogs and chickens and bring in firewood for the stove." Holly spouted enthusiastically. "We always did those chores at home."

"Since we have been gone for a week, Chance will need to see to things around here, while I must go to town for supplies and some suitable clothes for Holly and Beth. I will need a pair of strong arms to load the heavier items on the wagon. Perhaps Nathan…"

"Well," interrupted David quickly as a lazy smile crept over his face, "I'll be glad to help you ma'am."

Reanna's voice stuck in her throat, which had suddenly gone dry. She glanced at Chance for help, but he simply shrugged his shoulders, unaware of the earlier episode with the poker and pot. She took a quick gulp of sherry, pondering her choices. But there was only one without arousing her husband's suspicions, and David knew it. She finally found her voice and answered.

"David, you are welcome to accompany me on the condition that I do not smell a drop of whiskey on your breath, and you will need some clean clothing. Chance, you must have something he could wear?"

As she turned toward him, Chance wondered at her strained expression, but answered, "I suppose I could find something."

He gave David a piercing look. "The conditions my wife mentioned are agreeable?"

David shrugged haphazardly. "Sure thing, brother."

Chance glared at David, deciding that he really did not trust his brother's ready agreement. "Not a drop of liquor!"

David nodded curtly, his smile changing quickly to a perturbed frown.

Reanna sighed again, hoping that she had not made a grave error in allowing David to escort her to town. Shaking off her uneasy feelings, she rose and shortly joined her husband in their bed.

As she nestled snugly in his arms, his voice came to her in a strained whisper. "Now, my love, you know why I never wanted you to meet them. My father and David are nothing but lazy, poor excuses for human beings. If they were not ignoring the younger children, they were punishing them for some imagined crime. They treat women as animals. I have seen my mother humiliated and abused by him more times than I can count when he was stone drunk on that whiskey, he loves more than anything else. I will never understand why she stays with him, but she refuses to leave him. There have been many times, Rea, when I have actually wanted to kill both my father and my older brother. I may yet if they stay long enough to drive me beyond my point of reason. I was still a child when I left home, but I have grown strong enough now to know that I must protect my belief in what is right, and I will enforce what is right in my own home even at gunpoint if need be."

They simply lay then, holding each other, and drawing strength from their endless love.

Finally, Reanna spoke, seeking to ease his strong feelings of hate. "Perhaps they just need a wild filly to put them in their place."

Chance placed a warm, gentle kiss on her forehead. "I love you beyond all else, Rea. Now maybe you would like to show this stallion what his place is. Ride the wind with me, my love."

The sensual tone of his voice caressed her soul as his hands so effortlessly ignited the sparks of desire in her body. They rode the wind, high, wild, and free, chasing, catching, and taming each other in the flaming passions of love and hate combined. And the wind of love did indeed lift them to the treetops before letting go, allowing their slow and gradual descent back to reality.

Reanna awoke to a pink tinted dawn and two pairs of eyes solemnly watching her. Collecting her awakening senses, she realized that the blue pair belonged to Holly and the brown to Beth.

Yawning drowsily, she murmured, "Good morning girls."

"We're hungry," said Beth.

"Hush Beth! Mama says that's not polite." Holly chastened before turning again to Reanna. "I can cook. I have to lots at home. But I was scared to go down when no one was up."

"Well, I am hungry!" Beth declared.

Reanna smiled at the child and sat up. "Well, I had better get up and dressed then, before Beth fades away."

Holly giggled, and both girls stood expectantly waiting at the side of her bed. Reanna smiled warmly at them as she gently shooed them out. "Girls, could you please wait in Springs room? I will come to get you when I am ready to go downstairs."

When they had gone, Reanna leaned over to place a gentle kiss upon her husband's dark cheek. He opened one eye and inquired, "Is that an invitation madam?"

"Chance! You were awake all along!" she accused him.

"Long enough to know that Beth is demanding breakfast, and Spring will soon be joining her, so we better get up before my priorities are unavoidably changed, and I am tempted to spend the day in bed with a certain copper haired vixen."

Giving her a swift kiss, Chance slid out of bed, followed by Reanna.

"I have my doubts about you going to town with David alone." Chance told her as he was dressing. "But as long as he is sober, and stays that way, he should not present too much of a problem. And having the dubious honor of spending the day with my father is not a particularly cheerful thought either. Maybe we should succumb to some dire malady and spend the day in bed," he teased.

She spoke over her shoulder as she drew on a pretty, though plain, emerald colored linen gown with short, puffed sleeves and a scooped neckline. The form fitting waistline hugged her closely, showing her trim figure to perfection. "We cannot just give up before trying Chance. Holly and Beth are so sweet, and I would like to continue their schooling while they are here, and you did promise your mother, after all."

She gave him a quick peck on the cheek before she bent to slip on her old boots, with the gun inside, on her feet. She had not worn them in over a year, but Chance was glad that she did so now. It never hurt to take precautions.

"I will get some tea brewing first for your mother. Hurry down so you can bring it to her." Reanna said as she hurried out the door.

As he shaved, Chance decided that if he could keep his father and David away from liquor, their visit just might work out after all. He still had many reservations, but Reanna's positive attitude went a long way in convincing him to try.

Rummaging through his chest of drawers, he withdrew several changes of clothes, enough for his father and four brothers. Whistling a cheerful tune, he roused the rest of his family, giving them the clothing.

Half an hour later, they were seated in the kitchen enjoying a meal of thickly sliced ham, scrambled eggs, and warm slices of bread liberally spread with fresh butter, and hot, strong coffee. As they ate, they discussed the various duties to be parceled out, and the assignation of each.

Stew and Nathan would take care of the barns, and the stock kept in each. Reanna, Jeremy, and Holly would see to the chickens, pigs, vegetable gardens, and housework, in addition to looking in on Ellen and keeping an eye on Beth and Spring.

Luke, and after today David, would ride out to check the fences and stock out on the range. Chance realized this would be the best way to assure their continued sobriety. He winced at the thought of spending so many hours in their company, but it was unavoidable.

Reanna joined David in the wagon, hugging Spring to her as she sat in the seat beside him. She gritted her teeth and stared resolutely ahead as David set the wagon in motion, determined not to succumb to the urge to run fearfully away from her brother-in-law.

Although she remained icily aloof, she gradually became aware of David's intense perusal. "The sun shinin' on yer hair sets it off right pretty-like. Ain't never seen hair that color before. Right pleasin', like copper."

The sudden sound of his voice startled Reanna and as he reached out to stroke her hair, she knew a moment of fear which was quickly replaced by rising indignation. Glaring furiously, she angrily slapped his hand away, only to have her arm caught in his iron, vise-like grip.

"Wasn't meanin' no harm, mam. Just temptin' to touch is all." His voice was deceptively smooth, belied by the anger that was apparent in his steely gaze.

She forced herself to focus squarely on him, meeting his gaze with a dangerous glint emanating from her own. "See that you keep your hands to yourself in the future."

Their eyes locked a moment longer, and then David slowly relaxed his grip, releasing her arm as he concentrated once more on driving.

She took a deep shuddering breath, glad that she had won this contest of wills so easily and, consoling herself with the knowledge that David lacked the added bolster of alcohol that would further his bad behavior. They accomplished the rest of the ride in silence.

Gaining the comparative bustle of Carson City, Reanna nodded to several acquaintances before David pulled the wagon up in front of the general store.

When Reanna introduced David to the proprietor, he merely tipped his hat in acknowledgment and silently began to load the supplies into the wagon as she indicated her purchases.

Walking stiffly beside him as he carried the last bag to the wagon, she tersely informed him that he could wait outside for her, as she would be quite a little while choosing suitable ensembles for his mother and sisters. Turning to reenter the store, Reanna missed David's narrowed eyes and muttered, "Sure thing, miss high and mighty, sure thing."

Reanna did not have long to wonder at the smug look on David's face as she helped Spring into the wagon and climbed in herself. Her eyes were immediately drawn to the half empty bottle of whiskey nestled between his feet. Her courage fled as she looked up at his self-satisfied smirk and slightly wavering control as he started the team back home. Refusing to start a scene in front of passerby however, she had no choice but to sit quietly beside him.

Halfway home, David pulled the wagon off the road and stopped, deliberately watching her reaction as he reached down and raised the bottle to his lips, taking a long draft before wiping his mouth with the back of his hand.

Clutching her daughter closely in one arm, Reanna reached surreptitiously down to her boot, drawing out her revolver and hiding it within the fold of her skirt.

David leered casually at her, a lazy grin curving his lips as he reached brazenly out to cup her breast.

A gasp of protest escaped her, and her eyes widened in shock before she drew her scattered wits about her and raised the revolver, leveling at his chest. Her voice no more than a whisper in the stillness, she ordered, "Drive the wagon."

Unbelievably she heard him laugh. "Just seekin' a little sport, honey. Ain't gonna hurt ya any."

Her voice was tight in her chest as she demanded, "Take your hands off me or I will shoot."

His grin disappeared. "You ain't gonna shoot your husband's brother. Now hand over that gun."

She lent her words as much force as she could muster, insisting, "Drive!"

David's hand shot out, making a swift grab for the gun, and the deafening explosion rent the air just before a spreading crimson stain appeared on the front of David's' shirt. The force of the impact jerked his body as blood sprayed over Reanna and Spring, who was wailing loudly in fright. He slowly raised his hand to hold his shoulder where the bullet had entered as he stared at her in disbelief, and his voice sounded more surprised than angry.

"Wily vixen! Got guts for sure …" He rasped haltingly before he fell back, overcome with pain.

Horrified by what she had done, Reanna held Spring tightly and sobbed as she tried to comfort the child, dazedly grabbing at the reins to control the restive horses as they snorted and pranced nervously. Reeling with shock and revulsion, she placed Spring squarely on her lap, bracing her on each side with shaking arms, and slapping the reins briskly, galloped the team the rest of the distance to the ranch.

Chance and the others heard the pounding of hooves long before the wagon careened into view. They were just going back to work after the noon meal when they heard the rapidly approaching vehicle, and Chance felt his world crashing down around him as he recognized the blood-streaked figures. He watched in frozen horror as Reanna hauled back on the reins, barely bringing the lathered, blowing beasts, and the wagon, to a halt before she, with a terribly frightened, screaming Spring, almost fell from the wagon.

She staggered forward, and Chance, galvanized to action, ran to catch her as she fell to her knees, and held onto her as she retched violently.

Luke and the others ran to lift David's moaning form from the seat, carrying him carefully into the kitchen and placing him on the table.

"Chance, oh Chance," Reanna gasped as she convulsed in great wrenching sobs, her rising voice tinged with hysteria, "I shot him! I shot your brother!"

His grip on her shoulder tightened and the venom in his voice was almost a tangible thing as he ground out, "If he hurt you …"

"No! No Chance, I'm alright."

She drew in a shuddering breath before continuing, in a calmer tone, "Please, all I want is to wash this blood from us. I will be all right. Truly, he did not hurt me."

He considered her for a moment, and then stooped to scoop Spring up into his arms before proceeding his wife into the house, bellowing for water to be warmed immediately as they made their way to the bedroom.

Ellen met them at the head of the staircase.

"Mother," Chance began, "You should be in bed …"

Ellen cut him off. "I heard the wagon come in, and I have seen enough through the window to know that one of my sons may be badly hurt. I am assuming …"

Here she paused and looked directly at Reanna. "That should news of this … unfortunate accident … become general knowledge, it may prove to be most embarrassing to all concerned."

She waited for Reanna's nod of confirmation before continuing. I am perfectly capable of caring for David, especially after raising five boys in the wilderness, and I will have more than enough help."

She hurried down the stairs, and they continued on into their room, where Chance readied the tub and Reanna's favorite soap in time for the buckets of water hastily brought up by Nathan and Stewart. Red faced, ashamed of what their brother might have done, they could not meet Reanna's eyes as they silently emptied the buckets of tepid water into the tub, leaving one full next to the bath for rinse water.

Mechanically, Reanna stripped Spring and herself of their bloodied clothing and climbed into the tub, dunking Spring, who loudly protested as her mother vigorously soaped her head and dunked her again to rinse. This was not the happy, game filled bathing she was used to, but Reanna was aware of little, other than the need to wash the sticky red substance from their skin and hair.

She was barely conscious of the fact that Chance toweled Spring dry, that he helped her to rinse her own hair, or that he was speaking softly to her, as if to a small child.

Reanna was horrified by what she had done. To shoot a man just for touching her! The memories of when she had shot Cal came back with force, painfully assaulting with its harsh accusations. She had truly enjoyed killing him over and over. But with Cal it had been self-defense. He would have killed her, and she had been left with little choice. David, however, had not threatened her life, yet she had not hesitated to pull the trigger, exacting an unfair retribution. Was she becoming so callous that she would shoot at anyone at the least provocation? Was she to become a cold-blooded killer? Why had she been so quick to shoot him?

Chance grasped her shoulders, giving her a gentle shake. "Rea, please, tell me what happened!"

She focused on her husbands worried features and then turned from him, speaking barely above a whisper. "He but touched me, Chance. I shot a man just for touching me! What have I become?"

He turned her to face him. "There had to be a reason, Reanna! He must have done more than just touch you. Did he threaten you?"

Finding it hard to meet his gaze, she stared down at the floor. "It was the whiskey. He had a bottle. I could smell it, and … and when he tried to touch me … I-I just panicked. All I could see before me was Larry McPherson, but it was not Larry. He is your brother, and I shot him for … Chance, I could have killed him, and he certainly did not deserve to die for what he did!"

He held her tightly in his arms, preventing her from sinking to the floor as she sobbed broken heartedly against his chest.

He sought to reassure her, choosing his words with care. "You did what you thought was necessary, Rea, for your own safety and that of Spring. Unfortunately, we do not always have time to weigh our options and consider the consequences of our actions, and I am sure David deserved what you gave him. I know him, and what he is capable of, and you had every right to defend yourself from his unwanted attention with the only means available to you. There is no reason to feel that you are the one who has done wrong."

He helped her to a chair and poured a liberal amount of brandy into a glass, handing it to her. She hesitated for only a moment before accepting it, relaxing slightly as she sipped the fiery liquid, and it began to spread warmth through her aching body.

Chance brushed her lips tenderly with his as he pulled the sheet up over Reanna, and Spring, who had climbed into bed and promptly fallen asleep.

"You rest now my love. You did only what you had to do."

When she had been claimed by a deep, dreamless slumber, Chance allowed his anger to surface. Silently, with a determined glint in his eye, he closed the bedroom door and descended the stairs, entering the kitchen in a furious temper. Ignoring the fearful glances directed his way; he stopped in front of David.

Clenching his fists at his sides, he threatened, "I should kill you myself, you drunken, good for nothing -"

"Please Chance," Ellen implored weakly, stepping forward to place her hand on his arm, "I know that what David did was terribly wrong, but he has paid for it, and I think that he has learned a valuable lesson, one that he will not forget."

David, white lipped in pain, sat uncomfortable in a chair, washed clean of blood and tightly bandaged. It had taken all of Ellen's failing strength to accomplish this, and she swayed weakly on her feet.

Chance resolutely tamped down his anger and moved to lift his mother's frail body into his arms. She glanced up at him and whispered, "David …"

Chance turned and coldly regarded David, who shifted nervously in his seat before Chance lifted his gaze to Nathan and ordered, "Bring him up."

Reanna opened her eyes to find Chance sitting anxiously by her bedside. He leaned forward, his dark eyes moving carefully over her face. "How do you feel?"

"I will be fine," she assured him as she moved to rise. She would not let him see the self-blame and guilt that wrapped her in shame as memory came flooding back in force. He would not understand.

"I really am fine, Chance. I will start dinner as soon as I dress, and I am sure that you have many things to do."

"Yes, I do." Chance answered slowly, suspicious of her calm demeanor.

"Well?" she queried with an arched brow. "Was there something else?"

"No, the children are all outside with Jeremy and Stew. David and mother are resting. I will take father and Nathan with me to see how Michael and Jared are coming along with the last section of fencing up on the east range and try to locate a mare that seems to have wandered off. She is due to foal any time now, and I would not like to lose either of them. We should be back by dinnertime though."

Reanna watched out the window as they rode away until they were swallowed by distance and the tall, lush grass that danced on the horizon. A soft sob escaped her lips before she straightened her shoulders and began to put away the clothing she had purchased for Holly and Beth. There was no joy in it, however. She no longer felt the keen sense of excitement, the anticipation of watching the girl's faces as they first glimpsed their new finery.

She went through the day and evening this way, wrapped in an icy calm, showing no emotion, as if she were separate, somehow, from herself. That night when Chance turned to her, wanting to comfort, to share their love, she remained passive, her guilt not allowing her to feel his warm passion. She simply allowed him to take her with no response of her own.

Three days later, Reanna remained in her frozen state. Everyone had eaten the meals she prepared without complaint, even though their fare was either burned or tough and stringy. No one, not even Luke, wanted to add to her troubled thoughts. She avoided David's room like the plague, and Chance stayed around the house, working on accounts, lists of supplies for his business ventures on the coast, anything that would keep him near her should she need him. After the first night, he no longer attempted to do anything more than hold her unyielding body in his arms.

Tonight, he knew that he must breach her defenses, to try and relieve her of her terrible doubts and self-blame. As she reached to turn out the lamp, he caught her arm, and gently pulled her to face him.

His voice was low, but deliberately firm. "Is the wild filly so easily broken then, my love?"

He was surprised at the depth of pain that burned within those wide green eyes, searing him with the sudden knowledge that he had not even begun to understand. The deep despair that threatened to drown her. Her voice was steady and toneless as she spoke from her icy shell.

"No Chance, not broken. Only confused, roped, frightened and confused." She turned from him, put out the lamp, and crawled into bed, effectively shutting out his sad, searching gaze.

She woke hours later bathed in a cold sweat, with her heart hammering and her breath rapid in her breast. She knew now what she must do. She had to face her fears squarely, and overcome them, if she were ever to know peace within herself again.

Sliding from bed, she groped in the darkness until she had her robe. Tying it around her narrow waist, she searched again and found a candle, lighting it to carry against the darkness of the house. Silently she slipped down the hall, easing open the door to David's room, and gliding inside. She set the candle down upon the bedside table, her heart beating erratically in her chest. Glancing nervously around the room, she noted with dismay that Nathan was sleeping in a chair in the corner of the room, almost swallowed in shadow. She had not expected anyone else to be present. Praying fervently that he would not wake, she turned and softly murmured David's name. He opened his eyes instantly, almost as if he had known she would come and was waiting for her.

At his whispered question, "A right purty vision, come to haunt my dreams?" she almost fled, but gritting her teeth, held fast against the urge, and felt her strength grow with the conviction of her words.

"I came to beg your understanding, your forgiveness. I will tell you why I reacted with such force to my fear of you."

"Ain't necessary. You may find this hard to believe, I know it sounds crazy, but I admire what you did; the way you put me in my place and showed me a thing or two about disrespect. Ain't many women I know that would show so much spunk, or be so ready to protect their virtue, if you get my meanin'."

His change in attitude heartened her and enabled her to proceed without the limb shaking terror with which she had begun.

"It is necessary that I explain things, that I might not feel the condemning weight of my own guilt or the censure in your eyes, imagined or not." She took a deep breath and plunged on. "Before Chance and I were married, I was kidnapped and held captive for six days by four brothers." She had decided to leave Billy out of her story. "I was raped and beaten more times than I can remember during that time and forced to suffer many other humiliations that will haunt me until the day I die. I survived that hell, and the long, hard process of recovery that followed. Whenever I think that I have put that wretched time behind me, something happens to bring the nightmare back."

"When they were not abusing me, those four men sat and drank whiskey and smoked tobacco. The house reeked of it, and so did they. I still cannot tolerate either of those odors, and I probably never will, for they instantly return me to that hell. That is why I shot you when … you had that look in your eyes … I could smell the whiskey. I panicked, perhaps needlessly. I am sorry for it, but now maybe you can understand why I lost my head."

She watched David carefully, judging his reaction as she talked. Shock had turned to faint repulsion, and finally remorse. His eyes, as well as his words, begged her forgiveness.

"You got to believe me Reanna, I ain't like those men. I might come on strong, but I would never hurt you like they did. I like to play with women, to see how far I kin get, if you get my meanin'. But I would never hurt a woman the way you was hurt, and I am real sorry you were. If I'da known, why, I'da never got that bottle of whiskey. You got my word that I won't take another drop long as I'm here. And you don't need to be afraid that I'll bother you again. I won't, and I don't blame you for shootin' me none. I deserved it; just glad you didn't kill me. But … the bullet has finally hit home. Just the way you meant it to."

Although he smiled his understanding, his eyes bore a hint of pain for; Reanna knew instinctively, his mistake and her past hurt. Realizing this, she felt suddenly that she and Chance had both grossly misjudged this man. He may be lazy, and a compulsive womanizer, but he was neither bad, nor evil, and would never push himself to the point of hurting someone.

Her feelings were shared by the man that stood in the darkened hall, who had followed his wife out of concern, but now returned thoughtfully to their room as silently as he had come.

Reanna returned David's smile, though somewhat tremulously. "I am truly sorry for your shoulder," she said with feeling as she bent to brush a kiss quickly on his cheek.

"Well, now that you and me are friends, I guess I can quit hidin' in this room. Fact is, I been afraid to face you, after what I done an' all. An' it was getting darn lonesome with just myself for company most a the time."

She smiled in earnest now, amused at the thought of David hiding from her. "Good night," she whispered softly. She turned to leave, and her heart skipped a beat as her eyes met Nathans through the candle glow. How long had he been awake, she wondered, as she quickly padded down the hall. How much had he heard? In the end, she decided that it really did not matter. She had put her own shame to rest long ago.

Chance needed no further assurances when Reanna returned. She had faced her fears and won. Her eyes, lit by the flickering light of the candle as she moved around the bed, sparkled, reflecting the bright flame. As she set it down, his smooth, languid voice caressed her. "The rope is broken. The wild filly goes free."

Her answering smile was brilliant, and his breath caught in his throat as she loosened her robe, allowing it to slide down over her smooth creamy skin to pool at her feet.

As she slowly lowered herself into the bed, he gathered her quickly into his arms, and she said, "The filly is free but not wild. She is tamed under her stallion's fierce love."

He gazed into her wide green eyes, seeking the sea, and finding it, he rejoiced. He kissed her warmly, and then his voce came as a soft breeze in her ear. "Come, lovely filly, and we'll ride wild together through the night."

His searing lips moved hungrily over hers as his hands roamed feverishly from her full breasts to her taut belly. She gasped in delight as he nibbled her earlobe, and his tongue, hot and wet, traced a burning path down the soft column of her throat.

She moaned softly and her voice escaped her as a whispering sigh. Chance heard her words, "Wild and free," and brought his gaze up to meet hers. She gasped in pure ecstasy when she saw the flaming red desire in his eyes.

She placed her hands against his muscled chest, pressing him down to the softness of the pillows. Straddling his lean hips, she took his hard length into her with swift greed, moaning low in her throat as he filled her. Now it was her mouth and hands roving in fiery paths as she attempted to tame her wild stallion. They rode together to ecstasy and shuddering fulfillment.

Her confidence in life and love restored once again, Reanna was back in high spirits the next morning. She woke early, plunging into her day with a newfound relish. Humming gaily, she set about preparing breakfast, and had all in readiness as the rest of the household roused and joined her in the kitchen.

"I will not be needing that today," Ellen announced, after noticing that Reanna was setting up a bed tray.

Glancing up, Reanna was pleasantly surprised to see Ellen, followed by David, up and about.

"As you wish," Reanna smiled at her mother-in-law and took the plate from the tray. "Please, sit down, you too David," she added pleasantly.

Still, no one said a word to her about the blackened bacon, or her bread that was heavy and tasteless, and seemed to be happy with eggs washed down with very strong coffee.

The men had gone outside, and Ellen and the children had gone upstairs to straighten the bedrooms when Nathan approached her sheepishly.

"I heard everything last night, Reanna, and I want you to know that -"

Reanna was quick to interrupt him. "I am sorry that you heard. I meant for only David to know, so I could make him understand. It is behind me now, and best left that way. I survived, and I think that I am stronger for it. Please, do not pity me."

Nathan stared at the beautiful, proud woman standing before him with her small chin raised defiantly and her hair glinting in fiery waves as the sunlight from the windows touched it, and suddenly he did not pity her, but admired her strength and courage.

"You are a very special lady, Reanna, and Chance is a lucky man."

"It is I who am the lucky one," Reanna whispered as Nathan crossed to the doorway and stepped outside.

The Norton's visit stretched on through the summer, and Reanna became good friends with everyone in Chance's family, apart from Luke, who seemed to prefer keeping a respectful distance between them. He was almost pleasant now that he had stopped drinking. He worked beside Chance every day and enjoyed learning all he could about ranching. He often took Ellen walking in the cooler hours just before dusk and would even gift his wife with small bouquets of wildflowers encountered in their ramblings.

Reanna could see now glimpses of the man that Ellen, with her soft and gentle ways, had fallen in love with. He was, after all, quite a handsome man when he was clean and sober. She had learned from Ellen that Mr. Nolton had started drinking when the small farm he had invested his savings in turned out to be rocky and barren, unable to sustain his growing family. Bitter and disillusioned, he had been forced to work where he could, doing odd jobs for what he could get; spending most of his earnings on whiskey so that he could, for a time, forget his failings. David had merely followed his father's example.

Reanna surmised that the lack of true friendship between them lay in the fact that she insisted on schooling. Every afternoon, during the worst of the heat, she and Ellen would gather the boys, with Holly and Beth, to practice reading and numbers beneath the shade of the vines of the patio. Even David was willing to learn, much to the disgust of his father. Luke still insisted that it was all a waste of time, but he dared not prohibit the sessions.

Ellen, and after her return, Lada, were teaching Reanna to cook, because after so many hard to swallow meals, Chance had finally decided to speak to her about the quality of their meals, for the continued general health of all concerned.

"I'm sorry, Chance," Reanna admitted as her cheeks flamed and she gazed self-consciously at her feet. "I have really tried, but … but you see … I do not know how to make anything but the eggs I fry in the morning. I never learned to cook."

Chance was confused, "But the first morning after Lada and Billy left, everything you made tasted fine."

"Lada had everything prepared, so that I only had to warm it on the stove."

Chance stared at her, too stunned to speak for a moment, and Reanna's cheeks turned a deeper shade of crimson as he suddenly burst into laughter. Lifting her head, she glared furiously at him as he continued to laugh so hard that he had to hold his sides. But when he doubled over, she decided that enough mirth had been had at her expense. Livid, she lifted the bucket of water she had drawn from the well and upended it over his head.

The cold water sobered him enough that he was able to ensnare her in his arms. Trying hard to catch his breath, as much from the shock of the frigid water as the laughter that still threatened, he gasped, "Oh Rea, to think … we have been married all this time … and I never knew … I just assumed … it is a good thing I have done the cooking when we have gone camping. Lord knows what you would have done over a campfire."

Raising her nose haughtily in the air, Reanna pushed from his arms and stalked into the house, not yet ready to forgive him his laughter at her efforts in the kitchen. She was not, however, above seeking help from those more knowledgeable than she, and so passed many pleasant hours in the days to come under the tutelage of Ellen and Lada, much to everyone's relief.

Tasha whelped her first litter, and Modock pranced as proudly as any new father when everyone gathered to admire the pups. Holly was especially fascinated by the dogs and spent all her free time with the new arrivals, becoming quite attached to the one that she had come to call Angel.

As summer drew to an end and it came time for his family to leave, Chance gifted his parents with the deed to one hundred acres of prime grazing land that he owned in California, as well as a flock of chickens and several head of cattle. A new and better beginning for the man he had come to feel a certain fondness for. Nathan, Chance had discovered, had a great desire to stay in Nevada, and work on the ranch with his brother.

It was decided then that Nathan would stay on with Chance and Reanna when the others left, and the morning came when they exchanged their sad farewells. In spite of the shaky beginning, Reanna had come to love them all, and as she bent to wish Holly a tearful goodbye, she drew forth the squirming bundle of dark fluff that she had hidden behind her back.

"For you," she said softly.

Holly gasped at Reanna through her tears, her eyes rounded in astonishment. "You mean it Reanna? I can really keep Angel?"

"You certainly may," Reanna answered gravely, "I know that you will take very good care of him and give him the love he deserves."

Holly kissed her goodbye, and when Chance came to say goodbye to Holly and Beth, he hugged them in his strong arms and kissed their cheeks tenderly. Reanna noticed he did not say a word and knew it was because he could not find his voice, so great was his sorrow at having to say goodbye to his two little angels, as he had come to call them.

He promised to visit them in a year, to see how they were faring, and amid shouted farewells and promises to write, they started their small caravan westward, heading for a brighter future.

Nathan had grown to love the workings of the ranch, and the distant grand vistas that met his eyes every morning. He was awake at dawn every day, eager to be out with only the varied notes of birdsong for company as he began his chores. He helped Reanna clean the dogs pen every morning and as the pups grew, he also assisted with their training. He also set aside some time every morning to continue his studies, more than willing even at his age to learn all that Reanna could teach him.

Lada had come to love Nathan as she would a brother, enduring his jokes and teasing with good humor, which irritated Billy more than a little, for Lada continued to keep their relationship on a polite, friendly basis. Finally, Reanna took pity on him and explained that, obviously, Lada did not look upon Billy as a brother, hence the distance, for she was still not ready to deliver her heart into the keeping of a man, especially a white man, after the hurt she had endured the only time she had done so.

Belinda had been out to visit a few times when the Norton's were all there, and when she came again about a week after they left, Reanna noticed the warming glances that passed between Nathan and her friend. When she was ready to take her leave, he hastened to escort her out to her carriage.

He came back so elated that Reanna, unable to contain her curiosity, asked him what had pleased him so. Blushing slightly, he announced that Belinda had agreed to dine with him the next evening.

The date turned out well, with Nathan singing Belinda's praise afterward, and was the beginning of his serious courting of her. They spent every weekend together, and Reanna rejoiced in the knowledge that Belinda was no longer waiting in vain for Billy to notice her.

When they finally received a letter from the Norton's, Chance impatiently tore it open and read it aloud. It was from Holly, she is doing the writing she explained, instead of mama, to practice her spelling and handwriting. Mama thought it was a good idea.

They and the livestock had arrived safely, and Papa, with the help of the boys, were building a small house before winter set in, one they could add to next year. Angel was fine, and Mama seemed much happier now, except when Stewart talked about joining the military. There had been some talk of war.

Chance and Reanna smiled, missing the lively chatter of Holly and Beth, but no more so than Spring, who had become quite attached to her playmates. Her parents, realizing this, doted on their only child, and everyone in the house spoiled her, although not to her detriment. She was a happy child, always a pleasure to be around.

They relished their life together, their love growing stronger and more intense as time went on, their only disappointment being that Reanna had not conceived again. They both fervently wished for another child.

Their love was constant; a tangible bond that was so intense that they felt nothing would ever be able to break the magical flowing current of their love. They could not know of the forces that gathered; did not know they would have many more rocks and waterfalls to get through before reaching the ultimate end of their journey.

Chapter 12

Balancing his lean form easily, Chance sat atop the highest rail of the whitewashed fence, the dark brown hues of the work clothes he wore contrasting sharply with the brightness of the sun-drenched surface. His dark hat was pulled low, shading the dark eyes that quickly assessed the merits of the young roan stallion that was laboring frantically to rid himself of Nathan's weight, squealing his outrage as the young man held doggedly on.

Grunting his approval, Chance allowed his thoughts to wander as he watched the stiff legged, bone jarring battel before him. Stewart had joined the military a couple years ago and was now a captain in the Union ranks in the War Between the States. Chance himself felt very strongly about the issue of slavery, as did everyone in his household. If not for Reanna, he knew that he would long ago have joined the cause, perhaps be fighting at his brother's side right now.

The rest of his family was doing extremely well. Once pointed in the right direction, his father had finally done something with his life. He now owned a large, prosperous farm and his mother taught in the small schoolhouse that the budding community had raised and was assisted by Holly, who had grown into a beautiful eighteen-year-old. According to Ellen, his willful sister had spurned several proposals of marriage, breaking hearts for miles around. How they had ever gotten his father to let them teach, he did not know, but it was just one more indication of the great change in Luke.

David and Jeremy worked the farm with their father, and had added four more bedrooms to the original dwelling, which was now a sprawling one-story home which topped a small knoll, with plenty of room for David's new wife, Emily, and their first child, soon to be born.

This thought brought a stab of pain to Chance's heart, for after five years of marriage, Reanna had not conceived again, and Spring was four and a half now. Although he accepted the little girl as his own, and loved her dearly, he truly longed for Reanna to bear his own child, and he knew that she desired the same. They rarely discussed it now, however. Having faced disappointment so many times during the past years, Reanna was resigned to what she considered to be her failure.

Lada called from the porch, summoning the men to dinner. Acknowledging her with a raised arm, his thoughts turned to Billy. He had left them last year, riding proudly away with Michael Dublin to join the war, and Chance had guiltily found himself wishing that he could go with them.

A worthy cause, but he could not march righteously off to war, salving his conscience by standing up for his convictions, while leaving the women to run a ranch of this size alone.

He focused again on the horse and rider before him. Exhausted, the lathered, panting beast stood with his head hanging as Nathan dismounted to lead the now docile stallion around the corral in a cooling walk.

Chance dropped easily to the ground and joined Nathan, who deftly removed the saddle. Stepping to the roans' head, he eased the bridle off, patting the horse's neck as he did so, keeping his voice soft and level to reassure the quivering animal.

"He will make a fine mount once he is broken to saddle. He is spirited, yet good natured, with a will to please. By the way, I am starved. How about you?"

"After that workout I could eat the horse," Nathan grinned, his teeth flashing white against his bronzed, dust covered face.

When Chance merely turned and walked toward the house, Nathan followed, observing dryly as they stopped to wash, "You know, brother, you have not been the most pleasant to be around lately. Is something bothering you?"

Before he could reply, the drum of hoof beats heralded the arrival of a rider, and Chance stepped forward to help her down as Reanna brought Guinevere to a halt before them, her long copper curls swirling in disarray about her shoulders.

She wore a split beige riding skirt, and a white linen blouse was tucked in at her narrow waist. A beige Stetson hat was perched atop her glorious head of hair, the wide brim casing her green eyes in shadow. She flashed him a wide smile, and he marveled again at her beauty, as he had from the first day they met.

"Sorry that I am so late getting back from town, but I have not returned empty handed. We have a letter from Holly." She turned and retrieved the envelope from her saddlebag.

Laughing gaily, she fairly danced into the house, tearing the letter open as the men followed more slowly in her wake. Unfolding the paper, Reanna eagerly began to read as she dashed into the parlor.

Chance joined her just in time to see her body stiffen as she raised a trembling hand to her lips. As she raised a tearful gaze to his, she woodenly lowered herself to the couch, unconsciously holding herself stiffly erect.

It seemed to Chance that he moved in slow motion as he walked toward her, those few steps seemed to take forever. His voice echoed stonily in his ears. "Reanna, what has happened?"

She opened her mouth, struggling to speak, but no sound issued forth. Frustrated, she held the letter out to him. And he hesitantly reached to take it from her, yet unwilling to give substance to the grief that etched his wife's beautiful features.

Reanna stood and walked numbly to the window, leaning her forehead against the smooth glass as her body was shaken with wrenching sobs. She wept not only from the words she had read, but also from fear. Her life, she knew, was to be altered forever, and there was nothing she could do to prevent it.

Chance finished the letter and fought to control his emotions. When he was finally able to move, he crossed the room to where Reanna stood and gathered her into his arms, pulling her to him. They clung tightly together, trying to lend comfort in the knowledge of their love.

His brother was dead, killed in battle. Captain Stewart Allen Nolton had died with honor on a far distant field in the state of Virginia. His mother lay gravely ill and was not expected to live much longer.

Chance harbored no doubts now about what he must do, but instead of easing his mind, the decision left him with nothing but regret. There was simply no other course for him to take. He had to tell her, to make her understand. His voice was ragged with emotion as he spoke.

"Rea ... I must go. I will go to see my mother, and then I am going to join Lincoln's army. I will leave tomorrow."

She had grown rigid in his arms, pulling away from him to glare in anger. Her breathing stilled, and Chance could see the wild beating of her heart in the pulse that quickened in her throat. He wanted to shake her, to force her from her shocked state, but instead he caught her as she went limp in his arms.

He placed her gently on the settee, feeling as if the weight of his own emotions would pull him down. Clenching his teeth against the pain in his heart, he turned and made his way to the kitchen.

"Lada, I need a cloth wet with cold water, quickly!" He ordered as he fumbled in the cupboard bringing forth the object of his search, he poured a generous draught of the fine brandy, and, tossing it down his throat, he welcomed the warmth that spread through his numbed body. He poured another and glanced up as Lada brought him the wet cloth.

"Stewart … he is dead," he flatly informed her as he grabbed the glass of brandy and turned to leave. He paused as Lada gasped in disbelief, but could not find any more words to speak, so turned and went back to his wife.

Placing the cool cloth on her brow, Chance tenderly smoothed Reanna's hair away from her face. A low moan escaped her softly parted lips and her eyes slowly opened as she regained consciousness. Her wounded gaze met his for a moment before she averted hers, and then with a small cry she sprang up and threw herself into his welcoming arms, desperately needing to hold tight, else she might sink back down into the black depths that threatened to take her breath again.

Nathan had gone upstairs to change and returned to find Chance and Reanna holding each other in a tight embrace. Spying the letter on the floor where it had fallen from Chance's grasp, he stooped to pick it up.

"And what does our dear sister have to … say …" his voice faltered as he read the painful words.

Bleakly he met his brother's gaze, coming to an abrupt decision, knowing that Chance had already done the same. "When do we leave?" he whispered.

Without a moment's hesitation Chance replied, "Tomorrow morning."

Nathan nodded and left them, deftly saddling a horse and, wasting no time, headed into town. Belinda had just consented to marry him, and now he would have to tell her to wait. For how long, he did not know.

Lada stood and stared helplessly at nothing in particular after Chance left the kitchen. Although the early spring day was warm, she shivered, as a chill crept over her. Turning, she ran to her room, and throwing herself down upon her cold, empty bed she sobbed uncontrollably. There was no one to give her comfort, for when Billy left, he had taken her heart with him. She had tried so hard to deny her feelings, and she had regretted her actions since the day he left. Gentle, caring Billy who asked for nothing but her love, and he, like Stewart, may never return.

Chance and Reanna sat at the table silently as Spring chattered gaily, unaware of the tension and despair that surrounded her parents. Reanna toyed with her food, pushing it back and forth on her plate as she tried to maintain her composure. Through an effort of sheer will she forced herself to smile at Spring's antics, but her head pounded, and her eyes burned.

Chance, her beloved, was leaving her, riding out of her life as suddenly as he had ridden in, possibly to never return. She searched his dark, handsome features intently for some crack in his calm self-control. She wanted to rail at him, to beat her fists against his chest. Unable to hide her emotions any longer, she smothered a sob as she bolted from the table and out the door.

Guinevere nickered in welcome as Reanna ran toward her. She flung herself upon the mare's back and kicked her into a gallop, heading away from Chance, away from the home they had made together, away from the painful farewell that was just hours away. Tears streamed unheeded down her cheeks to dry in salty trails, and her burnished curls flew in wild abandon about her face and shoulders as she urged Guinevere to even greater speed.

The gallant mare responded eagerly, stretching out and racing toward the towering mountains, carrying her mistress as swiftly as her ancestors had borne proud desert chieftains across the miles of scorching sand and dunes that they called home.

Reanna slowed the pace as the terrain became too rough to safely run the mare. She was on her father's land now, riding the same land she had ridden all her life. Effortlessly they glided through the fragrant pines, silently threading their way ever higher until they paused at the edge of the sunlit clearing. Dismounting, she slowly led Guinevere to the other end of the small meadow, gazing out over her private empire of lofty evergreens and newly budding poplars.

She had not been to her Cliffside retreat since … Swallowing past the lump in her throat; she vividly recalled the desperate attempt she had made to end her life, only to have Chance save her from harm. She had lived and grown far beyond the frightened girl who had stood here last. Her lower lip trembled as tears welled once again in her eyes to flow down her smooth cheeks.

Suddenly remembering something else she had picked up in town, she stepped around Guinevere and reached into her saddlebag, pulling out the bottle of wine she had purchased to celebrate receiving the letter from Holly. Since it no longer represented happiness in any way, it might just as well be used to, temporarily at least, ease the pain that clutched at her heart.

Setting the bottle on the ground, she unsaddled her mare and, dropping it to the ground, settled herself in front of it crossed legged, using the saddle as a backrest.

Using her teeth to work the cork from the bottle, she gazed sadly out at the distant horizon as she sipped steadily at the heady draft. The late afternoon sun turned her copper curls to fire and shimmered upon the tears which streamed down her lovely face, as it bathed her in golden light.

Damn you, Chance Nolton, she thought fiercely. Why must you go? I cannot bear to have to say goodbye.

She shivered as another wave of fear and loneliness washed over her and took a long swallow of the fruity beverage that was just beginning to numb her senses. The sun was swiftly hidden beyond the mountain peaks as it sunk in the western sky, tinging that great expanse with pink briefly before darkness settled a velvet blanket overall.

The bottle of wine was empty. The tears dried on her face, and her eyelids grew heavy. She slept, unmindful of the evening chill, or of the horseman that appeared at the edge of the clearing.

He sat still and silent upon his coal black horse, a darker shadow among those cast by the whispering branches of pine. After some minutes the horse and rider advanced into the clearing.

Guinevere, eagerly cropping the fresh spring grass, raised her head, her ears pricked forward, to study the dark intruders before she nickered a greeting and returned her attention to the tender green shoots.

Reanna had not stirred, but lay bathed in moonlight, in a deep sleep. Her finely arched eyebrows, long thick lashes, and heavy, glorious hair contrasted darkly with the creamy white beauty of her skin.

The rider dismounted with lithe grace, his eye drawn to the deep shadow where her shirt had opened, barely exposing the fullness of her breasts as they rose and fell with her even breathing.

He drew his breath in sharply, hunkering down beside her as his warming gaze traveled the length of her slim form. He reached out to touch her but stopped suddenly as he noticed the empty wine bottle lying next to her.

His hungry gaze flicked back to her face, and he grasped her shoulder, shaking her gently as he repeated several times, "Rea, wake up," to no avail.

Bending his head to taste the lush softness of her parted lips, he drew back in surprise as the fruity odor of the wine escaped on her breath. Obviously, she had imbibed quite a bit.

He studied her carefully for a time before a slow grin split his face. He stood and turned to the dark horse standing so patiently by his side. "Lancelot, I do believe that my wife is dead drunk!"

Chance had carefully packed for an overnight expedition, but as lightly as possible, bringing only the most necessary items. He quickly laid out a bedroll and, bending down, effortlessly scooped Reanna up in his arms and carried her to it, placing her carefully upon it before drawing a blanket snugly up to her chin.

In no time at all he had Lancelot unsaddled and was pulling a softly snoring Reanna into his warm embrace, a grin of amusement turning up the corners of his mouth as he joined her in restless slumber.

Birdsong rang on the crisp morning air as the sun rose to clearly etch the tops of the pines against the sky. Reanna snuggled against the warmth at her back, sighing contentedly before her eyes flew open in surprise, and she turned almost fearfully to meet the amused dark eyes of her husband.

"Chance!" she exclaimed, "How did you get here? I do not remember…"

His deep laughter interrupted her questions, and at her look of outrage, he replied, "I am not surprised that you would not remember anything about last night, Rea. You seem to have had a bit too much to drink."

"Yes, I suppose I did. But you still have not told me how you knew where I was."

"You seem to forget, my dear that I have spent years tracking, and hunting men down, and you did not exactly bother to cover your trail."

"I read Spring a story and put her to bed last night, and when you did not come back, I asked Lada to care for her, and came after you."

He rose to lean on his arm, peering intently down at her. "I still leave this morning. It is up to you to decide how we are to say goodbye."

He had leaned closer to her, and Reanna searched his face with her wide-eyed gaze. She knew that he was committed to leaving, just as she had had to go to Daniel all those years ago.

"I'm sorry I drank too much and passed out, Chance, our last night togeth…" her throat contracted, and she could not go on. With forceful will, she blinked back the tears that threatened to fall from her eyes, refusing to spoil their last hours together.

Chance held her tightly and murmured words of love, and soon was unable to deny the deep hunger that burned in his dark gaze, and with the potent desire that suddenly and forcefully swept through her body, Reanna groaned and wrapped her arms around his neck, murmuring urgently, "Love me Chance. Please, love me."

Chance eagerly pressed his mouth down upon her soft, yielding lips, almost bruising them as he pressed her body down beneath his.

They were breathless as he broke their tight embrace to hurriedly discard their clothing. Tearing her blouse off in his haste, he buried his face between the soft mounds of her breasts and inhaled deeply, breathing in the light, warm scent of roses that always seemed a part of her.

As his hands roved over her creamy skin, they seemed to touch every part of her, igniting a fierce longing, and his lips followed, his tongue searing a blazing trail across the taut peaks of her nipples before plunging to the deep valley between her breasts and down the smooth expanse of her stomach to her inner thighs.

Reanna gasped and moaned in pleasure. She raised her hips to meet his downward thrust as he impaled her, and her small sounds of delight urged him on as they mated violently, all the emotions of anger, hurt, and love flowing from their hearts through their bodies, each attempting to take a part of the other with them.

They lay entwined for a time as Chance gently stroked Reanna's silky hair, neither of them willing to intrude upon the warm glow of satisfaction that surrounded them with words of their parting.

Finally, Reanna gave voice to her fears, knowing that she must face the inevitable. "Chance, I am frightened. I cannot run the ranch alone. What if I —"

Her doubts were silenced as Chance kissed her long and thoroughly before raising his head to answer.

"Rea, I have no doubt you can do anything you set your mind to, and you were brought up on the largest ranch for miles around, so you should have no problems keeping everything running smoothly. And you will not be alone. You have your father and your Uncle Bob to consult should any need arise. You must learn to trust yourself. You have the knowledge, and the strength, use them. As for your being alone, I know that it will be difficult being apart. There are no words necessary or even possible, to express the deep love we share, and no words exist to express the deep sorrow of our parting. There is but one way we can even come close to expressing these feelings."

As he bent again to kiss her, she could see the flaming red desire that smoldered once more in his dark gaze.

Their union this time was intense, but leisurely, with each of them savoring every part of the other. Even after they joined, and Reanna felt full of him, she begged him for more.

"Chance, please, closer, more. It is not enough."

Chance murmured against her ear, "There will never be enough of either, for the other."

She felt as if her life was leaving her and flowing into him. But then she felt his life force flowing into her, and his heart inside her, and she knew that they would both be able to endure this trial.

"I have to leave," he said quietly, as he watched the thin wisps of clouds that scuttled across his line of vision as he stared up at the sky.

"Yes," she agreed flatly, and rose to slip her clothes back on.

Sighing, Chance decided to follow suit and soon they could postpone no longer, so leading Guinevere, Chance held Reanna loosely before him as they rode Lancelot through the bright sunlit morning toward home together.

"You do understand why I am not coming home again before I enlist?"

The sudden question startled her, after their long silence, and she was slow to answer. "Yes, I think I do."

"It would just bring more pain, saying goodbye twice."

"I know."

As they drew close to the house, they could see Nathan waiting, hat in hand, next to two saddled horses, and Reanna's heart contracted painfully. He so resembles Chance!

Chance dismounted and turned to help Reanna slide from the great height of Lancelot's broad back, holding her tightly against his chest as he did so. He bent his head to rest it on the fragrant silk of her hair and swallowed past the lump in his throat as he set her carefully upon her feet. God, how he hated to leave her! Reluctantly he set her from him and, grabbing the reins, turned and led the horses down to the corral.

She watched as he smoothly tugged the saddles off before she turned and stepped to Nathan. He hugged her tightly to him and she bid softly, "My heart is being carried away by two this day. Take great care, Nathan, and give your family my love and condolences. Godspeed."

She pressed a warm kiss to his cheek and turned to step into Chance's waiting arms as he joined them. He kissed her passionately, as if seeking to take part of her with him, and then clutching her hard to him.

"Godspeed, my heart, my life, return safely to me." Her voice was harsh with unshed tears, and she strove desperately to control the urge to break down completely.

Suddenly Spring burst from the kitchen door, and her short legs pumped furiously to launch her small body at Chance, who grinned and caught her easily, hugging her to his large frame.

"Are you leaving now Papa?"

Chance glanced at Reanna and said, "I explained everything to her last night. I told her that I would very likely be gone a long time."

He turned to his little daughter again and answered, "Yes, I am, and I want you to remember your promise to be extra good for mommy."

"I will take good care of her Papa," the child promised earnestly, "and we will write you letters together. Will you write to us too Papa?"

"Of course I will, sweetheart. I will miss you both very much." Giving her a last hug, he whispered, "Goodbye sweetie," and set her down next to Reanna.

He and Nathan swung up onto their mounts, as they tossed their heads and chomped at their bits in their eagerness to be off.

Looking down at his wife, his face cast in harsh planes as he struggled to control his emotions, he whispered simply, "Goodbye Reanna," before they turned the horses and slowly cantered away.

Lancelot trotted back and forth along the length of the white corral fencing in agitation, and his piercing whinny followed the men as they rode away, as if to question why he was being left behind.

His cry died unanswered on the morning air as Reanna sunk to her knees beside Spring. They clung to each other, finding comfort as they held one another, their brightly burnished heads bent together as Reanna softly stroked her daughter's hair.

Sniffling, Spring pulled away from her mother and raised her small chin, "we should be brave … like Daddy."

Recognizing the truth of the child's words, Reanna looked deeply into the eyes that so nearly mirrored her own and smiled sadly.

"Yes, we should, my darling, and so we shall be."

She spent the next several days in a flurry of activity from dawn to dusk, attempting to ease the ache in her heart.

Nighttime was the worst of her agony, and she found it impossible to sleep for the first few nights without her beloved. Finally, sheer exhaustion dictated that sleep overcome her, despite the coldness that she felt inside – and all around her. The coldness of her empty bed.

It was a month later, on what had become her weekly trip to town that a letter from Chance awaited her at the post office, but she did not open it until she was home and seated comfortably on the patio with a glass of iced tea.

Tired and dusty as she was, her fingers eagerly tore open the envelope, and her hands trembled as she began to read.

They had made it to their mother's side as she was drawing her last breaths, but Chance and Nathan had both been able to wish her farewell and sent their love with her before she passed away. They buried her on a sunny hillside overlooking the farm.

Reanna drew a quivering breath, glad now that Chance had gone as soon as he did and continued to read the rest of the letter consisting of words that spoke of Chance's great love for her ... how much he missed her.

She folded the letter, smoothing the surface with her hand, and raised it to hold against her chest as silent tears slid down her cheeks, tears of grief for her gentle mother-in-law who had become her friend, and tears of fear that she would not see Chance ever again. He and Nathan had taken the next available stagecoach to begin their journey east, and she imagined that by now they had already reached their destination.

The days flew by swiftly as Reanna and Lada threw themselves wholeheartedly into working the ranch. There were gardens to be tended, herbs to be dried, stalls to be cleaned, fencing and stock needed to be checked, and fresh berries to be picked.

Reanna had to acknowledge the signals that her body was sending her. She had not had her menstrual flow for two months now, her breasts were fuller, and she was queasy in the morning.

She was most definitely pregnant, the knowledge of which brought her greatly conflicting emotions. She and Chance had wanted a child so desperately, for so long that her joy at carrying his child knew no bounds, but to find out now, when he was so far away seemed a cruel jest. He probably would not be home for the birth.

She decided to write him the news just as soon as she received word from him on where he could be reached. Knowing that he was to be a father would give him great joy, and more reason to take great care with his life. Her worst fear, which she tried very hard to keep buried inside, was the fear that her beloved husband would be killed in the fighting. She convinced herself that the fates would never be so cruel as to take him from her now and heartened herself with positive thoughts.

A few days later Reanna sat astride a nervously prancing Guinevere, grimly surveying the damage. Three fine, big calves had become bloody, half eaten carcasses staring from sightless eyes as the buzzards circled overhead. "Damn!" she swore.

There had been at least one calf slain each night for several nights now. She had found enough tracks around some of the kills to determine that this was the work of several large wolves, probably young males that had been unable to find mates and were now traveling in a savage pack. They were killing not only for food, but for the pleasure in it, consumed by blood lust. At this rate they would be losing much of their profit for the year, for the wolves could reduce the numbers of their heads dramatically within a few months. Something had to be done, and soon.

Deciding to see if she could get help from her father, she headed toward his ranch. She had not seen him in quite a while because of her hectic days, and it would be a good time to let him know about the baby.

"Papa, do you think you could spare a couple of hands? There are wolves slaughtering our calves every night, and if I allow them to go unchecked, we will not have much of a herd left by the time Chance returns."

Raymond sighed, obviously distraught. "I can send Pier and one other man, Rea, for a couple of days. I wish I had a few hands to send that could stay with you, but I would not trust any of them with you and Lada there by yourselves. All of the good, hard-working men have gone to fight in the war or are trying their hands in silver mining, and we are left with naught but ruffians and deserters from the army. I would not want you alone with them. Maybe Pier could stay with you, especially now that you are with child."

"No Papa. I would not think of separating Pier and Carmelita. We are getting along just fine, except for this problem with the wolves."

For the next few nights Reanna, Pier and a man named Jake rode silently through the darkness, patrolling the bunched groups of cattle, hoping to catch a glimpse of the quarry they sought.

Three nights later their patience was rewarded as they sat downwind of a closely bunched herd, carefully scanning the surrounding area, six ghostly shapes slipped furtively from the cover of some nearby trees.

Tongues lolling and fangs gleaming wickedly in the bright moonlight, they broke rank and moved, as if of one mind, to surround a calf that was on the outside edge of the herd. Together they made a highly efficient killing machine.

Sensing danger, the calf and its mother faced the nearest predators as the rest of the cattle began to move restively, lowing in fear, further assuring that the two men and woman on horseback would not be noticed.

They raised their rifles to their shoulders, taking aim as the wolves closed in on the calf, which had lowered its head in an instinctive gesture of defense, a copy of the same stance taken by its mother.

Gunshots screamed in the still air, breaking the drama of the pathetic tableau as three of the lean, slivery shapes dropped to the ground.

The remaining wolves swerved abruptly, desperately attempting to regain cover as the three riders galloped furiously after them. The cattle, bawling in fright, began to stampede, their sharp hooves trampling the lifeless bodies of the dead wolves into the ground.

The wolves raced swiftly, but close upon their heels rode death, and one by one they fell as shots rang out to accurately find their mark. They would come to kill no more.

Reanna fell back into the normal routine of ranch life, and as the cattle grew sleek and fat, so the tiny life within her continued to grow.

Occasionally she would find a fencepost down, with cattle scattered everywhere in free abandon. With Spring before her in the saddle, she and Lada would manage to round up the wandering beasts and reset the post, using the horses to pull it upright.

These were the days when she thought that she could not go on, for the child sapped much of her strength, and when she crawled, aching and exhausted, into bed at night, her heart yearned for her beloved husband. She found little solace in sleep, for her dreams were plagued by Chance in battle, surrounded by his enemy.

He had written her several times; informing her where he was stationed and touching only lightly upon the battles he fought. He, for the most part, told her of the interesting people that he met. He was, she knew, trying to protect her from the real horrors of the war.

Just as she sought to protect him by not telling him of the child, she had decided that it would only cause him worry for her welfare, and guilt that he had gone. He had enough to do, she realized, with just trying to stay alive, to return to her unscathed.

*   *   *   *   *   *

The late summer day promised to be another dry, scorching one. Heat bugs droned and the morning sun burned her face as Reanna stepped from the kitchen door to draw water from the well.

Raising the wooden bucket full of clear, cool water from the dark depths, she could not resist cupping the liquid in her hands to splash on her face. Sighing wistfully, she thought of how much cooler it would be in the mountains. The heat was making her feel more than her fifth month along in her pregnancy.

Again, her gaze was longingly captured by the cool promise of the mountains when suddenly her gaze shifted, and she swung abruptly to the side. There, she faced what had been only a movement, almost out of her range of vision.

Shock and fear froze her motionless for a time as she watched the great billows of smoke rising into the cloudless sky. This was something she had not considered, but it had been an exceptionally dry summer, and she should have known that a range fire would be entirely possible.

She spun and raced back to the house, screaming for Lada, who met her at the door.

"Quickly! Ride to my father's and take Spring with you. Leave her with Carmelita. Have my father bring as many men as possible, with picks and shovels. There is a range fire out on the east range! Please hurry!"

Reanna dashed past Lada, calling urgently to Spring as she deftly tied her hair into a tight braid. Turning, she hurried back outside to the barn, where she began to saddle horses. Lada soon joined her with Spring, and the two women were quickly ready to ride.

Lada helped Spring onto one of the horses, then handed Reanna, who had already mounted, a shovel, whispering, "Good luck, Reanna. I will return as soon as possible."

"Thank you. I think, if we hurry, we may catch it in time."

Looking across to Spring she said, "Be good for Carmelita, my darling." And setting her heels to her horse, galloped in the direction of the smoke, while Lada rode swiftly for help.

Reanna rode as close as she dared to the fire, sliding from the back of her horse to begin digging a wide path, flinging the grass she dug out to the side closest to the fire. The intense heat from the baking sun soon had her drenched in perspiration, but she struggled on, pausing only to wipe her brow with her sleeve, or to catch her breath.

The smell of the smoke grew stronger, and it seemed to Reanna that she had been working for hours before she glanced up to see a wagon and several riders racing toward her. The men leaned down to grab picks or shovels from the wagon and separated, fanning out to form a straight line. Jumping from their nervous mounts, they immediately set to work, expanding the swath of fresh soil that Reanna had begun.

Raymond had barrels of water loaded into the wagon, and as Reanna paused to sip at some, her shoulders sagged in weariness. The smoke hung in the air like a faint haze, burning her throat raw as she filled her lungs with air, which had grown hotter as the day went on.

It seemed that she had been digging forever, throwing clumps of tall dry grass from her for days, but finally she looked up with satisfaction at Lada who had been working toward her. The patches of dark earth they had been digging formed a solid protective line against the advance of the hungry flames.

The men straggled back to the wagon one by one, tired, sweaty, and dirty, to eagerly ease their parched throats and splash the now tepid water over their heads to run down their flushed faces.

Raymond, assured that the wagon and most of the hands, along with the women, were well away, ordered the grass along the cleared area set afire in several places.

The flames, unable to find substance in the dirt, would burn toward the original fire, consuming all in a voracious blaze until the two met and burned out, extinguished for lack of more fuel.

Reanna and the others watched, exhausted, to be sure the fire was contained. A ragged cheer went up as they saw that their efforts had not been in vain, and they turned to ride back to the Dublin ranch and the dinner that Carmelita would have ready.

Raymond rode alongside Reanna, eyeing her in concern. "Reanna, you worked very hard today. You kept up with the men and never once complained."

Reanna barely managed a smile; she was so exhausted. "Yes, I suppose I did."

"I want you to stop it."

She peered quizzically at him with her face smudged with dirt. "Father?"

"You are with child, Rea. I know that you are determined to succeed on your own, but you will lose that child if you do not slow down. I want you and Lada to stay at my place tonight, and tomorrow I want you to go into town and hire someone to help you."

"Chance thinks that Lada and I can manage just fine."

"Chance does not know that you are pregnant," Raymond snapped. It angered him that his daughter would not write to her husband of her pregnancy. A man had a right to know that he was going to be a father.

Reanna sighed, "All right father. I have to go see if there is a letter from Chance tomorrow, so while I am in town I will see if I can find someone."

"About time," Raymond muttered.

"What did you say Father?"

"Nothing Rea."

There was no letter from Chance. She had written him every week and had received only two letters and no word in over two months. She was beginning to worry. Why didn't he write?

She did, however, hire one of the men hanging about outside the saloon. He claimed to have three years of experience working on a ranch, and he was not drunk, as some of the other men she had seen had been, and she had no choice but to take him at his word.

He said his name was Pete. He did not offer his last name, and Reanna did not ask.

He was fairly tall, with hazel eyes and sandy hair and a spattering of freckles across his wholesome, friendly features.

Reanna was to meet him in an hour to ride back to the ranch. He would use the time to gather his possessions, and she would stop in to have lunch with Uncle Bob and Aunt Martha.

She questioned her uncle about Pete and learned that he had drifted into town about two weeks ago. He seemed pleasant enough and caused no trouble. Beyond that, Uncle Bob could tell her nothing.

Pete met her outside the general store and accompanied her back to the ranch, where she quickly showed him through the barns and gardens and introduced him to Modock and Tasha.

He showed Reanna, and later, at the dinner table, Lada and Spring, nothing but respect and polite friendship.

Reanna was well pleased, congratulating herself on the wisdom of her good choice.

A week later, however, as she lay awake in bed, she heard the restless stomping and nickering of her horses coming from the barn. She rose and peered through the open window but could detect little beyond the fact that something was in with the horses.

A feeling of unease crept over her, and she slipped on her bathrobe, belting it at the waist, and picked up the rifle she had leaning in the corner of the bedroom. Thinking that another wolf had acquired a taste for livestock, she loaded the gun and crept downstairs and out the door quietly, so as not to disturb Lada and Spring.

As she slipped from the house to the well under cover of darkness, she stared in disbelief at the figure on horseback that drove the remaining horses, including Lancelot and Guinevere, from the barn and opened the gate of the corral, ready to disappear with them into the night.

Reanna paused, her thoughts whirling in confusion. This was not the same man who had played with Spring all week after his chores were finished. He could not be the same young man that had smiled so easily, who had been so eager to help with even the smallest, most mundane of jobs.

It had all been nothing but a deliberate ploy to gain their trust, and how easily he had managed it!

But now he was herding the horses through the gate, and Reanna had to act. She stepped from behind the well, and her voice was loud in the stillness. "Pete!"

He looked her way and flashed a cold, triumphant grin as he raised his gun. "Get back into the house Reanna. Just get back in and be quiet, and no one has to get hurt."

In answer she raised her own gun and fired, but at the same instant she felt the bite of a bullet as it slammed into her arm, and she dropped her gun as the searing pain flooded her right side.

She fell back, sinking to the ground as she screamed for Lada, and the horses, frightened by the gunfire, scattered, and thundered away into the night.

Pete was dead. He lay unmoving where he had fallen, yet Reanna kept glancing back to where his still form rested on the ground as Lada helped her into the house.

Still stunned by what happened, Reanna sat quietly while Lada cut the bloodied sleeve from her bathrobe and gently inspected the wound. Satisfied that Reanna would live, Lada cleaned and bandaged the wound, and fashioned a sling for Reanna's arm. She then helped her upstairs and poured a generous portion of brandy, ordering her to drink it all before Lada helped her to bed.

"I will ride into town and tell your uncle what has happened. He can come for the body. At least Pete's horse is still here, and saddled, so that I can go right now. Will you be all right?"

"I will be fine," Reanna murmured before she closed her eyes and slept.

Reanna woke the next morning to a throbbing pain in her arm, but that did not bother her as much as the dull, nagging ache in her abdomen. She knew something was not right, and she feared for her unborn child.

Lada came in to check on her, and finding her awake, fussed and fretted over her until Reanna could stand no more.

Last night she had killed a man, she was in pain, she was worried, and she wanted only Chance. In lieu of that, she just wanted to be alone in her misery.

She did not want to offend Lada, so she explained, as gently as she could. She needed fresh air and solitude just for a little while. She wanted a good long walk, and with Lada in agreement, she headed for the outdoors.

She noted that the horses had all been returned to the corral. Uncle Bob must have rounded them up last night. They probably had not gone very far. She gazed up into the sky, seeking some small comfort from nature as she watched for birds soaring the heavens, but there was nothing but endless emptiness against the heat of the morning sun.

Reanna entered the cooler realm of scented needles and tall, silent giant trees, as she walked among the shadows of the forest, gradually climbing higher as she wandered at will.

Suddenly the pain in her abdomen increased, and then became so intense that she doubled over, gripping her middle. She cried out, screaming her fury at the fates when she felt the moisture leaving her body, and knew she was losing the life that she carried within her.

Chance's life. His child.

No! God, no! Her mind screamed in denial.

She could not go on. She would surely die. She was sick to death of missing Chance, of waiting in vain for letters that did not come. She was tired of acting strong, when in truth she was full of aching misery. Now, to lose this child, carried her beyond the limits of endurance.

She fell, broken, to the ground, sobbing and howling her misery and pain as she rocked and clutched her stomach with her free arm. Her world became a haze of pain as the strength slowly ebbed from her body along with the blood that flowed from her faster now, taking with it the only thing that had kept her going these long, lonely months.

The haze parted, and she was dimly aware of a sense of calm stealing over her. Her cries subsided, and the tears began to dry on her face. She became quite still. She felt a forceful presence beside her. Opening her pain filled eyes, she saw Mansunama bending over her.

He lifted her into his strong arms and carried her back to her house.

It did not seem odd that he laid her tenderly on her bed, and that she wordlessly yielded to the ministrations of both he and Lada as they cleaned her up and bound her lower body in clean rags.

Not knowing that she did so, she slept, feeling almost peaceful now, somehow, but awoke with a start sometime later to find Mansunama in the chair next to her bed.

"How do you always know when to come? It seems that you are always here just when I need you the most."

Mansunama moved to sit on the bed, taking her hand into his. She could feel the strength and power of time and knowledge eternal that pulsed through him, within him, and flowed into her.

"You know that I have dreams to tell me when those closest to my heart are suffering, and knowledge comes, sometimes, borne upon the wind. I do not question the fates that have given me this power but accept it gratefully."

"The earth has also given me a gift; the aura of the woods and mountains to give strength, and to heal those that are in need. I may only give of my magic when I know it to be the right choice. It is right now, Reanna, for there is no one else to help you. Chance is far away, and does not know of your pain, or of your deep grief."

Reanna shut her eyes against the reason in his gaze and sobbed, "Why could you not heal the child? Allow me to keep it, to give it life?"

She opened her eyes and was ashamed as she saw the shadow of pain that crossed his face.

"I am sorry. I did not know in time. It was not meant to be this time, Reanna."

Tears sprang to her eyes, and Mansunama held her in his warm embrace, rocking and soothing her as she sobbed until she could cry no more.

He comforted her without words but filled her with his presence and his love.

When she quieted, he drew back to gaze deeply into her eyes. "I will stay with you Reanna, until Chance comes back. You need me."

His tone brooked no argument, but Reanna would not have refused his offer, in any case. He alone had the power to see her through these darkest of times until Chance came home again.

Chapter 13

Reanna's body recovered quickly from the miscarriage and the gunshot wound. Although she still grieved deeply for her loss, the presence of Mansunama and his unwavering support made everything easier on her.

After a month, they were working the ranch together day by day, and Reanna had regained her strength. Everything ran more smoothly since Mansunama had come.

Her worst worry, one that she considered almost constantly, was for Chance's safety. Four and a half months with no word. Billy and Nathan had not written either, and both Reanna and Lada feared for the men.

Mansunama could not give them the answers they sought or offer an explanation for their men's long silence.

As summer turned to fall, they would often gather on the porch after dinner to enjoy the cool evening air and admire the colors which had just begun to tint the mountainsides between the evergreens.

Lada and Spring would listen, enthralled, as Reanna and Mansunama played their guitars, filling the air around them with the magic of their music. They played and sang so well together that it was as if they knew each other's inner feelings and thoughts.

Reanna tried to convince herself that it was just because they had spent their childhood together, sharing each other's dreams and secrets.

She enjoyed his company immensely, finding that she was even able to laugh again and to feel again the pleasures that life could bring.

Mansunama was certainly helping to ease the passing of a very lonely time. But she could not ignore the desire in his dark eyes as he watched her, and the small ways he had of asking, without words, if she would allow him to get closer.

At times like these Reanna would force herself to leave him and seek the privacy of her bedroom. She knew without a doubt that she could find it too easy to love this proud man if she allowed herself to get close enough. That she would not do, for her heart belonged to Chance and she truly wanted no other.

The months slipped by, with the long winter sending howling blizzards and deep snows, and Mansunama would be gone for days, or even weeks at a time. His people needed him, and he could not desert them just to spend time with Reanna. He was their only medicine man. Honor and duty compelled him to care for the sick and elderly in his tribe.

Spring arrived with warm breezes and melted the snow, setting the fields, ranges, and meadows abloom with wildflowers, and still there was no word from any of the men.

Reanna was nearly frantic with worry, but she strove to hide her fears from the others.

Spring's birthday came and went with no word or letter from Chance. She was five years old now.

As usual, Reanna stopped for the mail on her weekly trip to town. Silently she prayed that this time there would be a letter from Chance, just as she did every week. He had been gone for nine months now.

There was a letter waiting. It was addressed to Mrs. Chance Nolton. It was from a Captain Nathanial White in Virginia.

Her heart beat wildly as she stared at the envelope in her hand, unable to open it. She knew with grave certainty that it contained bad news. She stood rooted where she was for so long the clerk grew anxious.

"Reanna, are you alright? Are you feeling ill?"

Startled, she glanced up. "Oh, yes, Mr. Tibble. I am fine, thank you."

She turned and walked out into the bright sunshine, but a chill had settled over her that had nothing to do with the weather and she shivered as she drove her wagon home.

Mansunama was waiting. He knew, she was sure, that there was something wrong. He silently helped her from the wagon, and they stood together as she slowly, hesitantly, opened the letter with shaking hands. She began to read aloud, in little more than a whisper, "We sincerely regret to inform you of the death ... Chance! It cannot be true!"

She began to sink to the ground, but Mansunama caught her under her arms and held her as she sobbed brokenhearted. She could not accept this, could not believe the words she had read.

Suddenly she straightened and stood on her own, wiping the tears from her face, and looked into Mansunama's black eyes, announcing, "It is not true. He is not dead. If he were, I would know. Inside, I would know. I would feel it. He is still alive. I will not believe otherwise."

The Indian made no reply, and Reanna pushed away from him, going to the barn without another word to saddle Guinevere. She did not glance his way as she rode out.

This year's calves eyed her in wide eyed curiosity from between their mother's legs as Reanna stopped to watch. Riding on, she topped a rise to find one of their herds of horses grazing below, the mares, sleek and shining in the sun and the foals gamboling playfully through the tall, nourishing grass.

Life, it seemed, was new, fresh, and vibrant. And her baby was gone, and Chance was dead.

No! He most certainly was not! But there was the proof. She had the letter from Captain White.

She sat and suffered the great pain and weight of her loss. There was little choice but to believe the words that were in the letter. Chance was dead. Her beloved was gone. How could he have done this? How could fate be so cruel as to allow her to face such suffering?

She slid from Guinevere's back and only after waving her fists at the heavens, damning, and cursing Chance for having dared to leave her alone on this cold, harsh earth, she finally wept in the midst of the silent, waving grasses, until her tears were spent, then rode the patient mare back home, where she left the horse in the yard and went wearily into the house and up to her room.

The house was empty. Lada had probably taken Spring to Raymond's. She threw herself across her bed, clutching a pillow tightly. "How could you take him away from me God? How could you do this to me?" She moaned into the pillow before she began punching it furiously, attempting to rid herself of the wrenching pain and anger inside.

Jumping up from the bed, Reanna marched to her dresser and, grasping her silver hairbrush in a shaking hand, threw it as hard as she possibly could, straight at her full-length mirror.

She caught a glimpse of herself just before the glass shattered, sending shards of glass about the room. Her hair was tangled, and her curls tumbled wildly down to her waist. Her clothes were wrinkled, and soiled from lying on the ground, and her eyes were red rimmed and swollen.

She grabbed the silver hand mirror, and then her sliver comb. They followed the hairbrush, breaking what was left of the large mirror from the frame.

She began to scream in fury and wrenching sorrow, smashing crystal perfume bottles, candles, and lamps with a vengeance. Nothing escaped her wild furor, even the windows were smashed.

As her box of jewels crashed against the wall, her eye was caught by the lovely necklace Chance had given her to wear with her wedding dress six years ago as it flew to the floor to lay amid the broken waste.

The lustrous pearl caught her eye, and Reanna stared dazedly at the simple beauty. A heart-wrenching cry escaped her as she sank to the floor and picked it up, clutching it tightly against her heart. Rocking to and fro, she sobbed out all the soul searing pain that was bottled inside.

In the quiet aftermath of the storm, Mansunama appeared and, helping her up, led her gently down to the kitchen, where he resolutely pried the necklace from her numbed fingers, and tenderly bathed the blood from the cuts from the shards of broken glass, and dunked her hands into a pot full of stinging, cleansing solution, the ingredients to which only Mansunama knew.

Reanna actually welcomed the pain when her hands were immersed, for it gave her something else to focus on for a few moments, and any pain was preferable to this pain in her heart.

She spent the next two weeks floating in a sea of utter desolation. She sat for hours on end staring at nothing. She had no interests, and ate as little as possible, merely toying with her food. She burst into tears at the slightest provocation, and found little sleep at night, waking from so many nightmares about Chance that she forgot what it was to have a full night's sleep.

Mansunama could no longer stand to see her suffer so. She was rapidly losing weight, and there were dark shadows beneath her eyes, eyes that held such pain and suffering that he could barely bring himself to meet her tortured gaze.

Tasha was about to have pups again, and Mansunama decided that this might be the very thing that Rea needed to pull her from her depression. He kept a close watch on the dog, and when the day came that she started her labor, he hurried to find Tasha's' mistress.

He insisted that Reanna come with him.

"You are perfectly capable of delivering pups, and handling any problems that should arise," Reanna stated dully.

"But you are the one that she loves and trusts, Rea. And that can make all the difference in the world. Come now," he insisted as he held his hand out to her.

"Someone that you love and trust," she repeated as she stared at him considering his words. Having learned to trust in Mansunama's instincts, she did not hesitate longer and decided to accompany him.

They watched the entire birth, from beginning to end. This was Tasha's fourth litter, so she had a fairly easy delivery, and needed little help.

Reanna watched the squirming, helpless pups as they were nuzzled and cleaned by their mother, and Mansunama noted the softening in her eyes as she gazed at the new lives in wonder.

Picking up a pup, he held it out to her in the palm of his hand. "You see Reanna, life does go on."

He spoke softly and gently, as if to a small child, but she felt the bite of his words as if Tasha had sunk her teeth into Reanna's flesh. She felt it strongly and realized that his words were true.

Life did go on, and so would she. She was alive, although she had wished otherwise these past weeks. Her tears came, and she cried while Mansunama held her tightly against him, stroking her fine hair and whispering words of comfort.

She was filled once again with his powerful aura and felt as if she had come to life once more.

They walked for some time, and when Reanna found herself baring her soul to him, it seemed quite right that she did so. Mansunama listened gravely to her every word, and Reanna felt much better by that evening than she had in a long while.

During the next two weeks she gradually began to work and care for the ranch again and even visited with some of her friends in town.

Kenny and Molly lent their sympathy and support, as did Uncle Bob and Aunt Martha.

Every time she saw Belinda, it seemed that they discussed the war and wondered at the fact that they had heard nothing from Nathan or Billy. They would end up holding each other, crying out their sorrows and fears. The strengths of these friendships, combined with hard work at the ranch, began the process of healing her broken heart.

Mansunama, she knew, was the greatest source of her healing strength. But she could not allow him the closeness that she sensed he wanted. She still felt her aching emptiness too strongly to allow anyone to become very intimate with her yet.

Much of her time was spent alone, roaming around the ranch on foot or on horseback, as if she were searching for something that constantly evaded her. Finally, it came to her that it was just restless frustration that kept her moving so.

Reanna had another reason to be grateful to Mansunama, for it was he who explained about death to Spring, and in the Christian's way. It just was something Reanna had felt unable to do.

After Spring understood that Daddy's spirit was in Heaven, she wondered why Mommy was so sad. Daddy was happy, wasn't he?

Reanna explained that she would miss having her husband, and that is what was making her sad.

Spring thought a minute, then answered, "I will miss him too, Mommy, very much, but I am glad that he is with God in Heaven, and if we are sad, that might make Daddy and God sad."

Reanna hugged her daughter tightly, unable to reply.

Although Spring would have everyone believe that she was not bothered by her father's death, including herself, there were many nights when Reanna awoke to find her daughter climbing into bed with her, not a usual habit.

Gradually, the sharp pain of her loss grew less, and Reanna knew that Mansunama was largely responsible. He would sit in the evenings and just hold her hand, and she could feel his strength, his earthy power, flowing into her. Somehow, she no longer felt a need to pull away from him. After so many months of grieving over her beloved's death she was ready to be healed, she wanted to be free of pain.

One night as they sat with Lada, relaxing after dinner, Mansunama picked up his guitar and began to play.

Suddenly nervous, Reanna rose from the settee and poured herself a glass of sherry, sipping it as she returned to her seat. The sound of raindrops drummed on the roof and splattered on the windows as they were driven by the wind.

Spring was fast asleep in bed, and Reanna and Lada were content to listen to the beautiful melodies that softly filled the room.

Reanna had not played since Chance's death and had no desire to now. The hour grew late, and Lada took her leave to seek her bed. Relaxed with the sherry and soft music, Reanna had decided to retire herself, when Mansunama began to play a very special song. She shivered as the haunting lyrics in Mansunama's deep voice surrounded her; the story of the golden eagle trying valiantly to heal his broken wings, to fly free as he was meant to do.

Mesmerized, Reanna listened, knowing that he sang of her plight, of her broken wings … and of how he could heal her.

Finished, the pure notes died away, and in the silence that remained Mansunama laid aside his guitar and stood, towering over her, and lifted her hand, pulling her to her feet to stand before him. His strong, gentle hands held her shoulders and fastening her wide green eyes with his intense black ones, he gazed deeply, drinking in her stunning beauty, and she could not turn away. His voice when it came, was low and sensuous, yet firm with authority.

"Let me help you to heal your broken wings Reanna, like the eagle in the song. It is time for you to fly. Let my love lift you to the heights of your hearts desires."

She attempted to shake her head in denial, but he leaned down to claim her lips with his own, a kiss full of passion, of love, of himself and Reanna was rendered helpless by the powerful feelings he stirred deep within her. He drew back slightly, testing her reaction, and she could only stare at him in wonder.

She was aware of the sounds of the raging storm outside, and acutely aware of the warm, powerful aura of the handsome man who stood in front of her. She wanted desperately to deny the fact that there could be anyone for her but Chance, but that did not seem to be true any longer.

Chance was gone, and Mansunama filled her senses with his being, with his love, she heard herself murmur, as if from far away, "Heal me then Mansunama. Lift me with your love."

He wrapped his strong arms around her and carried her to the bedroom, kicking the door closed and laid her gently on the bed. She watched as he leisurely slipped from his buckskin vest and breeches as he came closer. He stood before her in savage, naked splendor and watched as her eyes traveled the harsh planes and sinewed muscles of his brown body before he joined her, taking her into his arms to offer her his love.

"I have been waiting for you for a lifetime," he breathed as he captured her mouth in an infinitely tender kiss, seeking, and gaining her heated response as desire, too long suppressed, welled up inside her. His fingers worked at the buttons of her blouse, and he soon slid it from her shoulders and away from her, his hands and mouth sampling her exposed breasts and smooth skin.

She released a long sigh of pleasure, opening her eyes to meet his hungry black gaze. She was momentarily taken aback that there were not brown eyes burning with the familiar red glow of desire before her. Closing her eyes against that memory, she slowly began her own enticing exploration of his body while savoring the feel of his touch.

He moaned, holding back his own desires as her hand found his engorged lance. Brushing her hand away, he feverishly feasted upon her flesh, teasing her breasts, and exciting every nerve in her body, finally reaching, and tasting of the wild nectar between her legs.

Reanna gasped, shocked at this invasion, for although Chance had come close, he had always stopped short of this unexpected delight. Her shock turned to unabashed pleasure, and she writhed, moaning in sweet agony.

Mansunama lifted his head, sinking his fingers into her long, tangled copper tresses, relishing even the texture of this treasure as he poised himself above her to sink the burning root of his desire into her willing body.

She cried out as he entered her, and their lips met again as he plunged repeatedly into her eager, welcoming warmth. They were swept in a whirling maelstrom and Reanna felt as if she were a leaf in the wind as she was buffeted, soaring higher and faster than ever before.

When he groaned into her ear "fly, my love," she was carried so high that the intensity of her climax was almost too much to bear. She screamed in utter ecstasy when she reached the peak of the mountain tops, but quite suddenly the wind stopped as she fell back to earth, landing with a sharp pain shooting through her heart as Mansunama shuddered above her. Her eyes filled with tears, she curled into a forlorn ball, unable to stop the sobbing that overcame her as her mind reeled in confusion.

How could it have been so wonderful with a man that she did not love as a husband? How could she have been lifted higher than she ever had been with Chance? Her husband, alive or dead, still possessed her heart.

Perhaps it was Mansunama's strong healing powers, the power he held of the earth and wood combined with the great love he held for her. She had accepted that love freely, but now was unsure she should have. Inexplicably, she felt certain that the Shaman would be hurt in the end. His arms wrapped around her, and she felt the soft texture of his long black hair against her wet cheek. She turned to look at him as his eyes anxiously searched her own. She attempted to explain her tears. "I fear for your heart, Mansunama. I will never love anyone the way I have loved Chance. I do not understand why we were able to soar so high, but I came back down quickly enough to the reality that I do not love you enough to call you husband. I do not wish to hurt you, but it is better to be truthful now. Can you ever understand, ever forgive me?"

He spoke gently, "I've known all of this right along, my lovely Reanna. I would give anything to make you my wife, but I know it is never to be. I have always known, but it will be enough for me that you share whatever love you have left in your heart, even that you have given me that for this one night. Now your wings are on the mend, this makes my heart truly happy."

Reanna wondered at the sadness in his voice, but hugged him tightly, relieved at his understanding. They slept embraced in each other's arms.

When they woke, just as dawn was breaking, Mansunama again claimed her body, this time slowly, driving her to ecstasy in the white morning light. Afterward, she hugged him, kissing him tenderly on the cheek before she climbed from bed to dress. He laid back against the pillows, watching her movements through hooded eyes. Reanna, catching his look, flashed him a bright smile before leaving to help Lada with breakfast.

Lada noticed the change in Reanna immediately; for she was humming cheerfully as she put the coffee on to boil.

"Reanna, you seem happier today than you have for the past year. Your medicine man must have strong powers indeed."

Reanna blushed at her friends knowing smile, hesitating only slightly before she smiled back.

"Yes, I suppose I am. Oh, Lada, he is so wonderful. What would I have done without him these last months or you either Lada? You have been such a great friend to me through everything."

Ladas's smile faded as she turned concerned eyes toward her friend. "Just don't ever forget that he is a very powerful man, strong and proud. He cannot ever belong to your world, and I would hate to see you hurt. I know he loves you but, but I have an uneasy feeling..." thinking better of spoiling Reanna's newfound happiness, she stopped herself.

"Well, never mind all that, I am truly happy for you." She embraced Reanna quickly, and then got back to her work.

That night Reanna found it impossible to sleep. Mansunama had decided to give her time, to let her come to him. He wanted her to be sure about their relationship with no pressure from him.

She remembered too vividly the warmth of his arms, of his hair against her skin; of his deep, dark eyes ... she tossed and turned all night, finally giving up near dawn as she decided to begin her day early.

The next night she was able to endure only an hour of her empty bed and wistful memories before she crept silently to Mansunama's room and slipped beneath the sheet, snuggling close to him.

His voice startled her in the darkness. It seemed as though he had been waiting, knowing she would come to him.

"My beautiful, loving Reanna, you were not meant to sleep alone. You are too passionate, and finally having tasted passion once again, you desire it. You do not belong in a cold bed with no one to share your feelings, but one warmed by a man who loves you."

She turned to him and felt a love for him; the love of respect and appreciation that his wisdom had brought to her.

She unabashedly pursued his love that night, and every night thereafter for a fulfilling and happy month-long adventure of pleasure and the healing of broken wings.

That blissful month came to an abrupt end one night when Mansunama awoke in a cold sweat, sitting up with a start. His gasp and sudden withdrawal from her arms woke Reanna. She sat up next to him; something was dreadfully wrong, and she shivered in the darkness.

"What is it? What is wrong, Mansunama?"

He left the bed and began to pull on his buckskins. "I must go. I must listen to the wind...it is something of grave importance."

Reanna hurried from the bed, swiftly drawing her bathrobe around her.

Mansunama, irritated turned to her, "You must stay here Reanna. I will need to concentrate, and I do that better alone."

"It is about us, is it not? I want to come. I want to know what you hear."

He stared at her a long moment, a deep, penetrating gaze. He turned, leaving her without a word.

She was determined to follow him, and after waiting a moment, did so, furtively keeping to the shadows as he led her far into the night, deep into the woods.

When he stopped and stood stock still with his arms raised to the heavens, she sat beneath the low hanging boughs of a nearby tree, silently watching and waiting.

Mansunama stood immobile for two long hours. His eyes were closed, and his face was raised, casting moonlight onto the handsome, sculpted plains of his features. When he finally moved it was to sink slowly to his knees, head bowed as if in defeat. Raising his arms he clutched his forehead, then as suddenly, his arms fell limply to his sides.

Reanna, cramped from crouching, longed to stand, and stretch, but dared not move. She held her breath as Mansunama finally pushed himself to his feet and began to walk toward her. Surely, he could not know that she had been hidden here. For the first time in her life Reanna felt fearful of this powerful medicine man. She had grown up with him, but there had always been much of himself he kept apart from others, allowing no one in.

He was walking straight toward her. His face was terrible to behold, as cold and unyielding as the barren mountain peaks, ravished by a grief that he was barely able to contain. Reaching her, he stretched out his arm to help her up. She could see the intense agony that filled his eyes. Her heart sank. Her world was spinning out of control.

His voice was harsh as it brushed her ear, "I am leaving you Reanna. When I am gone, you will understand."

Reanna was suddenly very frightened and incredibly lonely. It felt as if he was already gone. "What is it? Why must you go? Please do not leave me Mansunama. Please don't leave me alone!" Her voice shook with the depth of her feeling.

A spasm of pure pain crossed his features. "You must believe me. This is the only way."

"No!" Reanna cried as she flung her arms around his neck and kissed him, desperately, passionately.

His arms came around her to pull her tightly against him. He kissed her long and hard before setting her away. "Give me your hand," he ordered. She was surprised, but complied, as he removed his knife from its sheath. Before she realized what he was doing, he had cut her hand. He let it go to cut his own then clasped hers again, palms together and fingers entwined to hold them close.

"Our life blood will mingle, as our lives and love have mingled. Now shall we always be a part of each other until the day when our spirits may pass from this earth. Take heart, my one and only love, for your future awaits."

Reanna was moved beyond words at the great honor Mansunama bestowed upon her. It was unheard of for a strong, proud warrior to share this honored tradition of mingling blood with that of a woman. She opened her mouth to speak but no sound issued forth.

Mansunama smiled sadly, gently tracing a finger down her cheek. "Goodbye Rea." he whispered softly, then turned and walked out of her life.

She did not break down. She would not cry. She felt empty and brittle, wondering at Mansunama's words. Her future? She had no future without him. Sighing heavily, she retraced her steps back home. She filled her lonely hours with work to alleviate her heartache. It wasn't working. She now realized she was pregnant with Mansunama's child, adding to her burden.

She became impatient and short tempered with herself and even with Spring. She had grown accustomed to sleeping in Mansunama's warm embrace and her lonely bed was pure misery. Only after putting in long, arduous hours of labor during the day did she manage to sleep at night.

The summer sun beat down mercilessly. On her knees in the vegetable garden, Reanna pulled weeds, swatting futilely at the stinging insects. She stopped to straighten, placing a hand to the small of her back. It was dreadfully hot, and she was tired. Raising her eyes, she noticed a man coming toward her. There was something vaguely familiar in his stride. Then he was standing before her, and it took a moment for her to focus.

This must be a figment of her imagination. It couldn't be... but it was. He was standing before her. With a glad cry she welcomed him. "Nathan!"

He crouched next to her in the dusty, dry dirt. "Lady, don't you even recognize your own husband when you see him?" She stiffened, the blood draining from her face, hardly the reaction he expected. He gently laid his hands on her shoulders. "It is me love, I am home Rea, God how I have missed..."

Reanna's face had gone ghostly white; she slumped forward, going limp in his arms. Her mind refused to accept that which her eyes and ears told her was true.

Chapter 14

Reanna regained consciousness slowly, becoming aware of her surroundings, but she dared not open her eyes. Was she mad? What cunning tricks would her mind play on her next? She was afraid to find out.

She could feel the smooth fabric of the settee beneath her. Someone had carried her into the house and placed her here, but who? Lada certainly did not possess such strength.

Someone was urgently repeating her name, and the voice resembled...but it could not be Chance. She was, most assuredly mad.

She could hear that beloved voice plain as day. Deep, smooth...she reached up and placed her hands over her ears, blocking out the voice. Why?! Why had she seen and heard him so distinctly?

Warm, strong hands grasped hers, easily pulling them down from her ears. She heard the voice again.

"Rea, my love, I am not dead. Lada told me about the letter you received. It is not true Rea. There has been a terrible mistake. I am here, and very much alive. Now open your eyes and look at me."

She heard his voice clearly, and very slowly, afraid of what would meet her gaze, she opened her eyes. They were filled with the vision of Chances brown eyes, and reflected in her pupils, his love shining plainly from them. She saw his dark, raven hair, the dark line of his mustache above his upper lip as he gazed down upon her in concern.

She reached up tentatively to softly brush his cheek with her fingertips, afraid that he would vanish with her touch. He was real. He felt wonderfully warm and alive beneath her hand. As if in awe, she whispered "It is true! You are alive!"

She sat up and moved slowly into his arms, haltingly choking out her words. "My God, Chance, it really is you!" Laughing and crying at once, she tried to get a grip on her spiraling emotions as she touched him everywhere, reassuring herself that he was, indeed, here before her.

His eyes glittered with many emotions as her trembling hands wandered over him, but foremost it was his deep love that shone through.

Her voice shook with the force of her feelings, "My love, my life, my heart. You are returned to me. Some miracle of fate has seen you safely home! Oh God Chance," her voice broke as she drew a long, quivering breath. "I believed you dead, gone from me forever. Hold me. Hold me tight, never let go!"

They embraced, clinging together tightly as Chance spoke. "Rea, I'm so sorry. Sorry that I ever left you in the first place. Sorry that I put you through such misery. I did almost die. God, when I think of how close I came to leaving you for good."

He continued, "There was a battle. We were losing badly. I was wounded and left for dead. I remember lying among the dead, the awful stench. I could hear screams and moaning all around me, the cries of the wounded. I thought I had died, but then I woke up in a bed, a real bed, with an elderly woman waiting to feed me some heavenly tasting broth. She and her husband lived not far from the battlefield, on a small farm. When the fighting ended, they came looking for survivors the soldiers may have missed. They were not on either side, just interested in saving lives, anyone's life. The color of a man's uniform did not matter. I was wounded badly in the gut by a bullet and in the chest by shrapnel from cannon fire. I had contracted a fever and lay delirious for three weeks. I was very weak, and it took months for my wound to heal and to regain the strength to be able to travel back to you. That was the real hell, Reanna, worse than the war, worse than anything I have ever had to suffer. To lie in that bed, day after day, for so many weeks, away from you! My wound became infected, and sometimes I would slip into some unknown world, but always Rea, you were forever in my mind, a bright beacon in my heart. All I wanted was to come home to you. I could not write, and the old couple did not know how to. As soon as I was able, I traveled to Washington and received a medical discharge. I came home as quickly as I could."

Reanna pressed a soft, warm kiss against his lips. "It does not matter anymore, none of it. You are home my darling, which is all that matters."

Their eyes met and Reanna rejoiced when she saw the glorious red glow in his loving gaze. It pulled fiercely at her heart. Her eyes filled with tears. Tears of joy, love, and life fulfilled. She exclaimed "I have my heart back. I feel our love so intensely that it causes pain."

Chance held her gently against his broad chest and buried his face in her long, dark, copper tresses, murmuring endearments of love. Reanna felt the sparks of desire igniting deep inside her body.

"Mama, Mama, Daddy's home! He's home!"

They both turned and Spring launched herself wholeheartedly into his waiting arms. They all cried as they hugged each other, overjoyed at Chances return.

They spent the rest of that happy day riding the ranch. Chance held Spring in front of him in the saddle, once again on Lancelot's back. He complimented Reanna on the care she had taken of the ranch in his absence. The fencing was all sturdy and the stock looked sleek and healthy.

Reanna told him about the fire and how they had worked so long and hard to control it. She told him about the man she had hired afterward, of being shot, and about the problem they had with the wolves.

Chance was astounded that she had handled these emergencies so well and knew a towering rage toward the man who had lied to his wife, shot her, and tried to cheat her.

Reanna did not tell him of the sorrow of losing their child. She tucked that pain away in a secret corner of her heart. She also decided she could not bring herself to tell him about the affair with Mansunama, not wishing to take the brightness from their day of reunion.

She finally summoned the courage to ask Chance if he had heard from Billy or Nathan, half fearing his answer. Unfortunately, he had heard nothing from, or about, either of them. He and Nathan had been separated when Chance was wounded. He had searched and asked everywhere he traveled, but no one knew of Billy's whereabouts either.

Chance told her about his family's farm, describing it in great detail. He had seen David's beautiful baby son, trying to hide the yearning he had for a son of his own, in deference to Reanna. But she saw it there in his face, and silently cursed the fates that had taken his child from her loins so many months before.

Her good humor was restored, and she laughed merrily when Chance regaled her with tales of the silly antics of Angel, Holly's dog as she played spiritedly with Beth. Neither of them brought up the subject of the war again, of its cruelties and hardships. It was enough that they were together.

They played with the pups before dinner, and Chance concentrated most of his attention on Spring. They laughed and played together, and Reanna realized how much he must have missed the child, with her precocious ways. After dinner, Chance insisted on putting his daughter to bed himself, a joy he had long been denied.

Reanna stayed behind to speak to Lada, who had appeared distressed during dinner. "Lada, what is it? What is bothering you?"

Lada's eyes stung with sudden tears as she answered, "Oh, Rea, I'm sorry. I do not mean to upset you, but I am so worried about Billy. The shock of Chance returning...why haven't we heard a word about Billy?"

Reanna hugged her friend tightly. "I know you worry about him, but my faith has been restored, and I believe we will be seeing Billy very soon, Lada. You wait and see; he will come home."

Lada smiled mistily, dried her eyes, then turned to busy herself with the dishes, Reanna by her side, helping.

Lada spoke in a soft whisper, "There is something else I worry about. Will you tell Chance of Mansunama?"

Reanna felt a chill pass through her. Nervously she stammered, "I'm undecided. I don't know that I could bear to tell him. Please, Lada, do not mention the Shamans name to Chance." Their troubled gazes met, and Lada pushed further, trying to make Reanna understand just how tenuous her position could really be. "Have you thought of the dangers of not telling him? The worst of which is the possibility that you may have a child?"

Reanna looked aghast, and sat, defeated, in the closest chair. Her face was ashen, and her hands began to tremble as the enormity of what she had done closed in on her. The thought that had so briefly passed through her mind, only to be quickly discarded, was suddenly being voiced out loud by another!

What would she do if...Oh God, she would have to tell him! She would never feel at ease with him now, knowing that her body had betrayed her heart and might yet punish her, in the cruel way nature had of betraying a woman's secrets. She looked around at the familiar kitchen, suddenly stifled. She couldn't breathe. "I... must get some air," she whispered brokenly, then fled out the door.

Chance came seeking her. He saw her in the moonlight, silhouetted against the corral fence, absorbed in watching the horses. Her long copper hair stirred softly in the gentle night breeze, and the softly rounded contours of her woman's body stood out through her clothing. Chance thought he had never seen her this beautiful, lovelier than he remembered. He walked to her and slipped his arms around her, pressing a kiss to the back of her head. When she remained stiff in his embrace, he was bewildered. "Rea, what is wrong? I have been gone so long that my touch has become too unfamiliar?"

She turned in his arms, holding him tightly. When she raised her face to look at him her eyes were filled with tears of regret and pain. Her voice was hoarse with emotion as she spoke. "I thought that you were dead, Chance. I never knew such an empty feeling or aching pain in all my life. I wanted to die myself. I love you beyond all else, beyond my own life. You must know that. Tell me that you believe it."

He stared down at her, his brow furrowed in concern, confused by her words. "Rea, I know all this as surely as I know my own love for you. I am here now though, my love, and I will never leave you again. Is that what you are afraid of?"

She turned away from him, unsure as to whether she could tell him more. Convinced now that something was truly wrong, Chance grasped her shoulders from behind, "Rea, what is it?"

She took a deep shuddering breath, steeling herself for what was to come. "When ..." She spoke slowly, seeking the right words, the words that would make him understand.

"When you were dead...when I thought you dead, I was dead. My heart was dead. But my body was not. I lived, and I allowed my body to betray and deny my dead heart."

She wrung her hands, and then clasped them tightly together in an attempt to calm her nerves. She hung her head in misery, and Chance had to strain to catch her softly uttered words.

"There was a man...Oh God! I... I needed the warmth and comfort of a man's arms. I was so lonely Chance, so alone. I shared my body, but you must believe, my heart was with you. Always. I never would have chosen to give my heart to anyone but you." She could think of nothing else to say. Her words lay like great weights between them. In the heavy silence she dared, finally, to look into his face, instantly regretting that action.

His face was hard and still, save for the muscle that twitched in his cheek, a sure sign of his anger. She was standing too close to miss the coldness, the betrayal that blazed in his eyes. He turned away without a word and walked slowly into the barn, returning in a short while mounted on Lancelot. He stopped before her, staring as if at a stranger, then kicked his mount into a gallop, disappearing in a cloud of dust, darkness quickly enveloping the horse and rider.

As the dust settled to the ground, Reanna sank slowly down with it. Her heart, having so recently been returned, was torn freshly from her breast. In silent agony she dug her nails into the earth. That is where she remained until the sun came up at dawn.

She could stand it no longer, the aching of loss all over again. She began to grow angry, then furious at Chances lack of understanding. Her loneliness had been for him, not anyone else. She had sought the only comfort that had been freely given by the one who wished to heal her. She had accepted it, felt the healing, and yes, had even enjoyed his love. But she had never given hers. It burned only for Chance.

Suddenly determined to find him, she first prepared herself a bath, soaking in the rose scented water until it turned cold. She then donned the soft blouse and skirt she had worn the night of their first union, the night of her uncle's party. It seemed such a distant past. She wore the necklace that Mansunama had pried from her fingers, wedding gift from Chance, and it nestled against the creamy softness of her skin. She brushed her hair, pinning it on top of her head, leaving a few stray curls to dangle softly around her face and neck.

She was ready to leave when Chance burst through the door. He stood before her, humbly contrite. Reanna did not know what to think, but her heart soared. He had come back!

"Chance, I... I was just going into town to look for you." She stopped, unsure of his reasons for coming back, but daring to hope.

"There is no need. I am home, home to stay. I am ashamed to admit I spent the night in a useless bout of drinking, cursing both you and the man who would dare to love you. Then when I thought, I mean really thought about you being alone, and believing me to be dead, well, I would not expect you to live the life of a nun. I would not want you to be alone, for you are too young and beautiful, too loving, and full of passion. Your words kept coming back to me, about your heart always being with me. I realized you spoke the truth, just as I know it would be the same for me. I hope you can forgive me for acting like such a cad."

Reanna, her eyes filled with tears of relief, rushed into his waiting arms. "Oh Chance, I am so glad you are back. I love you Chance!"

Chance's feelings mirrored her own, and he showered her upturned face with soft, tender kisses. Suddenly, their long-denied passions exploded wildly. With shaking hands, they hurriedly undressed each other, impatient in their fierce desires.

When Reanna felt his rough, calloused hands upon her smooth skin, she felt such intense pleasure that it hurt. She was moaning in ecstasy as Chance effortlessly lifted her and carried her to the bed, stretching out next to her.

Reanna looked into his eyes, purposely seeking the familiar red glow of desire she knew would be there, that she had not seen in so very long. The sheer intensity, the very depth of his burning gaze shook her, as her breath caught in her throat. She held his gaze throughout their entire mating, relishing the sight of him once again before her.

Chance had been far too long without her. He entered her and was through all too quickly, though neither of them minded, for they had both felt the same urgency. It proved to be a short, but extremely sweet pleasure.

They were both claimed by much needed slumber afterward, and when they woke, there was no need of words between them. Their eyes spoke all of their love. A kiss, deep and searching, and the warm pleasure of their bodies pressed together lit the fire once again. This time they fanned the flames slowly, each of them leisurely tasting, touching, and savoring the feel of the other.

Reanna felt the new scars he carried, three of them on his chest from the burning shrapnel, and a smaller one, lower on his abdomen, where the bullet has passed through. She bent and kissed each one, trembling with the knowledge of all the pain he had been through and the realization of how close he had come to never returning to her.

When he entered her this time, she cried out at the joy of his homecoming. They were carried away by the wind which fanned the flames of their desire, lifting them farther than they had ever been together, above the mountain peaks. Reanna felt herself slowly and gently floating back to reality after this union, back to her beloved's warm embrace.

Much later, after securing a promise from Reanna to stay where she was, Chance left the room. He returned a short while later with coffee and warm bread and butter and an assurance from Lada to care for Spring for the rest of the day.

He flashed her a wicked grin and with sly eyes explained, "So, my lusty wench, you may spend the rest of the day leading your bounty hunter on a long, enticing search of your most fervent desires."

Reanna returned his smile. "My only desire is you, my rogue knight."

Chance bent close above her, gazing into the green pools of her eyes that sparkled with a hint of the sea. "Your desire is my desire."

His lips claimed hers in a hot, passionate kiss, and then pulled back, gently teasing and exploring, lightly brushing her lips, then pulling back before teasing her more, until she could no longer bear the game.

Sinking her fingers into his thick, raven hair, she pulled his head down to stay him with a deep, penetrating kiss, skillfully using her probing tongue. They were caught up in the wild, searing flames of passion once again, consuming each other in a quest stronger than any other they had yet shared. They were swept up to dizzying, spiraling heights many times that day, and within the next night. They found they had little need of sleep, the more intense, urgent need being to share their long-denied desires of love.

The next month was filled with activity as Chance labored to catch up with many things that had gone undone in his absence and culling the herds of fat cattle for the coming winter.

At the end of that month, Billy finally returned from the war to the loving, and at last, willing arms of Lada. He was white and pinched, suffering from a fever, but otherwise unchanged.

Lada saw to the care of him herself, brewing teas from herbs which she bade him drink, and cooling his body with cool cloths. Under her tender care he recovered, losing his pinched look, slowly gaining weight and strength.

Reanna and Chance rejoiced at their friend's romance, for it was easy to see how happy they were. In each other's company their eyes told all as they gazed lovingly at each other whenever they were together.

Some disconcerting news also arrived that month. Three of the properties that Chance owned along the coast in California had burned to the ground. Three fires in less than two months' time was enough to raise Chances suspicions. He wanted to plan a trip to investigate, but he was loathe to leave Reanna again so soon after he had returned. He did not want her to become involved in anything dangerous either, so decided it was best to stay put for the time being. Those losses would be absorbed by his other business properties and his ship, so he forcefully decided to concentrate on the ranch and his reunited family.

One day, as Spring sat in the saddle with her father, she mentioned having ridden with an Indian. Chance had an instant vision of Mansunama as the child elaborated, "A great, tall Indian."

Chance tried to tamp down the feelings of jealousy and rage that Spring's words made him feel. He consoled himself by thinking the Indian had just come for a visit while he was gone to war, that was all...just a visit. He wondered then, why Reanna had not mentioned it. She probably just didn't think it important enough, he reasoned, and so pushed these unpleasant thoughts from his mind.

The dawning of a new month brought with it a new worry, this time for Reanna. She had learned to recognize her body's rhythms and signs all too well. Now her body was telling her something she did not wish to hear. However, she had little choice but to listen, so decided she must go see Dr. Farley.

After breakfast, she informed Chance that she would be going into town to visit with Belinda and check for mail. Chance had no argument and asked no questions, much to Reanna's relief. She was so distraught, she had worried he would know something was amiss, so when he left the house, she breathed a sigh of relief.

Leaving Spring with Lada, she rode Guinevere to town, stopping first at the mail office, delaying her visit to the good doctor as long as possible.

Her heart pounded, and she thrilled with excitement when she spied the letter from Nathan. She swiftly tore it open to read the words in greedy haste, feeling a mixture of relief, joy, and sadness as she perused the contents.

Nathan was in the hospital recovering from a serious leg wound. He was almost healed and ready to leave, to come home. But he could not walk well and was working hard, day after day, to learn to walk with the aid of a cane, and to mount and ride a horse. Nathan revealed that the hardest part was dismounting with a leg that was stiff and unyielding, causing him much pain. It was good to be alive though, and he would return as soon as he was able. Before she left, she collected Belinda's mail for her, and was overjoyed to find a letter from Nathan to her friend also.

Belinda was so thrilled that there was finally some word of her beloved that her eyes filled with tears as she tore the envelope open. Reanna left her to read the happy news in privacy. Her heart beating wildly, she sought the doctor's office as if going to her doom. She breathed in deep gulps of air, trying to quell her nerves.

After his examination, Doctor Farley peered at her, thoroughly confused. "Rea, you are with child, but Chance has been back little more than a month, and you seem to be much further along than that."

The unspoken question died on his lips, as Reanna, pale with shock, stood on quivering limbs and walked out of his office. She did not wish to face the accusation in his eyes when he realized the truth. She was shaking so badly; she could barely make her way across the street to Guinevere. Upon doing so, she clutched the mare's silky mane in her trembling hands, burying her face against it, her body overcome with wrenching sobs.

Heedless of the inquiring looks cast her way by passersby; she leaned into the mare until she could see clearly once again. Wiping her swollen eyes, she mounted Guinevere once more and turned her toward home.

Her mind reeled with shock and pain. She trembled in fear at having to face Chance with this news. He would be crushed, she knew. She was crushed. Not so much because she carried this child, but much more because of the pain it would cause her beloved husband.

Strangely, she felt the instant maternal instincts that she had known when she carried Chance's child. She dared not admit, even to herself, that she was happy to have Mansunama's child growing within her as she told herself it was more like an honor. Like the feeling she had experienced when he had mingled their blood, a privilege of the gift of his love.

She laughed a harsh sound of self-derision. What privilege this, to see her beloved's heart broken? No privilege, no honor...just terrifying pain and guilt. The sun was hot on her head. She should have worn her hat, trying to think of anything but Chance's face when she told him. It was useless. His features swam before her eyes.

Stifling a sob, Reanna kicked her heels into Guinevere's sides, causing the mare to leap suddenly into flight. Leaning forward, she kicked her again, and the mare answered with a quick burst of speed. The landscape was a blur as horse and rider tore down the dusty road, leaving visions of hurt and anger in their wake with brown particles of dry earth that hung suspended in the air. Hooves drummed loudly in her ears, the wind of passage tearing at her hair, and Reanna closed her eyes and mind to all but the thundering mount beneath her.

Suddenly Guinevere swerved and screamed in terror. Reanna felt herself, with a sickening lurch in her stomach fly through the air, her breath knocked from her as she hit the ground with a heavy thud, landing on her back. She opened her eyes. Guinevere was screaming from a distance, it seemed. Her vision focused on the mare as the horse repeatedly reared up, then came down to pummel something into the ground with her sharp hooves. A snake. Guinevere gave a last stiff legged pounce, and then lowered her head to sniff at the broken reptile. Tossing her white head and giving a last disgusted snort, she turned to gallop down the road.

Pain surrounded Reanna, cloaking her in a gathering darkness. The world swam before her eyes and she closed them, no longer able to fight against the tides of pain. She welcomed the darkness...

Chance rode Lancelot leisurely into the yard, pleased with the number of cattle they would be able to sell. The ranch was certainly doing well, and they would realize a handsome profit this year.

Suddenly he stiffened in the saddle, his eyes narrowed in concentration as he spied Guinevere hurtling toward the ranch yard from the direction of town. His heart lurched with fear as the mare drew closer with no sign of Reanna. Terror gripped him as he kicked Lancelot to an instant burst of speed; never pausing as he passed the froth covered Guinevere to retrace her path from town.

He found Reanna where she had fallen, and his insides twisted in shock as he noted the dark red blood that stained the fabric of her skirt. She was unconscious but breathing. He lifted her as gently as he could, and blood ran down to drip with clear, sickening taps upon her leather boots. Had she been shot? He could not find a bullet wound. She must have been injured when she fell from her horse. He knew he had to get her home and stop the bleeding, whatever the cause. It was too far to town, so he would send Billy to fetch Doctor Farley as soon as they reached the ranch.

He pondered what could have happened. Then the answer and sudden understanding hit him with sharp, painful clarity. He looked down at her still, pale face and wondered, for the thousandth time, who the man was. He reached the house after what seemed like hours, keeping his horse to a slow walk so he would not jostle Reanna unnecessarily. Shaking his head to clear his rage, he carried her to their room, shouting over his shoulder for Lada to help him, and for Billy to get the doctor.

Chance and Lada cleaned Reanna, making her as comfortable as possible. Lada confirmed Chances suspicions of a miscarriage. His only outward sign of emotion was the muscle ticking in his jaw. Without further words, he retired to his study, poured a large glass of brandy, and sat behind his desk as he sipped it, staring out the window with a menacing scowl.

The doctor, echoing Lada's words, added that there was nothing they could do but wait for her to regain consciousness, and for the bleeding to stop.

Reanna moaned and stirred slightly as she regained her senses that night. Slowly, all the thoughts and memories of the day before assailed her and anguish replaced confusion in her muddled state of mind as she felt the blood flowing from her body.

She began to cry, and Lada came and took her in her arms, whispering soft words of comfort. "There, Rea, it is for the best this way, my friend, even though it does not seem so right now."

Reanna was hurt and felt angry at Ladas words. Yes, she thought dully, they would all think that, but it was not so for her. This was her child, and it had been created in love.

She realized that she truly did love Mansunama. Not in the same way she loved Chance. She did not have the same desperate need for Mansunama that she had for Chance. But she loved the Shaman in a warm, gentle way. The same way she loved the beauty of the woods, the earth, and the wind. He was a part of her childhood, a part of her. She loved this child of his, even though she realized it would have been painful for Chance. She could not help her love. She swallowed painfully in the darkness, turning away from Lada, and sank back once more into a welcome world of exhausted, empty blackness.

The next time she opened her eyes it was daylight. Lada was there tending to her and gave her a glass of water and spoke softly to her friend. "Rea, the bleeding has stopped. There has, as yet been no actual miscarriage. You still carry the child. I do not know how, but you do. It is controlled by a force far greater than we can understand, it seems."

Reanna's heart was flooded in relief, and it showed in the depths of her green eyes, but with that relief came renewed fears about Chance's reaction. There was no help for it. She felt strongly about the child, so she told herself that Chance would love it too, and accept it, the same way he had Spring.

After all, he was the one who had told her about loving a child as part of oneself, no matter the begetter.

Chance woke to an uncomfortable stiffness and stretched gratefully as he rose from the chair behind his desk, where he had fallen asleep in the early hours of the morning.

His head ached. He had consumed the full bottle of brandy. The bright light that filtered through the study window pricked his eyes, and he felt ashamed by the feeling of relief that claimed him, though he did feel pity for Reanna. It was hard for a woman to lose a child, and she had been waiting so long to have another. He could not stop himself from thinking that it was for the best. How could he stand to witness her bear another man's child again, especially since she had given herself willingly. He would save her from her pain if he could, but if he were to be perfectly honest, he was glad that she had lost this baby, and for these thoughts, he hated himself.

He entered their bedroom to find Reanna sitting up, bolstered by the pillows of the bed. He sat gingerly on the edge of the mattress, fearful of causing her any pain. He gently placed his hands on her slender shoulders as he gazed into her eyes. "I am truly sorry for you Rea. Are you alright?"

"I will be fine after a few days rest Chance, but how do you feel?"

"I love you Reanna, I am just worried about you. I know that your body will heal, and though I cannot deny that I am relieved you will not carry the child of another man, I know how hard it must be for you."

Reanna interrupted, the feeling of dread at his words making her voice sound harsh. "I did not lose the child."

Chance felt as though he had been slapped. "What?!"

Pain twisted in her breast as she noted his unwillingness to accept this news. She continued in a softer tone. "The bleeding has stopped. I still carry the child...How can you feel relief at the loss of a child, Chance? You are the one who tried so hard to convince me to feel otherwise when I carried Spring. Why would you not feel the same this time? You know that I..."

Chance's face was hard and rigid, his muscles tensed tightly in frustrated anger as he stood, jerking quickly away from her as if he had been burned. He stared down at her through a haze of rage, choking out his words.

"It is not so much that you willingly gave yourself up to another man's passions as it is the hard, cold fact that it seems I am to ever watch you bear fruit from other than your own husband. Call it callous pride, call it anything you want, but I will not stay to see this child born." His voice gained octane as he became more certain that he could not bear this new twist of the fates. "I cannot stand the sight of you growing large with another man's child, and I cannot stand the light of happiness I see in your eyes at the knowledge that you will have this child that is not of my making."

He turned and strode angrily from the room, slamming the door in his wake. The sound echoed in Reanna's head like crashing booms of thunder until she heard Lancelot's hooves beating the ground, racing away.

For two days Reanna waited expectantly for Chance to return. When he did not, she knew that he was really gone. Her beloved Chance had left her.

She heard the song of the golden eagle in her head as her mind swirled with visions of the eagle lying crippled in the dust with broken wings, unable to fly. She heard the harsh, pathetic, eerie cries of the great bird. They rang and echoed in her mind and in her ears, down into her soul, loud and unending.

She had become one with the broken eagle yet again, and it was her own voice sounding his cries as she lay crumpled and broken upon her bed. She knew now the true pain of losing her heart and her love. Death had not been able to separate them as entirely as hurt and anger did now.

Chapter 15

Chance sat alone in the thick night darkness, staring into the flames of his campfire as they licked greedily at the dry wood he had just added, the sharp snapping of the fire fading from his hearing as he dealt with his conflicting emotions, his thoughts reeling in disorganized abandon.

Running away, which was certainly what he had done, and trying to leave his pain behind was only causing him more of the same. Yet he could not go back right now. He was not sure when he would be able to return to the life he had left behind, if ever.

His male pride had been too damnably injured. Anger, hurt and a sense of betrayal and frustration warred within his breast with many opposing emotions.

He loved Reanna beyond all else. That had not changed. It was that fact that caused his heart to wound so deeply, but he had meant it when he said that he would not be able to witness the birth of this child she carried. It was too much to ask, to see the woman he loved once more bear the fruit of another man.

With a snort of self-disgust, he wondered who the child would resemble this time. Not knowing the identity of the father, and not wanting the knowledge, he could not fathom just what his reaction to the child would be if he ever laid eyes on it, especially considering that his wife had seemed so happy with the prospect of it.

No, he could not bear to go back.

He had been forcing himself to concentrate on other things these last two days. Riding hard, he had thought grimly of his varied businesses along the California coast, of the fact that they had burned. That is where he would go, to take up his old life of roaming at will. First, he would head to

Sacramento to check on his holdings there. Then he would get to the bottom of those fires. Perhaps when all was in order, he would even once again captain his ship to distant ports, instead of paying others to take care of these … pleasures, as he had once thought of these endeavors.

He smiled in the darkness, but the action held no warmth as he felt the old mantle of cool indifference once again settle over him, a man of no feelings. He had grown too soft under Reanna's spell.

Yes, he had plenty to do, more than enough to keep his mind and body occupied, and he would not dwell on painful thoughts.

With his future set in his mind, he pushed memories of Reanna to the furthest recesses of his thoughts and lay down to find the peace that comes with deep slumber.

He slept, but found no peace, as his dreams held only visions of his lovely wife. Strangely, he dreamt that she was one with the eagle of her songs. The eagle with the broken wings and shattered dreams.

Reanna lay in bed, thinking about what she would do. For days she had remained in a shocked, dazed state of mind, unable to believe that Chance really had no intentions of returning to her.

Today she realized that she must finally face the truth. Chance was gone. He was not coming back, not unless she did something about it.

The more she thought about it, the angrier and more determined she became. She would be damned if she would allow him to walk out of her life, away from her love, and throw their hearts to the wind only to crash to the ground and be shattered. She had a good idea that he would head to the coast of California to investigate his holdings. Where else would he go? Certainly not to his father. That, she decided, would bring him too much sorrow, knowing the questions that would be raised by Holly and Beth. No, he would not seek shelter with his family. He would go to the coast and Reanna was determined to go and find him.

Mentally making plans for the trip, she got up and washed, then began to dress, donning a brown riding skirt and soft cotton blouse with matching brown piping around the yolk, shoulders, and cuffs. She was just doing the last buttons on the front of the blouse when she heard a hesitant knock on the door.

"Come in," she called, and then gasped as the door was slowly pushed open. She automatically started forward to hurry into his arms. Then caught herself abruptly as she noted the cane he leaned upon.

"Nathan!"

Nathan smiled, although his eyes showed the sorrow he felt for his brother's troubles. "Reanna, just because I am not Chance, does that mean you cannot greet a returning soldier properly?"

Reanna ran to him and held him tightly, tears spilling from her eyes as she gazed up at him. "Have you been to see Belinda? Does she know that you are home?"

"Yes, of course. She was my first priority. But what is all this I hear of you and Chance? My brother, it appears, has taken leave of his senses and left for parts unknown. Do you want to talk about it? I don't know if I could help, but let us give it a try, shall we?"

He gently led Reanna to the bed, and as she sat down, she found herself relating the whole story to him, along with many tears of despair.

Dashing the tears from her eyes, she looked directly into his and said, "Today I finally decided that I must stop these tears and go to find him. I have much to say to him, and I will ask Uncle Bob or Jared to accompany me. I will not take the stage to California, for I would rather have my own horse, Guinevere, with me. I am sorry to have to leave so soon after your return. I have missed you terribly, Nathan, but I am sure you understand."

"I understand one thing, Reanna. I will not let you go without me."

"Nathan, I cannot ask that of you, or of Belinda. She has been waiting so long to have you back home again. You just can't leave so soon."

She looked at his face etched with concern, so much like Chance that it made her heart tighten in pain. "I … I do not think that I could stand … to have to keep on looking at you … Oh Nathan! You look so much like him that it causes me pain!"

She had turned, presenting her back to him, but he knew that her lovely eyes were filled with tears. He moved toward her, and laying his hands on her shoulders, gently but firmly insisted, "I may look like him, but I am not him, and I will not let you go searching the countryside for him without me. You will get over the pain of looking at me, because you have no choice, and you know that in the end, we will find Chance. I love you, sister, and I would do anything to help you. Besides," he frowned, "I have a thing or two I would like to say to your husband myself. So, we will find him together, you and I. that would not be so terrible, would it?"

Touched by his concern for her, Reanna turned and was enfolded in his strong embrace. Looking deeply into his eyes, she questioned softly, "And what of Belinda?"

"I have no fear that she will understand, and hasten me on my way, for she loves you very much, and would not see you unhappy."

Reanna gently pulled from his arms and began gathering her bags and clothing. "It is settled then, Nathan. We will leave as soon as you have had a chance to explain to her."

While waiting for Nathan, Reanna delivered Spring to her father's house so that Carmelita could look after her, leaving Billy and Lada free to look after the ranch. She had no idea how long she would be gone, weeks, or even months. All she knew was that she would not give up until she had found her beloved husband and convinced him to come home.

When Nathan returned, it was with Belinda in tow. Smiling sheepishly, he attempted to explain, "Reanna, she refuses to let me go without her."

Belinda, her face wreathed in smiles, defended her actions. "He has been away from me for far too long Rea, and I will not allow him to leave me again so soon. I can ride and shoot with a certain amount of accuracy, and you may want another woman along. Nathan told me of the child," she murmured softly.

Suddenly very glad of her company, Reanna hugged her friend, at a loss for words.

Nathan had also picked up the mail while he was in town, and now handed it to Reanna, who shuffled through it half-heartedly, then was glad she had taken the time to do so when she spied a message from Chance's business associate in California. Reading the letter, her face paled, and she silently handed it to Nathan.

It seemed that a rash of fires had taken place again; more businesses burned to the ground, all owned by Chance Nolton. It was obviously the work of some yet unknown arsonist, out to ruin Chance. Only now it was not just arson. The fires had resulted in three deaths so far.

The three of them exchanged worried glances and mounted their horses to set off. They had to find Chance, to warn him before it was too late. Someone was obviously trying, regardless of the cost, to lure Chance to California. Reanna felt the chill of fear. Someone wanted to ruin her husband very badly and would stop at nothing to see the deed done.

They pushed their mounts, riding hard for seven days. Reanna did not even notice the scenic country around her that she had so enjoyed on her first trip to California, seeking to pass through the mountains of the Sierra Nevada's before they were caught by any early snows. Her only thoughts were those of Chance, of finding him in time.

Painfully, and to her chagrin, with a small amount of envy, she watched Belinda and Nathan together, missing her own beloved so much that it made her heart ache whenever her companions exchanged loving gazes or smiles.

They began their search in Monterey, the southernmost site of Chance's burned-out holdings. They planned on working their way north, all the way to Sonoma.

Reanna was positive that they would find him easily, for he was well known in this section of the country, where he had spent many years. She just prayed that they would be in time.

They also decided to hire some men from the Pinkerton agency to investigate the burned-out sites of several of the fires for signs of sabotage, in case law enforcement officials had missed some clue that would lead to the identity of the culprit.

Reanna felt something gnawing at the corners of her mind, as if she knew, or should know, the answer to this puzzle, but for some reason the solution evaded her.

Chance traveled from Sacramento to Sonoma, where he planned to begin his search south, down the coast. The three fires that he knew of had all taken place in this general area. He would look into the causes, and then decide whether or not to rebuild each of the business before he left port on his ship in Monterey. He remained determined to stay busy with travel, for to stay too long in one place would invite painful memories.

Chance sighed heavily and leaned back in his chair. He had just finished questioning a former employee, one of many that he had interviewed in the past several days. He had come up with nothing. Everyone, including the sheriff, agreed that the sights had been checked thoroughly, and there was nothing to suggest foul play. One of the fires appeared to have been caused by lightning. As improbable as it was, the fires had to have been a misfortunate coincidence.

Well, at least he was free in his own mind to continue his journey down the coast. He would leave instructions to begin rebuilding his losses; the men in his employ could not stay out of work indefinitely.

Reanna, Nathan, and Belinda found different news as they spent the next six weeks traveling and investigating the other fires.

One was known to have been deliberately set, but there was no proof of who had done it, and two others were considered suspicious. They were no closer to finding an answer as to who was responsible, or how they could prevent further damage to their income properties. There was no way of knowing where the arsonist would strike next.

And they were no closer to finding Chance. No one they talked to had seen him.

When they reached San Francisco, Nathan suggested that they stay a few days, as he felt that they all needed a good rest, especially Reanna, who was looking quite peaked.

They held to the belief that they would cross paths with Chance soon, before it was too late, perhaps even in this bustling port city. It was, though, becoming increasingly hard to hope that they would find him easily, so Reanna began to feel very depressed and hopeless. There was no comfort for her.

Chance had begun to have much the same feelings as Reanna. Wandering for two months had not brought him the solace he desired, and every night now his dreams were filled with images of his wife and the golden eagle, broken and alone. The nightmares became impossible to ignore, plaguing him even during the day as he began to worry about her and Spring.

Remembering Spring's birth brought him the fear that Reanna could die in childbirth, and he would not even know. The more he thought about it, the worse his fear became, and he realized that he had made a grave mistake in coming here and staying away for so long.

How could he have been so cruel, so thoughtless of his wife's feelings? He still loved her beyond all else, that fact would never change.

This realization struck him with a smarting blow, and he now saw that it was out of love, out of her loneliness for him, that she had been able to accept the comfort of another man's arms. The enormity of his mistake and foolhardy action cut him with pain, carving his knavish heart in two. He decided to return, to beg her forgiveness, which he did not deserve.

"Hold fast, Rea, my love. I am coming home to you." That thought was a beacon, guiding him through the silent night.

As the trio reached Albany, Reanna was reminded of her last visit here with Chance, and her mind was filled with painful memories.

Luckily, Chance had no businesses or properties in this town, so they passed through quickly, but as they rode on,

Reanna felt the pull of something at her mind. Something she could not quite remember. She had more pressing concerns however, such as the whereabouts of her husband, and so she dismissed her elusive thoughts as unimportant.

By the time they reached Sonoma, Reanna was in the fifth month of her pregnancy. Travel was growing more difficult, they had still found no trace of Chance, and she was becoming increasingly more despondent and unsure.

That evening as she sat at dinner with Nathan and Belinda, she voiced her doubts. With tear filled eyes, she blurted, "I can no longer go on like this. It was foolish to think that we could ever find him. He probably did not even come to California, and if he did, well … he just does not want to be found. Oh, what good is love when all it causes is suffering and hurt?" She buried her face in her hands, sobbing uncontrollably.

Exchanging a long, compassionate glance, Nathan and Belinda helped Reanna from their dining table and guided her up the stairs of the hotel to her room.

Nathan, at a loss for comforting words, felt much the same as Reanna, and left her in the care of Belinda as he returned to the dining room to drink in morose silence as he watched the door, hoping that Chance would walk through that opening, and knowing that his brother would earn Nathan's fist in his face if he did.

Reanna was beyond comfort and tired of the dusty days on the road. She lay curled upon the bed, and cried until she fell into an exhausted slumber, only to awaken sometime later with a start.

She had been dreaming of Daniel Macon in the prison at Albany, and suddenly, unbidden, rose the memory of the marshal there. Remembering the tone of hatred in his voice when he had spoken of Chance, she shivered, recalling her mistrust of him at the time. He just might be the person responsible for the fires. It would be worth checking him out, she thought, for he had the perfect cover, and they had nothing else to go on, no leads after all this time.

Belinda leaned forward in the chair where she had been sitting near Reanna's bed. "What is it, Rea?" she asked, her concern evident in her voice.

"I just thought of something that I should have remembered long ago. The marshal at Albany, he hated Chance. Enough to ruin him, I would wager. We must go there right away. We may just find the answer to the fires there."

They made the return trip to Albany in two and a half days, stopping only when dusk came upon them, and it grew too dark to see. Their progress was slowed slightly now, due to Reanna's condition. Nathan insisted they take it easy for the safety of the baby.

Reanna was desperate to be doing something to help Chance, and she allowed her slightly burgeoning figure, and her well-meaning brother-in-law, to impede their progress as little as possible.

They checked into a hotel in Albany and wasted no time in finding a restaurant in which they might discuss their course of action after Reanna had identified the marshal as, indeed, the same man she had met on her previous trip.

It was a touchy situation. They could not very well accuse a prison marshal of the crimes Reanna was now sure he had committed without positive proof. Perhaps she could pretend to make a bargain with the man, to wheedle information out of him by letting him think that she was interested in him. He had certainly seemed interested in her when she last saw him.

Nathan, Belinda, and even Reanna herself, were doubtful of a successful outcome, for Reanna's condition was now obvious, but, unable to offer a different solution, Nathan finally heaved a resigned sigh.

"If anyone can make a man forget that she is pregnant, it would be you, Reanna. He will but gaze into your green eyes and be lost. But seriously, you must promise to be careful. If what you suspect is true, you will be dealing with a very dangerous man. Are you sure you want to do this?"

'Very sure," Reanna answered quietly, with a determined glint in those sea green eyes.

In the morning they all walked to the prison, and while Nathan and Belinda eavesdropped, out of sight, Reanna drew a long calming breath and went inside.

Stepping over to the large, paper strewn oak desk, Reanna forced a sweet smile to her lips and lightness to her voice. "Well, good day Marshal Magellan. I have come to inquire about a prisoner."

The marshal raised a heavy brow and gave Reanna a sly smile. "Well-l-l, Mrs. Nolton, I must admit to being surprised to see you here." His gaze flicked past her to the door. "And without body guards this time?"

Now it was Reanna's finely arched brow that rose in surprise. "I am pleased that you would remember me Marshal. But how did you know that I am married to Chance Nolton?"

"Ma'am, I make it my business to know everything there is to know about the famous Chance Nolton, and his wife, who is one of the most beautiful women that I have had the pleasure to meet." He smiled once again, showing yellowing teeth.

At his words of praise, Reanna's voice lilted with a suggestive note, "Why Marshal, I am flattered. What else have you made it a point to find out about me?"

Silence drew uncomfortably out as the marshal stared at her, weighing her words. He opened a drawer in his desk, and, withdrawing a lethal looking knife, began to clean his nails. Seemingly absorbed in his task, Reanna started slightly when he suddenly stood and threw the knife back into the drawer, slammed it shut, and then came around the desk, stopping in front of her. He was as large as she remembered, a blond giant of a man with a handsome, clean shaven face and cold, steel blue eyes. She felt a shiver of trepidation but swallowed her fear.

"I know that your husband left you, although I certainly cannot fathom his reasons." He laughed shortly. "But let's talk about why you are here, instead. What is it you want?"

Reanna answered levelly, "I came to find out about Daniel Macon. I wondered what ever happened to him. Of course," she added quickly, "that is not my main reason for coming. I really wanted to see you. You see, I could not help but notice your interest in me on my last visit." She smiled, but her heart was pounding wildly with fear as the marshal laughed unpleasantly.

"Yes, I guess I did show an interest then. Well, your friend has been hanged." He looked pointedly at her rounding middle. "But if you are looking for someone to care for you, and that brat you carry, then I'm afraid you have come to the wrong place. Or is there some other reason for your sudden longing to see me?"

Reanna gathered her courage and, keeping her smile fixed brightly in place, teasingly fingered the lapel of the marshal's jacket as she answered him softly, "Truly, sir, a lady does get quite lonely without a man around, and when she knows that there is one who might protect her, and warm her bed … well …" She let her voice trail off as she looked at him suggestively.

He stared back keenly through narrowed eyes, their depths cool and calculating. "And was there something else you seek to gain from our … association, other than a warm bed?"

Reanna widened her eyes in feigned astonishment. "Why, what other gain could I possibly seek? Of course, I would like a divorce from that bastard after he walked out on me, and I hoped that you might recommend a good lawyer. I want to get all I can from him, ruin him. I hate him for walking out on me." Her anger sounded genuine, and she even managed to produce a few tears.

The marshal leaned closer to her, so close that she could feel his breath hot against her skin as he spoke, and his eyes bored into hers. "I have had word that your husband headed home … two weeks ago. And you are not there to receive him. If he wanted to reconcile, would you still hate him? Want to see him ruined?"

Reanna did her best to hide the shock she felt at the news that Chance had gone home. "You do seem to keep tabs on our lives, sir. I cannot help but wonder why. What interest does Chance Nolton hold for you?"

His voice was low and insistent as he ordered, "Answer my question."

Reanna looked him squarely in the eye, her voice determined. She had to find out if he was responsible for the fires. "I will never forgive him for what he did. To leave me alone after putting this child in me … Even if he came back now, it would be too late. I could never give him my trust. Yes, I would still like to see him ruined."

The marshal raised his hand and toyed with a lock of her heavy hair. "What if I told you … no, suppose we visit in a more private place, Reanna?"

Reanna looked thoughtful for a moment, and then asked sweetly, "I wonder if you could be of more use than I first thought. You could help me to ruin him, couldn't you? He will allow me nothing other than the ranch once we divorce. Perhaps you could somehow help me to get his other investments to fail. Would you be interested in making a deal?"

"Just what sort of deal, Reanna?"

"Surely, I have made myself more than plain, sir. You agree to help me ruin him, and I warm your bed in return. If you hate Chance half as much as I do, then it should be well worth your while."

"Sounds fair to me. I will meet you in your hotel room tonight. I assume that is where you are staying. If you do not have a room, then get one. We will discuss this further over coffee tomorrow morning. Unfortunately, you will be kept too busy to make any plans tonight, although I know you are as anxious as I to see your husband's demise."

Reanna almost groaned in frustration. This meeting was not going anything like she had planned. The thought of sleeping with this man repulsed her, and she could never go through with such a scheme, even to save all of Chance's holdings.

The marshal had not divulged his involvement in the fires, and she could not think what to say next. Her guard slipped for just an instant and she showed her revulsion.

The marshal found what he had been looking for. "What is it, Reanna? Are you having second thoughts? Or is it the fact that you have not gained the information that you came here for?"

Reanna looked at him in stunned surprise, and then quickly tried to mask her expression, but it was too late.

The marshal, with anger clearly written on his features, grabbed her arms, and turning her around, forced them behind her back. His clipped words came from behind her.

"I do not hold kindly to being lied to, lady. I know the reason your husband left you. It is not his child you carry, and it seems that you hold a certain Indian in great esteem."

Reanna stiffened in his arms, and he laughed once again.

"It seems that I have surprised you yet again. I have had you watched for months you see. And now I know that you came here today to trick me into revealing information about who is sabotaging your husbands' holdings, and that you suspect I am involved … well, you see my position. You shall have your answers, but I am afraid they will do you little good, for you will be locked up, and I intend to have my way with you at my leisure. There is no sense in rushing a good thing, now is there?"

As he turned her once again to face him and bent to kiss her lips, Reanna began to struggle wildly, taking the marshal by surprise, and broke free long enough to reach down and pull her gun from her bootstrap. As she brought the revolver up, he twisted her arm away from him and thundered for the guards that were stationed outside the cells in the back of the prison to come and take her.

Reanna managed to pull the trigger and get off a shot to warn Nathan and Belinda before the marshal wrenched it painfully from her grip, and her two friends burst through the door to see Reanna being held fast between two burly guards. Nathan drew his gun to fire at one of them, but missed, and he did not get a second chance. There were suddenly guards everywhere, subduing the three of them before leading them away to be locked up at the marshal's order.

He had known of their plan all along.

*   *   *   *   *   *

Chance arrived home, tired and travel weary, only to hear from Billy and Lada that Reanna had gone to California to look for him two months ago. Chance was furious.

"Damn that little fool! What the hell is she thinking of, traipsing all over the countryside while she is with child!"

Then guilt and remorse washed over him as he realized that it had been his rash actions that led her from home. He left, once again, for California just as soon as he was able, in search of the trio who were hunting him, noting that even Lancelot was less than eager to be going this time.

Patting the great stallion's neck, he murmured, "I see that you also want nothing more than stay at home. I fear that we have both grown tired of our wandering days. With any luck, my friend we should be able to come back home, soon, for good."

He decided to return to Sonoma and work his way down the coast once again, and soon picked up their trail. It was easy to trace their steps, for many had taken note of the beautiful red-haired woman on the graceful white mare.

When he reached Albany and found that they had stayed a night there after being up the coast, he was sure that he would find them further down south, diligently combing the countryside for his whereabouts.

As he rode south, he found that it was longer and longer lengths of time that had passed since they had been seen. Puzzled, he continued southward to see exactly where they had started their search, and maybe find some clue to their ultimate destination. He reached Sacramento and found that it had been two months since anyone had seen any of the three, he became frantic with worry. Where were his wife and brother?'

Seeing little else he could do, he decided to hire some investigators to help in his search and found that Reanna had been there before him. "Your wife hired us to find the person responsible for burning several of your warehouses. It seems that they were all deliberately set, not accidents as they were originally thought."

"Fires?" Chance asked dazedly. "Here?" In his search for Reanna, he had forgotten his original purpose in coming to California.

"Yes. Jack Seymore, your business partner, informed you of the fires several months ago. You mean to say you never got his letter?"

"No," whispered Chance, as a cold chill settled over him.

"Mr. Nolton, I hate to say it, but your wife and brother may have become victims of foul play. This arsonist, whoever he is, is a very clever man, and your wife struck me as being too brave for her own good."

Chance felt as if his world was spinning away from him.

*   *   *   *   *   *

He moved off her, and she felt tears pricking the backs of her eyelids. How had she been reduced to this? it had been like this every time he had taken her to his private office, as he liked to call it, and seduced, no, raped her.

A room away from the other cells, with a stout door instead of bars, used for isolation or interrogation of prisoners, bare but for the small cot upon which they lay. A cold, dank, windowless room.

She shivered and her tormentor turned toward her, placing his large hand against the soft whiteness of her breast. "I have decided that I am going to marry you."

He laughed at her obvious surprise. "Is it so startling, my dear? I intend to go far, and you will be by my side. You are beautiful, passionate, and graceful. I find that I desire you greatly, despite the fact that you carry another man's child."

Reanna was truly frightened by his zeal and the look of madness in his eyes when he spoke of his plans.

"But I am already married!"

"And I will have his lovely widow, and with her, all of his holdings. I will be a rich and thoroughly contented man."

Reanna gasped as the meaning of his words hit her. They had been right. He meant to kill Chance. When she began to weep, he threw her apparel toward her.

"Get dressed," he ordered her tersely, as if he could not stand her tears.

Reanna moved quickly to obey, and kept her head bowed in fear as he walked her back to the cell that she shared with Belinda.

One look at Reanna's ashen face told Belinda all she needed to know, and she rushed to comfort her, rocking her friend as gently as she would a child.

"You poor thing," she murmured softly, and glanced up to meet Nathan's look of impotent rage as he gripped the bars that separated the women's cell from his own, so hard that his knuckles were white.

Correctly divining his thoughts, Belinda softly said, "There is nothing we can do." With a choked sob, she turned back to Reanna, who fell into an exhausted slumber within a few short minutes.

Later, Reanna woke with a scream, bathed in a cold sweat. Belinda was quickly by her side, and Nathan limped stiffly to the bars, his leg having grown stiff during the night.

Reanna was frantic, but remembered to keep her voice lowered so that they would not be overheard by the guard, who was looking their way suspiciously.

"Nathan, Belinda, I had a dream, a message. Mansunama came to me, and Chance is in grave danger. He had returned to look for us, and the marshal has hired men to kill him. Chance, quite a few years ago now, when he was a bounty hunter, killed the marshal's brother. When we were here last, and Chance was shot, it was another of the brothers who tried to kill him. Chance recognized the man who shot him on the beach, but he never knew that the marshal was related, as the marshal must have changed his name, and there is little resemblance between him and the brothers that he feels he must avenge."

Looking with steely eyes at Nathan she said, "Nathan, we have to find a way to break out of here. Your lives, and Chance's, depend upon our escaping as soon as possible."

Nathan creased his brow in thought. So far there had been little chance for escape. The prison was patrolled by armed guards, and although there was only one in the cell area at night, he had no way of knowing how many were stationed on the other side of the door.

Reanna's voice interrupted his thoughts. "Nathan, I have an idea. When the marshal comes to take me again, it must be our opportunity for escape."

Nathan's look of concern changed to one of tight-lipped rage at her words, and his face so resembled Chance that Reanna felt a tremor of fear pass through her. She reached up to gently touch his cheek.

"Please, Nathan. There really is no other way. I have no choice but to go with him. I know that you would stop him if you could, but it must be up to me now. After I and the marshal are gone, you must somehow attract the guard's attention. Feign illness or choking perhaps. When he comes close enough, you must disarm him and get the keys. Release Belinda, and the both of you meet me in the front office. I have only seen two other guards in that office at night, but they may be our greatest problem. If they overhear anything, then we will lose the element of surprise."

At Belinda's increasing look of dismay, Reanna hastened to add, "I know that this is a long shot, but if we do not do something, then Chance, and perhaps both of you, may die. And he will find a way to force me into becoming his wife, all without damaging his public image."

The people of Albany thought of their marshal as a decent, law abiding solid citizen, but Reanna had discovered just how ruthless and cruel he could be.

"If I can lure those two guards into that private office somehow ..." continued Reanna, thinking aloud.

Nathan and Belinda finally relented, it being the only choice they had, so, nervously, they waited for their chance, and it came three days later when the marshal led Reanna away for further 'interrogation'.

Ten minutes later, as Nathan lay on his cot, he began writhing and grasping his stomach, moaning in severe agony. Belinda, rushing to the bars of her cell, begged the guard to come and take a look at her poor, sick fiancé.

As the burly man bent over him, Nathan sprang, and wrestling his gun from its holster, brought it down with force upon the man's skull. As the guard slid silently to the floor, Nathan grabbed his keys, and locking the cell door behind him, rushed to set Belinda free.

He spared her a cocky grin as they rushed to the door. "Some performance, huh? I think that I have missed my true calling."

"You will not have any calling if we do not make it out of here!"

They slowly, carefully opened the door to the outer office.

Reanna, meanwhile, did a little acting of her own. After the marshal eagerly divested himself of his gun belt, then his shirt, she doubled over, gasping dramatically.

When he rushed to her side, she hissed through clenched teeth. "Quick! It's the baby! I will need help – Ahhh!" Reanna gasped as if a new spasm of pain had gripped her. "Please! I need a doctor!"

He hastened to do her bidding, crossing to the door to summon a guard as Reanna swiftly retrieved his discarded, and momentarily forgotten, gun. As the marshal turned back to comfort her, she brought the barrel of his revolver down with all the strength she possessed, knowing that she would have just this one chance. He crumpled to the floor, and she did not stop to examine the bloody head wound as she called out to the remaining guard.

"There is something wrong with your Marshal! He wanted a doctor, and now he has collapsed!"

Surprising herself with the ease of her ruse, the guard burst through the door, completely dismissing Reanna as he bent over his superior in concern.

He never knew what hit him, and afterward when he recovered, the marshal would be hard pressed to explain the lack of some of his clothing during the questioning of a female prisoner. Just enough doubt about his moral character to ruin his chances of election to any public offices.

Nathan, with Belinda in tow, met Reanna in the front office, and in silent accord they slipped through the front door and out onto the street. Keeping to the shadows, they stopped to survey their surroundings, and then Nathan motioned to the two women to follow him as he stealthily crept through the darkest area of the streets, working his way to the livery. It was closed for the evening, but Nathan soon had them inside, saddling their horses which were luckily still there, and riding through the night, away from the nightmare that Albany had become.

As they rode from town, Reanna could not help but think, wryly, that they had acted just like a band of outlaws, and she wondered where Nathan had picked up the skill he had used to break into the livery. She prayed that those they left behind were only knocked senseless, and not dead, for then they truly would be outlaws, wanted for murder.

"I know exactly where to go," explained Reanna as they rode. "In my dream, Mansunama made it clear. I recognized several buildings. Chance is in San Francisco."

Her companions never thought to doubt her word. Mansunama's powers were, by now, well known to them.

Chance was rapidly running short of possibilities. He had pursued every lead, and still found no sign of the trio he sought. It was dark and beginning to grow late, and Chance, exhausted by fear and guilt, decided to call it a day and check into a hotel, which he set out for after stabling Lancelot in the nearest livery.

As he wearily trod the boardwalk, a shape emerged from the shadows and appeared suddenly as a man directly in front of him, pointing a gun to Chance's head. He heard two hammers cock behind him. He was surrounded.

So, his turn had finally come. There was nothing he could do with three guns on him. Reanna's lovely face swam before him as his heart sent out his love.

"You are a dead man," the figure before him hissed, and the thunder of guns firing rent the night air.

Chance hit the walk with a thud, rolling to the side as he swiftly pulled his gun from his holster, wondering at the fact that he was still alive, and that his would be executioners lay unmoving.

He peered into the darkness, thinking that he had surely gone mad when he heard Reanna's voice. "Chance!"

Then she was before him, tears trailing down her cheeks, her hair falling about her face in wild disarray, and she had never looked more beautiful to him. She did not smile, but waited expectantly with lips parted, for some sign of his acceptance, or denial of her.

Chance slowly pushed himself to his feet, and holstering his gun, reached out to gently stroke her cheek before he pulled her roughly to him, embracing her tightly. His voice was husky as he choked out, "my God, Rea, my love. You are here. I had begun to think ... Thank God that you are safe."

He began to cover her face with soft kisses, and Reanna laughed and cried her happiness as she wrapped her arms about his neck and pulled him to her.

Nathan and Belinda approached, and Reanna stepped back to allow the two brothers time for a greeting, and they embraced for a moment.

"Well, little brother, shall we go have a drink while you tell me how you all happened by in so timely a fashion?"

They all walked arm in arm to the hotel and ordered a drink. As their separate stories unfolded, Chance was once again grateful to Reanna's warrior friend Mansunama, for having sent her the dream message.

Chance and Reanna found it difficult to keep their eyes on anyone but each other and Nathan was reassured that the two would resume their happy marriage.

"I apologize for acting like a boor, and almost costing you your lives," Chance said, "And now, if you don't mind, I wish to retire for the evening with my wife."

When they were snuggled together in their bed, Reanna asked, "Chance, have you truly forgiven me?"

As he looked deeply into her sparkling, sea green eyes, he reached out to stroke her long copper tresses and answered softly, "You have done nothing to be sorry for, my darling. It is I who must ask your forgiveness. I do not know myself, how I could have been so cruel, Rea. Please forgive me."

She snuggled closer to him. "It is enough that you are safe, and we are together once again, my love. I ask nothing more."

Reanna sent a silent thanksgiving to Mansunama then, before they slept, with Chance's arms securely wrapped around his wife.

Chapter 16

Reanna sat in the parlor with her feet up on a pillow. She had grown too large to do much else, and Chance had strictly forbidden any arduous activities, but she did not mind this time as she had with her first pregnancy, for she looked forward to the birth of this child.

She had chosen a book to read but found she could not concentrate. Sighing, she gave up and leaned her head back, allowing her thoughts to wander as she stared into the flames of the fireplace, lit to take the damp chill from the early spring morning.

They had set off for home the day following the attempt on Chance's life. Reanna had wanted to stay and enjoy the salty air of the seashore, but Chance was adamant about getting home as quickly as possible, before Reanna grew too large to travel. He did promise her a return trip as soon as they were able.

Nathan had decided to stay in town to be closer to Belinda, so Chance and Reanna had arrived by themselves at Ray Dublin's ranch to reclaim Spring. She had been impossibly spoiled and doted upon and was proudly sitting astride her very own dappled gray pony when her parents arrived. She immediately climbed down to nestle in her mother's waiting arms. "Mama, you are getting fat!" the child exclaimed, noting the bulge in Reanna's stomach.

Reanna glanced up to see her fathers surprised expression and hastened to explain, "Oh father, I have not told you..."

"We are expecting another baby." Chance broke in, and Reanna was suffused with a warm glow at his words. "You see Spring," he explained as he hoisted her into his arms, "the baby is sleeping in mommy's tummy right now, and when it is born you will have a brother, or sister."

Reanna could tell by his voice that he still found it hard to accept, but he was claiming the child as his, and she prayed that he would come to love the baby after it was born, as he loved Spring.

"Well, this calls for congratulations!" Ray announced enthusiastically, and they all burst into laughter when Spring announced, "I want a girl! I want a sister, not a mean ol' brother!"

Continuing with her musings, she thought of Nathan and Belinda, who had been married a month ago. It had been a small but beautiful wedding, with the bride and groom so obviously in love that Reanna had to smile, remembering it. Nathan had purchased some land adjacent to Chance's, where he and Belinda planned to start a ranch of their own.

Billy and Lada were planning to marry in the near future and would live with Chance and Reanna on the ranch, but in a house of their own. Reanna smiled contentedly. It was good to have her family and friends nearby.

Modock and Tasha produced two litters a year now and Reanna was able to sell them all at good prices, which pleased her, for although Chance had given her the dogs, breeding, and raising them was her own venture and her success gave her a measure of pride.

The only thing that hindered her complete happiness was the slight change in Chance's behavior. Barely perceptible, but there, and she knew him so well, she could not help but feel it. Whenever the baby was mentioned, he would suddenly change the subject. There was something missing in their intimate unions as well. He seemed to be holding back slightly, as if unable to fully enjoy their passion as he had in the past.

A sharp twinge of pain intruded upon her thoughts, and she placed her hands over her protruding stomach as she gasped in surprise. Just then Spring burst into the room with

Modock bounding at her heels. Struggling to her feet, Reanna shooed the dog out the French doors that led to the garden and led Spring into the kitchen for some cookies.

Billy and Lada had gone to Virginia City and would not return until the next day. She hoped she would not give birth before then, for she so wanted Lada, with her calm demeanor and gentle ways, to assist with the birthing.

To pass time Reanna tried to show Spring a few new cords on her guitar. She had been teaching the child for the past two months and Spring showed promise of playing as well as Reanna did someday. A new contraction gripped her, stronger than the others that had come while she and Spring were playing. She glanced out the French doors. A damp, swirling mist had started, encompassing the outside world in a soft gray light. She stood, deciding it might be best if she put Spring in for a nap and lay down to rest herself.

She closed Spring's door and walked to her own room to rekindle the banked fire. When she had a good blaze going, she stood to make her cumbersome way to the bed, doubling over as intense, unending pain in her back and middle suddenly incapacitated her. Gasping for breath, she felt the burst of warm liquid escape, the birth waters breaking and running to the floor.

Finally, the pain abated enough to allow her to strip from her gown and don a clean, loose fitting nightgown of fine gauze, gathered at the scooped neckline to flow softly around her form. She heard her door open and turning, gasped in surprise. Mansunama stood there filling the doorway. He crossed to her silently, easily scooping her up to place her gently upon the bed.

Another pain crested within her, and she closed her eyes against it as a soft cry escaped her lips. When it finally passed, she opened her eyes to see Mansunama still at her side. His black gaze resting on her was somehow reassuring.

He spoke softly, "Rest Rea, I will clean up and help you with the birth." He turned away to place water on the fire, and then placed his knife in the coals.

Reanna worried, "I did not know you would come. I am glad you have, but what of Chance? What will he think?"

The Shaman turned and answered harshly "Did you think I would let you bear my son alone?" He continued more gently, "Your husband is a strong man, a good man, a great warrior among your people, with a great love for you. Have you never spoken to him of us?"

"He does not know who the father is," Reanna answered lamely.

"He will know when he sees my son."

"How do you know it will not be a daughter?" she asked, more sharply than she meant to as another pain caught her unaware.

"You will bear me my only son," he stated with finality. "I am now married to Red Deer." He stared at her lovely face, his eyes reaching deeply into hers, loneliness and desolation apparent even in his voice as he continued "She is not the one I would have chosen to spend my life with, but she is young and will be a good wife and mother. She will bear me only daughters. You, who have my heart, will give me my only son. It does sadden me that we can never be together, for I would want all of your total love, and that is something that only Chance Nolton will forever have."

"Oh Mansunama, I do love him so! I wish I had not lost his child. I wanted it so badly. I was so alone, believing my husband as well as my baby lost to me. If it were not for you, I would have died that day. You helped me to realize my maternal love for Spring. You saved Chance's life in San Francisco. We owe you more than we could ever repay, for how can one put a price on life or love? If, in giving you a son, I can in some small way compensate for all that you

460

have given me, then I am honored to do so. And, you will see, Mansunama, you will come to love Red Deer."

Mansunama raised his hand to lovingly touch her cheek, his black eyes full of such pain that for a moment Reanna forgot her own. Then he swiftly assumed his full dignity, his expression becoming inscrutable, before he turned away to stare into the snapping flames of the fire.

Meanwhile, Chance rode hunkered down in the saddle, peering through the shrouding mist at intervals to check Lancelot's progress. He could just discern the outlines of the house and barn, so it would not be long now. A hot meal and crackling fire were all he needed.

The kitchen was warm from the woodstove, but where was Reanna, or dinner for that matter? He decided the girls must be napping so he padded up the stairs as silently as possible, knowing how easily Reanna tired these days.

A man's voice reached his ears and he paused outside the doorway to listen, surprised as the simple words hit him like a rock. "Did you think I would let you bear my son alone?"

Chance leaned back against the wall, the shock of recognition great. Mansunama! He should have known. Of course, Reanna would turn to him! Unable to stop himself, he did not make his presence known, but listened intently to their words. "I wish I had not lost his child." The pathetic sadness in her voice tore at his heart. She still grieved their lost baby, even now. Suddenly he realized that his beloved had survived those days only because of Mansunama.

He closed his eyes, his first rage at Mansunama draining from him as he caught the telling sadness in the Shaman's voice, his words, "You, who has my heart." Chance could feel the heavy burden of unrequited love that rested over the tall, spiritual warrior. At the same time, he felt joy in his heart that Reanna truly had never turned from him, even when she had thought him dead. He was not worthy of such love, love that proved to be a beacon, shining brightly through even the darkness that is death.

"We owe you more than we could ever repay..." The soft words he heard from Reanna tore at his heart, humbling him with their selflessness and he, too, decided they owed much to their Paiute friend. He knew the Indian would never know the measure of true happiness such as he had found with Reanna. He drew a deep breath and schooling his features to hide his knowledge of their exchange, entered the room.

Chance, pale himself now, wiped the beaded sweat from Reanna's brow, worried at the pallor of her skin. She was growing weaker, her strength flowing from her as she strained to give birth. She had tried for hours, struggling in painful silence as she clenched her teeth down on the piece of rawhide that Mansunama had given her when her contractions increased unbearably.

"We must do something!" Chance said hoarsely to Mansunama. "She cannot last much longer like this!"

"We must get her up" Mansunama said as he leaned down to help Reanna from the bed. "You must walk" he instructed her, and Chance came around the bed to support her as well. They helped her walk around the room, slowly, for what seemed to be hours. Finally, gasping, Reanna cried, "The baby! It is coming!"

"Squat down," Mansunama said calmly, and she had no choice but to obey as he pushed down on her shoulders firmly. She closed her eyes, grunting with the effort of the birth. Chance crouched behind her, holding her shoulders firmly and allowing her to lean against him for support.

Mansunama placed thick padding under Reanna, just as she strained again, expelling her breath, and the baby's head emerged. As she pushed again, Mansunama had placed his large hands beneath the tiny head and guided his son into the world.

Chance held his wife and soothed her as he pushed her hair from her face, awed by witnessing the miracle of birth.

"You must cut the cord" Mansunama's voice cut through Chance's thoughts, and he rose to slide the sharp knife and cleanly sever the cord, as the majestic, dark skinned man turned to clean the tiny boy with a warm, wet cloth.

She slumped against Chance, exhausted and he pressed a kiss to her brow, and then scooped her into his arms to deposit her gently on the soft bed, covering her with a sheet.

Mansunama laid the baby, cleaned, and wrapped in a blanket, into Reanna's arms, his eyes full of yearning as he looked down into the little face before relinquishing his hold. He straightened, and after a hard glance at Chance, turned and left them as silently as he had come.

Reanna gazed after him, then down at her son. When she realized how much the baby resembled his Indian father, her heart sank. She glanced at Chance, at once afraid that he had noticed too, but only pleasure showed in his eyes.

"We have a beautiful son, Rea. Everyone will assume that he gets his dark coloring from me."

Reanna's voice was weak as she answered, "You are beautiful, and perfect, my love. Please forgive me for the pain that I have caused you..." Her head fell back against the pillows. She was thoroughly exhausted, but her gratitude showed in her eyes. Chance leaned over and pressed a warm kiss to her forehead. "No pain, Rea, only love and relief that you are here with me." He took the baby and laid him in the cradle, then cleaned the room as best he could. He left Reanna to rest, and then went to tell Spring the news.

"Well," he said to his daughter, "you have a brand-new baby brother. Shall we celebrate with a tea party? Then we can find something for our dinner."

"Cookies?" Spring asked hopefully. Chance laughed. "Not for supper, little one, but maybe after."

Later that night when Chance crept in quietly to check on Reanna, he found her sleeping peacefully. Moving to the cradle, he gazed thoughtfully down at the baby. Yes, he should have known all along. Not just anyone for her, but a man of great strength, love, and earthly wisdom. A true warrior and healer, able to delve into worlds that Chance himself could only imagine existed. He realized that he loved this child, just as he loved Spring, part of Reanna, of her love and life, her beauty and warmth. He still sorely wanted to see her bear his own children, but they had time. For now, he accepted Reanna's two children as his own and would never deny them. Still, he prayed for the day that he would see his own child born of his beloved.

The next morning, Reanna sat in bed, contentedly nursing her son. Bright sunlight flooded the room, a welcome change from yesterday's gloomy weather. She hummed to herself, and the door opened as Chance entered the room with Spring, who was anxious to meet her new brother, having long forgotten her preference for a sister.

Spring gazed at the baby in awe for a moment and then smiled as she noted innocently, "Mommy, he looks just like Mansunama. How come he doesn't look like me and you?"

Shocked that even a child would notice the resemblance, Reanna raised fearful eyes to Chance, but all she saw was his back as he walked from the room, closing the door quietly behind him.

Reanna's emotions were in turmoil. She loved this child, was even grateful for this gift of Mansunama's love, at the same time feeling regret and shame for what it must be doing to Chance. There seemed little she could do though, but to hope no one else would voice the same thoughts as Spring. Spring, after all, had seen Mansunama nearly every day for the months that he had stayed, but there was no one else that familiar with him, except Lada. She sighed and prayed that the love she shared with Chance would be strong enough to survive whatever trials lay ahead.

Raymond Dublin arrived to view the new addition and did not comment on the baby's appearance. "Rea, he is beautiful. I am overwhelmed to have such fine grandchildren. My dream of living long enough to see them has been fulfilled."

"And you will, without a doubt, live to see many more." she said as she hugged her father while silently thanking him for his acceptance of the baby.

Later that afternoon, feeling much stronger, Reanna donned a fresh bed gown and brushed the tangles from her mass of hair. Chance stood in the doorway, his dark, handsome face inscrutable as he stared at the charming picture she made. He approached her, his intense brown eyes holding her wide green one's captive while he brushed his fingers through her thick copper tresses. When he spoke, his voice was soft and smooth.

"I am sorry that I walked out earlier, my love, but when Spring noticed the baby's resemblance to Mansunama, it suddenly hit me just how hard it will be if others question the boy's appearance, not only for us, but for him as well. I, however, have come to terms with it all now, and you do not ever have to worry about my acceptance of the child, or my complete support if you should need it for any reason. I love you, Rea, and that will never change, no matter what. I do have one request though. I wonder what you would think of naming the child after my brother Stewart. I came so late to know him as a man, yet love him I did, and that is something that I must thank you for."

Reanna was deeply touched that Chance would care to name this child after one he loved. Her eyes brimmed with tears as she reached up to hug him tightly, speaking in a voice that shook with the force of her emotions. "I think that is a perfect name for our son, Chance, thank you."

In the following two weeks, all the Nolton's family and friends came to meet the new arrival, and not one brow was raised, nor question asked, as to the baby's parentage. Reanna was grateful for her friend's unquestioning loyalty.

They discovered Marshal Magellan had hanged himself in one of his cells after the authorities had caught one of the men responsible for the fires, and he had named the marshal as the man who had hired him. Knowing what his punishment would be for arson and murder, he chose to take his own life, a beaten man.

Reanna's days were taken up with the duties of a new mother. She had resumed her schooling of Spring in reading, writing, and playing guitar. Each evening when Chance was done working, the child would eagerly show her father all that she had learned that day. Chance was amazed at her quick mind and easy grasp of all she was taught.

Before she realized it, a month had passed since the birth of little Stewart James, and Reanna's young body hungered for her lover's touch. She knew that Chance would wait until she felt herself ready to receive his love and she did not intend to delay.

She bathed in rose scented water, soaking her long, slender limbs until the bath water turned cool, then toweled off and donned a soft gown of sheerest emerald silk that hugged the enticing curves of her voluptuous body like a glove, hiding just enough of her curves to invite further exploration. She brushed her mass of fiery hair until it shown and snapped with a life of its own, silken gossamer falling about her white shoulders.

Chance entered their bedroom looking haggard and ill-kempt after an exhausting day. It was branding time again and he had been deliberately putting in overlong hours the last few days so that he would be too tired to notice how much he wanted to ravish his wife.

When Reanna laid aside her hairbrush and stood, moving provocatively toward him, the look of exhaustion faded from his features to be replaced by one of open desire, only to be quickly guarded. It was too soon. Suspiciously he asked, "Where are the children?"

"Both sleeping soundly," Reanna answered, smiling as she correctly divined the reason for his discomfort. Her soft, full lips and small pearly teeth beckoned him enticingly, and he swallowed past a sudden constriction in his throat.

"Rea, so soon? Are you sure it will be alright?" His voice was husky with desire.

"It will be, my lord, after I have bathed you." She smiled and the sea glittered softly in her eyes as she stepped into his embrace, breathing her words into his ear, "Even one more night without you is too long. Come, my darling, I have prepared your bath."

Chance, his thoughts of sleep forgotten, lithely divested himself of his dirty, sweat soaked clothing. Reanna caught her breath at the sight of his perfectly formed, muscular body before he lowered himself into the tub of warm water. His eyes devoured her as his reddened gaze swept her length. The flames from the hearth touched her skin with a rosy glow and reflected iridescently on the thin layer of silk as it highlighted her curves. "My Lady," he whispered hoarsely, "come and wash your Lord." He held the washcloth out to her.

Wordlessly, she knelt, and leaning over the tub, began to gently wash his shoulders and back. He sat with his eyes closed against her tempting charms, unwilling to hasten their pleasures.

As her hands dipped lower to toy with his hardened member, he slowly opened his eyes to find that she had leaned ever closer. Drawing his breath in sharply, he reached up to cup her full breasts, which threatened to spill from their silken prison, wetting her gown so that it clung like a second skin. He lowered his dark head, and his warm tongue found her nipples, lapping warmly at them through the silk.

A low moan escaped Reanna's throat, and Chance increased his ministrations, half pulling her into the tub with him before he raised his head and stood, scooping her up into his arms and crossing, dripping wet, to the bed. He lay her down, immediately covering her soft length with his own hard one, before catching her lips in a bruising kiss. His mouth seared a trail to her ear, where he nibbled, breathing rapidly, trying to control his raging lust. He whispered in her ear, "My love, my heart. I do love you, Rea."

She moved against him, the thin fabric, now soaked, serving only to heighten their desire as it burned between them, hiding nothing, but denying that which they both sought to attain as his engorged member strained against it.

With a low growl of impatience, he rose from her, grasped the gown between her breasts, easily ripping the offending garment down the front, pulling it swiftly from her as she rolled toward him. She pressed her lips and tongue eagerly down the length of him, tasting of his warm, wet skin until he could endure no more. He drew her up, rolling her to her back as he entered her wet, burning sheath, teasing the taught peaks of her nipples with his tongue once more, as he began to move upon her.

She cried out in pleasure and strained upward, begging him for more, and he pushed in further, filling her, until their moans and cries of ecstasy sounded, and it was music to their souls.

Replete in their pleasure, they lay entwined, sighing in satisfaction, and slept.

Before long, life on the ranch was back to a normal, daily routine. Billy and Lada were married. The wedding was a beautiful ceremony that none who attended would ever forget. Their intense love of one another so apparent, they shone.

Jared came to stay with the Nolton's permanently, finding a renewed appreciation for ranch life after his return from the war. He also enjoyed the children, going out of his way to teach Spring new games, or show her something that he had found while out riding that he thought might interest her.

The day of Bob and Martha's annual picnic drew near, so Chance, Reanna, and Jared left the day before to help with the many preparations, leaving Spring with Billy and Lada, who would arrive the next day at the party.

As the women were preparing goodies for the party, Chance read a letter from Holly they had picked up on their way through town. "I am running the school now, and David and Louise are expecting their second child any day. I hope it's a girl this time. They still live here on the farm, helping Pa and me to look after things. Jeremy has become an apprentice to the local blacksmith and loves the work. He also has six girls sweet on him, and he goes calling on them all! But do not say that you heard it from me. Love, Holly."

They all laughed merrily as they pictured the shy Jeremy trying valiantly to juggle his time between six young ladies and learning a trade at the same time. Chance said, "Well, I will leave you ladies to your work, and I shall see to mine," as he left the house.

Reanna and Martha chatted and worked when they were suddenly interrupted. Chance's harassed words brought their conversation to an end. "Rea, can you do something with Stewart? He must be hungry; he will not stop fussing and I have tried everything!"

"But I just fed him on the way over." She reached out to take the crying infant from Chance. Holding him, she smoothed her hand over his head. "Chance, he feels awfully warm. I think he has a fever."

Aunt Martha placed her hand on the baby's forehead. "Why, he is burning up! We must get him into a cool bath, and then I have some herb tea we can spoon feed him. It should take the fever down." They tended the child, to no avail. He began to vomit while his eyes held a dazed look. He became lethargic and his fever still raged.

"Chance, maybe you should fetch the doctor," Martha worried. The women kept their vigil while they waited. Reanna clutched the baby to her breast, pacing the house and praying for his tiny soul as he began to slip in and out of consciousness.

When the doctor arrived, he thoroughly examined the child, but was at a loss. "There is nothing more to be done, just try to keep his fever down. It does not look good."

A strangled sob escaped Reanna as she placed a hand to her mouth, sinking into the nearest chair. The doctor's words echoed in her mind, and shock numbed her body. There was nothing to be done for her precious babe. This could not be true.

Morning came as the sun climbed high in the cloudless blue sky. Reanna sat rocking her baby, clutching the tiny, hot body to her chest. There was no change in his condition. The night had dragged on as she bathed him over and over with cool water, coaxing spoonful's of herb tea into him when she was able. Still, he lapsed into an unconscious state and back without warning.

When, on the third day, there was still no change in the child's condition, Reanna began to grow desperate. She was watching the life drain from Stewart's tiny body. Helpless, as she stood gazing down at him, she began to pray to God, and finally, unable to bear up under the strain any longer, she broke down, sobbing violently. When she fell to her knees, it was not to God she prayed any longer, but to Mansunama.

"Why do you not come? It is your son who lays here dying slowly while I am forced to watch, unable to help or ease his suffering. You must know, you must feel that your son needs you. Please, please feel his need; hear my desperate plea, Mansunama. You must save him."

She stayed where she was, unable to stop the terrible sobs that wracked her body, and that is where Chance found her. Kneeling to the floor, he gathered her in his arms and held her tightly, attempting to comfort her. It was an impossible task since his own heart was heavy with hopeless apathy.

Reanna finally gathered her courage together and gazed deeply into her husband's worried brown eyes. She spoke, her tone deadly serious, "Chance, our boy is dying, and I can no longer stand helplessly by and watch. I must go find Mansunama! He alone may have the power to save him from this illness. It is the only hope we have Chance. I do not know why, but the Shaman healer does not seem to know about this, or he would have come, I am sure of it. I must find the reason for his delay and let him know how desperately we need his help. I will leave immediately."

Chance made absolutely no response, but sat rigidly by her side, his face averted as he worked the muscles of his lean jaw, suddenly furious at his inability to help those within his care. She left him without another word.

As Reanna made her way to the Paiute encampment, she worried, not having been there for many years, but determined to find her way. She ventured deep into the forested realms, looking for some familiar signs. Suddenly, a strange warrior appeared before her, blocking the narrow path she followed. She let out a startled cry, and then met his cold perusal with as much dignity as she could muster. She spoke slowly in the Paiute tongue, explaining her urgent need to see her friend Mansunama, the Shaman healer. He then led her into a large clearing, the Paiute village. The warrior stopped her and called out loudly for the Shaman.

When the medicine man approached her, he spoke softly, "Rea, why have you come here?"

She answered, pain in her voice, "Why have you not come to me? Our son, he is dying. I thought you would know, as you always seem to know these things. Please come with me and try your healing magic. Nothing else is working. Please, Mansunama."

"I did not know, perhaps because my wife was giving birth to our daughter, and it was a difficult birth. We were very worried about her. She and the babe are fine now, and out of danger. I will come with you and do what I can for our son."

Reanna yanked on his arm, trying to pull him onto her horse, no patience to wait for him to gather his own. He hopped on her mare, sitting behind her as he whispered, "So be it, sweet Rea."

Much later, Mansunama gazed down at the frail, emaciated form that was his son. He told Reanna, "Leave us."

Feeling uneasy with his melancholy mood, she turned and left the room, leaving the baby in the Shaman's care. The strength, what little remained, drained from her body as she leaned against the door she pulled closed behind her. Weak with exhaustion, her knees gave way beneath her. She sank gratefully to the floor, where she remained silently throughout the long, tedious hours of her solitary vigil.

Chance did not enter the house and Reanna felt little disposed to seeking him out. She listened to the rise and fall of Mansunama's voice as he called upon the spirits, entering a world that had meaning only to him, as it had for his ancestors of countless years past, of wisdom and magic that eclipsed the trappings of time to rest within his hands.

Reanna dozed fitfully while Mansunama remained ensconced with Stewart, for a full five hours. Constantly the deep timber of his voice served to offer hope where there had been none, and she wondered many times where he drew the strength to continue with his unstinting efforts.

Finally, Mansunama stepped from the room to meet Reanna's green eyes, full of hope shining bright. "I am sorry, Rea, I have done all that I can. The fever is down, but otherwise, no improvement. You can only wait. I must return home now, I am sorry." He finished hoarsely as tears sprang to her eyes. He was aware that she had expected him to cure the child completely. He reached out to gently brush away the tear that trailed down her smooth cheek, and with an aching heart, he silently took his leave, feeling far older than his years warranted. In the yard, he stopped in midstride as Chance hailed him, leading a tall, black stallion in his wake.

"I know you do not have your horse. I give you this stallion, the son of my Lancelot and Rea's mare you rode in on yesterday. He is four years old now and will carry you well.

The Shaman expertly eyed the young horse, taking note of his superior form. He stroked the dark velvet of the tapered muzzle as he met Chance's dark gaze. "This horse is worth a great deal of money. Why do you give him to me?"

"He belongs with a great man," Chance answered simply, and handed Mansunama the reins. "Besides, I have much to thank you for, and I have never properly expressed my gratitude." He looked the warrior in the eye as he continued, "You could have taken Reanna away with you while I was gone. She would never have had to know that I still lived."

Some emotion, Chance was unsure of the nature, flickered behind the tall Indian's fierce gaze as he raised his eyes to the distant mountains where he made his home. "My way of life, the ways of my forefathers, are gradually coming to an end. Reanna belongs to this world and the life you can give her. She never belonged to the dream of my making. There is, however, one thing I would ask of you. My son if he survives. I would like your word that you will bring him to me every summer, so that I may begin to teach him the ways of a tribal Shaman, when he is not learning in your white man's schools. In this way, he will have the best knowledge of both worlds, and perhaps in time become a great healer, a doctor of all people."

"Consider it done," Chance assured.

Chance found Reanna sleeping in a chair next to Stewart's crib. He sent her to bed and stayed the night with the baby, who, by the next afternoon, had improved considerably. Reanna found she was able to smile for the first time all week, and ranch life went back to its normal routine, while the Nolton's rejoiced, thankful for a healthy family.

Chapter 17

Reanna tilted her face upwards to catch the warming rays of a bright, brazen spring sun, her eyelids closed against the white light. She inhaled deeply, enjoying the scents typical to early spring. Freshly turned earth in the vegetable garden, the hint of melting snow and fragrant pine that wafted down on gentle dancing breezes from the higher elevations of the mountains. She listened to the various calls of the birds, their songs sharp and clear as they trilled in celebration of awakening life and smiled softly as the voices of her family rounded out the perfection of the afternoon. Lowering her head, she sought them out with her clear, green gaze.

Spring was sitting easily astride her birthday gift of a few days ago, a sorrel mare that she had promptly dubbed Lucky Lady. Reanna sighed wistfully as she watched her daughter patiently put the mare through her paces. It seemed just yesterday that the ten-year-old had been an infant in her mother's arms, and now she was confidently circling the corral on her own horse, dark copper curls bouncing in carefree abandon, green eyes dancing with excitement, her face lit by a brilliant smile.

"How fast the time fly's past!" Reanna thought. "Life is so good, so rich, and full of wonderment. I regret that I must someday grow old and leave it all behind."

With a shake of her head, she dispelled her melancholy thoughts and focused her attention on the comical sight of two brawny men, each abreast one side of a dapple-gray pony that Stewart was now learning to ride. Suddenly spurting forward, their arms outstretched, their faces a study in terror as they each instructed their young charge, loudly, on the best way of slowing his mount, ready to catch him should he fall.

Jared sprinted over to join Reanna at the fence, a wide smile playing across his face as he watched Chance and Nathan race after the pony, with Stewart, giggling, perched atop a miniature saddle. Bonnie, a gift to Spring from Reanna's father, Raymond, was an unusually gentle mount, responding docilely to Stewart's commands. The boy had discovered the joy of racing his mount into the wind, even though the pony was small, and the racing no more than a trot.

Stewart, always sensitive to the feelings of others despite his fierce zest for life, took pity on his father and uncle and slowed Bonnie to a walk, very competently for a five-year-old, and noted the immediate relief on the faces of the two men. Chance grabbed the boy from the saddle and set him on his feet, rumpling Stewart's dark hair affectionately, and Reanna was reminded once again of the fleeting passage of time. She wanted to catch it, to hold it to her breast, to never let it go on. Alas, all she could do was to live and savor every minute to the fullest, to enjoy all that life offered. The children would all too soon be grown, going their own ways.

Stewart resembled Mansunama more each day, with his high cheekbones, sculpted nose, and firm chin, and she ached to present Chance with a child of his own.

She had miscarried twice in the past five years, early enough that Chance had never known. She had become extremely depressed after each one, but with the steady warmth of Chance's love, and the busy schedule of their daily lives, the pain of sadness had dimmed to be replaced by the hope that maybe next time...

Her monthly flow had been interrupted again. Reanna decided soon she would visit Doctor Farley and prayed that this time she would carry the child safely.

Although Chance tried hard not to let it show, Reanna had seen the deep longing in his dark eyes when Billy and Lada became proud parents of a healthy son last year.

The Nolton's life was rich, and full, and now, if she could just give her husband a child of his own, their life together would be perfect.

A month later, Reanna stepped from the doctor's office, her face alight with happiness. She was three months pregnant and ecstatic with joy. She rode Guinevere home, almost bursting with the need to share her news with Chance but deciding it may be better if she did not tell him for a couple more weeks, just to be sure she would not miscarry again. He would be so disappointed if something were to go wrong. So, she hugged her secret to herself, but alas, her eyes glittered with anticipation, her smile was extra bright, and their lovemaking took on a new, carefree abandon.

A few nights later, as they lay entwined in each other's embrace, Chance asked lightly, "How long do you plan to wait before telling me, Rea?"

She propped herself up on an elbow and gazed at him, her eyes wide with surprise, and questioned him, "Tell you what, my dashing sir knight?"

Chance, pride evident in his voice, for he had already guessed her secret, bantered, "Why, milady, I am surprised that you wish to keep a secret such as this all to yourself. Why have you not told me of the child you carry?"

Reanna sat up indignantly, her eyes flashing in accusation as she demanded, "Chance Nolton! How did you know? Have you seen Doctor Farley?"

His chuckle rumbled softly before he answered. "Rea, you have been flitting around like a bird on the wing. Your face glows with pleasure, and your body, my dear, speaks its own language. I would have to be a fool not to have guessed it. What I do not understand is why you have not told me sooner. Certainly, you knew I would be thrilled by such news."

She lowered her eyes and spoke softly, her voice barely a whisper in the stillness. "That is just it, Chance. I knew that you would be thrilled, and I wanted to wait and be sure, certain that I would carry this child, to avoid disappointing you.

His smile vanished, and he cupped her chin in his hand, raising it so that her eyes met his as he also sat up. "Ah, Rea, my love, that is not something you should have to carry on your own shoulders, this fear of something going wrong. You would spare my feelings at great cost to yourself. Although I do admire your selflessness, I want you to promise me that you will never try to hide anything like this from me again. We need to support and comfort each other in times of crisis as well as times of joy. This, by the way, is just what I feel right now. To know that you carry my child, our child, when I had given up hope that it would ever be."

He pulled her to him, and their emotional embrace quickly led to renewed passion as they were caught in the flames of heated desire. Their tumultuous joining soon lifted them and carried them on a swelling tide to bursting fulfillment. They slowly drifted back down, pleasure and contentment lulling them to sleep.

The months passed by swiftly, in a flurry of activity, but not quickly enough to suit Reanna. She was anxious to bear her child so that she might hold the precious life within her arms. This child that would be part of her beloved husband, created from a deep, abiding love.

Chance's brother David wrote that he would be coming with his wife Louise and father for a visit, and they arrived a month before Reanna was due to give birth. Reanna's pleasure in their arrival soon turned to anger, however, when she noted the reaction of Chance's father toward Stewart.

It was quite obvious that he would never accept the child as his grandson. Although he said nothing at the time of their introduction, he had looked at the boy with contempt in his eyes, and then turned that contemptuous gaze to Reanna. She had stared, taken aback for a moment, before she grabbed Stewart's hand and led him from the room. She tried to cool her temper by taking her son for a walk before she could make one of several scathing remarks that came to her mind.

She had never been able to get particularly close to Luke Nolton, never feeling more than a casual kinship toward him, and she now felt a growing resentment at the prejudice that had gleamed in his eyes.

Reanna was very uncomfortable through dinner that evening, for Luke's accusing stare met her eyes whenever she happened to glance his way. Later, when they all gathered in the parlor, she only played one song, at Chances request, before pleading exhaustion and excusing herself to retire. Her wariness was legitimate, so heavy was she with child, but she had felt a more powerful need to escape Luke's disconcerting gaze.

For nearly a week she was able to avoid a direct confrontation with the man, avoiding his company when at all possible. One morning when Chance had taken David and Louise out to town, Luke begged off going, pleading a headache, and waited for Reanna to come downstairs.

Assuming that everyone had gone, Reanna was brought up short as she entered the kitchen to find Luke still seated at the table. "Well, Mr. Nolton, Stewart and I were just going to bake some cookies. Would you like to join us?" She gave a nervous laugh to cover the dread she felt at having to be in his presence alone.

He did not look at all amused but stared at the two of them in distaste. When he spoke, his tone was not at all pleasant. "You whore! How any son of mine could stay with you after you bedded with a stinkin' Injun is beyond my understanding. You are nothin' but filth, and that red bastard of yours should not even be allowed in this house. This is a white man's world and you both belong with those savages, livin' like the animals you are!"

Before Reanna could form a suitable reply to his venomous words, Luke pushed his chair back with a loud scraping noise. Jamming his hat furiously onto his head, he stormed from the house.

Waves of shock and guilt swept through her, and Stewart began to cry large, silent tears, the pain of betrayal clearly evident in his large black eyes. She sank weakly into the nearest chair, enfolding Stewart in her arms and pulling him as close as her large girth allowed, the terrible words still ringing in her ears, stinging with their truth. She had foolishly lulled herself into thinking that Stewart would be unquestioningly accepted by the world, when truthfully, there would always be those who were heartless and cruel in their prejudice, with their narrow minds.

Gradually, she became aware that Stewart was questioning her. "Why did he say that Mama? Why doesn't Grandpa like me? Is it true that we are dirty Injuns?" Her heart broke at the heartache plainly visible on her son's small face. She gently smoothed his hair back as she tried to think of the best way to reply.

Forcing an encouraging smile to her lips she told him softly, "It does not matter, Stewart. Mommy and Daddy love you very much, and Uncle Nathan and Spring, and Grandpa Dublin, so do not worry about what Grandpa Nolton said. You are my son and Chance is your father, and we are all different from each other on the outside. But inside, where it matters, we all feel love the same, and, the word is Indian, and they are not dirty!"

This seemed to satisfy the child for the time being. He sniffled and wiped his eyes. Relieved that he felt better, she also realized, however, that she had a real problem on her hands. Whether she faced it now, or sometime in the future, she was not one for leaving problems unsolved for long. She would have to find an answer soon.

Before she could think about when, and in what way, she would tell Stewart of his real parentage, however, there was the more pressing issue of keeping the boy out of Luke's way for the remainder of his stay, and in the interest of Chance and his brothers, avoiding another confrontation with the man herself.

Chance noticed her distracted state during the next few days, and wondered if there was something bothering her, but when the gift he had ordered for her to celebrate the approaching birth of their child arrived, he knew something was very wrong with his wife.

He made a grand show of presenting her with two wriggling, excited Gordon setter puppies, a male and female, as Modock and Tasha were growing too old to keep breeding. Everyone gathered together in the yard to be part of the surprise. Chance affected a most courtly bow, "For milady, the fair mother of my children, and" he pointedly looked at her bulging belly, "those as yet unborn, a gift worthy of a queen." With an exaggerated flourish, he lifted the cover of the mysterious box, and out tumbled the silky, dark pups.

Spring giggled, covering her mouth with her hand, while the rest of the gathered audience smiled at his foolish antics, and the way he was so obviously besotted with his beautiful, very pregnant wife.

Chance did not notice the resentful glare that his father directed toward Reanna. He did, however, thoughtfully note her subdued reaction to his lively gift, already scampering off at the children's heels, as they ran and tumbled about. Seeking to yet lighten her mood, he turned to Modock, who was sitting quietly by Reanna's side, distrustfully eyeing the new arrivals. "You, master Modock, are assigned the onerous task of keeping those two out of trouble." Modock licked his jowls nervously, lowered himself to sit at Chance's feet, and looked up at him mournfully.

Reanna smiled and stepped to him, brushing a soft kiss across his cheek. "Thank you, they are lovely."

Disappointed as he was at her lack of enthusiasm, he could not very well question her in front of everyone, but he knew now something was terribly wrong. That evening, in the privacy of their room, he confronted her. "Rea, what is troubling you? Is it the baby? Is something wrong with...?"

She hastened to assure him, "No. No, nothing like that Chance. I guess, I am just getting anxious for the baby to come. I'm all right."

Chance narrowed his eyes, reprimanding her silently before he chastened her with words. "You are doing it again, Rea. Something is wrong, and you seek to spare my feelings. I thought we had agreed not to do that to each other again. Now tell me what is troubling you, my love."

Reanna sat slumped on the bed, staring at her hands as she twisted the corner of a sheet nervously in her fingers. "It is just that I am so worried about Stewart, Chance. That there will always be those, like your father, who would malign him with vicious tongues, or worse. Your father kindly brought the matter to my attention, at the same time deeming it his responsibility to bring the child's differences to light, in front of him."

Chance glowered at her, a dangerous glint in his eye, and steel in his voice. "If he has hurt the boy, so help me, I will..."

Reanna interrupted him, "It was inevitable that he find out Chance. We both knew that. He would have noticed the differences in a few years himself anyway. It is just that I would have chosen to explain it to him in a gentler fashion than your father used. Perhaps we can just bring him to meet Mansunama sooner than we had planned. He is a little young to understand it all now, but if we are honest with him, if he learns to have pride in his Indian heritage, and in Mansunama, it can only serve to make him a stronger person, better able to fend off the hatred that feeds on the misery of others. And please," she begged him, "do not say anything to your father. A fight between the two of you would only serve to hurt Stewart more. He will feel that he is responsible."

Chance was thoughtful for a long moment before he answered. "You are right, my love. As soon as you are able to travel after the baby is born, we will bring Stewart to meet his father. As to my own loving Sire, I will overlook his indiscretion this one time, but I cannot promise that I would do so again."

Reanna tried to throw her arms around his neck but could not reach past the wide girth of her swollen stomach. Smiling in the humor of her predicament, Chance leaned over her so that he was close enough for her embrace.

"Oh Chance," she sighed, "you are the most wonderful man in the world, and certainly the best father a child could ever hope for."

"Most certainly," he agreed, looking into her earnest green gaze with amusement.

Contented now that they had formed a course of action, Reanna allowed herself the luxury of a huge yawn, and settled down to sleep. Pulling her close, Chance enfolded her in his embrace.

"We will tell him that he is a very lucky boy to have two such wonderful fathers," she murmured sleepily.

"Incredibly lucky, indeed." Chance agreed in a whisper, as he nuzzled her earlobe. She giggled, and Chance whispered, "Sleep well, my love."

Chance watched his father carefully over the next few days. He had become so absorbed in Reanna and the upcoming birth of his child that he had failed to observe the subtle nuances of emotion around him, a luxury he would never had allowed himself in years past. It could have proven to be a deadly mistake.

He caught the side long looks that his father angled at Reanna, and at dinner one evening he intercepted the unguarded, venomous glance that Luke directed toward Stewart. The boy wriggled uncomfortably in his seat and cast his eyes, shame faced, down to his plate. Chance had seen enough.

He leaned toward his father, and in a deceptively calm voice asked, "Is there something that you wish to say father? Speak up. We are all family here."

Reanna could sense the barely concealed rage that simmered below the surface of Chance's iron-willed control, and mumbling an excuse, hastened the children from the kitchen, leaving them in the parlor with Lada.

David and Louise suddenly found something of great interest on their plates and gave their food their undivided attention. Nathan leaned back in his seat, ready to observe the explosion he was sure would come. Luke seemed to take nothing amiss, and at Reanna's hasty exit, decided he had better set his son to rights, since Chance had asked.

"First of all, that little half red savage should not be allowed to eat with decent folks and that injun lovin' wife of yours..."

With a growl of pure rage, Chance shot out of his chair and reached his father in one long stride. He grabbed Luke's shirt front, hauling him up out of his chair, and smashed his fist into Luke's jaw, sending the older man sprawling to the floor.

Shaking his head sharply to clear his blurred vision, Luke rubbed his sore chin and picked himself up just as Reanna made it back to the doorway of the kitchen, gasping in pain as a sudden contraction seized her. She clutched at her middle, focusing in disbelief on the remarks made by Luke, and of Chance ready to deliver another blow.

"She is no good, Chance, I'm telling you! She'll ruin you. Why, she's nothin' more than a who..."

Chance's fist sent Luke to the floor again, and Chance attempted to pounce on him, but David flew from his chair in time to hold his brother back. Luke was wise enough to uphold his silence this time, and Chance forced his words through clenched teeth, "She is my wife, and the boy my son! Do not ever make the mistake..."

"Chance, the baby!" Reanna cried, as she suffered another spasm of pain. Chance had been about to shove David away from him, intent on reinforcing his angry words with his fists. At Reanna's painful cry, however, his expression changed dramatically from livid rage to instant, tender concern, so swiftly that Reanna was forced to smile. "Chance, I think someone should go for the doctor," she suggested.

"I'll go," Nathan offered, and Chance nodded gratefully before turning a baleful eye to Luke. "You will collect your belongings and leave this house and consider yourself lucky to be alive after forcing my wife and son to endure your insults and malicious looks. Believe me; it is not from any great love that I put up with you. In fact, I do not want to ever see you again."

Luke quivered in righteous indignation as he painfully picked himself up off the floor but offered no argument. Casting a last contemptuous glance at his father, Chance turned to assist Reanna up to the bedroom. Louise hurried to set water to heat, and David grabbed Luke's arm, grimly hauling him from the house. Lada rewarmed the children's dinner and they all settled down to eagerly await the birth of this newest member of the family.

Three hours later a lusty cry heralded the arrival of his newborn son, and Chance bathed Reanna's brow with a cool cloth, grateful that his wife's struggles to deliver the baby were now at an end. The doctor handed the baby to Louise who bathed the infant with warm water. "He is a beautiful baby and is the perfect image of you Reanna."

Chance smiled tenderly down at his wife, his gratitude and love shining in his dark eyes. "I thank you for my son, madam," then turned puzzled eyes to the doctor as the older man happily informed him, "I would not be thanking the lady quite yet, son."

Reanna groaned in pain, and the doctor informed her, "Keep pushing, Rea. Push, harder! That's it, here it comes." She dug her nails into Chance's arm and with a small cry of triumph, brought forth another tiny life.

"A girl!" proclaimed the doctor heartily.

"Twins!" breathed Chance in amazement as he regarded Reanna's soft, glowing features in tender awe.

The doctor and Louise slipped out to share the news with the rest of the family, leaving the proud new parents alone to admire their squalling infants. "Have you changed your mind about the names?" Chance inquired.

"No", Reanna replied, "William Raymond and Audra Ellen. I just never expected to be using both of them at once."

Chuckling, Chance agreed. They had decided on William Raymond for a boy, after Billy and Reanna's father. Audra Ellen was for both Chance and Reanna's mothers.

"Chance," Reanna began tentatively, changing the subject, "I am sorry about that terrible fight with your father yesterday."

"Don't be!" he snapped; his eyes suddenly hard. "As far as I am concerned, I have no father. I have lived without him over half my life. It will not pain me to do so again. Besides, I have all that I could ever want or need right here with you."

David and Louise stayed on a few more days to help where needed. Finally, though, they said their goodbyes, for they had left Holly and her husband to care for the farm and children. It was time that they collect Luke from the hotel in town and start for home. Bundled against the cold, their breaths frosty in the morning air, they waved, before they disappeared from sight.

"I shall miss them," Reanna sighed. "It always seems so long between visits."

"Mmmm," Chance agreed, "and now back into the house with you before you catch your death. Nathan and I have work to do."

The winter passed, every moment filled as the men repaired and cleaned all of the equipment and tools of the ranch, and scouted the ranges in the snow, searching for any signs of predators molesting the stock. Reanna and Lada were kept occupied with the task of keeping a growing family fed and well cared for.

Winter waned, finally releasing its last tenuous grasp on the land to the advent of spring. With the warm weather came the thorough scrubbing, airing, and polishing of every surface of the house. Spring cleaning added to the normal household duties, along with the planting and care of the vegetable garden. The men worked long, grueling hours, driving the stock in from winter ranges, roping and branding, culling, and gelding, any of the young males, horses and cattle.

It was after one such lengthy, back breaking morning that Chance, Nathan, and Jared, brushing the dust from their clothing, sat down to the noon meal with ravenous appetites. Reanna, her face flushed from the heat of the stove, distractedly served them scorched cuts of thick steaks, causing Chance to eye his plate distastefully. Sawing into the tough slice of meat, he asked irritably, "Where is Lada?"

"She is out picking berries for dessert this evening," Reanna answered tiredly, pushing a sweat dampened curl back from her face.

"I see," said Chance, "and you just could not manage a simple meal on your own without screwing it up!"

Reanna stared, stricken at his tone, and her face reddened more. Chance pushed his plate away and plunged in a heedless, quarrelsome voice, "And when, may I ask, are you going to begin training those pups? When they are too feeble to be able to learn any commands? I really think you could give them more attention."

Reanna drew herself up stiffly. Nathan and Jared shifted uncomfortably in their seats as the silence drew out. In a harsh tone, she replied, "I could use a little attention myself Chance. I've got all I can handle and more inside the house. I do not have time for dogs, or for myself!" She dashed the tears from her eyes and cast a glare in the direction of her husband before fleeing through the kitchen door, onto the porch, where she stopped, attempting to regain some control over her roiling emotions.

Chance could have bitten his tongue. What had possessed him to act in such a foolhardy way, berating Reanna because he was hot and exhausted, when she must surely feel much the same. He pushed back his chair and rose to follow his wife, damning himself for acting like a fool. He pulled her gently against him and brushed her cheek softly with a kiss. "I'm sorry sweetheart. Can you forgive me for being such a boor?"

She looked into his drawn, miserable features, and her anger quickly fled. "No, it is I who am sorry. It's just that I am so tired all the time, and with the four children demanding so much attention, I can't help but get a little edgy myself."

"Come with me," Chance ordered, and grasped her hand, pulling her after him as he strode purposely around to the side of the house. "There is something I want you to see." He drew her through a whitewashed arbor and stopped. "Look, Rea, all the roses you planted two years ago are in full bloom. Have you had time to enjoy them?"

"I had not even noticed them," she answered softly, staring about in surprise. "Why, they are beautiful!" she breathed, as Chance plucked a deep pink specimen from its thorny branch. Placing the fragile flower in her hand, he said, "You labored for two years to achieve the results of this garden." With a sweep of his hand, he indicated the myriad of blossoms. "Inhale the fragrance, touch the softness, and appreciate the beauty." She buried her nose in the flower she held, inhaling deeply. She brushed her cheek against the soft petals. When she raised her head and met his eyes, her own glowed with pleasure.

"I want you to hire someone to help with the children," he suggested, "so that you have more time to yourself, time to enjoy each day."

"Well, I suppose those two scamps that you try to pass off as pups could use quite a dose of training, and with someone to take charge of the children, I would be free to do so," Reanna admitted. They embraced tightly, then walked back to the house smiling brightly, only to meet with total bedlam, in what had been a quiet kitchen.

The twins were screaming, Stewart had spilled his milk all over himself and the floor, and when Spring tried to help him wipe up the mess, they had succeeded in overturning his plate of food all over the floor. The pups had dashed into the house when Chance went after Reanna, leaving the door ajar, and had tripped Nathan when he got up to help the children. They were now wrestling with each other on top of Nathans prone body while they growled in playful abandon. Jared had risen from his seat and surveyed the catastrophe with a look of what could only be described as horror.

Chance and Reanna looked at each other and burst out laughing before Chance moved to remedy the situation. He picked up Audra and handed her to Reanna, scooting the pups out the door as he did so. Nathan picked himself up with as much dignity as was possible, muttering something about living in a den of miscreants, only to break out in hardy laughter as he noted the look on Jared's face.

"You take the twins up and nurse them, Rea; I will take care of the rest. When you have the babies down for their nap, take the afternoon off to do whatever your heart desires. Go visiting, or shopping, and see if you can find someone brave enough to take charge of these little terrors," he eyed the children askance.

Reanna spent some time with her father and Carmelita, then with Molly and Kenny Beckett, in a pleasant afternoon of laughter and the latest gossip. Molly suggested Reanna ask her old friend Avis to help with the children. "Since her father passed away last year, Avis and her mother could use the extra income," Molly confided.

Avis was, as Molly had predicted, eager to take the position. She would travel back and forth from town to the ranch with Jared, and in periods of inclement weather, stay over. She would start the very next week.

Reanna returned home with a lighter heart, and a feeling of accomplishment. As soon as she arrived home, Chance suggested that they bring Stewart to meet Mansunama the next day. "It is warm enough to make the trip with the twins, and time that Mansunama meet his son." Chance murmured against her soft, silky hair as he pulled her close within his arms, and Reanna agreed, raising her lips to meet his softly questing kiss.

When they arrived the next day at the Indian camp, they were met by a sentry, as on Reanna's last journey here, who led them to the Indian village, then reined in their horses to wait while he went to summon his Shaman.

Chance kept his huge stallion under control while William nestled close to his chest in a pouch that was securely slung over his father's shoulder. Reanna sat astride her white mare, her hair hanging in glorious waves to her waist, half concealing Audra, strapped to her mother in the same way William was to Chance.

The silent warrior they had followed into camp finally emerged from a large hut in the center of the village, with Mansunama right behind him. Regally stretching to his full height, he strolled purposely toward them, his fierce black gaze resting first on Reanna, silently approving the long length of leg encased in the soft moccasins she wore, his eyes raising to the baby she carried. He glanced at Chance, making note of the second child sleeping against the broad chested man.

"She has given you two. You have a good woman, Chance Nolton."

Chance nodded in agreement before inclining his head toward Stewart. "We have brought someone to meet you, to stay for the rest of the summer, if you so desire."

Mansunama looked at the small boy on his pony, and as their eyes met, the shock of recognition swept through the tall, earthy Shaman. Peering back at him was a small miniature of himself, his son. He invited them all into the large hut, introducing them to his wife, Red Deer.

When they were seated, Mansunama asked, "What have you told him?"

Chance answered, "We told him he is a very lucky boy. That he has two fathers, and that it is time to meet his second father, who happens to be a very important, wise man, who also happens to be an Indian. He is a little young for any more explanation right now."

Mansunama tore his gaze from Stewart to focus unwaveringly on Chance. "Yes. You have done well. I thank you." He glanced back to Stewart, who sat solemnly under his steady regard. "And how do you feel, my son? Would you like to stay here with me for a time? There is much that you should learn, much that I would teach you."

Stewart considered this other father, and as their eyes met, something pulled at the boy, an ageless love, an earthy rhythm, and a slow, tenuous smile curved his lips. He glanced toward Reanna, and at her slight nod of approval, directed his attention to Chance. "We will come back for you in a few weeks," he assured the boy, and Stewart sat a little straighter. "I will stay father," he decided and Mansunama smiled down at his son.

"But we will have to give you your tribal name while you are here," the Shaman stated, as he contemplated his young son. "What do you think of the name Full Moon, for tonight, your first night here, there will be a full moon gazing down as you sleep." He then focused on Chance. "Come, I will show you Dark Angel and the many fine sons and daughters he has sired," glancing at Stewart, he said, "you too, my son. We will give the women time to visit and tend their babies."

When the men were gone, Red Deer smiled shyly, and Reanna was prompted to ask, "Does it bother you, the fact that Mansunama has this son?"

Red Deer did not hesitate. "No. Every man should have a son. I love my husband very much, and want to bear him many sons, but I seem to be able to produce only daughters. I am happy to see him with a son and will treat your child as my own."

Reassured of Stewart's welcome, Reanna was able to relax and enjoy the afternoon, drinking cold herbal tea, playing with the children, and chatting with the native women. All too soon, the men returned, and it was time to say goodbye to the son she would be leaving for the first time. An ache wrenched her heart as she knelt and hugged him close. Tears brimmed her eyes as she brushed his cheek with a kiss. Stewart presented his parents with a wavering smile as he tried very hard to be brave and not cling to his mother.

They mounted their horses and waited as Mansunama approached, leading two perfectly matched palominos toward them. He placed a comforting hand on Stewart's shoulder as he spoke to Chance. "I want you to take these horses as my gift to you, for raising my son as you would your own, and for giving him the opportunities presented by the white man's world, even though he will encounter some who will not like him for the blood he carries. These are," he indicated the two horses, "the daughters of Dark Angel, granddaughters of my Wildcat, my old palomino."

"Thank you Mansunama," Reanna breathed as her gaze traveled over the trim lines of the two golden horses.

"It is I who should thank you, Reanna, for the gift of my son. Our way of life is rapidly coming to an end, but my knowledge of healing will live on in Full Moon." His black gaze delved deeply into hers.

"Goodbye, Full Moon," Reanna spoke to her son in quiet dignity. Mansunama and Full Moon stood together, watching until Chance and Reanna were no longer in sight.

A few weeks later, at Lake Tahoe, alone for a few days while Avis watched the children at home, Chance and Reanna wandered in silence, engulfed by nature's exquisite beauty. They were young and free as never before, shedding the responsibilities and worries of everyday living, giving themselves to the wild, untamed grandeur that surrounded them.

Reanna sat and played her guitar, her clear, light voice lifted and spread around them, in tune with the birds and wildlife that pulsed with the breath of life. She stopped as she spotted a great, soaring, golden eagle overhead, and watched as it glided high above them. The huge bird uttered a high, regal, lonesome cry, and the call echoed as the sound reached the walls of the mountains.

Then, Chance stood before her, rising as tall and handsome as any knight of yore, with the sun at his back, as if he were magically transformed from the king of the eagles to a man. As he bent toward her, his eyes bored into hers, dark brown and glowing with the red heat she so loved to see at times such as this. When they felt their love for each other so strongly that it burned, consuming them both with its fierceness. Their lips met, igniting the banked flames as their tongues entwined, then parted, tasting, and exploring.

Chance moaned low in pleasure, the sound mingling with Reanna's sigh of delight. Then she gasped for air as his lips left hers to trail downward to possess her breast, his hands working feverishly to remove her clothing. He pressed his hot lips to the swollen peaks of her breasts, his wet tongue flicked at the rosy tips, swirling about them tauntingly.

The fevered pursuit of his tongue trailed lower, across her abdomen and down to her womanhood, where he kissed her, tasting the sweetness there. She writhed beneath him, trembling uncontrollably as she was engulfed by an ecstasy so sweet that she cried out, as almost unbearable tremors shook her, overwhelming in their intensity.

Momentarily content, a sigh of pure bliss escaped her, then her hands and mouth sought her husband's pleasure as she hurriedly removed his pants. His manhood was hard and throbbing, and he thrust forward to enter her, but she resolutely pressed him back to the ground as her searing lips trailed the length of him, burning and tormenting him. Feeling that he could stand no more of the exquisite torture, she raised herself above him then, to slide down upon his fullness, filling her warm, wet depths with his full length, riding him, increasing the tempo until they both felt their loins erupt in a spiraling blaze of glory. Their two hearts beat as one, and they were lifted higher than ever in their love. Above the tallest mountain peak, high into the heavens, where only the golden eagles had the privilege to soar. The two lovers soared alongside the eagle, high, wild, and free, for what seemed an eternity.

Afterward, as they lay entwined, still floating in a realm of bliss, Chance murmured, "Sweetheart, our love truly holds a magic of its own."

Reanna rejoiced in his words, for she knew their love had indeed, reached the ultimate peak that was possible between two mortal beings. She thanked God in his heavens, she thanked the earth, and Mansunama, and she thanked the great golden eagle, for she knew that it would forever more be thus between herself and her beloved Chance.

The words of her song came to mind, "and the great golden eagle rose high into the heavens, there to soar ever proud, ever free, for all eternity," and her own wings were indeed, finally healed, forevermore.

Made in United States
North Haven, CT
22 June 2024